"In war, it is not the men who make the difference, but the man."

Napoleon Bonaparte

IN PURSUIT OF GLORY

By William H. White

Cover art © 2006 Paul Garnett
Author photo © William H. White, jr.
Artist photo © Paul Garnett
Illustrations © 2006 Paul Garnett
Photos of Medal issued to the officers of USS *United States* for their victory over HMS *Macedonian* courtesy of USS Constitution Museum, Boston, MA.

Graphic design and production by:
Scribe, Inc., 842 S. 2nd St., Philadelphia, PA 19147

Printed in the USA by:
Victor Graphics, 1211 Bernard Drive, Baltimore, MD 21223 USA

Questions regarding the content of this book should be addressed to:

TILLER Publishing
605 S. Talbot Street, Suite Two
St. Michaels, Maryland 21663
410-745-3750 • Fax: 410-745-9743
www.tillerbooks.com

DEDICATION

This volume is for the one in twelve, with love.

ACKNOWLEDGMENTS

As with any endeavor, most of us need the help of others to accomplish our task. This effort is no exception and I would like to set forth those whose efforts on my behalf contributed to the accuracy, characters, and history you shortly will read.

In Washington, DC, **Dr. David Winkler** of the Naval Historical Center arranged for me to have the guiding hand of **Jean Hort** to assist in my research of Commodore Barron's court martial. She found the necessary documents and, when I ran out of time to study them in their library, copied the many pages I needed and mailed them to me.

In Boston, **Dr. William Fowler**, noted author, historian, and then Director of the Massachusetts Historical Society, assisted my effort with information concerning the advancement of a nineteenth century midshipman to lieutenant. Also in Boston, **Linda W. Wiseman**, authority on American decorative arts and architecture, traveled to Newport, RI to find a suitable house for the grand ball to which Oliver, his captain, and his messmates are invited. She found the perfect one, still extant, built prior to the American Revolution, and used by French General Rochambeau, where it is said that he assisted George Washington in planning the battle of Yorktown.

Best-selling author, **William Martin**, very kindly offered a read of the manuscript, made some suggestions for improving it, and provided a most generous "cover quote" for the printed work. **Dr. William Dudley**, former director of the Naval Historical Center in Washington DC and naval historian par-excellence, did the same. I am indebted to both of these good men for their willingness to share, not only their knowledge, but their reputations as well.

Harrie Slootbeek, USS Constitution Museum, Boston, provided the photographs of the medal commemorating Decatur's victory over **Macedonian**, as well as the description of Isaac Hull's arrival on Long Wharf, taken from a contemporary account.

My daughter-in-law, **Felicity McGrath, Esq.**, found a book on Ebay, a bit after the conclusion of writing, that proved so helpful I absolutely had to add some of the wonderful (and well annotated) bits of history to this story. The book was a long-out-of-print edition of naval correspondence between 1805 and 1807 and it will make an ongoing and most useful addition to my personal research library. Felicity, thank you so much!

Of course, my good friend and extraordinarily talented artist, **Paul Garnett**, whose rendition of the **Chesapeake Leopard** Incident adorns the cover, has added immeasurably to my effort by creating an eye-catching and dramatic image surely destined to catch the browser's eye on a bookshelf.

Finally, sailing pal and long time ally, **Joe Burns,** read what I thought was the finished manuscript and found a variety of errors in syntax and grammar that only a long-time copy-writer could. Thanks, Joe.

There are several others who helped with the creation of characters depicted in these pages; they will remain nameless, as not all of the traits I borrowed from them are of the "first character" and their unwitting contribution to the story should remain a subject shrouded in mystery! But I nonetheless also owe them a debt of gratitude.

If this book is successful and enjoyed, it is to the credit of these good people who provided of their many talents to ensure it. Of course, this is a work of fiction, and while I have made every effort to remain true to the actual history, errors or mistakes are in no way the fault of the generous folks who gave their help.

To them, I offer my heartfelt thanks and to you, the reader, I can only hope you will enjoy the story and, perhaps, even discover a few historical gems you might have previously overlooked.

A final note of thanks and apology to those who have read my previous books and enjoyed them: I thank you for your loyalty and enthusiastic reception of each new effort. Obviously, without you, the reader, a writer has no audience for whom to write and would wither and die on the vine. So again, I offer my heartfelt appreciation for allowing me to continue to do what I love. And finally, I offer my apologies for having kept you waiting for this sequel to **The Greater The Honor;** it was too long in coming and I hope you find it was worth the wait!

William H. White
Rumson, NJ 2006

PROLOGUE

*A*t seven o'clock in the morning of 22 June 1807, the United States frigate Chesapeake (36) *won her anchor from the mud of Hampton Roads in Norfolk Virginia and set sail for the Mediterranean Sea. On board, in addition to stores and supplies, spare yards, cordage, and materiel for the Mediterranean fleet, was Commodore James Barron, en route to take command of the Squadron, which had been maintained in that sea since the Barbary Wars. Also in the ship was an indeterminate number of former Royal Navy sailors, deserters from their own British ships.*

Immediately the frigate had cleared the Virginia Capes, she was stopped by the British two-decker, HMS Leopard *(50), and peaceably first, then forcefully, boarded; four of the deserters were removed to the Royal Navy ship.* Chesapeake, *severely wounded, returned to Norfolk with three dead and over a score wounded, including the commodore.*

After a Court of Inquiry, convened in July, 1807 by Secretary of the Navy Smith, ruled sufficient grounds, Captain James Barron, Commodore; Master-commandant Charles Gordon, Captain; Marine Captain John Hall; and Warrant Gunner Hook were all court-martialed for their actions in the brief, but sharp and deadly, conflict.

The populace was outraged at the overt hostility from a nation with which America had enjoyed a twenty-five year peace; demonstrations, riots, speeches, and all manner of outcry ensued. Indeed, even the two governments roiled and blustered over the incident, not embarking on a plan for reparation and calm until the passage of almost two years; it would take another two years of negotiation before the British and American governments would arrive at a satisfactory conclusion to the event.

This delay of reparation and, of course, the attack itself are widely credited with fanning the smoldering fires of resentment toward Great Britain extant since the American War of Independence, embers that would ultimately burst into flame on 18 June 1812 with a declaration of war by the United States against Great Britain.

CHAPTER ONE

"His career's likely finished with this. Being court martialed for surrendering your ship, Oliver, is certainly not the way to win the admiration of the Navy department . . . or your fellow officers, I'd warrant. Might even get himself hung for his efforts!"

Lieutenant William Henry Allen's words struck me a bit premature as the court he referred to had only just convened one deck below where we now stood, on board USS *Chesapeake*; the gun announcing its commencement had fired not ten minutes before. They also seemed some harsh. The unspoken aura of cowardice hung over the ship and its crew like a pall, but so far, had remained *unspoken*. I called him on his hard opinion.

"Henry, you don't have any more idea than I do of how this will finish. I agree that surrendering one's ship, prematurely or otherwise, is a serious charge and some scandalous on top of it. But his career finished, or him hanged like a criminal? I think it might be more prudent to wait until the hearing's done and Rodgers, Decatur, and the others have decided the issue. Besides, Captain Gordon and the Marine . . . uh, Captain Hall, are also being tried. And the gunner. Perchance the court will lay some of the blame on them rather than letting the commodore stand alone." My breath made a white cloud which hung in the air between us as I spoke.

"Aye, and with Rodgers on the court, in point of fact, the *president* of it, I should think it a foregone conclusion that they will vote to convict. And your own friend, Captain Decatur, sits at the table, as well. There's no love lost 'twixt the two of them and Barron!" Allen made a wolfish smile as he, in *his* mind at least, proved his earlier pronouncement.

"Well," I responded quickly, searching my memory of the names on the court for one who might balance the enmity of Rodgers and Decatur. "What about Captain Bainbridge? He sits on it as well. You might recall,

Henry, when he was court martialed for losing the *Philadelphia* frigate a few years ago, Commodore Barron supported his cause and voted to exonerate. So at least *one* of the captains should take a friendly stance to him."

Without providing him an opening to counter this brilliant utterance, I then continued my argument, fairly hoisting myself on my own petard. "Besides, I'm sure you know that Decatur tried several times to get his own self excused from this affair. I heard he wrote to the Secretary of the Navy sayin' he'd already made up his mind that the commodore had faltered in carrying out his duty. But the Secretary claimed there weren't enough captains on the court and he surely would not let Captain Decatur off. And I'm told that he even mentioned to Barron's counsel that he had already made up his mind as to the case, but the chap did not exercise his right to protest. Maybe Decatur will maintain a neutral mindset."

He simply humphed at this last, not willing to give any ground. I, however, continued to give ground, which, ultimately, caused him to break into a smile which broadened into an eye-crinkling grin.

Then just to be sure I had overlooked nothing in the way of undercutting my own argument, I pressed on, adding further and, unwitting, concession with each word.

"I don't know the minds of the others, but I know Rodgers has never thought highly of Barron, so you may be right that he and Cap'n Decatur will sway the court's opinion. We'll have to wait, I guess."

Allen, his smile now gone, his eyes stony and flat, stared at me for a long moment, obviously annoyed with my unwillingness to take his opinion as my own. He muttered something and, though close, I only managed to catch a part of it; ". . . gardless . . . his actions . . . shameful." With no further comment, he turned his back on the ship to study the far shore of Lynnhaven Bay.

He pulled the collar of his deep blue great coat tighter around his neck as a sharp gust of the raw wind rattled the ice in the rigging and sent a chill that penetrated us to the bone. I turned as well, saying nothing, and we stood together, his hands on the bulwark, mine in my pockets, and individually, silently recalled the events that had conspired to place us (and many others, also to be called as witnesses) here, on USF *Chesapeake's* decks, secured to a pier at the Norfolk Navy Yard with ice-laden hawsers on this bitter cold and raw day in early January, 1808.

I also wondered if, perchance, I had been a bit familiar with my friend; after all, he was a lieutenant and I only a midshipman, a senior midshipman with over four years service to be sure, but still a midshipman. After he had won his promotion to lieutenant and the accompanying epaulet or, as we called it, his "swab," he had generously encouraged two of us (now, with his move to the gunroom, the senior midshipmen aboard) to use the familiar form of address. Until this minute, I had felt comfortable in doing just that, using his middle name (he preferred it to William) as I had when he lived in the midshipmen's mess. Now I wondered if it was the subject or my forwardness which might be responsible for his sudden foul mood.

Had the horrors of the past June not occurred, we would have been today on a routine patrol in the warm and sunny Mediterranean Sea, a return to the waters of my first cruise. And while June wasn't actually so long ago, so much had happened since the wounded *Chesapeake* had limped back into Norfolk, that the summer seemed as far in the past as the year and more I spent as one of "Preble's Boys" fighting the corsairs off the Tripolitan coast of Africa.

When we sailed from Norfolk last June, America was at peace; it had been some two years since we had agreed to a treaty with the Bashaw of Tripoli, our most recent antagonist, giving us no expectation of confrontation or hostility with any. And certainly not a confrontation in our own coastal waters!

I remembered my own shame that June day as one of the participants, a midshipman only, but an officer in the eyes of the Navy, and still could feel the disgrace of our action as sharply as I did then. I could not help but compare Commodore Barron's behavior with that of my first (and now again) captain, Stephen Decatur, to whom honor was everything. Even as I looked aloft on this decidedly different day at *Chesapeake's* taut and orderly rigging, with the blue and yellow court martial flag held straight out by the biting wind, I saw only the shambles left after suffering twenty minutes and more of broadsides from a fifty-gun ship of war. The rig then had been all ahoo and her decks littered not only with fallen spars, blocks, and bits of the rig itself, but also with the still unstowed stores and equipment necessary for a long commission. Most vivid though, was the sight of the shroud-covered bodies of three of her crew and twenty wounded, each crying out in pain. And the gore, still wet, that stained the pale, pristine pine of our decks.

How different the ten-year-old frigate looked today, restored to her unwounded appearance. As different as today's Oliver Baldwin was from the one who had left Boston in September of 1803. According to the navy yard, the ship was "as good as new." But even I knew the vessel would forever carry the burden of having been surrendered after firing barely a shot, just as I would carry with me to the end of my days the memory of war. The older hands, both aboard and ashore, muttered about a "jinx" and "bad luck," two sobriquets that already had made most difficult finding sufficient numbers of skilled seamen for her crew. Even before the shameful incident of June, *Chesapeake* had borne the stigma of a "bad luck ship;" she had stuck on the ways, not just once, but twice, while being launched just across the river in Gosport. And when finally she did slide into the water, a yard worker had been killed, struck by a timber balk kicked out by the passage of the ship. Then just last spring, before our fateful meeting in June, her fore t'gallant yard had fallen to the deck while lying at anchor off Alexandria. That incident had resulted in the deaths of a seaman and a boy and injury to four others.

Yes, Chesapeake *had earned her unsavory reputation*, I agreed.

". . . Sir? Mister Baldwin?" An insistent voice jerked me back to the present. I turned to find a smartly turned-out Marine, standing rigidly to attention, and wearing a somewhat annoyed look. Perhaps it was just the cold (he wore no cloak or great coat, as I did), that caused him to grit his teeth, making a thin line of his lips. His right hand remained close to his hat and I quickly doffed mine in response to his salute.

"Yes? I'm sorry. You wanted me?" I could not help but remember how this same scene would have frightened me half to death on *Argus* back in '03, when I was a struggling fourteen-year-old lad, first embarking on his employment as a U. S. Navy midshipman.

"Yes, sir. Actually, them below wanted you. I am to bring you into the court martial. Follow me, sir, if you please."

The Marine turned, assured that the summons of "them below" was sufficient incentive for me to be but half a step behind him, and strode purposefully aft toward the hatch which would take us down one deck to just outside the Great Cabin and the august assemblage within. I made a woeful face, only part in jest, at Lieutenant Allen and stepped off in the man's wake, catching the wink and nod of encouragement from Henry as I turned.

At least he still ain't so upset. Guess I wasn't on the wrong side of propriety in arguing with him.

In spite of the cold, the thought of facing and being questioned by some of the most distinguished and celebrated officers of our Navy made me break into a sweat and tightened my stomach. Even though I knew I shared none of the blame being heaped upon the commodore, Captain

Gordon or the others, I could feel the cold trickle make its way down my back. I shrugged off my great coat, hanging it on a peg next to several others belonging, I assumed, to those already in the Cabin. My hat, I tucked carefully under my left arm.

My escort rapped his knuckles sharply on the closed door and I heard a muffled acknowledgment from the other side; he opened it and nodded to me. I stepped into the room and stood for a moment taking in the sight before me. The large Cabin—it took up the full width of the ship— was illuminated by sparkling brass lanterns, each giving off a smoky yellow light which augmented the dim winter daylight struggling in through the large quarter gallery windows. Above each flickering lamp was a dark stain on the overhead, a result of the low grade of whale oil available to the Navy. The dark wood paneling added to the gloom. Most of the furnishings that I had seen in place when the Cabin served only as the apartment to the ship's captain (or commodore) had been removed and had been replaced with furniture more appropriate to this occasion. The effect was to make the Cabin appear even larger and more imposing than it already was.

Seated at a long table across the after end of the room were several men I recognized from my time in the Mediterranean with Captain Decatur: Commodore William Bainbridge, my brother Edward's commander in the late *Philadelphia* frigate; Master Commandant David Porter, first lieutenant in the same ill-fated ship; Captain John Rodgers; Lieutenant James Lawrence, who had been first lieutenant in *Enterprise* during my time aboard the schooner; and, of course, Captain Decatur sitting immediately to Captain Rodgers' right. Rodgers was, as Henry had mentioned, president of the court martial and, while not actually a judge or magistrate, functioned as one and was in charge of the proceedings. There were six others at the table who were unfamiliar to me. Each man wore a solemn and grim expression. Their severe expressions left no doubt as to the gravity of the gathering.

Commodore Barron, deep in conversation with a man seated beside him, a civilian in proper frock coat and cravat, sat at a smaller table facing the court and in the middle of the room. Between the two tables was a chair. Empty. In the back of the room were a dozen and more chairs, some occupied, but about half were empty.

"Mister Baldwin, if you will step forward and be sworn, you may then take a seat." Captain Decatur smiled slightly as he spoke and gestured toward the straight chair.

"Aye, aye, sir." I mumbled as I made my way to the center of the room, past the chairs occupied in part by officers and a few civilians whose roles I could not determine.

When I got to the designated chair, I made as if to sit down, but another gentleman in civilian garb whom I did not know—*Why were there civilians in what appear to be important roles here? Was this not a Navy matter?*—appeared at my side and pointedly cleared his throat. I caught myself before my bottom made contact and stood erect, at attention, my hat again tucked under my left arm.

Must be some kind of clerk or something.

"Place your hand on this Bible, if you please." I did as I was told and, in the process, managed to let slip my hat from where I thought it had been secure. As I bent down to retrieve it, the back of my leg hit the chair and knocked it over with a crash whose noise was exaggerated by the exquisite silence that had prevailed until my misadventures began. When I stood up, my hat now held firmly in my left hand, I started to step back a bit to stand up the chair. I was suddenly exceedingly warm, and realizing that my face was likely scarlet only compounded my discomfort. From the corner of my eye, I caught the horrified looks that seemed to be pasted on every face at the long table. Looks that quickly gave up their struggle for gravity to a suppressed ripple of quiet laughter, augmented by those sitting in the back of the room. Another side-long glance told me that even the commodore and the civilian, whom I took for his lawyer, had been unsuccessful in suppressing a modest level of gaiety.

"I'll take care of that, Midshipman. You just stay put right there." The tall civilian who had been about to give me the oath spoke as he bent to right the fallen chair, allowing a barely audible grunt to escape his lips from the effort. Commodore Rodgers rapped his gavel sharply on the table, stilling the undercurrent of quiet mirth that filled the room. And, with the chair once again in its proper place and order restored, the gentleman again faced me and held out the Bible.

"Do you swear to tell the truth to this court, the whole truth, so help you God?" He spoke much louder than was necessary for me to hear him and his foul exhalation bespoke some considerable hours of revelry the night before.

I recoiled involuntarily, but answered, "Yes, sir."

"You may be seated." I sat. Without further mishap.

Gradually the heat drained away from my face and I knew my color was returning to a more normal shade. But now, in the absence of my earlier embarrassment, I was suddenly aware that my stomach was churning in a most alarming fashion and a sense of foreboding and apprehension threatened to overcome me. It called to mind that dark night, now almost four years back, when I waited with seventy of my shipmates to board and fire the frigate *Philadelphia* and experience my first taste of naval combat. Hoping for a look, a nod, or a smile of acknowledgment from one of my former superiors, I studied the stern faces lining the long table to my right. There was not a glimmer of recognition from any and I wondered if I had only imagined the earlier smile from Decatur. To my left was my former commodore, James Barron, who was still busy speaking to his counsel and paid me no mind whatever. My stomach continued to roil, making noises I was sure all in the room could hear quite plainly, and threatened to cause me accident of a most embarrassing nature; the pork I had enjoyed at breakfast was surely now less pleasant as I tasted it again, swallowing the excess of wetness in my mouth.

"Mister Baldwin." Captain Rodgers' stentorian tones broke the silence, causing me to start. *At least talking will hide the rumblings of my poor belly!*

"Sir," I responded.

"You were aboard the United States frigate *Chesapeake* in June during her late encounter with the British vessel HMS *Leopard*?"

I nodded, my throat now quite suddenly too dry to utter a sound.

"You must respond aloud to any questions asked, Mister Baldwin. The secretary can not record a motion of your head." This from Lieutenant Lawrence.

"Yes, sir. Yes, sir, I was aboard *Chesapeake* at that time. Sir." It came out more as a croak than the voice of a confident and seasoned midshipman. Indeed, one who had faced death several times over before his fifteenth year had ended. Somehow, this was different.

"And what were your duties in the frigate, sir?" One of the lieutenants at the table asked.

"I held partial responsibility for the second division and also did some recruiting duty at a rendezvous prior to our leaving port . . . here, from Norfolk. Sir." I seemed to be regaining some element of composure and relaxed slightly; these questions weren't so hard. Perhaps my fears were quite misplaced. After all, it wasn't *me* on trial here. Even the rumblings and churnings of my midsection quieted a trifle.

"Mister Tazewell, you may proceed with your witness." Captain Rodgers nodded to the man in civilian garb who merely responded with a curt, "Sir."

I looked about, trying to determine what was to happen next and who was Mister Tazewell, when the civilian gentleman who had given me the oath approached my chair and stood directly in front of me.

Well, I thought, *he's* not *just a clerk. Must be important.*

As his stature was much greater than my own, especially as I was seated, his devilish breath caused me no distress. I looked up at his countenance, scowling as it was, either from his effort to regain some dignity in the face of my own earlier antics or the continuing effects of his apparent over-indulgence I knew not, and I wondered idly whether he had ever experienced a confrontation with an enemy intent on killing him. I thought not.

That I had been aboard in a capacity which rendered me fit to recount the misadventures of that ill-starred and short-lived commission had been established by the several questions of the court martial board and now, the haughty Mister Tazewell, standing rigidly before me would, it appeared, manage my questioning. (I soon discovered he was the *judge advocate*, and, as such, responsible for most of the conduct of the trial.) He cleared his throat and began.

"Midshipman Baldwin: do you recall the events of 22 June, the year just passed and where you were and what occupied you during those events?"

I nodded. *What a silly question. And what a pompous ass! Of course I was there and will likely never forget those events and my role in them.*

"Mister Baldwin, you have been instructed already to *speak* your responses. The secretary can hardly be expected to be looking up at a witness while he is trying to take down *verbatim* testimony." Tazewell bent down and spoke his rude words directly into my face, exhaling as he did so. I turned my head, appearing to look at the court, and managed to avoid much of his foul exhalation.

"Yes, sir. Of course I remember. How could I not?"

"Yes . . . well! Perhaps you might share with the court your recollections from that day and all that transpired." His face now wore a sneer, perhaps an effort to discredit my having won a victory, small to be sure, but a victory nonetheless. He waited as I gathered my thoughts. I concentrated on not smiling at this pompous buffoon. All thoughts of my uneasiness were banished from my mind as that horrifying day came into sharp focus.

After studying him for a moment, I shifted my gaze to the court and caught the eye of Captain Decatur. He offered a barely perceptible nod of encouragement. I took a breath, relaxed some, and began.

"Yes . . . well." I stopped, realizing that my utterance would appear to mimic his own of only a moment before. A look at his face told me I was right. *Too late! Press on, Oliver. And don't smile; this is serious!*

"We made sail, sir, shortly after six bells in the morning watch, about 7, I think." I added that in case he was unaware of the meaning of "six bells in the morning watch" and received a tiny smile from Lieutenant Lawrence for my trouble. "It was a fine clear day that augured well for a satisfying commission. As you no doubt already know, we had a significant number of civilians aboard and they were all on deck watching our progress as we made our way on a favorable breeze down the Bay toward Cape Henry and thence to the Atlantic."

"Assume I know nothing, Midshipman, and tell your tale as you recall it. Leave nothing out."

Littleton W. Tazewell (I discovered, somewhat later, his full name, and that he was an attorney prominent in Norfolk legal as well as governmental circles, which likely accounted for an appointment to his current role) again aimed his words directly into my face, his noxious breath emphasizing each syllable. Assuming he knew nothing would surely not be difficult.

"Aye, sir." I paused again, gathering my thoughts and recalling the events of that awful day . . .

Suddenly, the Great Cabin, the panel, and the lawyers all vanished like a puff of smoke in a fresh breeze; I was there again, standing just off the quarterdeck, watching the shoreline slip by and only occasionally watching the off-duty sailors as they struggled to make some order out of the piles of stores, cordage, spare sails, yards and supplies, not only for our own use, but also for the Mediterranean Squadron which we would join upon our arrival. The civilian passengers and the group of chattering Italian musicians (their services no longer required by the American government, we were transporting them home) took up most of the remaining deck space and seemed constantly in the way, but they were enthralled with the goings-on both aboard and ashore and remained quite oblivious to the sailors' entreaties to ". . . Please step aside, sir, (or ma'am) if you would." And ". . . beggin' yer pardon, sir, would you kindly step over there?"

Set to the t'gallants—that is we had almost all of our sails spread and drawing—we made a fair turn of speed down the Bay with the fresh west-southwest breeze billowing our sails out to larboard and keeping the sheets, braces, and bowlines nicely taut. Before noon we had made

Lynnhaven Bay. As we approached, Henry pointed toward the starboard bow and spoke for the first time in an hour and more.

"Look there, Oliver. Looks as if the Royal Navy is fixin' to give us a welcome!"

Indeed, when I looked past his outstretched arm, I saw, anchored, HMS *Bellona*, signal flags snapping in the breeze, and HMS *Melampus*. Beyond them, HMS *Leopard* also swung to her anchor.

"And you like as not can see all their ports're open." Henry continued to point, in case I had missed the open gunports gaping like so many missing teeth in an otherwise attractive smile.

"It's right hot, Henry. They likely got 'em open just to get some air into the ships. We're not at war with the British." Hostility, at least hostility directed at an American ship, could not have been further from my mind. I watched idly as signal flags broke out from the cro'jack yard of *Leopard* followed by increased activity both on deck and aloft. Clearly, she had been ordered, likely by some senior officer on *Bellona*, to get underweigh and was complying.

By then, *Chesapeake* was past the Bay and only a cannon shot from the entrance to the Atlantic Ocean. As we paid off to head for the Capes of Virginia and put the wind more astern, we could feel the swells that rolled in as they gently lifted our bow, then passed under us with a sibilant *hiss*.

"Sir. The pilot boat is closing on us from astern." The quartermaster called out to Captain Gordon.

Henry and I both looked and, to be sure, the rakish pilot schooner was making on us. And so too, was HMS *Leopard*.

"Mister Brooke," Captain Gordon bellowed to our sailing master. "We'll be comin' up directly to take some speed off her. Clew up the main and fore courses, if you please. Mister Johnson, stand by to receive the schooner alongside to weather to pick up our pilot."

I could see men scurrying aloft to the encouragement of Mister Brooke, as others, Bosun Johnson's men, opened the gate in the starboard bulwark and heaved down the heavy manropes which the pilot would use to make his way down to the considerably lower deck of the schooner sent out to fetch him. *Chesapeake* slowed as her sail area was reduced and a tops'l was braced around and backed.

As the pilot schooner made our side, none aboard either vessel could miss the fifty-gun, former ship of the line, HMS *Leopard*, as she fairly flew by, also to weather. Her gun ports were still open.

The Virginia Capes, Henry and Charles, were now abeam larboard and starboard and, with the wind having backed around to the southeast, we were obliged to tack to avoid running onto the hard. With the fifty-gunner a musket shot off our wind'ard bow, Captain Gordon was obliged to bear off some to run under her stern, then, once past, harden up in an effort to regain the ground he had lost to weather. *Leopard* carried on for several minutes and then tacked, quickly regaining the ground she had lost and maintaining her windward gage.

"That's certainly rude behavior. I wonder what could be in his mind." Allen commented to me on the Royal Navy ship pointedly keeping to windward of us, clearly a hostile posture; normally, a vessel passing or wishing to speak another friendly ship would stay in a non-threatening leeward position.

"Not only rude, Henry, but you'll notice her guns are run out as well. And I don't see any tompions. I think they might be . . ."

"That chap is serious, gentlemen. He aims to come on board of us. Lookin' fer his deserters, I'd warrant." Sailing Master Brooke gave voice to the very thoughts Lieutenant Allen and I each had held unspoken. We had all heard of, and, indeed, had seen many deserters from the Royal Navy. Some scurried inland just as fast as they could to avoid the ever-present press gangs, always eager to collect the bounty recaptured deserters brought; others sought to get back to sea quickly, either in the United States Navy or a merchant of any convenient flag. I knew our sailors, especially those who had enjoyed past service in the Royal Navy, appreciated the kinder, more humane treatment they received as sailors under the American flag.

"Do we have any aboard, Mister Brooke?" I asked in perfect innocence. After all, I had personally recruited forty or fifty of the sailors we shipped and believed that I had signed only eligible seamen, and a few landsmen, to our muster book. I did not know whether any other recruiter might have been less vigilant.

"Cap'n Gordon asked me that very question, Mister Baldwin. I give him the same answer I'll give you: ain't real sure, but I know them in the rendezvous was told 'no deserters.'" He shifted his gaze back to the British ship, growing larger and more daunting with each passing moment and pointed with his chin. "Looks like they gonna send a boat over. And they's an officer fixin' to tell us what it is they might be after, looks like."

Indeed, I could see quite clearly that a gang of sailors had already swung a small boat from its resting place to hang over the ship's larboard bulwark, and aft of them, an officer stood atop the rail near the quarterdeck, a hand resting on the mizzen shrouds. He raised a speaking trumpet to his face.

"Aboard *Chesapeake*! We have dispatches from our commander-in-chief for the commander of *Chesapeake*." With his position to our windward, the voice floated over the water, losing not a shred of its hostility or sneering superiority.

There was a flurry of activity on our quarterdeck and I saw one of my messmates from the midshipman's cockpit scurrying down the hatch, obviously to fetch the commodore who had appeared topside only once since leaving Norfolk. That had been to glass the three British warships lying in Lynnhaven Bay.

Now on the quarterdeck, coatless, Commodore Barron stepped to the bulwark and stared aghast at the British ship, sailing only a long pistol shot distant. A few sharp words, which I failed to hear, were offered to Captain Gordon and then the commodore, clambering atop the carriage of a quarterdeck long eighteen-pounder, cupped his hands around his mouth and shouted back to the British officer, "We will heave to so you can send your boat on board." He again spoke briefly to Captain Gordon and returned to his Cabin below.

Now our wind'ard side was lined with curious sailors, a few officers and midshipmen, and all of the passengers save a few who had retired to their cabins, already suffering the ill-effects of our being at sea. We all watched as the cutter, bearing an officer of the Royal Navy, made good time across the still calm sea toward our side.

"Topmen aloft! Hands to stations for shortening sail!" The sailing master's cry dissolved the group at the rail as we all moved to comply. As I stepped to the mizzen (my station for sail handling), I studied our captain for some indication of what he might be expecting. He paced side-to-side on his quarterdeck, never taking his eyes off the approaching boat. His jaw worked as though he were chewing something and his clenched fists relaxed regularly only to clench again immediately. When he turned towards me, I could see a trickle of sweat making a track down the side of his face, clearly not a result of the warm, but quite pleasant, weather. From time to time he shifted his gaze to the British man-o'-war, now hove to some sixty or seventy yards away. Without their tompions, the plugs that kept water out of the barrels, the gaping maws of her battery were plainly visible and made for a menacing look that would surely intimidate an enemy.

Must be fixin' to organize some gunnery practice after they deliver the dispatches to Cap'n Gordon. Good thing we're not at war with England; the weight of that broadside would render most of our size into matchwood!

But still, I was made uneasy by the sight of those powerful long guns, two decks of them, poking out the side of the ship right at us! Their open muzzles made for a daunting display.

As *Chesapeake* heaved to, the cutter made its way around our transom and coasted expertly to a stop alongside the manropes to leeward. I could not help but notice that the cox'n was skilled in his trade as the small boat stopped exactly in position and in perfect concert with the frigate. As Gordon made his way forward to greet whoever it was sent from the Royal Navy ship, I watched a lieutenant step smartly onto the battens on the frigate's side and climb easily to the break in the bulwark, assisted by the manropes. He and our captain arrived at almost the same moment.

There were salutes and some stiff posturing, but, of course, from my position at the mizzen mast, I could hear not a word they spoke. Then the two officers started aft. Gordon's gaze settled on the first midshipman he saw.

"Mister Baldwin. Escort Lieutenant Meade of the Royal Navy to the commodore's cabin, if you please. He has a letter for Commodore Barron." Captain Gordon, seeing I had little to do, save gawk at the goings-on, summoned me.

I hastened to the quarterdeck, saluted Lieutenant Meade and, with a quick, "Follow me, if you please, sir," led him to the hatch which would take us to the gun deck immediately outside the Great Cabin. Upon which door, I knocked.

"Commodore, sir, this is Lieutenant Meade of HMS *Leopard*. He has brought a letter for you, sir."

Barron heaved his bulk up from the chair and stood as we entered the Cabin. At something over six feet in height, he towered over the English officer, whom he greeted with a scowl and a grunt. Doctor Bullus, whom I noticed taking his ease in a comfortable chair in the quarter gallery, merely looked up, a quizzical smile in place, and remained mute.

"Sir." Meade began, obviously intimidated by the size of the man as well as his seniority, "I have been sent with this letter from Captain Humphreys of HMS *Leopard*. I believe you will find it quite reasonable. Also this copy of an order from Admiral Berkeley, our commander-in-chief on the North Atlantic Station. Captain Humphreys asked me to express his hopes that this matter could be resolved in a manner such that the harmony between our two countries might remain intact." He thrust toward the commodore a sheaf of papers; prominent on the top, I noticed, was a folded sheet bearing a red wax seal. Not having been dismissed, I stood silently just inside the door and watched the events unfold before me.

The commodore made a cursory appraisal of the letter and glanced down at the Royal Navy officer. "This contains a list of your deserters, Lieutenant. What possible interest could I have in the Royal Navy's inability to hold on to its sailors?" Barron's tone was so disarming, I was sure that Meade had been caught unprepared. Barron's gaze returned to the documents he held and it was apparent, even to me, that his question had not required an answer.

"Sir. As you can see, it requests me to muster your crew and determine whether or not they are in your ship." Meade had warmed to his task; his tone was arrogant and not in the least conciliatory.

"Midshipman . . . Baldwin, isn't it?" Barron looked at me quickly. I stood stiffly to attention and nodded in silence. He went on. "Step to the quarterdeck and ask Master Commandant Gordon to join us, if you please."

I practically fell over myself in my haste to carry out the commodore's bidding. In no time at all, I was back, the captain with me.

"Captain Gordon, Lieutenant Meade, here, seems to think we have some Royal Navy deserters aboard. At least his captain does. Here is the list of them. Any familiar to you?" The commodore, now seated, thrust the paper at Gordon.

The captain took it, his gaze never wavering from the commodore's. He responded without so much as a glance at the papers he now held.

"Sir. Most of the men have only been aboard a matter of days. We have barely assigned them stations on the watch, quarters, and station bill. I could not say whether we have any Britishers aboard. But I will say," and here he turned from the commodore to face Lieutenant Meade full on, "that I instructed our recruiters most plainly that they were not to enlist any deserters from the Royal Navy." As he finished speaking, he glanced at me, no doubt recalling that I had been an officer in charge of a rendezvous and responsible for the presence aboard of some forty and more of our recent arrivals.

"Very well, Mister Gordon. I shall write a suitable response to Captain Humphreys. You may return to your duties." As he spoke, Commodore Barron was dipping a quill and drawing a sheet of paper from the drawer of his desk.

Gordon left, I stood silently in my place near the door, and Lieutenant Meade stood rigidly where he had been all along, in front of the desk. The scene recalled in my mind a time many years back when I had been called before the headmaster of the academy I attended in Philadelphia. I had stood at attention in front of the man's desk while he appeared, for what seemed an eternity, not to notice me. Clearly the headmaster had been proving his great importance – and my complete lack of any – to me. And so, it seemed, was the commodore.

The silence, punctuated only by the noises of a ship hove to in a calm sea and the scratching of Barron's pen, endured. The splash of a wave breaking against the ship's side, the rattle of our rigging, now slack, now under a strain, and the slap of flaccid canvas offset the silence and offered a counterpoint to the "snick, snick" made by the commodore's quill as it moved in fits and starts across the vellum.

Barron wrote quickly, pausing often to scowl at the young man standing before him, then returning to his task. Each of the first few times Barron looked up, Meade started to extend his hand as if to take the completed letter. After several false starts, the young lieutenant simply stood still, his eyes, like my own, focused on the distorted image of the sea beyond the quarter gallery windows.

"Come in!" Barron grunted in an annoyed response to a knock on his door.

"Sir, Captain Gordon's compliments, sir, and there's a signal from *Leopard*. Recalling their cutter, they are. Sir." The seaman, the messenger of the watch from the quarterdeck, stood loosely as he moved to the motion of the ship and twisted his hat in front of him.

"Very well, sailor. Thank you." Barron didn't even look up as the messenger tugged at his forelock in salute and turned to leave, then thought better of it and stopped.

"Should I tell 'em something, sir?"

Meade appeared discomfited by the message just delivered and answered. "I expect I should be getting back, sir. Cap'n Humphreys is not one to be kept waiting."

Barron continued writing. "Stand fast, Lieutenant! I am just about done here and you, and your impatient captain, shall have your answer to these outrageous demands. Allow you to muster my crew, indeed!" This last was muttered and I barely caught it. Remembering the waiting seaman, he lifted his head and, louder this time, instructed him tersely, "You may tell Mister Gordon that Lieutenant Meade will be along directly."

Finally, Barron put his pen in the stand, sprinkled some sand on the completed paper and stood. When he blew the excess sand off, a goodly portion of it hit the British officer.

"Here, young man. Go back to your captain with this. I am sure it will satisfy him. Mister . . . Baldwin, you may escort Lieutenant Meade to his boat. And kindly ask Mister Gordon to come down on your return." Meade followed me out the door.

Not only would I ask Mister Gordon to come down, I would personally bring him! I had witnessed the start of this play and was most keen to see how it might finish.

"Here is the answer I sent back, Mister Gordon." Barron wasted no time on pleasantries when Gordon and I stepped back into the Cabin. (I kept my earlier post close by the door so as to remain as unobtrusive as I might.) "And here is a copy of their admiral's order seeking return of their sailors. You will note that Admiral Berkeley has not ruled out the use of force should we not accede to his demands. I submit you ought to get your gun deck clear as their intentions seem likely to follow that course. No telling what lengths that man, Humphreys, might go to in the interest of carrying out Berkeley's orders. And get the ship underway."

Gordon, his face darkening perceptibly, hastily read the British admiral's orders to his subordinates. I, of course, had no idea what words were written on the papers, either by the British captain or the admiral, but they must have been some sharp to provoke the reaction they did in my two senior officers. Captain Gordon returned the several pages to the commodore and, turning, motioned to me to follow him.

As the captain and I heard the Cabin door close behind us, he said to me, "Mister Baldwin, get the word passed to put the crew at quarters. Quietly, if you please. There will be no drum this time. No sense alerting the Brits we're ready for them."

I hastened forward on the gun deck to carry out my orders, repeating to any I met, men, midshipmen, and officers, the captain's instructions. I was dismayed when I heard the Marine beating his drum, calling the men to quarters as he was trained to do. I quickly silenced him which confused the men, mostly landsmen and former merchant seamen who, unlike the Marine, had never been trained in what was about to happen. Many, in fact, turned about, intent on returning to previous tasks, thinking the call to quarters to be a false alarm.

Baggage, furniture, huge casks, and boxes littered the gun deck as completely as the spar deck, making it nearly impossible for anyone to move about freely. Finding room for the guns to move backwards against their side tackles when fired seemed hopeless, but had to be accomplished if we were to fire them and then re-load. Fortunately, we had conformed to Navy policy and all the guns had been loaded prior to our departure; it would be loading the second shot, should such a happenstance prove necessary, that presented the problem.

"Mister Baldwin. See about getting some of this area cleared so we might fire the guns! And get some powder and shot up." Henry Allen, my immediate superior and the one actually responsible for second division and the six guns assigned to our care on either side of the ship, shouted from across the deck as he struggled to push people and crates out of his way. I noticed he wore his sword and had a pistol tucked into his belt.

Rounding up a few men I recognized from having recruited them at Mrs. Pickney's Rooming House and eatery in Norfolk, I directed them to wrestle the hogsheads and crates away from our guns. Another I sent to the magazine. It was then that I noticed the hawser – it had to have been our spare anchor cable—as great in girth as a man's thigh, laid out in neat fakes behind five of my six guns, ones which would likely be on the engaged side, should it come to that. A glance told me it would be a hundred fathoms and more in length and impossible to handle. The loops of the cable made an intricate pattern of lines and curves which might have intrigued a landsman; I had no interest in the beauty of the design that lay before me, only how best to move it. Clearly, it would take a great deal of time and men to shift the cumbersome rope out of the way. Lieutenant Allen's agitated state told me that should the British be intent on mischief, we would not have anywhere near enough time to accomplish such a Herculean task even though we might have the seamen available. I focused on the one cannon not blocked by someone's lack of foresight in where they had stowed the cable and began personally to shove a large and heavy crate far enough away from it so when the gun fired, it might have room to recoil unimpeded.

After some minutes of heaving and sweating, I received help in the form of two sailors who joined in my efforts and together we got the crate out of the way and began to wrestle another to a spot clear of the gun carriage. Around us, the confusion of shouted orders, curses, and efforts to clear the deck swirled in a cacophony of chaos. Many of the men had no idea of where they were supposed to be, let alone what to do once there. They milled about, their questioning shouts to equally confounded shipmates adding to the ruckus and confusion.

"Mister Baldwin!" I heard Henry's voice above the din. I looked up and saw him closer, but still struggling to make his way through the tangle of stores and men to where I was engaged in my exertions. "Powder horns, Mister Baldwin! Hang it all! We will need powder horns. Fetch them up from the magazine, if you please."

Lieutenant Allen's outburst gave a clear indication of his agitated state; like Captain Decatur, he is not one given easily to blaspheming. I threw a sloppy salute at my superior and, dodging the knots of confused, milling sailors that seemed to choke the entire deck, ran as quickly as I could through the litter to the first hatch that would take me down three decks to the magazine.

The confusion there, if possible, was worse than I had found on the gun deck. A ragged queue of powder monkeys, boys, and aggravated sailors pushed and shoved, shouting to Gunner Hook, each other, and any in earshot, that they needed ". . . powder horns, gunner. A few bags as well."

And ". . . powder here, Gunner. Mister Aldrich sent me and he ain't one to suffer any tarryin'!"

"Cartridges, Gunner. And quick! Ain't none topside. Them Brits gonna be shootin' at us quicker 'an ever."

Shoving worried and angry sailors out of my way, I struggled to get close to the magazine. With the help of my uniform, I gained a position at the front, stunned at what I saw there.

The gunner was quite confounded. He stood back from the door and well into the magazine, away from the waving hands that reached toward him. He held a powder horn in one hand and, on a rude table to the side, an open cask of black powder stood. Empty horns littered the table and the deck. A few felt bags, empty, lay in rumpled uselessness behind him near an open barrel of powder, a scoop showing at the top. His white face, vacant stare, and slack jaw gave testimony to the horror he felt at not having made up cartridges for the cannons and filled powder horns to use for priming them.

I yelled at him. "Gunner! Gunner! Fill that horn and give it to me. Now! HOOK! DO IT!"

I would never have dared to speak to Gunner Tarbox in *Argus* with that tone of voice, but then, Tarbox would never have been caught so ill-prepared.

The man looked at me and took a step backwards. Suddenly he fixed his eyes upon me, a flicker of recognition in them. His hands shook and, as though he were a trapped animal seeking escape, he frantically shifted his gaze from the horn he held, to the small cask before him, then back to me. It seemed an age before his desperate look gave way to understanding and, as if working under water, his hand moved toward the cask. As he pulled the plug from the horn with his teeth, his eyes, wide and unblinking, again met mine and he started to pour the powder from the cask.

"Yes, Gunner. That's it. Fill it right up and then another. Quickly." I tried to sound encouraging, mask the terror I felt at being alongside a fifty-gun ship which might begin firing at us from pistol-shot range at any moment. The man turned to his task, the tip of his tongue replacing the horn's plug between his teeth, as he concentrated on not spilling the powder. In my mind, images of Gunner Tarbox, with the great booming voice and his orderly magazine on *Argus,* overlaid what was before me. In my days in *Argus*, I didn't appreciate the imposing gunner; now I would have given anything for the terrifying Tarbox to materialize and hand me a powder horn!

After an eternity, during which I was jostled and shoved without regard to my rank, Hook stuck out a great paw grasping two filled powder horns. Swatting and elbowing away the other grasping hands seeking to grab the precious horns, *my* precious powder horns, I managed to seize them, incurring the voluble outrage of my competitors, and press them to my chest. Then I fought my way through the mob, grown larger now as more gun captains and officers recognized our dangerous situation, and struggled to the ladder, proud of my success. I surely would not have dared to act in so ungentlemanly a fashion in *Argus* or *Enterprise*! But as a still untested youngster in those days, I had yet to experience the devastation and terror of cannon fire at close range.

Hardly had I regained the gun deck, when Captain Gordon himself appeared, heading for the hatch I had just left.

BOOM! BOOM! The sound of cannons discharging was as loud as if they had been fired from our own ship. *Leopard*, now some sixty yards to weather of us, had fired on us! We were not at war with England, or anyone else for that matter. What could they be thinking? We all ducked instinctively, holding our collective breath as we waited for the crash and splintering of wood as the two iron balls—*were they twenty-four-pounders?*—found their mark. For that brief moment, a sudden and exquisite silence rang throughout the gun deck.

Mercifully, none struck the frigate; a voice cried out that they had fired one shot across our bow, followed by one to our stern. Immediately, the cries and shouts, confusion and disorder returned. The captain, white faced, pushed me aside, causing me almost to drop my precious cargo, and grabbed at a boy, a powder monkey, just emerging from the ladder with two felt bags, each filled with six pounds of black powder. Without so much as "Sorry" or "By your leave" he snatched the cartridges from the startled youth and ran aft to a starboard side battery.

But before he had taken five steps, a breathtaking explosion filled the air and *Chesapeake* shuddered, then reeled under a broadside from *Leopard,* this one clearly intended to bring us to grief. Happily for those of us below the spar deck, they had aimed high, and the shot tore through our rigging, wreaking havoc aloft and alow as it cut through shrouds, sheets, braces, ties, and lifts. Almost before the thunder of the broadside ended, we could hear over our heads the heavy *thumps* and screams as falling blocks and broken spars fell to the deck, killing or cruelly wounding the sailors unlucky enough to be in the wrong place.

"Allen! Baldwin! Get that gun firing." Gordon screamed as he ran up a ladder to the spar deck, his frustration at trying to be in several places at once evident in his voice. I noticed, without conscious thought, that he no longer held the two cartridges.

BOOM! Another broadside erupted from the British ship. This time, we felt the full effect of it as the heavy iron shot, at least fifteen of them, slammed into our hull. The ship stagggered, seemingly shaken by a huge unseen hand. Some of the British iron flew into the open or nearly open gunports, upturning some cannon and dismounting others, while more of the twenty-four pound shot plowed through the cargo still lying helter-skelter all over the deck. A few managed to fly into our sailors, killing two instantly and gruesomely, and leaving others desperately wounded and screaming in agony. A shower of splinters tore into a near-at-hand landsman who let out a blood-curdling yell and fell over, clutching at his stomach; a jagged sliver of wood, some two feet and more, extended out from between his gore-covered hands. I stared, open-mouthed, at the man and the spreading pool of crimson staining our pristine deck, quite unable to move for several moments. The confusion of the gun deck swirled around me, fueled by our fear and the cruel wounds evident throughout. Before any could recover, return to whatever efforts remained of trying to return fire, or even regain a shred of composure, *Leopard* fired again. Another broadside, and, again into our hull with equally devastating result.

I saw Lieutenant Allen, covered in gore, struggling with the train tackle on the gun I had earlier begun to clear. As I watched, he grabbed two sailors, shook them violently into their senses, and directed them to cast off the tackles opposite him. I noted that his appearance had shocked the seamen as much as it had me. Shaking off the stupefying shock which had held me in an immobilizing embrace, I ran to help him.

"Henry! What has happened to you? You have been shot!" I screamed above the din around us.

He looked at himself, obviously surprised at my outburst and, I think, some startled at the sight of his front and arms scarlet with blood. Then he shook his head.

"Not mine. One of the lads was quite undone by a ball. Likely to have been a twenty-four-pounder. Caught it square on, he did. Must have splashed onto me." He pointed over his shoulder where a body, its upper half mostly gone, lay in a widening pool of crimson.

I was again shocked into speechless immobility at the sight and, though utterly horrifying, I found myself quite unable to tear my eyes away from it. The man, from the top of nankeen trousers down, looked quite normal; had I noticed the legs splayed out from behind a gun carriage, I likely would have admonished their owner to get back to work. What remained of the upper portion of the poor unfortunate was scarcely recognizable as having belonged to a man; bits of flesh, some pale and bloodless, others crimson with the man's life blood, were strewn about as though by a careless child. Pieces of bone lay starkly white in the deepening pool of blood and a nearly intact arm, its sleeve as ragged as the arm itself, had landed incongruously atop a hogshead, seemingly placed there for later use.

Allen's voice, insistent and urgent, penetrated my horror and I turned away from the spectacle to face my officer. He appeared oblivious to the carnage, indeed, paying it no more attention than had it been an up-turned bucket. His voice, directed at me, as well as those near at hand, was raised over the cacophony and, as he grabbed a pair of sailors (they appeared to be as stunned by the devastation as I) he shouted in a voice crackling with urgency, "If we can get this gun trained around, by the Almighty, we can gave 'em a taste of our own iron!"

The fire that burned in his eyes, even in the dim light of the gun deck, and the ferocity of his tone drove the dreadful specter of the severed body from my mind and replaced it with one of us returning a hot fire. That, and Henry's words, inspired me to an effort beyond my limits and with the aid of the two sailors, we manhandled the eighteen-pounder long gun around to aim at our tormentor. Using one of my powder horns, Henry spilled a small quantity into the touch hole of the gun, then looked about frantically.

"My God! We've no match or loggerhead! Fetch me a linstock, Oliver . . . or anything to touch a spark to 'er. A bit of slow match, a flint, anything." Allen's frustration at standing behind a loaded and ready cannon with no means of touching it off gave his voice a sense of exigency that sent me scurrying fore and aft in search of the needed flame, slow match, or, indeed, anything, anything that might serve our purpose.

When my frantic rush brought me back to the gun empty-handed, Henry was gone, apparently on a similar quest. Suddenly he re-appeared, stumbling and tripping over fallen sailors, boxes, and rope, a smoking loggerhead from the galley held aloft.

He jammed it into the little puddle of powder in the touch hole and received not so much as a sparkle for his efforts. The wood was not hot enough to ignite the powder! Throwing it down in disgust, he ran off again, only to return a scant moment later with a glowing coal from the galley camboose balanced in a soup ladle.

"Stand back!" he warned us, and, blowing on the coal, which responded with a small burst of flame, he dumped the now flaming ember into the touch hole. He was instantly rewarded with the sputtering of the powder there and, in a second, the explosion of the gun.

With a deafening roar, the cannon discharged its ball and a six foot tail of fire, immediately slamming backward in recoil, to come to rest against the now straining breach tackles.

"Again! Swab 'er out and load another!" Henry's cry penetrated the ringing deafness that always follows a firing, but the ramrod he brandished aloft left no doubt in any mind as to his meaning. I threw a sponge at one of the men who quickly shoved it into the barrel to extinguish any lingering sparks. The rest of our short crew turned to with a will, quickly preparing our gun to speak again.

"Below there! On the gundeck. Hold your fire! We've struck our colors!" A voice—it sounded to me like the commodore himself—shouted down the ladder to the gun deck loud enough to rise above the clamor and confusion that still reigned throughout.

Another voice, equally loud and commanding, echoed the first. "We are surrendered! Cease fire!"

I looked at Lieutenant Allen and I am sure his slack-jawed incredulity must have mirrored my own expression.

Struck? We had struck our colors after three broadsides? What had possessed someone on the quarterdeck to do such a thing? And, more puzzling, who? Surely not Commodore Barron! Though that first voice most assuredly belonged to him.

Together we ran for the ladder to the spar deck, manhandling out of our way the still bewildered sailors who were dumbstruck, either from the three broadsides we had just received and the chaos and carnage that lay all about, or our precipitous surrender. In deference to his rank, I let the lieutenant gain the deck first but was close in his wake.

On deck, we were greeted with the same confusion and frantic desperation as we had just left. Fallen spars, blocks, chain and rope lay strewn on the deck amid the crates, bundles, casks, and hogsheads, unmoved since leaving Norfolk that morning. Twisted among the wreckage were men, wounded in varying degrees, but all crying out in their agony. Large pools of gore stained the previously immaculate, nearly white deck and gave testimony to the carnage wrought by the falling rigging and chain-shot. The lower mizzen mast was missing a great piece, almost like a bite had been taken of it, apparently gouged out by an iron ball. Both the main and the fore masts were wounded as well, though not as badly. Our sails were cut by the grape and canister we had received in the first full broadside. The main topmast, its shrouds having mostly been carried away, teetered as the ship rolled in the still mercifully easy seas, and lines, cut from aloft, hung in useless disarray throughout our rig. Amid the pandemonium, men and officers pushed and shoved, lifted and shouted, as they attempted to get to the men pinned under the fallen rigging.

Henry and I were dumbstruck! He stood open-mouthed as the scene registered; I am sure my expression was no different. I had seen nothing like this carnage and disarray even after a several hour running battle with Tripolitan gunboats. And this was the result of fifteen minutes of gunnery! I later discovered that we had been hulled in twenty-one places.

"Mister Allen. You will accompany Mister Smith in the boat, if you please." The commodore's voice, icy calm, penetrated our sensibilities and Henry stepped off to the larboard side where the cutter had been secured under the gate in the bulwark. I noticed several splotches of crimson on the commodore's white breeches, but he seemed not to be concerned about them and I followed the progress of my friend and the first lieutenant as they disappeared through the bulwark. They soon re-appeared, seated in the sternsheets of the cutter, as they were rowed across the short span of open water toward *Leopard.*

Why were our first lieutenant and a junior officer being sent to the ship which had just pummeled us into wreckage? Should not the victor come on board his conquest and claim his prize? I pushed aside unanswerable questions and watched the boat.

Had Father not warned me against wagering those many years ago when I first left Philadelphia and the sheltered life I led in their house on Held Street (he also warned me about blaspheming and the effects of strong spirits, but neither warning had stuck with me for long), I would have wagered all I had that not a man among us took a breath while every eye topside was on the cutter and the two officers as they made the side of the British warship.

Within moments, our first lieutenant and Henry Allen were back in the cutter retracing their course to *Chesapeake.* And followed by two boats from *Leopard* carrying in their sternsheets at least three (that I could see) Royal Navy officers.

As our boat drew closer, I could see both Allen and Lieutenant Smith were clearly agitated; they talked with great animation, their eyes shifting constantly from each other to the two boats following, to the still gaping muzzles of *Leopard's* guns menacing our ship, and finally, to *Chesapeake's* quarterdeck where Barron paced in great vexation, smacking his fist onto his open palm.

By contrast, Captain Gordon who I had last seen tearing topside from the gundeck as our own special hell began, and who was the one likely to answer to the Secretary for the surrender of his ship, was white-faced and quiet; stunned, I would reckon, and perhaps even unable to grasp the enormity of what had just transpired. The work on deck, stopped by most to follow the actions of our officers, had resumed; the surgeon's mates treated a few of the wounded and carried others below to be looked after by Doctor Bullus and our surgeon. Topmen were aloft sorting out the tangle of broken spars, shredded canvas, swinging blocks, and dangling ropes, securing any that might suddenly give way and drop to the deck and cause further injury to the crew.

Surrender! What possibly could they have been thinking! An American warship surrendered after receiving three broadsides and only one shot fired in response! Decatur would surely not have behaved in such a disgraceful way.

My mind continued to reel with more and more unanswerable questions. I shifted my gaze haphazardly, not knowing whether to keep an eye on the two British boats or my colleagues in our own boat. Standing close at hand, equally incredulous at the shameful drama in which we were all now players, my fellow midshipmen and a clutch of seamen seemed to suffer the same indecision.

Our boat made the side first and, as the first lieutenant rushed aft to the quarterdeck, Henry Allen came and stood where a knot of junior lieutenants and several midshipmen had gathered. I moved to join that agitated group.

"Henry, what happened over there? What were you sent to do? Present the captain's sword in surrender? What did they say?" Joshua Belcher, a midshipman slightly senior to me, cried out. From the corner of my eye, I could see Lieutenant Smith making his report to Commodore Barron and Captain Gordon. Scowls, wide-eyed horror, and, finally, incredulity greeted his report.

"Aye. Smith and I were sent to tell them in *Leopard* that *Chesapeake* was surrendered and their prize. Captain Humphreys—he's commander over there—personally told us he had no interest in taking our ship as a prize. 'We're not at war with you Jonathans and she wouldn't be adjudged a fair prize, in any case.' Those were his words. Smith very nearly collapsed when he heard that. 'Why ever did you fire on us, then?' he asked. 'You have British seamen aboard who are deserters from the Royal Navy and it is our intention to return them to where they ought to be. After a proper court martial and punishment is meted out, of course. To that end, Lieutenant Smith, we will *again* send a boat on board your ship, muster your crew, and find our missing sailors. We expect your cooperation . . . or at the very least, your non-interference. After we have recovered our property, you are free to carry on as you will.' Then the pompous ass turned, gave a few orders relating to their boats and some officers, and marched himself right aft to the quarterdeck, where he still stands, I'd warrant."

"*Muster our crew?* That's what started this whole affair in the first place!" I couldn't help my self; Barron's words—and he must have put them in the letter he sent to Humphreys as well—still echoed in my head. Of course, none of the others had been privy to the meeting between Meade and the commodore and suddenly they all spoke at once, questioning me on my knowledge.

By then the two boats were alongside and the British officers on our deck. Without a lot of fanfare, we were pleased to note. One of them, a tall fellow with a large sharp nose with spectacles perched on it, stepped onto the quarterdeck and, quite ignoring Captain Gordon, faced the commodore with all the bearing of a Roman gladiator standing over his victim. That he arrived on that hallowed deck without so much as a 'by your leave' added insult to injury. We could not hear their words, but the effect of them became apparent as soon as the bosun blew shrilly on his pipe and called for "All hands to muster in the waist, and look lively, there! Form up by division."

My colleagues and I went to the break of the quarterdeck while the hands assembled, mostly grumbling and growling. Two British officers and a master's mate stood rigidly facing forward, their hands clasped tightly behind them. They seemed quite unmoved by the wreckage strewn about the deck before them or the obvious stains of blood which they had taken some pains to avoid.

I noticed they wore swords and two of them, the master's mate and one of the lieutenants, had pistols stuck into their trousers. *Do they really think they will need those? We have surrendered and, unlike the corsairs off Tripoli, will not begin the fight again.* I felt the same sense of outrage that, I am sure, burned in the breast of every man aboard.

The three officers moved through the ranks of our sailors and marines, stepping over fallen blocks, cordage, and bloodstains, still shining wetly, all wrought by their untimely broadsides. One of the officers, a lieutenant, would stop directly in front of each man in turn, staring into his face, then questioning him and inspecting him closely. Each response was checked against our muster book and then the name was compared to a paper the master's mate held. Every man-jack in the crew received equal attention.

And then the British boarding party searched the ship. The whole of it lasted for over three hours while we lay hove to under the still gaping guns of *Leopard*.

When it was done, the British had discovered four men whose names appeared on their list. They also found another eight whom they identified as British, but whose names were not included in their orders. We all waited, with growing impatience and indignation, as a boat went to Humphreys and returned, bearing instructions to bring only the four named deserters. Along with the orders was a letter to James Barron, which, I later discovered, deplored the whole event, and offered whatever assistance might be required by our cruelly wounded ship. Indeed!

After the three officers left with their prisoners, among whom (I found out later from Lieutenant Keane) were three Americans who had indeed deserted HMS *Melampus* to which ship they had been impressed a year before, Barron sent Henry Allen, by himself, back to the British vessel in a further—and futile—attempt to have Humphreys accept his surrender. Never before or since have I seen such outrage as enveloped Lieutenant Allen, or any other in memory, for that matter. His face scarlet, eyes hard, and fists clenched tightly, he was quite unable to give voice to his feelings beyond a sputtered ". . . a shameful disgrace" and " . . . humiliation beyond description." He busied himself with trying to restore order to the gundeck. His efforts also gave our sailors employment. Allen worked feverishly, quite obviously trying to exorcise the demons of our dishonor from his mind, moving barrels and boxes by himself which normally two, or even three, men would have been hard-pressed to handle. And all the while his scowl never left his face, or his mutterings his lips.

During the late evening, Barron called the officers and midshipmen into the Cabin. He sat at his desk, his waistcoat unbuttoned and his jacket thrown over a chair. His normally round face was drawn and, while he wouldn't have stood upon any of our entrances, he sat very still, casting nary a glance at any of us as we arrayed ourselves before him. His hands remained folded in front of him with two fingers forming a steeple. I noticed his breeches still showed the crimson stains I had seen earlier, immediately after our surrender. Overhead, we could all hear the sounds, hammering, thumps, muted shouts, of the work necessary to bring the vessel into condition sufficient for sailing the fifty or so miles back to Norfolk. It made a telling counterpoint to the silence that pervaded the Cabin.

After allowing us to read Admiral Berkeley's order, the British captain's letters and his own response, he asked our opinion of the day's events. Charles Gordon, Captain, at least in our minds if not that of the commodore, spoke first.

"Sir," he began, cautiously. "Your . . . action spared the effusion of blood, beyond that which was already lost."

Barron nodded and looked next at our first lieutenant, Ben Smith, who looked impassively back at him, then shifted his gaze to the darkness beyond the quarter gallery windows. He remained mute. Barron's gaze didn't waver nor did he change his expression.

"We have disgraced the flag!" Henry Allen spoke in a quiet, obviously strained tone; his effort at self-control seemed more to underscore than hide the humiliation and rage that still consumed him. And even though he did not raise his voice even a little, his contempt for our commodore's action was plain to all.

Now Barron's eyes, indeed, his whole body, snapped around to face Allen, but he said nothing, preferring to fix the lieutenant with a blistering stare. His arms trembled, whether in an effort at self-restraint or anger, I knew not, but his whole body spoke eloquently in reaction to my friend's words, words which we all thought but had not the courage to speak. I was proud to know Henry and even prouder still when he did not flinch a single muscle in his being, but rather stared straight back into the commodore's glaring eyes.

"Hmmph! That will be all. You are dismissed." Barron's icy tone left no room for question and, as one, we all stood and filed out of the Cabin. Little conversation followed, save a few carefully guarded smiles and nods to Henry for expressing what we all had felt.

Thanks to light and contrary winds, we were employed for two days making our way back to Hampton Roads where we set our starboard anchor in seven fathoms at a half past the noon meridian on the twenty-fourth of June.

CHAPTER TWO

The Dream had returned. I awoke in time to hear four bells chime indicating two on the clock in the middle watch. Despite the winter cold and damp that permeated the entire ship, including the midshipmen's cockpit below the gun deck, my tangled bedding was soaked in perspiration and my nightshirt a sodden mess. Sweat ran down my face and back the moment I sat up to swing my legs onto the deck. I shivered as the cold, stale air hit me and, as I dropped to the deck, I grabbed my great coat off the peg by the door and wrapped it around me. Having been visited by the Dream many times (though happily, not recently until tonight), I took the only course which, in the past, had allowed me to clear my head; I sat at our mess table.

There was a dim pool of warm, yellow light thrown by the well-trimmed lantern hanging to one side of the table. With the wick turned down so low, it emitted hardly any smoke at all, and enough light to identify chairs and seachests. The shadows cast by the lantern's glow danced in an exaggerated imitation of the small movements of the lamp itself as the ship swayed gently against her mooring lines. So consumed with my plight, I barely noticed the shapes of the shadows, nor did I particularly care whether or not I sat in the light or the dark.

Gradually, my heavy coat offset the chill I had earlier experienced and, while my physical being grew more comfortable, my inner one remained as tangled as had been my bed linens; for, try as I might, I could not cast the images from my muddled brain, images that, in their horror, had dragged me up to consciousness from a sound, but evidently restless, sleep. The Dream had not held me since the early fall; in fact, it seemed to go away about the time the repairs to the cruelly wounded frigate were complete. And now, it was back in all its vivid awfulness and just as sharp and frightening as ever it had been: our encounter with the British man-o'-war.

Except that, in the Dream, the events played out as though all the elements of it were underwater; each of the iron shot that slammed into *Chesapeake* was clearly visible, leaving the muzzles of the English cannon in great gouts of fire and smoke, coming at us, languidly floating through the air, and the splinters that flew into my shipmates' flesh seemed almost to drift from the bulkhead as the ball struck, and make their way in a most leisurely manner into the men nearby. I would try to scream and push them aside, but to no avail as my screams and my own movements mimicked those of the splinters and balls. I saw Henry Allen receive his soaking in the gore of the sailor who took a twenty-four-pound ball in the chest, marveling that each droplet of blood and shard of flesh moved slowly, effortlessly, and in exquisite detail. This was perhaps the most chilling part of the Dream as I had not actually witnessed the original event, only the aftermath. My trip to the magazine for a powder horn was chaotic, even more so than the actual, and made me cry out in anger and frustration. Instead of the clutch of seamen gathered at the magazine, there were hundreds, all pushing and shoving, ignoring me completely, blocking my way and causing me to waste precious time in fulfilling my mission. All the while, balls from the British ship pounded our vessel unmercifully, wreaking havoc far worse than what we had, in the event, experienced. The horror of it was so real, so vibrant in its detail, that even here, in the midshipmen's mess at two in the morning, I could taste again the noxious, sulphurous smoke that blew down on us from our antagonist. My nose wrinkled as I again smelled the freshly spilled blood and again my own bile rose to my throat in protest of the revulsion that seemed to consume me.

In each repeat of the Dream, when Henry and I came topside, we found, amid the shambles of the spar deck, the commodore and Captain Gordon standing on the quarterdeck, laughing hysterically and pointing at our tormentor, even closer in the Dream than it had been on that frightful day last June. Not only was my Dream peopled with my fellow Chesapeakes, but also with random faces from my past: James Stevens and Thomas Wheatley (now both dead) from *Enterprise*, my brother Edward, still draped in the chains of his captivity in Tripoli, and even the master of the academy I attended in Philadelphia before becoming a midshipman. Edward moved about the gundeck, clanking his chains and exhorting us to hurry our preparations lest the Tripolitan corsairs board us, as they had his own ill-starred frigate, *Philadelphia*.

Must have been telling the story at the court martial I mused, trying to make some sense of why, after so long an absence, this dreadful nightmare had chosen now to pay me a visit. *Thinking about that shameful day and dredging up all the horrifying details had refreshed the memory and now here it was again.* I tried, in vain, to think about other things, pleasant memories like my reunion with Mother and Father after returning from the Barbary Coast. But that, too, held unpleasant associations; Edward was still captive in that dreadful dungeon, held by the Bashaw of Tripoli, his fate uncertain. While my parents were delighted at *my* return and welcomed me with open arms to their fine house on Held Street in Philadelphia, Edward's absence cast a pall over what might have been a joyous occasion. Other happy memories flashed through my mind, only to be pushed away by the vivid memory of the Dream and the actual events that had incited it.

I turned my mind to yesterday's court martial proceedings. After I had told my story to a silent and attentive panel, interrupted only by the scratching of Barron's pen and that of his lawyer as they took notes of my tale, Mister Tazewell, who had been resting his backside against a table throughout most of my monologue, stirred himself and stepped to his earlier position in front of me.

"Mister Baldwin. That is a recitation worthy of a youthful memory. Pray, in your opinion, was *Chesapeake* able to fight beyond the firing of your single gun? After the surrender, I mean"

I at first had thought his remark about my memory a compliment; after brief reflection, the reference to my youth caused me to bristle silently. I was eighteen years of age (nearly nineteen!) and well-seasoned by my four years of service. Surely few would mistake me for the raw fourteen-year-old who sailed in *Argus*! I recognized the heat rising in my neck and face and struggled to overcome the perceived slight. A deep breath helped.

"Yes. Unquestionably she could fight. Which is why Mister Allen and I, along with everyone else aboard were so stunned that we had surrendered." I controlled myself and answered in an even tone.

"And why, do you imagine, were not the other guns fired? Were they not loaded prior to leaving port as would be expected?" Tazewell continued.

Do I imagine? I did not imagine anything, you fool. I know *why they did not fire. The gun crews had little idea of what to do or even where they should be. We had no powder up even had the sailors been at their stations. Calm down, Oliver. Getting your dander up ain't the way to answer. Deep breath, now and just answer the question.*

With a conscious effort, I calmed down, though my insides continued to churn.

"Yes, sir. They were indeed loaded. We had no match on the gundeck and few powder horns. Or cartridges, for that matter." I answered evenly. "And the deck was lumbered with stores." I added.

"Very well. To your knowledge, was any report of the incident you have just described, beyond that of the commodore, sent ashore?" Mister Tazewell spoke quietly, perhaps sensing my well-disguised (I thought) reaction to his earlier comment.

It seemed a strange question to pose to a lowly midshipman until I remembered the paper with his account of the action that Henry had asked us all to sign. I had been reluctant until I saw the scrawl of Lieutenant Ben Smith, our first lieutenant prominently at the top of the list of those who had already signed. I nodded to Tazewell.

"Aye, sir. I believe a letter was sent to the Secretary giving an account of the attack. It was carried ashore by the doctor . . . Doctor Bullus, and Captain Gordon in the pilot boat the very afternoon we returned."

"And who wrote this letter, Mister Baldwin?"

"Sir, I am not sure. But I believe one of the officers wrote it."

"So this was different and apart from Commodore Barron's official report of the affair?"

"I assume so, sir." I knew what the letter had said; Barron would not . . . could not have called for his own arrest for his negligence.

"Very well, Midshipman. During your telling, you mentioned that you saw Captain Gordon on the gundeck carrying several cartridges for the long guns. Are you quite sure of that?" Tazewell studied my face for a reaction to being questioned on a detail on the day's events.

"Yes, sir. Quite sure, indeed. But he left them and ran topside immediately the shooting started."

"Did you think it odd that the commanding officer would be dashing about the gundeck laden down with powder cartridges with the ship about to go into action?"

"I was surprised to see him there, sir. But things were so confused and we were all quite befuddled that I don't recall what I thought at the time. I might not have thought anything . . . or had the time to."

"Very well, Mister Baldwin. That's all I have for now. You told a very complete story, I think." Tazewell actually smiled at me and turned to sit at the table reserved for his use.

"Mister Taylor. Any questions for Midshipman Baldwin?" Captain Rodgers' deep voice summoned my next interrogator, the civilian counsel to the accused, from the commodore's table.

"Indeed. Mister Baldwin: that was a fine recounting of a sad affair." Taylor spoke quietly as he rose, ponderously, from Barron's table to stand facing me. The chair groaned, as if relieved to be shed of his weight.

I studied the man's round, florid face, noting the deep-set eyes which seemed to study me with the same intensity as I watched him. His red-veined nose, prominent on his face, along with the roundness of his cheeks, seemed to make his eyes recede even further into his skull. I wondered idly if this man ever laughed . . . or even smiled. His paunch was contained by a straining waistcoat. The thought of his buttons shooting off the garment when he took a breath made me smile, but inwardly, as grinning like some fool at this point would serve only to do me ill.

What more could I possibly offer? I have told them everything I can remember. Not likely to forget any of it for a long time, either!

I watched Taylor for some sign of what was coming. Was I about to be on the receiving end of a broadside? My stomach, quiet now for so long, began again its rumbling and churning, threatening once more to cause me embarrassment.

"Are you familiar with the signal flag codes of the Royal Navy, Mister Baldwin?" Barron's counsel again spoke quietly, quite matter-of-factly, as though we were two friends chatting during a casual encounter.

"No, sir. I am not at all." *Why would he be asking me about British signal codes? I am sure they are as closely guarded secrets as our own are.*

"I believe you mentioned that HMS *Leopard* got underweigh in response to orders from HMS *Bellona*, did you not?"

"Yes, sir."

"And yet, you just told us you were not familiar with the signal codes used by the Royal Navy. How did you know the flags you saw on *Bellona* were, in fact, telling another ship to carry out some action?"

"Well, sir. We saw the flags on *Bellona* answered by *Leopard* which then won her anchor and made sail. Seems logical that was what the flags had meant." I felt a small trickle of wetness make its way down my back and realized that under my short pigtail, my neck was quite wet.

"But you didn't know that at the time, hmmm?" Taylor continued to press, leaning closer to me.

"No sir, not actually." The trickle of sweat on my back was joined by rivulets down my sides. Both of them.

"Did the signals mention anything about attacking your ship? Or did you not know that either?"

Rodgers banged his gavel and spoke. "Mister Taylor, you may find that type of badgering to be productive in a civilian court ashore, sir, but I will not countenance it here. Midshipman Baldwin has already indicated that he is not privy to Royal Navy codes."

Taylor merely glanced at the panel, nodded his head, and continued.

"When you came onto the spardeck, Mister Baldwin, where did you observe the commodore to be standing?"

"He was on the quarterdeck, sir."

"And how would you describe his spirit at the time?"

"His *spirit*, sir? I am not sure what you mean."

"Was he hiding, sheltering from the action? Was he in control and in command?"

"I was not on the deck during the action, sir. I was at my post on the gundeck. And not in a position to see the commodore. When I came topside *after* the firing had stopped, he was standing on the quarterdeck giving orders to lower a boat and man it. He was not hiding, sir. He did seem to have been hit during the shooting, sir, as I noticed on his breeches some bloodstains."

"In fact, bloodstains that, while he made little of the wounds that caused them, were the result of sufficient damage to his person to keep him bedridden for four months after returning to Norfolk." Taylor raised his head, scanning the panel and the gallery, and his voice, making his point about the commodore's bravery ring in the otherwise silent room.

After a lengthy pause, during which not a soul moved nor made any sound, he again returned his attention to me.

"Mister Baldwin," he had lowered his voice to a conspiratorial whisper, so quiet I had to strain to hear. "Did your responsibilities include ensuring the guns, at least those over which you had charge, were ready to fire, save the delivery of shot and powder? Hmmm?" He stared at me, looking down his plump nose and over the spectacles, now lodged at the end of it.

What is he trying to do? Put the blame on me for our inability to return fire? It was one of my guns—and Henry's—that did fire. The only one that did. I had nothing to do with the cargo scattered all over the decks!

Unable to contain myself, I said as much, though my tone was calmer than certainly I felt. "Sir. The guns in my charge *were* ready to fire. In fact, one did. My responsibility did not include stowage of deck cargo; that would have been taken care of by the first lieutenant and the purser. And while it would have been convenient to have the firing locks installed prior to leaving Norfolk, it was not my place to give orders of that nature to Gunner Hook. The guns were still able to fire using the old method of touching off the powder with the use of slow match or loggerhead." I stared back at him in a manner that some might have called both impudent and rude; certainly in a way that I would never have dared only a short four years ago!

"Yes, of course. Well, then you are to be commended for firing the gun."

"Sir. It was not I who fired the gun; it was Lieutenant Allen who managed that. I only helped." Taking undeserved credit went against all I had been taught as a child.

"Oh, very well, Midshipman." His tone sounded quite exasperated. He slowly removed his spectacles and studied me for a moment; his lips formed a thin, straight line in counterpoint to his round face. Then, he shifted his glance to a sheaf of papers he held, squinted his eyes and, ultimately returned his eyeglasses to his nose.

After a moment he looked up and addressed me again. "I believe you gave testimony to the effect that you were assigned recruiting duty at . . ." He paused, leafing through the pages he held while he consulted his notes. "Oh yes, Missus Pickney's Rooming House. A rendezvous, was it not?"

Where was he going with this?

"Yes, sir. I did. And I was."

"Were you given specific orders by Master Commandant Gordon to the effect that no British deserters were to be signed?" He raised his voice slightly, causing me to start.

"We all were given those orders, sir. 'No British deserters.' And as far as we know, we followed them. Sir."

Now it's my *fault we had those British runners aboard* Chesapeake. *And how was I to know that any among the crew were deserters, British or otherwise, should they choose to lie about it? Which apparently several did. But I didn't recall having signed the four captured by the officers in* Leopard.

"Hmmm. It would appear not, Mister Baldwin. Unless of course, those four sailors slipped aboard the frigate unnoticed and on their own!"

I simply looked at him, deciding it could not possibly go well for me were I to argue with him.

"Mister Taylor. May I remind you, sir, that Midshipman Baldwin is *not* the one on trial here. He is only a midshipman, and, with Lieutenant Allen, considered one of the few, the *very* few, who performed honorably." Captain Decatur's tone was some harsh and my inquisitor recoiled visibly in the face of it. And Taylor then turned, and waddled back to his table and sat down next to the commodore. A whispered comment passed between them, their heads close.

After being shown my written testimony, which I was required to approve by signing it, I was excused and told that, should I wish, I could take a seat in the back and listen to the proceedings, which I did, grateful for both Captain Decatur's help and the conclusion of my questioning.

Tazewell's next witness was Lieutenant Allen and, while the Marine fetched him along to the Cabin, we were able to move about a bit, stretching and limbering stiff joints. Henry appeared quickly, curtailing our respite, and after being sworn, he was seated in the same chair I had just vacated. Without incident.

The remainder of the day centered on Henry's story, which agreed in every detail with my own. As it should have. With my role now that of spectator, I was able to indulge myself in the luxury of watching the participants, gauging their reactions to the words my colleague spoke; I had foregone this activity for obvious reasons during my own time in the witness chair.

Barron spent about the whole time alternatively shuffling his papers and scowling myopically at Allen. From time to time, he would shift in his chair, seeking a more comfortable position for his sizeable bulk. Each time he did so, the chair protested loudly, causing the members of the court martial to glance his way. I noticed that when Decatur, Rodgers, and Lawrence did so, their gaze was not kindly. Nor was Barron's when he studied Lieutenant Allen. I was coming to believe the long-standing rumor that the commodore viewed with contempt all of his junior officers and thought them less than capable.

Henry held nothing back when he described his two visits to the British ship. The judge advocate questioned him closely on his being sent back a second time to insist that Captain Humphreys accept our surrender and take *Chesapeake* as a prize. The lieutenant became as agitated as he had been on that June evening though he managed to control himself more readily this time; his neck and ears grew scarlet and I could see his fists, clenched tight as ever could be, rigid on the arms of his chair. His whole manner had changed; his words were clipped and quiet and his gaze, as far as I could determine, was fixed on the commodore. While I could not, from my seat behind him, observe the cast of Henry's eyes, I was sure they were hard as flint. He left little doubt in any mind that he had had no desire to have become a player in our shameful disgrace.

When Henry finished his recounting of the day, minimizing his heroic role in firing the single shot *Chesapeake* managed to fire, Captain Rodgers offered the commodore's counsel the chance to question him, and again, Mister Taylor pushed himself erect and strolled the few steps to face his witness. The two studied each other for some moments until Barron's lawyer cleared his throat and, scowling through his spectacles still sitting precariously on his ample nose, consulted one of several sheets of paper he held.

"Lieutenant: during the time immediately prior to the ship getting underweigh from Norfolk, did the commodore visit the gundeck?"

"Sir, I have no idea of whether or not he did. I was not there all the time. He might have. I would expect he likely did, but I did not see him." Henry answered thoughtfully.

"What you might, or might not, expect, Lieutenant, is of little interest to me; let us just remain with the events of that day and leave the speculation to others, hmmm?" Taylor's voice sounded more like a growl.

He shot a blistering glance at his witness and continued in a more amiable tone. "Was Captain Gordon aware of the lumbered stated of the gundeck before *Chesapeake* sailed, or had he not visited your province either?"

"Aye, the captain knew well that the deck was lumbered and the guns blocked."

"And this, then, or the lack of powder horns and matches was the cause of your inability to fire in a timely manner?" Taylor pressed.

"Both, sir. We managed to secure powder horns and something with which we could touch off a gun, but we could not change the lumbered condition of my division quickly enough to respond to the British fire. There simply was not time."

"Did you hold the usual drills in dumb show at the great guns prior to your departure, Mister Allen?"

"No sir. There were no drills at all."

"And whose responsibility would that have been, Lieutenant?"

"Well, the captain would have ordered them, but the first lieutenant would have seen to their execution."

"Do you know why these drills were not done"

"We couldn't have carried them out even had they been ordered, sir. The guns were not all mounted on their carriages nor were the men assigned to their stations for quarters. In fact, we were still receiving men from the rendezvous and mounting guns right up to the time we sailed."

"Hmmm. Who had the task of ensuring that powder horns, matches, and the other implements of firing were available on the gundeck, Mister Allen?"

"That would have been Gunner Hook, sir. He was in charge of the magazine and responsible for filling the horns whether or not the new firing locks were installed." Henry had become quite calm during the course of his examination and answered each question in a neutral voice.

"We have heard from Mister Baldwin of the condition of the frigate after receiving the broadsides from *Leopard*. We also learned from him, a midshipman, I might mention, that, in his . . . valued . . . opinion, the ship was quite capable of fighting in spite of the wounds she had sustained. Would you agree with his assessment, sir?"

I bristled at Taylor's slur to my earlier response, feeling the heat rise up my neck. The officer next to me, a lieutenant I did not know, sensed my discomfort and lightly touched my arm. He smiled and nodded in a conciliatory way, neither of which helped me calm my agitation.

Henry set his gaze on his inquisitor. "Absolutely! Without question, she could have fought, were the decks cleared, powder, shot, and match available, and the men directed to fight. Her condition was not such that surrendering was the only option." Henry was no longer as calm as he had been. Neither was I, still bristling from Taylor's comment about me. "Thank you, Mister Allen. That will suffice for today, I think. You may return to your duties. It is possible I will have a few more questions for you at a later date." Taylor's ingratiating tone left little doubt that "a later date" would be coming rather sooner than later. With a nod to the panel, the civilian lawyer returned to his seat next to the commodore.

"Gentlemen: I apologize for the lateness of the hour. This seems like an appropriate time to adjourn for the day; we will recommence this court at two bells in the forenoon watch on the morrow. As a final note, I would personally like to commend Mister Allen on his actions and courage." Rodgers smiled and from my position behind Henry, I could see his ears again turn a bright scarlet as the words of praise were uttered. Words that were surely true, but, in Henry's mind, quite unnecessary.

Rodgers continued, addressing the pompous judge advocate, who apparently had recovered some during the day from his ill-feelings of the morning. "Mister Tazewell, please ensure that Master Commandant Gordon and Captain Hall will be present and able to give their testimony at that time along with any others you may wish to call." Rodgers shifted his gaze to me (causing me to blanche a trifle) and then to Henry. "Midshipman Baldwin and you, too, Lieutenant Allen: you will be in attendance on the morrow as well, if you please. In the event any further testimony should be required." And he banged his gavel down on the table.

The room emptied and Henry caught my arm as I made for the ladder to the spar deck.

"I understand you most likely gave them enough to cashier Barron just by yourself, Oliver. My testimony only confirmed what you had already told them. A colleague, who enjoyed your performance from the gallery, mentioned only just now that he had kept an eye on the commodore while you were telling the story, especially the part about surrendering the ship. The old boy barely blinked throughout the whole tale! Seemed some contemptuous I hear. I would not expect an invitation to dine with him in the near future!" Allen's eyes fairly danced with glee, whether at my discomfort at being the source of Barron's undoing or just out of the joy of seeing his earlier prediction bear fruit.

"There's much more testimony they'll likely want to hear, Henry. I just told the story the way it happened . . . as did you. Besides, I would expect the commodore'll have a few things to add his own self. He will be allowed to tell his side of it, won't he?" I didn't want to think about me being the one to "put the nail in his coffin;" as I said to my friend, I had only stated the events of the day as I had been instructed. And I was sure that all of the other officers and midshipmen would be called upon to answer questions about the condition of the ship and the action itself. The more I considered it, the more I became convinced that this trial was a long way from over. Little did I know then!

We stepped out of the hatch onto the spar deck. The weather had worsened as the evening approached; heavy clouds hung low in the sky and the chill dampness cut through our clothes even though the wind had all but quit. Intermittent rain fell, laced with sleet which made a curious *ticking* sound as it bounced through our rigging and clattered as it hit the deck. I could make out, through the gloom of the quickly darkening sky, patches of ice that clung to our rigging and spars; icicles had formed along the fighting tops, wet stalactites that glistened dully as the daylight finally gave up its struggle and surrendered to the darkness. After the closeness of the Cabin, the cold was momentarily refreshing, but I knew neither of us would stand about on the deck for very long.

"Oh, there's no doubt about that! I am sure that Decatur and Rodgers would not want to miss the chance to question him face to face." Henry responded to my concern. "But I will be interested in what Cap'n Gordon has to say; Commodore Barron was, in reality, only a passenger on the ship, but he usurped the captain's authority as soon as we were clear of the harbor here. I reckon Cap'n Gordon might have something to say about that!" He hugged his arms around him and shifted from side to side, occasionally stamping a foot to warm it.

"Mercy, but it's cold out here! What say you to a bite of dinner, Oliver? And, since it is as late as it is, perhaps a glass or two? I have told Joe Ripley I would join him for the meal, but I suspect he will have already dined, given the lateness of the hour."

"Ashore, Henry? That would be fine. I was some surprised to note the time when Cap'n Rodgers ended the session; I had no idea how long we had run. I guess I must have taken too long to say what I said."

"Go and find Lieutenant Rowe and get his permission for us to take our leave, Oliver, while I just check the gunroom for Ripley." Henry turned and stepped off for the hatch and ladder that would take him two decks down to the officers' quarters.

I went in search of the new first lieutenant who had arrived in *Chesapeake* only a few weeks back, just before Christmastide, it was, to replace Lieutenant Ben Smith. Our former first lieutenant had passed over from an illness in October. I recalled, as I made my way forward, that we had all made grim observations then that he had died from shame, a result of our June meeting with *Leopard*.

I was waiting at the gangway, having secured the blessings of the first lieutenant, when Henry appeared, trailed by Lieutenant Joseph Ripley. The two were still buttoning their heavy blue great coats, standing up the collars in an effort to keep the snow from their neck. And they both wore broad smiles, apparently having shared something amusing as they made their way up from the gun room. I soon found out what.

"Well! Mister Baldwin: the midshipman who will be the undoing of a commodore!" Ripley clapped me on the shoulder and spoke in a robust tone causing several hands who had been idling in the waist to look up from their own conversations. For my own part, I could feel the heat rise up my neck, face, and indeed, right to the top of my head!

"Wha . . . what do you mean, sir. I have done nothing of the sort." I stammered. Ripley had not been aboard during our ill-fated meeting with *Leopard,* having joined the ship in September while she was still undergoing repairs.

"Oh, I have heard . . . in point of fact, it's already well known in the ship, that your testimony was some damning of the good commodore! You made him quite clearly the villain of the piece!" Ripley, already known for his penchant for being a bit theatrical, was grinning broadly, enjoying my discomfort. The white cloud of our exhalations hung in the still dampness, as if holding our words suspended between us.

"Oh, sir! I did nothing of the kind. Tell him, Henry. Tell him I only described what happened on the gun deck . . . about the crates and hogsheads . . . and that anchor cable . . . we had to move and getting the powder horns from the gunner. And about you firing the gun." I appealed to my friend for help, but a glance at his own huge smile told me to expect no succor there.

"Perhaps Oliver would like to invite his friend, Commodore Barron, to join us, Henry? Do you think he would accept your invitation, Oliver?" Ripley was now enjoying his sport while I struggled to find a suitable retort that would be respectful enough of his position, but would put an end to his game. Several came to mind, but none I dared to utter. I remained mute, discomfited by his teasing and my own frustration at being too junior to respond suitably.

By the time we had reached a tavern and eating establishment, Ripley had tired of his repartee and the conversation turned to more mundane topics including where the ship would be sent once the trial had ended.

"Perhaps to the Mediterranean as originally planned. Though I wonder if they would make Decatur take over the Med squadron as they had intended for Barron. Besides, is he not still in command of the navy yard here as well as *Chesapeake*?" Ripley offered.

"Aye. I don't believe any has relieved him of that chore. But considering command of a ship well secured to the pier ain't too taxing, shouldn't be more than a man like Decatur could manage. Leastways until this court martial began. But I am sure they will find someone to assume command of one or the other before it's time to unmoor and head out." Henry shot a glance at me, then continued. "And of course, should the Secretary send us to that theater, it would likely be to the delight of young Oliver, here. Right, Baldwin?" Henry smiled at me, but gave me no chance to comment. "He spent his first cruise there, fighting the Bashaw's corsairs with Decatur, Lawrence, and the late Dickie Somers. One of "Preble's Boys" he was. And from what I have heard, did himself proud. Killed a few of those rascals in hand to hand fighting, I am given to believe."

"Is that a fact, Oliver! I had no idea. I knew you had been out before, but had thought it just here in our own waters." Ripley's voice seemed to hold a level of respect I had not before noticed. "Tell us about your adventures over there. A good yarn will go a long way to livening up our dinner. Were you one of Decatur's group of cutthroats who burned the *Philadelphia* frigate, or had you not arrived in time for that bit of excitement?"

"I was there, yes. And I was one of the "cutthroats" as you put it. My brother had been assigned in her with Bainbridge and was being held in the Bashaw's dungeon along with the rest of the crew. I guess Cap'n Decatur figured I'd want to go on account of that fact alone." I didn't mention that I had volunteered, several times, in fact, for the undertaking.

"There were seventy of us, crammed into a little ketch Commodore Preble had named *Intrepid*. Through a clever ruse, which I believe Cap'n Decatur dreamed up, we made it right alongside the frigate in the dark hours and boarded her quick as ever you please." A shudder passed through me as I recalled my first taste of war, of men killing each other in close combat.

I collected myself and went on with my story. "Overwhelmed the Tripolitan cutthroats—they really were the cutthroats, not us—and set explosives throughout the hull. We made it back into our ketch just before the fuses burned down and the ship blew up with great gusto. Quite spectacular, it was. Even cooked off some of her long guns causing them to discharge, some toward the water, but several toward the Bashaw's castle and fortress. We thought it fitting the old girl fired the final broadside in her own defense." I finished my short recitation with a smile, more to cover my own discomfort at again having to tell the story.

I did not mention, however, that never before or since have I been so terrified! I could still close my eyes and see that huge black-bearded pirate swinging his great curved scimitar at my head.

The two lieutenants talked knowingly to each other about the events of the Tripoli War even though neither had been involved, leaving me to leaf through my own memories of that horror. I sat quite mute while those fearful months, augmented by my concern for my brother, raced through my mind like a stream turned torrent; their conversation swirled around me, meaningless, mere back-eddies in the flood. Occasionally I heard bits and snatches of their wild ruminations but offered neither corrections nor additional details of my own involvement. By the meal's end, I had again slain the dragons of my memory and had refocused my thoughts on the events of the day, wondering what more I might be called upon to offer to Barron's court martial.

"Oliver . . . Oliver! Are you still with us, man? I said, 'Where is your brother now? I assume he survived the deprivations of the dungeon in Tripoli?" Lieutenant Ripley studied me with hooded eyes, perhaps a bit beguiled by a surfeit of the wine which had flowed quite liberally during the meal.

"Oh sorry, sir. I was thinking on something else. Yes, Edward was released with the rest of the Philadelphias and returned home in the fall of 1805. We were both given extended leaves as the Navy had no need for either of us right then. It was after I was ordered here, to *Chesapeake,* in the spring of last year, that he received orders to New York Navy Yard. Building gunboats under Cap'n Chauncey, I believe." I stopped, remembering Edward's reaction to his orders, and our parents joy at his apparently "safe" assignment.

Realizing both lieutenants were waiting for me to continue, I went on. "Yes, that is what they were doing there, building gunboats for our harbor defenses, same as in Rhode Island. Edward was not happy to be engaged in such shore-bound employment, and more than a little bit envious of my orders to a frigate; he would have much preferred being at sea. But, as he pointed out when we both were home over Christmastide, I appeared to be doing little better!"

That brought a laugh from my colleagues and after several more rounds of wine—now a thick, heady and aromatic port that recalled for me some I had consumed in Gibraltar—were bought and consumed, we made our way back to the navy yard and our unlucky ship. Whereupon I unsteadily removed my clothes, donned my nightshirt, and retired to my cot. Where, ultimately, the Dream again found me.

Running through the day's events seemed to relieve my angst and chase the horrifying images that had awakened me an hour and more before. I rose from the cockpit table, shed my coat and climbed back into my cot, wondering what the new day's testimony would reveal as I fell back into a mercifully dreamless sleep, ignoring, in my fatigued and still modestly intoxicated state, the cold and damp bed clothes.

CHAPTER THREE

The Cabin was beginning to fill with the participants in the trial as well as spectators curious as to what this second day of testimony might reveal. As ordered, Henry and I had taken seats in the back of the Cabin among the growing number of civilian and naval men who had developed an interest in the proceedings. Although Allen's experience in courts marital was nearly as scant as my own, he seemed able to answer most of my whispered questions as we waited for the court to be called to order. My latest query wondered at the wisdom of including civilians in what was clearly a Navy matter.

"Likely on account of the Navy Secretary wantin' someone who ain't biased like Decatur and Rodgers to do the prosecutin', Oliver, and who has the lawyerly skills to keep 'em on course. And Barron, I would reckon, wanted someone good enough to keep him from the brig or the noose. Better a civilian magistrate or lawyer than some navy . . ." His whispered, but sardonic answer was cut off by Rodgers' gavel.

The dull *thud* of a forward gun, the call to order by the president, and the second day of James Barron's court martial began. As the proceedings were still new and exciting for me, I hung on every word and studied closely those participants I could see. I noticed that Mister Tazewell was more animated today and moved differently than he had yesterday; quite obviously, he was not suffering from the same "hot copper" he had earlier experienced at the start of the trial. Mister Taylor and his client each wrote furiously, as they had during most of the previous session. The annoying *scritch, scritch* of their quills, initially quite audible in the silence of the room, quickly blended with other background noises and faded.

After the opening remarks and an inquiry about witnesses being present, Rodgers had inquired of Taylor whether or not he wished to further question Lieutenant Allen.

"Just a few items to go over, Captain, if you please. Won't take more than a few minutes." Taylor, it occurred to me, smiled for the first time as he made his request; the forced friendliness seemed incongruous and particularly ingratiating. Henry was summarily called to the chair.

"Lieutenant Allen," Taylor began immediately Henry's bottom had settled into the seat, "I would like your opinion of the condition of the ship after she had suffered those several devastating broadsides from the English vessel. Was she fit to continue the engagement or was she, and her men, too cruelly wounded to respond? And please be good enough to also address her ability to sail, sir."

Henry collected his thoughts and shot a glance at the commodore before he answered. Whether or not it occurred to him that he, and I, had answered the same question yesterday seemed not to matter. "The frigate was sore wounded, sir. Especially aloft and, as we later discovered, her ability to handle any significant amount of sail, was severely curtailed. The shrouds were badly cut up and lifts and ties shot through. All three masts had been wounded, the mizzen the worst. In her hull, she was wounded to the point of taking water, but not to the extent that would deprive us the ability to return fire."

"Thank you, Lieutenant. And how would you describe the condition of Commodore Barron when you saw him after the firing had stopped? Was he cowering or standing in a posture of command? Was he giving orders? Did he have control of the situation?"

Again Henry paused and thought before he responded. And again, he shot a look toward Barron, who now studied the lieutenant with a baleful stare.

"Commodore Barron was standing on the quarterdeck, sir. He seemed not to notice that his own person had suffered damage, but studied the progress of the work being done to free the men trapped under the spars and rigging that had fallen to the deck. He directed their activity and also ordered a boat lowered and crewed, the boat that shortly carried Lieutenant Smith and myself to *Leopard*." Henry's voice hardened and his whole person seemed to stiffen as he uttered this last part.

"And Captain Gordon, Lieutenant; how was he responding to all of this?" Taylor pressed Henry for more detail of that frightful afternoon.

"I don't recall what the captain was doing. I believe he was also on the quarterdeck, but I don't have any memory of what he might have been involved in. The commodore was clearly in command."

"Thank you, Mister Allen. I think that will answer my needs for now. You may step down, sir." And Taylor smiled again.

Tazewell, on direction of the president, called his next witness and the process repeated itself throughout the day. We did get a short recess for dinner early in the afternoon watch. And so it went, questions repeated and answered, in seemingly endless procession.

That had been some three weeks ago and, on most of the following days, we had heard a succession of the ship's officers and midshipmen, even a few of the seamen and petty officers, testify, answering questions about where they were, the condition of the ship, the condition and *spirit* of the commodore, and who might have known we had British deserters in the frigate. It had all become quite repetitious and both Henry and I were often finding excuses to be elsewhere. But today held the promise of interest for us. After a waning level of participation by the spectators, today's gallery was very nearly full; clearly, others felt as we did.

And one could feel the tension in the expectant crowd; whispering, gestures, and knowing glances bespoke a significance to the day's testimony. Certainly, Henry and I were eager to see what would happen when the captain took the witness chair.

I was surprised to notice that, while the gallery was fraught with the excitement of anticipation, the others, the daily communicants, if you will, seemed unmoved by the prospect of hearing Gordon's version of the attack and the events that led up to it. Each man looked much the same as every day before; some wrote, or scribbled on bits of paper, or talked in subdued tones among themselves. Rodgers and Decatur chatted quietly, perhaps sharing an amusing anecdote that caused them both to smile. James Lawrence, today gesturing with motions that could only be describing the maneuvering of two ships, talked with Judge Advocate Tazewell. Perhaps he was explaining how *Leopard* had come up to weather of us last June, or perhaps how the tiny *Intrepid* had made the side of the captured *Philadelphia*. And, as on every day previous, Commodore Barron was deep in conversation with Robert Taylor, referring frequently to writing in several papers he shuffled on the table before them. Taylor nodded frequently and mumbled incoherently as Barron pointed to this and that line on the vellum sheets.

The dull *thud* of the bow chaser that fired a half-charge of powder to announce the start of the day's proceedings was followed quickly by Rodgers' gavel, stopping the buzz and hum of the several conversations quite abruptly.

So abruptly that the commodore was caught short in his own deep discussion with his lawyer. He had been speaking a bit louder than a whisper to be heard over the shifting of chairs and murmured conversations and seemed not to notice that the room had gone silent, except for him.

" . . . and be sure to question him closely on that. The man is an incompetent rascal, out to get me." The commodore's voice filled the Cabin and, when he realized that he alone had continued speaking, he shut his mouth and clenched his teeth as he looked around the room, obviously seeking someone. Taylor nodded and patted the commodore's sleeve in most patronizing (I thought) way.

"We are in order. Judge Advocate, are all persons who are required to be in attendance present?" John Rodgers directed his question to the haughty Mister Tazewell.

Tazewell rose, drew himself up to his full six foot height and stood to attention. "Sir. All those called are present. Either in the court or just outside. Sir." His tone seemed almost bored; after all, he had been asked the same question every day of the trial and had given the same answer each time. Then he sat, folding himself into the straight chair much the way a long-legged bird might settle onto its nest.

A brief conversation ensued between Decatur and Rodgers and then the latter spoke, again to Tazewell.

"Call Master Commandant Charles Gordon, if you please."

A brief stir among the spectators, occasioned by craning necks, shifting chairs, and hushed comments, won the rap of the president's gavel, and silence and decorum returned. A moment later, Captain Gordon strode into the Cabin, marching straight to the witness chair. He was sworn and seated. This was what had brought Henry and me to sit in the back of the room today and we both, like most others, leaned forward so as not to miss a word of what was said.

"Mister Gordon, you were commanding the United States frigate *Chesapeake* in June of 1807?" Rodgers wasted no time in getting right down to business.

This was not the captain's trial; he had been called to testify as a witness in Barron's court martial and would receive his own separate trial next. As would each of the others accused.

After Gordon answered Rodgers' question in the affirmative, the president offered something that quite surprised me.

"Should you be asked a question you feel might incriminate you or otherwise serve to work against your own case in this matter, Mister

Gordon, you may decline to answer it. Further, should I feel you would be ill-advised to answer, I will so inform you. And the court will infer nothing from it in the case before us. Do you understand?"

I was astounded! I elbowed Henry and whispered as loudly as I dared, "What does that mean? How can they not infer the man thinks himself guilty if he fails to answer? Won't they . . ."

"Hush, Baldwin! I'll explain it afterwards. Listen to what Gordon has to say." Henry's tone, even in a whisper, left no room for further discourse.

Rodgers had asked the captain about Barron attending the frigate in Washington, and I 'hushed' as he answered.

". . . from the Washington Navy Yard, sir. The commodore had come aboard prior to our departure, but then left to return to Hampton while we sailed the frigate and our passengers down the Potomac."

"Was the trip down river uneventful, Mister Gordon?" This from Decatur.

I was not surprised to notice that Gordon colored some at the question.

"Uh . . . hardly, sir. It was fraught with difficulty; we were some sixty or seventy men short in the crew and those we had were mostly landsmen. During a stop in Alexandria, their inexperience resulted in an accident with the foreyard which killed two and cruelly wounded a third."

Rodgers now nodded his head at Judge Advocate Tazewell who continued the questions.

"Why had you stopped at Alexandria, sir? Is it not but a two hundred mile trip from Washington to the Hampton Roads?"

Gordon looked at Tazewell with an obvious contempt, one of a seafarer to the questions of a shore bound lawyer, and a civilian at that. "As you likely are unaware, sir, there is a bar at the mouth of the Eastern Branch over which I had to bring the ship. With a full complement of stores and our main battery in place we would have been unable to clear it, so shallow is the water even at a full tide. Alexandria is the first place one might stop to take aboard that which we had been forced to leave behind in the interest of our draft. I had arranged for some of our battery and the stores to be shipped overland to that port, while the remainder of the cannon were sent on directly to Norfolk. I also used the stop to finish some carpentry work left undone by the Navy Yard."

"But, Mister Gordon, had not a goodly part of your stores already been placed aboard . . . or carried in one of your boats?" Tazewell pressed.

"Even with a light ship, one without her battery, we ran on shore during the forenoon watch and had to lighten her further to haul her off.

That, sir, is why some of our stores were in the boats." Gordon spoke quietly through a set jaw.

"So, after several days there, in Alexandria, you made the balance of the journey without incident?"

Now is when the trouble will begin. "Without incident," indeed! We had hardly begun!

"No, Mister Tazewell, it was not 'without incident.' We had an outbreak of a sickness which laid low nearly eighty-five of my sailors, causing us to be even further shorthanded. Those men remained on the sick list for the entire trip."

"Anything else, sir?"

"It is customary for a vessel passing below Mount Vernon to fire a sixteen gun salute to the late president." I was sure *everyone* knew this, but Gordon's tone clearly indicated he did not expect his inquisitor to be included in that group.

"I am well aware of that, Mister Gordon. And did *Chesapeake* fire her requisite salute? Without undue difficulty?" Tazewell appeared to enjoy his role as the cause of Captain Gordon's discomfort.

"Gunner Hook had overfilled the flannel cartridge bags with powder; about half of them would not fit into the guns. Others had swollen from the dampness and could not be rammed home. About half of our wads were made to the wrong caliber as well and were quite useless. I ordered him arrested and confined for later court martial. We did, however, fire the salute from the cartridges and wads that could be used. In so doing, we discovered that some major share of our powder was bad, quite unusable; it might have been over a half of it. I am told that we received it from the Navy yard in an unusable state. It was shortly thereafter that Seaman Winslow fell overboard and drowned.

"Several days later, we took aboard our passengers, Doctor Bullus and his family and staff, and Marine Captain Hall and his wife, causing us to stop yet again. They were to travel with us to the Mediterranean. Doctor Bullus, I might mention, was unable to restore any of my stricken sailors to robust health. Indeed, one of them shortly passed over. With the water at our location being shallow, we were obligated once more to delay our voyage while we buried the unfortunate ashore.

"Further down the river, some forty miles from the Navy Yard, we ran aground yet again, Lieutenant Allen not having trimmed the ship properly, in spite of my orders to ensure a proper bow-heavy posture."

Henry, beside me in the chairs set out for the spectators, grew suddenly rigid, his face coloring. I felt, rather than saw, his fists clench and his upper arms, indeed, his whole body, become coiled, tense.

The captain continued his narrative of the trip down the Potomac without further mention of my friend, who gradually returned to a posture of ease. "After kedging her off, we anchored, as there was no wind and a making tide. During that night, five sailors took a boat and deserted the ship. I sent a crew of Marines after them in the jolly boat and, while they recovered the stolen boat, they were unable to locate the deserters. And their own boat crew ran as well." Gordon stopped, as if overwhelmed by his own bad luck. He seemed to be slumped in the chair, a marked contrast to the tall, straight figure he made at the start. He took a breath and, in a quieter voice, continued. "Two more of the sick passed over just before we had gained Hampton Roads. As we were, at the time, in sufficiently deep water, they were buried at sea with the usual ceremony. We anchored in Hampton Roads during the first dog watch on four June. It was a hellish ride we had, sir. Just hellish." Gordon had lost his spirit; I would have expected him to explain 'dog watch' to the judge advocate.

"Mister Gordon." One of the lieutenants on the court martial panel spoke out. And received a sour look from our judge advocate for doing so. "Was Commodore Barron not aboard during any of this ill-starred passage down the Potomac?"

"No, Lieutenant. As I mentioned, he had left the ship for Hampton before we left the Washington Navy Yard. He returned aboard two days after we made the Roads. Doctor Bullus, along with his entourage and Missus Hall went ashore there, preferring the accommodations at an inn to those aboard the frigate." Gordon spoke up, only mildly irritated that he should be asked to repeat himself.

Tazewell waited a moment for further comment from the panel, moving his stare from one member to the next. When he realized that there would be nothing further from the officers judging the trial, he began his own prepared string of questions. "Mister Gordon, what work remained to be done in order for *Chesapeake* to depart and carry out her . . . your commission? And was it accomplished?"

"We had not loaded sufficient stores for a passage to the Mediterranean nor had we loaded the provisions and equipage we were transporting to the fleet there. The one which Commodore Barron was to take command of. Additionally, we had spars to rig and the eighteen-pounder barrels had all to be mounted to their carriages, a particularly tedious job of work given we were so shorthanded. And of course, I had to find a new gunner and powder to replace that which had proved useless."

"Did you make an effort to remedy the problem of the shortage of sailors?"

"Of course, sir! I had two rendezvous established, one at Missus Pinckney's Lodging House and one at the Anchor and Horn, a taproom just outside the Navy Yard. As I recall, Mister Baldwin was put in charge of the former while one of the lieutenants—Keane, it was—ran the other. They were told in no uncertain terms not to enlist any Royal Navy deserters no matter how short of crew the ship was."

Now it was my turn; I felt the color rise in my neck and cheeks as Gordon uttered those condemning words. And Allen's nudge to my arm did nothing to assuage my guilt.

How was I to know if a sailor was a Royal Navy deserter if he claimed otherwise? And I imagine Lieutenant Keane got a few at the Anchor and Horn as well!

"As I recall, you told us you had arrested the gunner and had him confined pending a court martial. Did you replace him in Norfolk?" Tazewell now lowered his voice, almost to the point where I could not hear his questions.

"No, I did not. I had no choice but to release Gunner Hook and reinstate him . . . in spite of his gross incompetence. There was no other to fill the billet. Were we to have any chance of mounting all of our guns to their carriages, not to mention the firing locks, I needed to have a gunner. But even with him—or perhaps *because* of him—we were unable to complete the job before we were ordered to sea."

Tazewell now stood erect, took a deep breath, and spoke loudly enough for anyone, even someone loitering on the pier, to hear him. "So, Mister Gordon. You set sail on an Atlantic crossing with an incomplete and incompetent crew, unmounted guns, and cargo and stores strewn about willy-nilly. Is that correct?"

"Yes."

"And who ordered you to sea, Mister Gordon?"

"Commodore Barron." A silence, elegant in its completeness, filled the Cabin.

I stole a glance at Barron who, for once, was not engaged in conversation with his lawyer. He stared at Gordon, his eyes hard as diamonds, and a killing look on his jowly face. Gordon, for his part, met the glare of his former commodore without a flinch, then looked away to see the members of the panel nodding as if in agreement.

"Mister Taylor, have you any questions for Mister Gordon?" The president broke the silence.

"As a matter of fact, I do, Captain. Only one . . . or perhaps two, if you please." Lawyer Taylor did not stand up, merely shifted his gaze from the panel to Master Commandant Gordon. "And who, Mister Gordon, informed Commodore Barron the ship was ready for sea?"

Gordon shifted in his seat, as if suddenly finding the hard seat of the straight-backed chair intolerable. But he looked at the commodore's counsel (or perhaps it was the commodore himself) and spoke quietly.

"I did."

"Why did you do that, sir? It doesn't sound as if that was the case at all." Taylor shot back, a smile beginning to form on his face.

"For a fair weather crossing, it would be no effort to stow the cargo and finish mounting our gun barrels. Since we were not at war with any country, we quite naturally expected no need for defending ourselves against any of hostile intent. Once the decks were clear and the work on the guns completed, including the mounting of the firing locks—no more than a few days out from the Capes—I had anticipated drilling the crew in gunnery, among other things. Additionally, sir, the commodore had received word from the Secretary that we were to make our departure with all haste. There was some considerable pressure to carry out his orders."

"But nonetheless, *Captain* Gordon, the ultimate determination as to the readiness of the frigate was yours, was it not?"

I wondered at Barron's lawyer suddenly referring to Gordon as *captain*. It seemed to catch Gordon all aback, as well.

"Well . . . in a manner of speaking, sir, it was. But Commodore Barron had said he would . . ."

"Thank you, Mister Gordon. That will do for now." Taylor smiled wolfishly and shifted his gaze to Captain Rodgers. "I would like to request a short recess, if you please, sir, to discuss some matters with Commodore Barron. I expect to continue with Captain Gordon's testimony following it."

Rodgers consulted a gold timepiece which he had extracted from his waistcoat pocket and looked up at Taylor.

"We can take a recess now. We shall stop for dinner and reconvene at a half after three. I assume that will give you enough time to 'discuss some matters with the commodore,' Mister Taylor?" Without waiting for an answer, Captain Rodgers picked up his gavel.

"We are adjourned."

The sharp report of Rodgers' gavel put the period at the end of his sentence and, almost as one, the members of the court rose and walked through the Cabin without so much as a glance left or right.

Henry and I also stood and, after waiting for the court to file out, fell in line behind Lieutenant Lawrence and made our way topside. Once standing in the cold air, refreshing after the closeness of the Cabin, I pulled out my silver watch and was surprised to find it barely a half one.

"Henry, we have almost two hours for dinner. What say we dine ashore today? I am not sure I can manage the swill the cockpit steward will filch from the galley. Besides, I am brimming over with questions for you!" Even though it was still nearly an hour before our usual meal time, my stomach was rumbling a protest at being empty.

"A fine idea, Oliver. I should check on a few jobs of work I ordered started today before we go; give me a few moments and meet me in the waist. It will be a pleasant respite from the gunroom fare as well!" Without waiting for an answer, Lieutenant Allen turned and made his way toward the bow of the frigate, speaking to a few sailors he passed on his way.

Lieutenant Rowe, still learning his way (there was a rumor that this was his first assignment to first lieutenant and I was inclined to believe it) was standing at the break of the quarterdeck talking with Captain Decatur and I waited at a discrete distance for the chance to speak.

After several days of quite mild weather, we had experienced a change for the worse only yesterday and some of the older hands had predicted further worsening before it improved. Now, here was the proof of their prognostication; it had begun to snow, large, wet flakes which quickly coated everything they touched. I noticed that both Rowe and the captain were beginning to be quite liberally coated even though they could not have been standing there for more than a few minutes.

Should be finishing up soon, I'd think. Were they going to be in a long discussion, I would expect they'd likely move under some cover.

I was right; with a crisp doffing of his hat, which resulted in a brief blizzard as its collected snow fell off, Lieutenant Rowe stepped around the captain and headed right for me.

"Sir: may Lieutenant Allen and I have your permission to take our leave ashore. Just for dinner, sir, as we will be returning to the court martial thereafter." I lifted my own hat and spoke as he drew close.

"Hmmm . . . what's that? What was it you wanted, Mister . . ." He stopped and looked at me, his puzzled expression telling me he had again forgotten my name.

"Baldwin, sir. Oliver Baldwin. May Mister Allen and I go ashore for dinner, sir?"

"Oh, my, yes. Mister . . . uh . . . Baldwin. By all means." Rowe doffed his own hat, recognizing my salute, and hurried on forward to carry out whatever orders the captain had issued.

I waited only a moment or two for Henry to appear and, leaving tracks in the fresh snow, which seemed to disappear almost at once, filled in with fresh snow fall as they were, we hurried through the cold streets, following the faint—visible only as slight indentations—tracks of our predecessors. We came to an eating establishment where, to our surprise, we discovered several of the lieutenants from the court martial panel already ensconced at a table. Including Lieutenant Lawrence, who noticed us come in and stood to wave us over. We shook the snow off our great coats and hung them on a peg by the door, stamping our feet as we did so.

"You may as well join us, gentlemen. There appears not to be an empty table in sight and we would be glad of your company." Nods around the table, along with a few smiles, encouraged us and, pulling up two more chairs in the space made for us, we sat.

Formal introductions were made for our benefit—the three lieutenants from the panel, of course, knew our names from our having testified early in the trial—and a silence descended upon the group. Naturally, the officers involved in judging the guilt or innocence of Commodore Barron and the others would be breaching a confidence were they to discuss the matter with us, and there seemed little else of import that any cared to converse on.

After several moments of awkwardness, James Lawrence spoke up, pointing at me with his knife. "Perchance you gentlemen were unaware that Mister Baldwin and I served together in that business with Tripoli some years back. Got his blooding in the *Philadelphia* raid and later accounted for a few other rascals from that cursed country of scoundrels and pirates."

More nods and mumbled comments greeted this statement as the others considered his remark around large mouthfuls of beef stew. Henry, of course, was well aware of my past and merely caught my eye and winked. I suspected he knew what would come next.

"Pray tell us, Midshipman, how you saw that action on our late frigate. I have gathered from other accounts that it was quite bloody considering its short duration." The man across the table from Henry and me looked at me much the same as a fox might view a hole in the henhouse wall.

"Sir," said I, "it was indeed bloody and brief. Twenty minutes, as I recall." *As I "recall?" I would never forget those twenty "brief" minutes!* I thought as my stomach turned over just from the thought of that ferocious night. *Am I to go through this every time I take a meal with someone I have not previously met?*

"Well, do tell! Lieutenant Lawrence said you were 'blooded' in the scrap, Baldwin. I assume he meant you killed one of the villains." My questioner prodded.

Lieutenant Lawrence responded with gusto before I could even take a breath. "Baldwin was quite literally 'blooded' gentlemen. He apparently engaged in some swordplay with one of the pirates and, in the process, got himself covered in gore. I distinctly recall seeing him, his shirtfront, waistcoat, arms, and, indeed, his face, all crimson from the rascal's life blood. Even called for our surgeon to have a look at him! Ha ha. Thought he had suffered some severe gash to his own being when first I noticed him, but it turned out he was unscathed. Clipped off the man's head, or nearly so, right, Oliver?" Lawrence was positively gleeful at the recollection of my sorry condition when I appeared after the fight.

Despite my earlier hunger, I was fast losing my appetite. The memory of that fight, my first staggering steps of mortal combat, flooded into my mind and I saw that huge, black-bearded, corsair coming at me with his scimitar held aloft, ready to split me stem to stern. I could again feel the tingle in my arm as my cutlass parried his blow. And I could almost feel the warm gush of his blood as, after several moments (it seemed like *hours!*) of cut and thrust, parry and strike, I landed a lucky blow to his neck. As Lawrence said, almost severing his head from his shoulders. My gorge rose up as I again tasted the metallic bitterness of the man's blood.

"It would appear that Oliver remembers the occasion all too well, gentlemen. He seems unable to utter a word! Oliver, are you quite all right?" Henry's concern (he knew well the story and thus had no interest in hearing it again) was evident and I knew he would quickly seek a way to change the subject.

After a moment or two, I felt the color return to my face and, with some considerable effort, finished chewing and swallowed the mouthful I had been caught with. "Aye, just fine, Mister Allen. Thank you." I smiled thinly and nodded to him.

"Then you must have been one of Preble's Boys, were you not, Baldwin? I believe he was commodore of the squadron that was involved in the *Philadelphia* scrap and that dreadful affair with Somers being lost in the fireship." This from another of the lieutenants.

"Yes, sir. I was in Commodore Preble's squadron. With Mister Lawrence and Captain Decatur. My brother was in *Philadelphia* with Captain Bainbridge." I answered, hoping they would let me finish my dinner without the Grand Inquisition. After all, Lawrence was there too, and no doubt had told them every gory detail of every engagement.

"Too bad about Preble; a good man he was. A dreadful shame he had to take ill and pass so quickly after being named a hero by our Congress. Hardly had time to bask in the glory of it! And just a few weeks after the shameful event about which we've been hearing these past weeks. Must have been the killing blow to a weakened constitution is all I can think. Dreadful waste, it is, to lose a man of his caliber." My first inquisitor took a long draught of whatever was in his pewter, after first raising it in, presumably, a silent toast to the late commodore.

"My stars! Look at the time! We have very nearly frittered away the entire time Captain Rodgers allowed. We must return to our duties, gentlemen!" Lawrence held up a large gold timepiece, as if to add emphasis to his remark.

I sneaked a look at my own—it was silver, and not so large as Lawrence's—and saw that it was not quite as close to the appointed hour as Lawrence would have us believe; in fact, we had a good half hour to make the five minute walk to the frigate. Perhaps he was rescuing me from his associates! In any case, they each stood, threw some coins on the table, and, with mumbled pleasantries, departed. Leaving Henry and me to finish our meal alone.

"Well! That was interesting! But I don't think we have to rush back, Oliver. We're not on the panel, and I am sure Taylor will continue to lambaste Gordon for the remainder of the day. You certainly drew the lion's share of the fire, my friend! You might think those poor chaps had never seen a shot fired in anger, so interested in your 'blooding' were they. I would have thought that James Lawrence might have given them all the details before this. After all, it's been almost four years since you and Decatur attacked the *Philadelphia* frigate, right?"

"Aye, Henry. Almost to the day, in fact. February sixteenth, 1804. I shall most probably never forget any of it, so indelibly etched into my memory it is. Just as are the events of June. And while I was on the receiving end of shots fired by the corsairs off Tripoli, they were nothing like what I . . . *we* experienced from *Leopard*. I had dreams about that for some months afterward." I did not mention that, over several of the nights since the court martial began, I had been revisited by the same cursed brother of Orpheus.

"You know, Oliver," Henry adroitly changed the subject, perhaps sensing my reaction to the memory, "I was wondering the other day about the men you and Keane took aboard from the rendezvous. How did those four—the ones that got took back to *Leopard*—convince you . . . or Keane that they weren't British deserters. They must have looked like sailors and likely used words common to a seagoing man."

"Henry, those men had to have come to Keane's rendezvous at the Horn and Anchor; I could swear that I never saw them until we were under way from Norfolk. I would have at least recognized them, had I recruited them, I should think." I had wracked my brain countless times over that question and had drawn the same conclusion each time. "You could ask him the same question. I would, but I am not sure he'd take kindly to a midshipman questioning him about it."

"You may have to, Oliver. Swear, that is. That you never saw those four sailors until after we had won our anchor. They might just call you back to answer a few more questions, you know. You recall what Cap'n Rodgers said . . . to you as well as to each and every witness, when we were excused." Henry spoke very seriously, making me jerk my head around to look sharply at him. Then he broke into a smile. "I wouldn't worry too much about how those four got into the frigate; that is not what Barron and Gordon and the others are charged with. Disgraceful behavior is what they're charged with, not to put too fine a point on it!"

It had stopped snowing when we left the tavern and the snow, where it had not been trampled by passers-by and horses, lay about a small finger's depth on the street. Elsewhere, the frozen dirt which, with a thaw, would quickly become a morass of sticky mud, showed through, rutted by the wagon wheels and carts which carried goods to the Navy Yard.

Commodore Barron was just sitting down with his lawyer when we quietly took our seats again in the back of the room. The usual buzz and hum of muted conversations filled the air.

Bang! Rodgers' gavel slammed down on the table and we were once again in session, Tazewell calling for Captain Gordon to again take his seat in the witness chair so that Mister Taylor might further question him.

What more could they possibly extract from the poor man? We have heard over and over about how it was the commodore who surrendered the ship, not

Gordon. Does Taylor think he's going to unearth some new bit of evidence, some uttering that will exonerate his client?

Taylor wasted no time in niceties. "Captain Gordon, let us turn to the matter of the British deserters who were in your ship. We have heard from several of your lieutenants that you were, in fact, aware of some of these men in your muster. Is that correct, sir?"

Gordon shifted in the chair. "Well, Mister Taylor, you must understand that *Chesapeake* was extremely shorthanded when we left Washington and even more so when we arrived in Hampton due to the desertions, sickness, and deaths we had experienced *en route*. I gave the matter of British deserters little thought as it is quite common for them to seek employment in our navy. Since we ran several rendezvous' during our time in Norfolk, it would be quite natural, I think, for a few to sign on, despite my admonition to the recruiters. I am certain that, were you to step aboard any American warship almost anywhere in the world, you would likely find British sailors, a few at any rate. But I was not aware, specifically, of any by name who had signed into *Chesapeake*."

"Given, then, that you acknowledge the presence aboard your ship of seamen from the Royal Navy, did you not think you might be at risk of a boarding by the Royal Navy in an effort to recover what, in their perception, was their property?"

"Mister Taylor," Gordon was sounding more and more exasperated with each passing moment. "Our country was, and still is, at peace with England. And all others. Why ever would I expect to be fired on by a British man-o'-war? There are other ways, *diplomatic* ways, of handling things of that stripe."

"And what about seeing the *Leopard* getting under weigh with her gunports . . . uh . . . triced up? I believe that is the appropriate use of the word. Did not that kindle a spark of suspicion in your breast, sir?"

"I thought nothing of it at all; it was quite warm and a common practice in both navies to open the gunports to improve the flow of air through the lower decks of the ship." Gordon's tone was stronger, more confident.

"Surely, sir, when they ranged alongside with *their guns run out,* something must have gone through your head that all was not right with the world!" Taylor voice went up along with this eyebrows at this question.

"Their guns were not run out until *after* Lieutenant Meade had returned to his ship. Nor did we observe their Marines bustling about taking up positions that could be interpreted as hostile. And then, if you will recall, Mister Taylor, I ordered the ship cleared and the men to quarters."

I felt an elbow in my ribs and turned to see Henry motion toward the door with his head. We were leaving.

"This isn't going to accomplish anything; we've heard all this before from all the others. He's trying to cast the blame all on Gordon and hope the panel will exonerate the commodore from any responsibility. I can't listen to his attempts to discredit the captain any more and it ain't likely they'll be wantin' to hear from us today!" Henry offered by way of explanation as soon as the door closed behind us.

"I'll see you later, perchance after supper for a glass ashore." This was thrown over his shoulder as he hurried off up the gun deck. I watched him for a moment, then took the ladder down another deck to the cockpit.

CHAPTER FOUR

Thirty days on the calendar passed, during more than half of which the court listened to endlessly repetitive testimony from essentially all the officers and midshipmen, and even several of the warrants and sailors. Mister Tazewell asked questions, Mister Taylor asked questions, and members of the panel asked still more questions. Many were called into the Cabin several times to clarify this or that issue or verify what one of the other witnesses had said. And still not a word from Commodore Barron in his own defense. The tension mounted as we all wondered when he would speak.

Of course, not every day was filled with testimony; some days, the court was called to order with the sharp rap of Rodgers' gavel only to be dismissed due to the failure of one or another of the witnesses to appear. A few of the several civilians who were called were particularly negligent in making a prompt response to the summons and created no end of delays, all of which were met with a quiet stoicism on the parts of both the panel and the civilian lawyers. Some still had not made an appearance, and likely would not, though what their testimony might add to the proceedings quite eluded me. And the other two accused, Marine Captain Hall and Gunner Hook, each testified either for or against the commodore as it suited their own purposes. Each was given the same right, as had Captain Gordon, to refuse an answer when they thought it might worsen their own situation, but I was as sure as I had been when Gordon testified that Decatur, Rodgers, and the others would recall which questions each had refused to answer (or been advised not to answer) when the other trials commenced. And, I expect, ask them again, this time without the benefit of avoiding self-incrimination!

Adding to the ponderous process was the need to have the secretary read back to each and every witness their own testimony at the conclusion of their questioning so as to be sure what they uttered had been accurately recorded. And then the written version would be signed and the witness excused.

Frequently, whole sections of the testimony from the original court of inquiry would be required to clarify this or that point. It sometimes appeared that there were notable differences as time, or memories, or individual needs, altered a participant's testimony from the first hearing to this one. This confusion, of course, would cause no end of recalling witnesses to state that this or that happened, or "he said this" or did that. It became quite dreary and tested one's appetite for the processes of Naval law to the utmost.

Fortunately, as Henry and I had already testified and been recalled once—well, Henry had; I had not—it was not through any need of the court that we endured so many days of mindless repetition, and when our initial curiosity was slaked, we could escape to see to our sailors, chat, or just get some fresh air. The others, Captain Rodgers, Captain Decatur, Lieutenant Lawrence and their colleagues on the panel were forced to suffer repeated descriptions of the pounding suffered by *Chesapeake,* the commodore's spirit, recalled conversations, and actions of the officers and men of the frigate, all while trying to look and act as if they were hearing something revealing.

Only Lieutenant Keane (he was called on day twenty-one) offered testimony that seemed to shed light on the touchy issue of how the British sailors, the very reason for *Leopard's* unseemly attack on us, got into the frigate. I listened in rapt attention, recalling that I had earlier surmised the men had not come through my rendezvous.

"Mister Keane," began Mister Tazewell, "we have heard from both Master Commandant Gordon and Midshipman Baldwin that you were placed in charge of the rendezvous at the Anchor and Horn Tavern, seeking recruits for the frigate prior to her departure for the Mediterranean Sea. Were you, in fact, so assigned?"

"Aye, sir. I was indeed. Terrible difficult it was to attract sailors, what with the merchant fleet paying 'em—even a landsman—half again what the Navy does. We were right shorthanded, though, and could ill-afford to be especially choosy as to them we enlisted." Keane spoke earnestly, shooting the occasional glance at Decatur and Rodgers.

"And, sir, did you, in fact, enlist the four men later taken by force of arms from the frigate *Chesapeake?*"

"I didn't have any idea those four was deserters from the Brits, sir. Of course, I guessed they was English, but they weren't likely to tell me they deserted the Royal Navy, now were they?"

"So you signed the four into the frigate, thinking they were merely English immigrants with seafaring backgrounds looking for berths, correct?"

"Aye." Keane seemed to shift in his chair more frequently as the questions focused on his recruiting the British deserters. Now his glance had shifted to the commodore, who looked up from his note-taking only occasionally.

Having proved that the men were, in fact, aboard the American ship but unknown as deserters, Tazewell abruptly ended his questioning of the lieutenant and surrendered the floor to his opposite number, Robert Taylor.

Here's where Keane is likely to get broadsided! I'd wager a fair piece that Taylor is going to try and shift the blame to him for letting the British sailors aboard in the first place, and causing the whole inhuman attack by the British. Just trying to get back what was theirs!

Taylor rose deliberately, making the few steps from his table to the witness chair take much longer than necessary. Then he simply stood in front of the edgy lieutenant and stared at him. Whatever resolve Lieutenant Keane might have had remaining in him vanished like smoke in a fresh breeze.

Keane knows what's coming! Barron's lawyer is letting him stew for a bit. Likely try to fluster the poor man . . . even more than he already is.

Finally, he turned away from the witness and, looking at the panel, asked in a most restrained voice, "Mister Keane, did it occur to you that, for several months around the time under our scrutiny, there were *three* warships of the Royal Navy lying in Lynnhaven Bay or perhaps that desertion is quite common in the Royal Navy should an opportunity present itself?"

"Never entered my mind, sir. There're always a few Brits there or in Hampton Roads."

"Did an officer of the Royal Navy have any discourse with you during the time you operated the rendezvous?"

"Uh . . . yes. Sir. That would have been Cap'n Townshend. He had command of *Halifax*, I recall." Keane looked from the panel to Barron and back to the panel again before returning his gaze to his inquisitor.

Looks like a cornered fox lookin' for a place to hide.

"Would you recount your conversation with *Lord* Townshend, if you please, Mister Keane?" A smile had started to form on Taylor's face. He obviously knew what was coming, but I didn't and leaned forward to better hear Keane's now much quieter voice.

"Yes sir. We passed on the street and spoke . . . just greetings of the day and the like. He seemed in great dudgeon, hardly answering my greeting and at first, didn't stop. Neither did I. After all, he was a post-captain and had no need to talk to me, a mere lieutenant. Then he called my name after we had passed and I went back the few steps to where he stood in the street. He was barely civil to me, asking about me enlisting his boat's crew, or some-such bilge. After he described the men he was after, I realized I had indeed enlisted his men and told him as much, but added that I didn't know at the time they was deserters. And one of 'em was going by a different name than Cap'n Townshend mentioned to me."

"What subsequently transpired, Lieutenant?"

"Beg pardon?"

"What *happened* next, Mister Keane? Did Lord Townshend simply walk away and let the matter drop?"

"Oh no, sir. He asked me to give 'em back. Said he couldn't have his men runnin' off to the American Navy every time they got the chance. I told him I had neither the authority nor the desire to turn his sailors back to him . . . and neither did the local magistrate. Then he said just to give him back one of 'em—Jenkin Ratford, it was he asked for—so he could hang him proper as an example to any other what might be thinkin' on runnin'. The cap'n mentioned something about the man Ratford making open threats on his person and fairly demanded I turn him over. I said I couldn't do that and he stormed off, even madder than he was when he started."

"Did you, in point of fact, Mister Keane, sign his man, Ratford? Hmm?"

A silence had descended on the room and Keane's pause before answering this damning question served to exaggerate its completeness. Even from behind the witness chair, I could discern Keane's jaw muscles working, working as though he were chewing something, a piece of gristle perhaps. Finally, the lieutenant seemed to shake himself and looked at his tormentor full on.

"At the time, I had no knowledge that I had recruited him. Sir."

"And why is that, Mister Keane?"

"There was no one signed our articles going by Ratford or anything close to that name."

"But he was aboard the frigate, was he not, sir?"

"Aye. We later smoked his ruse; he had used a different name when he joined the ship. John Wilson, it was."

"And how did you discover Wilson and Ratford were one in the same person, Lieutenant?"

Keane looked away and wiped his mouth with his hand, effectively muffling his answer. The attorney raised his own voice and requested that the witness repeat his response so the panel and the recorder might hear it also.

"The tattoo on his arm. 'Jenkin Ratford,' it was."

"You mean to tell me that this man, Ratford, came into your rendezvous seeking to enlist in the American Navy with his name tattooed on his arm in plain view, and yet you signed him aboard under a different name? Why on earth would you do that, sir?"

"I don't recall having seen a name or anything else tattooed on his arm at the rendezvous, sir. He gave his name as Wilson and that's what I wrote down. Why would I expect a man to lie about his name?"

"Why, indeed, sir!"

Lawyer Taylor looked at the panel, exasperation plainly evident in his entire demeanor. It was as if he were asking the Court how it was possible our ships could sail with such imbeciles aboard as officers. I think everyone in the room might have pondered a similar question. Finally Barron's attorney turned back to his shamefaced witness.

"Mister Keane: let us put Ratford's sudden appearance on the frigate"—a ripple of laughter was gaveled down by Captain Rodgers— "aside for the moment and return to your conversation with Lord Townshend. You recall, sir, we *were* discussing your conversation with him prior to the Ratford issue."

Keane nodded, looking quite miserable.

"Splendid! Think back, if you please, sir, to the conclusion of that brief encounter.

"Did Captain Townshend, perhaps, threaten to *retrieve his sailors by force*, should it become necessary, Mister Keane?" Taylor leaned in close to the witness, his voice menacingly quiet.

"Well, he did say something like that, but I didn't think nothin' of it; everybody makes threats and I knew the Brits wouldn't come on board of one of our ships by force."

"You *knew*, did you?" The caustic tone and Taylor's raised eyebrows brought another ripple of subdued laughter from the spectators which was again quickly gaveled into silence by the president.

Taylor pressed on. "Did you tell anyone, your captain, for example, that you knew you had British seamen—at least four of them, and who knows how many more—aboard *Chesapeake*? And that a Royal Navy captain was most upset about it?"

"No sir. Didn't seem necessary and . . . well, nobody asked me. "Sides, I and everyone else—or most everyone else aboard—knew we had a passel of Brits aboard. Whether they was all deserters or not, I don't reckon any among us knew for certain. But we all seen British sailors marching up and down the streets in the city waving our flag and shouting slogans aimed at getting British sailors to sign American articles. British officers hadda seen 'em likewise."

"Did it not seem somewhat odd to you that a captain in the Royal Navy, a lord, no less, would stop a lieutenant with whom he had a barely passing acquaintance and inquire about some common sailors? And that, despite having possibly witnessed British sailors marching as you say, he was quite angry about it? To the point of making threats about using force?"

"Well, sir. I didn't give it much thought. Either his remarks or the men. We needed them, they showed up at the rendezvous wantin' to enlist, and I signed 'em up. I had heard that some of those we signed were Americans who had served on British ships but had been pressed by the Royal Navy off'n merchants. I forget whether the story had 'em in British or American merchants. Made no difference in the event; they were in the American Navy now."

"I see." Barron's counsel impassively studied the lieutenant for some time without saying a word; it had the effect of adding to Keane's discomfort and he shifted his weight yet again on the hard chair. The creak it made was the only sound in the Cabin; even Barron had stopped his incessant scratching with the pen.

"So you knew, sir, that there were British deserters aboard the frigate when you sailed from Norfolk. And so did the British. And that the commander of one of the English warships had threatened force to retrieve them, and you mentioned not a word of this to any. Is that not correct?" Without waiting for an answer, Taylor continued. "Small wonder the Royal Navy stopped the ship, then." Taylor said this last most quietly as he was returning to the commodore's table. As he sat down, he spoke again.

"That will be all, Mister Keane. I have no further questions for you." Mister Taylor turned toward his client and muttered something, his head close to Barron's. I didn't catch it, but I am sure we all heard Barron's reply quite clearly.

"Bloody incompetent rascal, he is. Just like all the others."

A brief muttered conversation then ensued between the commodore and his lawyer while members of the panel shuffled papers and spoke quietly to one another.

Henry turned to me and, in barely audible tones, whispered, "Well, looks as if Taylor's found his scapegoat, Oliver. I never thought Keane to be the tallest mast in the harbor by a long shot, but he done himself proud this time; his answers surely took even his mentals down a rung or two! I'd warrant that Keane is wondering if his name is to be added to the list of defendants, the way Taylor laid into him. Lambasted the poor bastard, he did! Still tryin' to shift the blame off Barron, I'd guess. Give the Court something else to think on 'sides hangin' his client." Henry's whisper seemed positively gleeful!

"I reckon all that's left is for Barron to take the chair, Henry, and recount his own version of his trying experience! I would hope that will see the end of our *trying* experience." I giggled at my intentional and clever play on words hoping that Henry would be equally amused; he remained unmoved by it and, with not even a smile, he pressed on.

"We're nigh onto a month of this and not a word has he offered, save having Taylor ask a few sharp questions to those called to bear witness to his disgrace. I can scarce wait to hear how *he* tells the tale!"

I whispered back to him. "Get this over and done with. Try the others and go back to sea, where we belong!" At least we agreed on that!

The one witness who I am sure the Court would have been desperate to hear was unavailable; our first lieutenant, Benjamin Smith, had passed over back in October from an illness. He had witnessed from the quarterdeck almost everything that had transpired and likely could have shed some light on some of the conflicting testimony the court had heard. He was, as well, the one Barron sent to *Leopard* with our surrender and, while Henry Allen had testified to that event, Smith might have added insight that escaped my friend on account of his emotional state. Of course, Mister Smith had been called to testify before the Court of Inquiry last summer, so perhaps what he might have had to offer was already in the record of that hearing.

Our current first lieutenant, Mister Rowe, had not been aboard during the disastrous and short-lived cruise in June, having been assigned aboard only when we were well into November. The sentiment throughout the gunroom and the cockpit ran that since we were well secured to the pier and unlikely to be heading out anywhere with a court martial hanging over us, the need for a first lieutenant had been scant. And we did, in fact, manage just fine without one for those several months. Of course, the Secretary of the Navy had wasted no such time at all assigning Captain Decatur to relieve both Captain Gordon and Commodore Barron. We barely had set our best bower in the Roads when that had happened!

Rodgers' gavel halted our, and several other, conversations, as he called for silence in the courtroom and announced that no further witnesses would be heard and we would adjourn for the rest of the day.

"Since Commodore Barron's testimony will be crucial to the outcome of this, and the subsequent courts, we would prefer to hear it in an uninterrupted fashion, at least so far as we can. We will reconvene on the morrow at two bells in the forenoon watch. We are adjourned."

Bang! The gavel ended the session and we all stood, grateful for the early respite from the tedium of the trial. At least, I was. And Henry and I were among the first of the spectators to gain the spar deck; we moved quickly to the rail to discuss the proceedings thus far. While we both held differing opinions as to the ultimate outcome, neither of us would accept a wager from the other on our surmises. Henry had, in his opinion, seen or heard little over the past twenty and more days of testimony that might change his earlier prognostication. I, on the other hand, thought the evidence and testimony offered thus far might find some favor with the panel, even with the well-known partisanship of several of its members, and perhaps Barron would simply be reprimanded instead of being hanged as Henry had prophesized. Surely Captain Gordon would bear a goodly portion of the blame for the condition of the ship when that fateful meeting took place, even if the commodore was proven guilty of infamous surrender. Time would tell.

CHAPTER FIVE

"May it please the court, Commodore Barron has prepared a statement in his defense and we pray the court that he might be permitted to read it himself." Taylor rose from his table after the usual preliminaries had passed.

The Cabin was packed; additional chairs had appeared and there were even a few men, mostly in naval uniform, standing along the walls on either side of the door. The morning sun streamed in undiminished brilliance through the quarter gallery windows and caused the brass and silver lanterns, of which only a few in the darker corners were lit, to glisten and shoot dazzling reflections around the dark walls. Candelabra of plate, their tapers fresh, remained unlit and likely would remain so until later in the day when the sun had passed its meridian and cast the aftermost part of the frigate into shade.

The commodore, his full dress uniform crisp and freshly brushed, sat with perfect posture at his table. For the first time since early in the court martial, that table was not covered with loose papers, pen stands, and ink pots; only a neat sheaf of pages was stacked carefully in front of him, papers to which his eyes dropped often during the beginning of the day's events.

"Very well, Mister Taylor. There can be no objection to his doing so if that is his wish. Commodore Barron may have the floor." Captain Rodgers raised his deep voice to carry over the startled expressions and comments which had instantly filled the room.

Quiet was restored immediately Barron rose and, with the stack of papers clutched in his fist, took a position in the middle of the floor, facing the panel of his peers, his judges. His gaze steadied on Captain Rodgers and, save for a brief glance at the papers he held, remained there as he began to speak, his stentorian tones filling the Cabin.

"Mister President and gentlemen of the court. After serving in the Navy for ten years, usefully, and with the approbation of the government,

I consider it my good fortune to be brought before you on charges implicating my honor and my life. After six months and more of silent, and not so silent, misrepresentation and misconception, I view this day as my opportunity to vindicate my honor before an intelligent and impartial tribunal. I shall use no unmanly attempt to interest your feelings or influence your generosity; my case shall be such as one officer may make to another without reproach and the officers receive without a blush. I shall direct my remarks entirely to your judgment, reason, and professional experience." He paused and glanced down again at his papers.

There was not a sound in the room. No chairs shifted, no feet scuffled, and, it seemed, even our breathing was subdued; even the scribe, who would normally be scratching away with his pen as a witness spoke, was still, knowing he would have a fair copy of the commodore's speech at its conclusion.

I stole a glance at the panel. Captain Rodgers studied Barron impassively, has face giving no clue to his feelings. Captain Decatur was not quite so neutral; his eyes were hard and his mouth, often so quick to break into a ready smile, made a thin line in his face. The others, Lawrence, Bainbridge, Porter, *et al,* showed little emotion or indication of their true feelings, if indeed any had reached a determination in their own minds of Barron's guilt or innocence.

After looking up and receiving a nod from Captain Rodgers, Barron continued his monologue, referring to his script only infrequently, and holding his eye contact with the judges as, I assume, he gauged from their expressions how they heard his comments.

"There are numerous charges against me, each with several specifications underlying it. I shall, for clarity and simplicity, enumerate each charge and specification, answer it, and move to the next. If I should seem to belabor a particular point, I would beg your indulgence as my defense is made not just for this court, whose members are well familiar with the duties and responsibilities of a naval officer, but for a reviewing authority who will surely not have enjoyed the same opportunities of being informed on those intricacies.

"The first charge against me is for 'negligently performing the duty assigned me' and of the specifications, there are two: that I 'did not visit the frigate *Chesapeake* during the period she lay in Hampton Roads before proceeding to sea as often as I was bound to' and that 'when I did visit her, I did not, as was my bounden duty to do, examine particularly into her state and condition.'

"These presuppose that it was, in fact, my duty to visit the ship often, to personally superintend her equipments, and to examine into her condition. I ask you, sirs, were these duties within my province? Was it, as a matter of fact, my duty, or the duty of another officer, to see to these concerns? It was designed by the Secretary that I should proceed in the frigate, following her re-commissioning, to the Mediterranean to take command of a squadron in that sea. Master Commandant Charles Gordon was appointed in command of the ship while she lay, dismantled, in the Navy Yard in Washington. Captain Gordon held the responsibility of overseeing her reconstruction, superintending her equipment, and conducting her thence to Hampton Roads. He continued in that station until the day of his arrest.

"It is apparent that the duties attached to me by this charge exclusively pertained to him, not to me, based on our respective ranks and commands. The President of the United States has established rules and regulations for the government of the Navy; a copy of them is supplied to all officers and midshipmen in our service. Those rules embrace all ranks from commodore to the cook and define quite clearly the respective duties of each in minute detail."

Barron stopped for a moment, turned to his table and retrieved a leather-bound volume I had not before seen there. Opening to a predetermined page, he proceeded to read the "duties of a commander or captain," pointing out again that Gordon held that rank. Of particular interest to all was the ninth article in that list of duties: ". . . at all times, whether sailing alone or in a squadron, he shall have his ship ready for an immediate engagement, to which purpose he shall not permit any thing to be on deck that may embarrass the management of the guns, and not readily be cleared away."

I know that I was not the only person in the room guilty of the sharp intake of breath that followed these words. It wasn't Gordon's trial, but it looked to me that here was the indictment that would seal his fate when the time came.

I nudged Lieutenant Allen and whispered, "Sounds more like Gordon'll be the one hanged, not the commodore."

He whispered back into my ear, "That's only one of the charges. I don't reckon the book says anything about surrendering when there's a fight to be made!" His whisper was as sharp as possibly a whisper might be.

I could not respond as the commodore was continuing to list more duties ascribed to the ship's commander, each representing an area in which Captain Gordon appeared negligent: "muster the crew at drills whether in port or at sea, examining the ship's company to ensure each is qualified to perform the duties assigned to him, ensuring that all hands are distributed to stations for quarters including the rigging, the great guns, and the powder magazine, and overseeing the whole conduct and good government of the ship."

Henry and I exchanged looks at this litany of Gordon's omissions, each of which appeared sufficient by itself to bring the captain to grief. Henry's smile was not so broad as before; perhaps he felt Barron was making a good case for his own exoneration, to the detriment of the commander of *Chesapeake.* The commodore continued reading his remarks in a tone quite neutral, considering the emotion that had attached to the whole affair right from the start.

"That a commodore is ordered to hoist his flag in any ship does not reduce in rank the commander of that ship; indeed, each has their own responsibilities, unaffected by the presence of the other. If it is insisted that the regulations do not apply to a commander in whose ship is embarked a commodore, I must then ask which regulations do apply? There are none, other than those I have read to you. And I might also ask, what duties *do* befall the commander of a ship with a commodore embarked? According to the charges against me, apparently *none.* The conclusion can only be inescapable: all captains, whether or not there is a commodore in his ship, are intended to be bound by the same regulations." Barron paused and looked at the panel. His gaze shifted from one member to the next as he studied their reactions to the first salvo in his defense.

During this pause in his recitation, the silence within the room remained unbroken. From without the Cabin, muted sounds of the ship, the cry of seabirds, and occasional shouts of men working above drifted into the silence with no more notice than the smell of the air we inhaled.

After shifting the pages he held to produce a new one for his continuing statement, the commodore then enumerated the duties assigned by the regulations to his rank, each of which were broad in scope and related, not just to one ship, but to all under his command.

"'He is obliged to inform himself of the properties of each vessel in his squadron, that he may make use of them to advantage as occasion may require.' Obviously this pertains to the qualities each ship may display so that, for example, the commodore, in appreciation of their respective qualities, might not send a dull sailer in chase. It does not require that the commodore examine into the minute detail or the arrangement of their interior as might be assumed by the first specification against me.

"The regulations also call for the commodore to visit the ships of his squadron or division and view the men on board, seeing them mustered, as often as he shall think necessary. I would call your attention, gentlemen, to that last expression, ' . . .as often as he shall think necessary.' You will also note, I am sure, that nowhere does the regulation require a commodore to rummage through storerooms, overhaul the rigging, pry into the magazines, or inspect the mounting of each gun. Those responsibilities derive to the captain of the vessel.

"It is apparent to me, and by now, I am sure, to you, that the framer of this charge demonstrated a want of clear conception of the relative duties of Captain Gordon and myself, or a most anxious desire to supply, by the number of charges, the want of individual force."

I noticed several of the judges nodding in apparent agreement with Barron's statement, including Captain Decatur and President Rodgers. I shoved my elbow, more sharply this time, into Henry's ribs and received an unfriendly look in response. His earlier assessment of nothing short of a hanging for the commodore appeared to be unraveling!

"If this is to be the tenor of his entire defense, I should not be surprised were he only to be given a slap for his disgrace and the shame he put on us, the ship, and indeed, the Navy at large. He's showing himself to be nothing more than a damn sea-lawyer!" Henry's whisper was some louder than necessary and I gauged from the looks he received from those in our immediate quarter that some were shocked he should speak thus, while others, nodding, appeared in silent agreement with his position. For my own self, I preferred to reserve my judgment to hear more of Barron's statement.

"Further, I would add," Barron was continuing to read from his papers, "that even though I have disproved in its entirety the first charge and its respective specifications, that fact of omission, that I did not attend the frigate prior to her departure from Norfolk, is entirely without merit. Between the dates of 6 June and the 21st of that month (when I ultimately went on board to stay), I paid two visits to the ship. As you heard in the regulation from which I read previously, it was my decision, and my decision only, when and with what frequency I should visit the vessels in my command. On my first visit, the crew were mustered and reviewed by me. I did more, though. I examined all her decks, looked into the state of some of her stores rooms, and inquired into her general condition to the extent I deemed necessary. Could I have done more without usurping the authority and responsibility of Captain Gordon? Would it not have displayed a lack of confidence in the man to have inquired further into details of his management? No, I did not clamber into the rigging, handle ropes, or inspect the yards; nor was I required to. A seaman's eye can determine the state of a vessel's rig merely by observing from the deck. This I did and found nothing to arouse dissatisfaction in its condition.

"On my second visit, which was cut short by plans made by Captain Gordon to hold a ball on board, I personally superintended the mounting of one of the quarterdeck gun carriages, gave instructions to several officers (who seem, in their own testimony, to have conveniently forgotten that fact) and quickly inspected the spar deck.

"And finally, gentlemen, on the day we sailed, I ordered the crew to be mustered and gave a general examination of the ship. Captain Gordon had reported his ship ready for sea; ought I to have doubted him?"

He stopped speaking, shifted the order of his pages again, and looked up, his gaze again taking in the whole panel. Some rustling of chairs, scuffling of feet, and a few murmurs of conversation filled the silence.

Henry seized the opportunity to make his escape, saying to me as he did so, "Stay if you will, but I can not bear to hear anymore of this. Next will come, should he hold to this course, the request for a medal to be struck, memorializing his gallantry in the action!"

I looked up into his face as he moved in front of me on his way to the door. His eyes were hard, his mouth a thin line and his jaw set. He had made no effort to lower his voice and most of those in attendance were able to discern his words and tone. Everything from serious nods to horrified gasps ensued and a few hateful looks followed my friend as he made his way to the door.

Barron either did not hear the comment or chose to ignore it and the resulting ripple of comment, as he launched quickly into the second charge against him and its six specifications. They all dealt with his neglecting to clear the ship for action in the face of a probable engagement.

"One of the more difficult tasks before you gentlemen is determining the operation of the human mind and its ability to review, after an event has occurred, the prognostics which might have foretold it, giving each its due weight. It is most common behavior and, indeed, human nature in its very essence, to attach a weight and importance to a prior event in the light of its aftermath which it would not have had at the time. Even a feeble mind will make this connection, one which would have defied even the highest intellect without knowledge of the result.

"On this subject, gentlemen, *you* have the benefit of history; I, at the time of the incident, could only speculate on the aftermath of a series of seemingly unconnected actions. That which has become fact for you could only, for me, have been inference. To judge me, you must remove yourself to the position in which I was placed on that morning and ask yourselves whether or not those circumstances would have led you to the conclusion that an attack was probable.

"Until the moment the *Leopard's* officer came on board *Chesapeake*, I most solemnly affirm to you that I had absolutely no suspicion of an attack. After he left, I gave orders to clear for action. That fact has been reported accurately by every witness."

I had to admit, the commodore made a most credible point: none of us who had been on deck and observing had any idea that we might be attacked. Only that the British ship was displaying rude behavior unjustified by any action of our own. I leaned forward, the better to hear Barron as he listed the reasons why none of the supposed "warnings" held any significance to him. Including the constant inferences that we had sailed with deserters from the British navy in the ship.

"It has been alleged by several witness that I knew, along with Captain Gordon, that we carried British deserters. That is, in part, true. I believe, gentlemen, that it is safe to conjecture that *every* ship sailing under an American flag, merchant or Navy, carries several deserters from the Royal Navy; in most cases, I believe it is equally safe to conjecture that that Royal Navy has abandoned all pretensions to these alleged deserters. That they stop our merchants to press American and, in some cases British, seamen can not be interpreted as any attempt to regain their own deserters in spite of their claims to the contrary. All too often it is proven that the very men they remove are, in fact, Americans, born and bred, who had never set foot upon the decks of a British man-o'-war.

"As to the view that I should have, upon observing the British squadron anchored in Lynnhaven Bay, been aroused to defend myself, I can only offer this. That same squadron was there when *Chesapeake* arrived from Washington; was Captain Gordon imbued with suspicion as to their intents? I think not, else we he would have acted differently then. The menace those ships implied has been mentioned by very nearly each of the officers in the frigate. I ask you, sirs, could it not be a case of attaching a significance, a weight, to an event *after* discovering its import?

Should that not be the instance, it must then appear as though each of the officers, indeed, every soul aboard, was remarkably negligent in the performance of their duties by not making Captain Gordon or myself aware of these misgivings." Barron paused, looked at the panel to gauge their reaction, and shuffled his papers again.

"The specification refers to the 'communications by signal from one of the British squadron.' Does the mere telegraphic communication from one ship to another signal *hostility*? I suspect a person, unaccustomed to naval affairs, might infer, from the solemnity with which these circumstances are urged, that such was the case. That same person might determine that signals are rarely used between ships of the same squadron and, when they are used, they are perfectly understood by all observers. This conclusion would derive support from several of the witnesses who mentioned that '*Leopard* got under weigh *by signal*.' Only Mister Baldwin, I believe, admitted he was, in fact, ignorant of the codes of the Royal Navy."

Goodness! He really was paying attention to what I said!

"I can only imagine, sirs, the surprise of that same person, unfamiliar in the ways of naval affairs, when they learn that communicating by signal is the ordinary mode of intercourse between vessels of the same squadron and that, at sea, scarcely an hour passes in which various signals are not made from one ship to another. It might astonish that same personage to notice that signals *regularly* are made between this ship, upon which we all stand, to various of the gunboats in the harbor. And that, without a book of explanation, those signals would be quite incomprehensible to any who noticed them.

"Since each of those officers who testified that *Leopard* got under weigh *by signal*, I can only wonder why the action then did not excite the suspicions it seems to have in the intervening passage of time. Indeed, sirs, nothing could have given these circumstances any importance but a previous suspicion. The Royal Navy has been in and out of our waters, it is well known, for many months, watching the movements of certain French ships of war, also within our waters. Ships have quit the anchorage often enough to arouse no concern, sail to without the Capes, and return. In some cases, they have actually intercepted French vessels, and captured them within sight of our shores. Is it not extravagant supposition to assume that the ships of a nation with whom we, as a country, have enjoyed the strictest amity, should suddenly and without warning, be sent underweigh to commit mischief on our flag, and at our very threshold?"

I had to admit, that it was certainly the farthest thing from my own mind that *Leopard,* or any other, would attack us that day. How my colleagues could testify to the contrary could only be explained by Barron's statement about attaching importance to an event after one had knowledge of the result. I found myself nodding in agreement and was surprised to find my sympathies moving in his direction.

Where is Henry now? He should be hearing this his own self!

I would have to attend closely the commodore's words so I could accurately pass them on to my friend. But not immediately, it seemed. A seaman, I recognized him as one of the new men recently signed, had made his way through the spectators and had handed a note to James Lawrence, sitting at the end of the long table. I watched as Lawrence, followed by each man to his right, glanced at the folded paper and passed it on until it reached the hand of Captain Rodgers; he unfolded it and scowled.

Holding up a hand at the commodore, causing him to pause in his recitation, Rodgers conferred briefly with Captain Decatur and then nodded.

"With your indulgence, Commodore, I would like to pause at this point in your statement for a brief recess. Not more than fifteen minutes, I assure you." Rodgers actually smiled at Barron as he spoke and, without further comment, banged the gavel on the table and stood up.

Barron was speechless; he stood, slack-jawed, as he watched the president accompanied by several of the members of the court, including Decatur, Bainbridge, and Captain Porter, file past him and out the door. To where, I had no idea.

The commodore turned about and faced his lawyer. His expression had changed from shock to a black fury and he leaned over the table to speak to the civilian. Even though Barron spoke with a tone prompted by his apparently shabby treatment by the court, I could hear only a few bits and snatches of his invective (for I am sure that is what was issuing forth, given his expression) over the hum and buzz of the murmuring that rose rapidly from the stunned silence of the gallery. And while I felt almost the same sense of outrage at the commodore's behavior last June as Henry, I could not help but sympathize with the man at this moment; one minute he was speaking eloquently and cohesively, debunking arguments made against him by almost everyone involved, and the next, he was cut off in mid-stride by a thoughtless and senseless interruption.

Could Rodgers and Decatur be so adamantly opposed to Barron's acquittal they would stop the recitation like that? Might even be illegal. Well, I guess one or another of the lawyers would've said something if walking out like that was against the rules. Where was Henry when I needed his wisdom now?

My head was reeling, filled with confusion, one minute convinced that Barron was being censured, singled out unfairly and the next, equally convinced that his actions last summer were beyond reprehensible and he deserved whatever he got. It seemed from the conversation I heard around me that others were equally horrified; some gloated at his discomfort and others—surely they had to be his confidants—were quite vocal in opposition to the court's action. But all had opinions to air.

And those opinions were becoming more and more voluble. They quickly reached the point were I could distinguish no individual words from any participant. Indeed, the room seemed to be consumed by a dull and constant roar, as each participant in the battle of opinion raised his voice to be heard by the person adjacent who, in turn, raised his voice, and so on. I may have been the only soul who held his tongue; not due to any lack of opinion, but due to the lowly rank I held and a lack of someone to whom I might offer that opinion. Instead, I simply stared, agog, I must admit, at those who jumped up and down, plucked at their neighbors' coats, and became more and more embroiled in the melee. So captivated by the antics of those around me, I failed, as did those around me, to notice the return of the panel members who had left.

Until the loud and insistent banging of Captain Rodgers gavel succeeded in gaining at first, the attention of only a handful of the less strident, followed by more and more until only one or two voices rang out in the silence. Those few fell into an embarrassed silence as quickly as they realized it was only their voices they heard.

"Commodore, I apologize for the interruption; I had just received word that Secretary Smith was on board the frigate seeking my presence and I felt it unwise to protract his idleness. As we all are aware, the Secretary is not famous for his patience. You will want to know, sir, the Secretary is most anxious for this affair to come to its natural conclusion and encouraged me . . . and Captain Decatur to hasten that conclusion."

There were any number of gasps from the spectators and Barron's attorney rose to his feet as Rodgers banged his gavel calling for quiet.

"Mister President: I would presume that this . . . this interference from the Secretary of the Navy will cause no lack of *juris prudence* on the part of the panel and my client will enjoy the full benefit of a court free from prejudice." Taylor remained standing as his comment stirred further murmurs from the gallery, which were duly banged into silence by Rodgers' gavel.

"Without a doubt, Mister Taylor. All the Secretary requested was to minimize the interruptions and, in his words, 'get on with it.'"

Obviously, the president missed the irony of his remark, but the smiles that appeared briefly on the faces of both Decatur and Captain Porter indicated they had not. Nonetheless, Commodore Barron rose to his feet again and after glaring at Rodgers and several members of the panel, he continued his monologue.

"As I had mentioned immediately previous to the brief recess, the mere presence of British warships in our waters was insufficient provocation to arouse suspicion to their intended mischief. None of the persons in *Chesapeake,* regardless of any testimony to the contrary by some"—here Barron paused and looked squarely at someone in the gallery, I could not see who—"could have held any doubt as to the continued placidity of those vessels of the Royal Navy.

"And further, the specification under this charge would imply that I had prior knowledge of some overt intent of the British to retrieve their sailors at the first opportunity. You will acknowledge, sirs, I am sure, that any tales of forewarning, to me or any in *Chesapeake* are unsupported at best and quite spurious at the worst, condemning by innuendo and unsupported imputation. No witness has been found to lend a shred of credence to this fabrication and, while I have answered it as though it were a valid criticism of my behavior, you gentlemen will, I am sure, see it as the ruse it indeed is.

"As further stated in the specification to this charge, it is suggested, nay, it is *stated,* that I should, by the maneuverings of *Leopard* once clear of the Capes, have recognized her hostile intent, a statement based solely on the opinion of others. The changes to *Leopard's* course were produced by the very same circumstances which caused *Chesapeake* to change her own course: the vagaries of the wind. The coincidence of the movements of the two ships was a matter of necessity precipitated by the proximity of land and changes in the wind. We had been standing to the southeast, as was *Leopard,* when the wind began to move into that direction. I changed course to the northeastward and by necessity, so did *Leopard.* For both of us, it was indeed the *only* course by which we could get off the land."

I studied the members of the panel for an indication of agreement to this statement, but observed only the unwavering stares and expressions devoid of any sympathy or even acceptance. Those around me, however, muttered in concert to each other; whether they agreed or not I could not fathom.

"With regard to the charge that I should have inferred that, from the actions of the Royal Navy ship, an engagement was probable, I can offer unflinchingly that had the United States been at war with Britain, the actions might have aroused some concern in my breast as well as in my fellow officers. But surely it can not be expected that such movement in a ship known to belong to a nation at amity with us ought to have excited the same suspicions. Once *Chesapeake* turned back toward the Capes to discharge our pilot, *Leopard* followed us under easy sail, making no attempt whatever to overtake us before we reached the limits of United States waters. As to her rounding up on our weather quarter as opposed to our leeward, which would have been in keeping with proper sea etiquette, I could infer nothing, save the rudeness of Captain Humphreys, as being responsible. And even that can be excused, one would suppose, by the sea honors still claimed by ships of the Royal Navy in their misguided arrogance."

A ripple of laughter broke the silence of the room and vanished as quickly as a gust of wind ripples a calm sea then moves on, leaving the surface again undisturbed. Even several members of the court succumbed to a thin smile. Barron looked up, seemingly startled by the reaction and, as the distraction ended, returned to his monologue.

"One might conclude that, while the individual actions of the British ship might arouse no suspicions by themselves, their combined consideration ought to have created a belief that an attack was designed. Here again, sirs, I can only offer that which I did before: in hindsight, an act can gain importance when the result is known and when viewed in the light of that result. And while some of the officers, whose testimony we have heard related many times over during the course of these proceedings, have imputed greater significance and hostility to individual actions than that which was called for, I would again offer that none felt sufficiently alarmed to mention those concerns to either me or Captain Gordon.

"And Captain Gordon himself, while claiming to have heard me utter words at table some two hours prior to any contact with *Leopard* indicating my suspicions of their intent, himself felt no onus to even attend the movements of that ship, or to examine the lumbered condition of our own gundeck and give the orders necessary to have his ship ready for an immediate engagement as called for in the regulations. None of the others present bore witness to his claim; indeed, how could they? I had offered absolutely no opinion as to the intent of *Leopard* either hostile or benign. One can not prove that which did not happen; Captain Gordon's is the only voice offering testimony to this utterance which, apparently, only he had heard."

Another ripple of laughter served to break the tension in the room and with it, I began to think Barron had won some of the panel to his point of view. The commodore cleared his throat, shuffled the papers he held and, looking squarely at Captain Rodgers, continued.

"Another thing in this matter is quite remarkable. While there have been some fifteen or sixteen witnesses who claimed no sense of foreboding coming from the overtly hostile actions of the *Leopard*," Barron's voice fairly dripped with sarcasm as he uttered the words 'overtly hostile action', "those who did claim an indication of some unfriendly intention from her are the self-same ones who originally preferred the accusation against me, and who have given a written pledge to the world, penned in secret and offered to the Secretary in the same manner to establish their charges. Would it not seem reasonable to think their memories of events might be skewed by that action? Their bias by itself should be sufficient to induce you gentlemen to receive those statements with considerable allowance. And while Captain Gordon is not among the number of my pledged accusers, a stronger motive operates on him. The web of his destiny is interwoven with my own. My condemnation is his acquittal; should it not be proved the catastrophe resulted from my misconduct, then the charge will inevitably fall to that officer, from whose neglect of previous discipline and arrangement, the surrender flowed."

A great intake of breath, a universal gasp, greeted these observations which Barron offered quite without rancor. For my own part, I was becoming increasingly convinced that much of the blame for our humiliation should rest on Gordon's shoulders and, while it indeed had been Barron who ultimately surrendered the ship, it was the captain's complete lack of preparedness which had precipitated it. Henry, I was sure, would vehemently disagree, a result of his animus for the Commodore. And while Barron was surely no Decatur, he could not have attained the status he did were he as incompetent as Henry would have me believe. I studied the faces of those members of the court who I knew held the commodore in contempt. Was there some softening, perhaps an understanding? Could the commodore make them feel the same Hobson's choice he had been faced with? He surely was gaining ground in my own estimation and *I was there*! I should share at least a measure of Henry's feelings still.

While I surely had felt all the same humiliation and rage that Henry had at the time, those feelings were beginning to ebb, exposing to me (and, I supposed, to others as well) the less emotional facts of the matter which, when examined in the cold light of unbiased scrutiny, seemed less damning to the commodore than they had.

After a pause, Barron continued in the same level tone, alternately gazing at his papers and the panel. "While I did not believe that hostile action would immediately follow the departure of the British officer who had borne his commander's missive, I did feel it appropriate to be prepared. To that end, I instructed Captain Gordon, who had reported to me promptly Lieutenant Meade had left the ship, that he should 'prepare the ship for action.'

"Clearly, while there is no specified and precise form of words by which an order to 'clear for action' might be given, my intent, regardless of Captain Gordon's testimony, could be interpreted in no other way. Even he, though he testified that he took my orders to mean to '*prepare* to go to quarters,' he subsequently issued his own orders instructing the crew and officers to '*go* to quarters,' an order that was, by all accounts, considered to be an order for battle.

"Captain Gordon also has testified that I did not issue the order to go to quarters in silence and without the beating of a drum until after the first gun had been fired by *Leopard*. All of the other witnesses, however, have concurred that the drummer had begun his beat before the *Leopard* fired and that Captain Gordon stopped the man while on his way from the Cabin to the quarterdeck. And all agree that the captain was present on the quarterdeck at the time we were fired upon.

"It was after I arrived on the quarterdeck to observe the actions of the British vessel that I discovered her tompions were out and her guns trained upon us. At that time, I gave Captain Gordon an additional order to 'hurry his men to quarters,' clearly a second communication of the original order. And while I did issue that order with the admonition to 'do it quietly, without the beat of the drum, I did not halt the drummer; that was done, and has been repeatedly testified to, by Captain Gordon. No one, nor any of you gentlemen I suspect, could impugn me for that; there are times when it becomes prudent to conceal one's actions from an enemy, whether to buy time, or simply not to provoke hostility. Clearly, were our drum to be heard on board *Leopard* there would be little doubt as to our own intentions.

"Captain Gordon has testified that it would have been unlikely that our drum would have been audible on the British ship and further, that their firing commenced before the drum was sounded. In both of these particulars, he is contradicted by every other witness. I leave it to the judges, experienced sea officers, to determine whether or not a drum might be heard across the water at a distance of fifty or sixty yards. Should I be adjudged censurable for ordering the ship to quarters quietly, then so be it. But the system of conduct which made such an order necessary was injudicious and improper."

The nods of agreement from the spectators seemed surely more universal and almost continuous, at least in my own mind. I could discern nothing from the expressions of those who bore the responsibility of judgment on Commodore Barron save interest and, from Captain Porter, a concern for the time; he had glanced at his watch more often than might have been considered appropriate by an impartial observer.

Barron was shuffling through his papers, perhaps seeking where he had left off in his defense. The spectators took the opportunity to mumble to one another, expressing their views of agreement or disagreement with his remarks. While I strained to pick out individual voices, I could make no sense of any, just an undercurrent of noise that seemed quite formless. I felt a hand on my shoulder.

Turning my head, I found myself nearly nose to nose with one of the Marine sentries who had guarded the Cabin for most of the past month. He withdrew in surprise at our proximity, as did I.

"Mister Baldwin, sir. You're wanted on the quarterdeck, if you please. Sir." His hoarse whisper was clearly audible to me and, I am sure, those near at hand.

"By whom?" I queried him, indeed puzzled that I should be sent for.

Were it Henry looking for me, he would have simply come into the Cabin and sought me out. Whoever could want me on deck?

The Marine simply shrugged and turned to leave, fully expecting, I am sure, that I would be close astern as he stepped out of the doorway and into the passage beyond. I was.

When I reached the quarterdeck, I saw only some of our sailors doing busy work or chores the bosun had set them to in an effort to occupy their time; there was very little needed doing as the ship had long since been put to rights.

And a good thing, too, I thought, *as we have such a shorthanded crew. We surely will need to do some recruiting if ever we are to sail the frigate again!*

A tall officer stood in the waist, his back to me. But even so, something about his carriage made him appear familiar. I studied him as I made my way forward; he appeared to be waiting for something or someone, and looked about him, seeming to take in all the details of the ship and her rig. A small valise stood by the bulwark, apparently his.

"Sir," I said as I came near. "Midshipman Baldwin. I believe you sent for . . ." I was cut off in mid-sentence as Edward, my older brother, turned at the sound of my voice.

"Well, Midshipman Baldwin. You are looking fit, I'd judge. I'd reckon this sea duty and sailing the vast waters of Norfolk harbor agree with you. And how goes the court martial?" The smile that lit his face was matched only by my own.

I started to doff my hat in salute, but Edward stuck out his hand and when I took it in my own, pulled me to him in a brotherly embrace.

As he released me from his enthusiastic hug, I studied his face for an explanation of his presence. He was still smiling broadly.

"I am very glad to see you, Brother. But why are you here? Have you been assigned in *Chesapeake*?" I realized how silly that sounded as I heard it, but it was the only reason I could manage in my surprise. Nonetheless, I continued. "Your requests to be released from duty building gunboats in New York were approved?"

His smile at our reunion faded, replaced by a most somber expression. "No, Oliver. I come to fetch you. Father is not well; he had an accident in the shop or on a ship he was fitting with furnishings. I could not tell from the message I received from Mother. But she was quite clear about both of us getting ourselves to Philadelphia as quickly as ever we could. So I managed to arrange a ride for myself on a dispatch schooner leaving New York the day before yesterday and here I am. I am hopeful we can find another to get us to Philadelphia or we shall be forced to use the stagecoach which will delay us even further." His earnest expression spoke more eloquently than did his words about his concern for our father.

"I shall seek permission from Mister Rowe at once, Edward. Will you come below to wait? Or would a look about topside be more to your liking?" Even though the weather had moderated greatly and could almost be thought of as warm, I had no idea how long it would take to secure the permission I needed to take leave of the ship, nor how quickly Edward might find us a vessel heading out of the Bay, up the coast, and into the Delaware. There was no reason he should stand out on the deck when he could be more comfortable below. Privately, I hoped he would want to see some of my ship as we had not been together on a ship's deck since I had received my warrant.

Besides, I thought, *this is* my *ship and I should act the proper host!*

"I think a look about would be very much in order, Oliver. I would like to see where *Leopard* put their shot, in any case. Lead on!" Edward smiled, perhaps sensing my desire to show off my home a bit.

Recalling that our first lieutenant had not been in the spectators' gallery in the court martial, I kept a weather eye skinned for him as I led the way around the spar deck. I also, as he had requested, explained as we walked, the damage done us by *Leopard* last June. He seemed genuinely surprised we had sustained as much as I described, even though I had written him in some detail about it and again described it to him and our parents just two months previously when we both celebrated Christmastide in Philadelphia. I answered his questions about the progress "Decatur and Rodgers were making in hanging James Barron" with veiled comments designed to hide what he would surely construe as my youthful naiveté in thinking that perhaps Barron had not been as much to blame as some thought but was being cast in the role of goat at the behest of his many detractors. Henry Allen not withstanding.

It was as we turned about on the fo'c'sle to again head aft that we came across the same Henry Allen directing some work being done to the larboard side bow chaser. He looked up at our approach.

"Mister Allen, may I present my brother, Lieutenant Edward Baldwin, late of the *Philadelphia* frigate and currently building Mister Jefferson's gunboats in New York."

"With all I have heard of you, sir, it gives me great pleasure to finally shake your hand." Allen, seeing that Edward had extended his own hand in lieu of a salute, responded in kind, a broad smile across his face.

"Aye, and thank you for that, sir. Oliver has told me on any number of occasions of your heroics in the face of *Leopard's* attack. I would add my own congratulations to the many I am sure you have already received. It must have been a dreadful experience, the whole episode, and one that I can well imagine, having been in a not dissimilar position in the late war."

"What brings you to Norfolk, Lieutenant, if I may inquire? Would it be an interest in seeing our illustrious commodore get his just desserts? I would offer, sir, that should that be your want, you would be well advised to hurry below before the event is history. The commodore must be close to finishing his litany of exculpatory explanations of his scandalous behavior by now and I am sure there will be few further witnesses called to add credence; most to date seem to have offered little in the way of assistance to the man." Henry's smile was gone, replaced by a grim expression leaving no doubt in the viewer's mind as to his stance on the matter.

"As a matter of fact, Lieutenant . . ." Edward was cut off.

"Henry, please, sir. I would be much more comfortable with your using my Christian name."

"Henry, then it is. And I am Edward." My brother smiled to his new friend. "As I was saying, Henry, I am here not for the court martial, though that surely is of interest to me. I have come to fetch Oliver, here, to Philadelphia with me. Our mother has sent for us as Father has apparently suffered a serious accident which has the potential of taking his life. It would not do for us to linger any longer than necessary in responding to her call. I have already inquired as to the availability of a fast schooner with room for us which might be heading for the Delaware Bay and onwards. Should that not materialize, we shall be obliged to take passage in the stagecoach, a certainly less than speedy conveyance."

"I seem to recall . . . yes, I do recall that a schooner with dispatches is leaving on the morrow for Philadelphia from Gosport, just across the way there. With a fair breeze on that vessel, you could find yourself in Philadelphia within three days, less should you find favorable tides in the Delaware. As she is a navy ship, I should think there would be little problem in securing a cabin for yourselves, especially with some help from our first lieutenant." Henry stopped for a moment, thinking, then looked at me.

"Oliver, ask Lieutenant Rowe for a letter and permission to use a boat and crew. I am sure he will suffer you the cutter in light of the urgency. I will entertain your brother until you return."

Henry spoke a few words to his gun crew about the work they had stopped doing while the three of us talked and, taking Edward by the arm, led him aft as he peppered him with questions about the Jeffersonian gunboats being built in New York. For my part, I hurried off in pursuit of my original mission, to find the first lieutenant, now with an additional request.

In Pursuit of Glory

CHAPTER SIX

" A h. Mister Baldwin. Welcome back. I trust you left your father well
. . . or at least on the mend?" Captain Decatur's greeting as I stepped
onto the frigate's deck caught me quite unawares. I did not know that he
knew of my departure and, even had he known, I was quite sure he had
many other, more important things on his mind than the comings and
goings of one midshipman.

He responded to my unfeigned surprise, though he seemed to err on
what had surprised me. "You recall, Oliver, that your father and I are old
friends. Mister Allen told me of his accident and I was sorry that duty prevented me from paying him my respects in person. I am also sorry to have
missed seeing Edward. He was well also, I collect?"

"Oh sir. Yes, sir. And thank you for asking. My brother is quite well
and likely back at his post with Commodore Chauncey in New York by
now. And Father is up and about, mostly through his own cussedness, and
hobbling about with the assistance of a stick. The surgeon is of the opinion that it will take some considerable time to replenish the blood he lost.
Father is still very weak, but determined to 'get back to normal' as he puts
it. It was a cruel hurt he suffered when the head flew off his assistant's
adze and he lost a fair measure of his blood on top of it. Razor-sharp, it
was and gave him what might have been a mortal wound. But he will
surely mend and, I am sure, return to his shop in the fullness of time. I
know my mother is in fervent hope of that happening sooner than later;
he is like a caged bear in the house, as you might imagine, sir."

Decatur laughed at the image of Edward Baldwin senior, cabinetmaker
of some note and provider to the Navy for furnishings of many of their
ships, unable to spend his usual twelve to fourteen hours daily at his profession. A large man, with a natural gusto for life and the voice to go with
it, he would be overbearing as a captive in his own home and most

demanding of his keeper, in this instance, my mother. Nor is he known for his patience, save when bringing to life his marvelous creations; in the shop, we have known him to spend an entire day shaping and reshaping the arm of a chair so that the curve of the arm will satisfy his craftsman's eye. I am sure that even Edward shared my feelings of relief at being allowed to return to our own duties, he in New York, hated though his duties are, and me here in the *Chesapeake* frigate.

"I am sure his clientele wish him back to work sooner than later, too, Oliver. I imagine that, should a better cabinetmaker exist in all of Pennsylvania, it is a closely guarded secret! I trust he still will continue to craft furniture for the Navy? When he is able, I mean."

"Oh yes, sir. I expect he will indeed. That has always been among his more satisfying commissions, I know. Of course, President Jefferson doesn't appear to be seeking new warships, only the gunboats my brother, Edward, and Commodore Chauncey are building in New York. And they don't seem to require the furnishings of a brig or frigate." I was unable to hide the feelings I had acquired during the month and more I was in Edward's company.

"Well, Mister Baldwin, I suspect our amity with Great Britain will grow less as they seem unwilling to quit harassing our ships for their supposed runaway seamen. This incident which has been holding all of our attention—indeed, the attention of the nation to judge by the newspapers—is only the most notorious.

"There continue to be others, though thankfully, not involving our Navy vessels. No, I fear that we may quite possibly be facing the might of the Royal Navy once again. But that remains to be seen, and surely is not something for a mere ship's officer to pontificate on. We will leave that issue for our diplomats and politicians to resolve, hopefully, without the need for shot and powder." Decatur looked ruefully around him, taking in the spar deck, seamen, ship's boats, and deck battery. Then he added, albeit much more quietly, "Though should it come to that, I expect some of us will not be unhappy!"

Then louder, ending my attendance to his comments, "I expect Mister Rowe will want to know of your return, Mister Baldwin. I am sure he will have much for you to do as we will be sailing within a fortnight under orders to enforce the embargo. I am glad you made it back to us." The commodore then turned and, without a further glance or, likely thought, in my direction, stepped aft, toward the quarterdeck and the hatch leading to his Cabin. For my part, I went in search of the first lieutenant to report my return aboard.

"Well, Mister Baldwin. You decided to return to your duties at long last, I see!" Henry Allen's unmistakable voice stopped me in my tracks as I made my way from the gun room, where my return was acknowledged by Lieutenant Rowe, to the cockpit to ensure my chest had been delivered by the sailor to whom I had entrusted it.

"Henry . . . uh . . .Mister Allen, sir, I mean." He frowned at my formality and I realized that he was only feigning an air he did not mean. "Yes, I am back only just now. I collect all is well? And I would assume that the court martial was brought to a satisfactory conclusion?"

I had immediately, upon approaching the ship, checked aloft for the court martial flag; the empty t'gallant mast where the yellow and blue pennant had become tattered and frayed, snapping in the winter gales daily for nearly all of January and a week into February when I had left for my father's bedside, told me the trial was done. How agreeable was its outcome would depend, I reckoned, on who was doing the telling.

"Well, I would reckon that might depend on 'satisfactory' to whom." Henry's warm smile retreated for a moment, as his words echoed my own thoughts, then returned. "Our illustrious commodore, while not hanged . . . or even cashiered for that matter, was suspended without pay for five years. A small price to pay for so great an offense as he committed, I'd warrant! And as we agreed . . . well, I predicted and you didn't *dis*agree, the other two officers—Gordon and Hall, got off with reprimands. *Private* reprimands, in fact. Of course, I had to testify at both of their trials. Same questions, almost to the letter, as I got in Barron's trial. Reckon the judges on the panel already found out all they needed to know during Barron's trial and the others . . . well, they had to do something, but it didn't seem all that momentous. Gordon's trial took only seven days and Hall's two.

"Gunner Hook chose not to hire a lawyer to defend himself, preferring to act as his own counsel. I don't have to tell you how *that* went! His trial lasted barely one day and the verdict was delivered almost immediately the testimony ended! Guilty! And out he went. Tossed to the wolves and good riddance, I say. Man was a fool and incompetent to boot!"

I could not believe my ears! The commodore thrown out of the Navy for five years! And, for not preparing his ship for sea and being ready to fight on a moment's notice, Captain Gordon got a reprimand, and a *private* one on top of it. Hall, the Marine captain, I neither knew well nor cared of his fate and Hook; well, from my own experience with the gunner during the attack, I could only agree with that sentence. But the commodore! I was astounded.

"I can not believe that, Henry. Five years suspension?"

"Hah! You *do* agree with me, Oliver! I was most certain you would see the error of your earlier position. It certainly was little more than a slap on the wrist for so heinous a crime. Surrendering one's ship without a fight, indeed! Should have been hanged, as I have said all along. Or tossed out *permanently* with that useless gunner! I would have thought Decatur and Rodgers and the others would have seen to it that that sentence would be a fit one and ordered it done. Course, the sentence they *did* order has not yet been approved by the Navy Secretary, so there's a chance he, or Jefferson, might see fit to stiffen it a bit. Aye, we can only hope."

My friend and superior had completely misunderstood my shock at Barron's sentence and I felt it prudent to leave the subject alone for now. No sense antagonizing him, friend or otherwise, unnecessarily. There would be ample time for that during long dull watches once we were at sea.

I quickly fell back into the shipboard routine that I had left some six weeks previously and turned to with a will, performing all the duties assigned me and helping to forge our mismatched crew into a fighting force. All under the watchful and practiced eye of our commanding officer, Stephen Decatur, but more often under the scrutiny of the first lieutenant.

Lieutenant Rowe was a quick study and had learned his employment with great alacrity, becoming a stern disciplinarian in the process. The contrast to his predecessor, Mister Smith, (and even that of Captain Gordon) was a constant topic of conversation among the midshipmen who, as might be expected by all but the most raw among us, felt the brunt of Mister Rowe's desire to excel, especially in the wake of our immediate and generally unsupervised and, some might even say, unruly, past.

And since Captain Decatur still held command of the Norfolk Navy Yard as well as the frigate, he left much of our preparation and pier side training to his first lieutenant. We also had the challenge of recruiting new sailors, as many of those who had sailed with us in June had been removed to other ships, it being unnecessary and wantonly wasteful of the Navy to maintain a full—or nearly full—sailing and fighting crew on a ship which would be secured to the pier for who knew how long.

Reprising my former role, I was again instructed to establish a rendezvous at Missus Pinckney's rooming house, given a carefully guarded chest of currency with which to provide advances to new recruits (many were quite literally destitute, a condition which frequently led them to a Navy rendezvous in the first place) as well as buy the occasional pint of whiskey or a meal for likely candidates, and instructed to " . . . be most selective and judicious in the choices of those you recruit." I took this to mean, again, "no British seamen." Which, of course, was *exactly* what it meant. Though how I was to be sure of the status of those I recruited escaped me.

Lieutenant Keane, apparently by his testimony in the late trial, had been determined to be unreliable in the execution of this order, and was excused from recruiting duty. The other rendezvous was administered by another midshipman, Daniel Mallory, a man of some greater years, but less experience, than I.

He was assisted in the management of his rendezvous, and the recruits he managed to attract, by *Chesapeake's* bosun, a robust and coarse fellow, known for his excesses in a remarkable number of bad habits, not the least of which was his ability to consume great quantities of distilled spirits, a fact that Mister Rowe either ignored or was unaware of when he assigned him the duty. Putting the bosun, encumbered as he was with his bad judgment and habits, together with an inexperienced midshipman and a chest of money with the stated purpose of (in part) standing recruits to the occasional meal and a "seal-the-deal" drink was laughable, and Mallory's stories, from the first day, became the high point of the evening meal in the cockpit or ashore, should that opportunity present itself.

"Some half dozen fine *citizens*—ragamuffins, they were—showed themselves at one point and the bosun, seeing an opportunity to enlist the lot of them, as well as indulge his own taste for strong spirits, took them all to an establishment other than where I could watch him, and was gone for several hours. Of course, a sizeable portion of our funds went with him, a portion he explained as ". . . necessary should I not be wantin' to get meself caught short, don't you know, sir." Mallory's Irish accent was a bit of an exaggeration of the bosun's brogue, but nonetheless, had us all holding our sides, laughing and hallooing every time he mimicked the man.

"I managed to recruit one or two myself (and without the need to buy them drinks, I might add) while he was gone. The pickings amounted to little but rascals and scoundrels, the leavings of humanity, and those likely to be on the other side of justice. What with the cold beginning to abate now, the higher pay available in the merchant fleet, and the somewhat unsavory reputation of our ill-starred frigate, I found few who could be enticed to chance a voyage, preferring instead to stake their prospects on the next merchantman to make the Roads. Should they, of course, be interested in maritime employment in the instance." He grew more serious in his narrative, and I recognized several of my own complaints which prompted me to give them voice.

"Aye, farmhands with no more idea of sailoring than I do of farming. Poor pickin's they are and not likely to gain much in the way of improvement." I began.

Upon hearing a measure of support from a "seasoned" recruiter, Mallory's dour face became even more so as he nodded vigorously in agreement.

I went on, stressing the importance of our employment. "But we can ill afford to put to sea with so many billets unfilled and, lubber or seaman, I would expect Cap'n Decatur will see to getting them drilled and trained into something resembling a crew before he looses a single line from the pier. He's some serious about his seamen, and his officers, I should hasten to add, knowing what they're about. We spent the entire time of our crossing to the Mediterranean in *Argus* drilling in everything from gunnery and hand weapons to sail handling and, for the mids and officers, navigating. And I'd warrant, should he tell the Secretary that *Chesapeake*'s not ready to make sail, it'll be taken to heart up in Washington. Especially after the late incident with the Royal Navy. "

As there was only one other midshipman in the cockpit with experience comparable to my own, I felt only the slightest twinge of guilt in pontificating in such a way. Even so, I did become aware of an unwanted comparison to both Judd Devon and Thomas Wheatley beginning to form in my mind.

Both were quite opposite one another (one being my friend and mentor while the other, Wheatley, was a boorish and disagreeable man of limited experience). They, and another (even younger than I was at the time) had shared the cockpit during the business with the corsairs of the Barbary Coast.

Uncomfortable with the possibility of being deemed a braggart, I turned the conversation back to Daniel's tale.

"Did the bosun bring the recruits back to the rendezvous to sign the articles?"

"Aye, he did that, and some the worse for wear, I'd warrant! But the five he brought in (one had either escaped or been too muddle-headed to make the walk back) were in even worse condition than the bosun. And not a one of them could write a lick. Barely had the ability to hold the pen to make his mark, so drunk were they! But scratch their marks in the book they did, and witnessed by my own self before they could change their minds. And then marched to the ship by the bosun himself." Mallory laughed at the memory of what the group must have looked like, being herded by a quite drunk bosun, as they clambered up the ladder to board the frigate.

"But at least they all made it aboard and with none wandering off along the way." Mallory added, seeing his shipmates preparing to laugh at the image he painted for us. "I had two chaps, seemed to have some experience from the way they talked, that came in to the rendezvous almost eager to enlist. Signed up quick as ever you please, and when they claimed to suffer such a shortage of funds as to not even allow supper, I gave them each a month's advance and sent them on their way. Never showed up at the pier, blast their eyes, anyway! Took the government's money and ran off. Likely made a business of it, showin' up at a rendezvous, takin' an advance, and then disappearing. Even sent Bosun Kelly lookin' for the pair the next day when I realized what they'd done."

He put on Kelly's accent again. "'Oh sir! Ye'll be wantin' to know I visited every pub and tavern 'tween here and the Navy Yard and nary a whisper did I hear nor did I catch me a single glimpse of them two. Even looked in to a couple of *houses,* sir, without a bit o' luck.' He actually winked at me as he reported this. 'Vanished like smoke, they done.'"

He switched back to his own voice. "And Kelly, from the look and smell of him when he returned, spent some considerable time in each and every tavern and *house,* (here Mallory winked at us!) likely waitin' on the two to turn up!" Mallory shook his head ruefully.

"I find that putting the advance pay in their hands *after* they report into the ship seems to answer some better, Daniel. You might give that some consideration." It had seemed so sensible to me, I would have thought any would do the same. Apparently not.

The cockpit steward, Munson, appeared in our doorway laden down with several platters of food for our midday meal. He placed them before Joshua Belcher, our senior (I was next in line, and as such, sat to his immediate right at table), and conversation dwindled to silence as we craned our necks to see what fare had appeared. Belcher served out what seemed to be a burgoo or stew of some type and, as the laden plates were passed from hand to hand, a bottle of not-bad wine worked its way down one side and up the other of the table. I had become used to taking spirits with a meal and filled my glass as well as Joshua's before sending the bottle down the table.

"You think the Secretary of the Navy will approve the commodore's sentence, Oliver?" One of the younger midshipmen, Taylor Scott, asked me around a mouthful of stew. "I would have thought they'da given him more than just a five year suspension."

"I have no idea, Taylor. But were I to offer a wager, I might expect that the sentence would be approved. Of course, President Jefferson could throw it out even if the secretary approved it. And do not forget, the court martial only convicted him of neglecting to clear the ship for action. None of the other three charges signified to the members of the panel. Reckon they figured Gordon was just as responsible for the surrender."

"I might have expected Gordon to be saddled with that charge—not clearing for action—rather than the commodore. Wasn't it his responsibility to see that the ship could operate properly? And how come, if Decatur and Rodgers had it in for the commodore so strong, they didn't sentence him for surrendering without firing a shot?" Mosley, a young, recently acquired addition to the cockpit, was on his first ship and had yet to leave the pier on anything beyond a rowing boat. Even so, it was rumored that he had spent his first full day aboard *Chesapeake* suffering from the effects of seasickness, which surely would continue to be the basis for an enduring round of jokes at the poor lad's expense. He masked his lack of knowledge and grasp of his employment with bluster and bravado, appearing to some, at least at first blush, as an eager and well informed young man.

"Mosley, you don't know anything. You're just repeating what you've heard others say. When you've at least left the pier, you might be entitled to an opinion. Until then, just listen. And remember that few, indeed, can operate their mouths and ears at once." Belcher glared at the young man who physically recoiled in the face of his senior's invective.

As for me, I resisted the urge to offer a comment that might be thought critical to Mister Belcher, recalling that another's inability to stifle a comment resulted in a duel, fatal, not to either of those holding the pistols, but to an innocent bystander. Instead, I determined to take young Mosley aside and help him in his new employment.

For now, I could only offer a mollifying appeasement. "I am sure that Captain Decatur and Captain Rodgers bent over backwards to be fair, given their well-known feelings for Barron. I would imagine that the sentence they imposed would be thought arduous enough. Even if there were some who thought Barron ought to get himself hanged for surrendering." Henry Allen's feeling as to what constituted a fair sentence was well known throughout the ship. I tried to sound knowing, but my shipmates were well aware of the fact that I had missed the end of the Barron's and all of the subsequent trials and thus the comments made by Captain Rodgers as he announced the sentences. Seeing the glances my comment drew from my messmates, I held my tongue, stifling the urge to offer anything further in defense of the seemingly light sentence.

Joshua Belcher, the only other in the cockpit who had experienced that dreadful June day, looked at me, winked, and said, "Aye, and Henry's right. Hangin' him would serve a right fine example for any who might consider a similar course in the future!" I knew he was only having some sport with me, as we had often discussed the outcome and he seemed to agree, at least on the surface, with my own sentiment.

"What will we be assigned to now, Joshua? I mean, the court martial is done; training is fine at the dock, but shouldn't we be sailin' somewhere and practicing what we've been training on for the past month? I don't know how much more of the dumb show with the great guns we can do. Seems mighty tedious, you ask me." Taggart, a quiet young man with a pox-scarred face who had joined *Chesapeake* only a few days after the *incident*, spoke for the first time.

He and I were about the same age, but Taggart had only been to sea as a midshipman for just over a year during the "quiet" time after 1805. So far, he had yet to experience hostile fire. He hailed from Massachusetts— Boston, I think—and had sailed in several merchants as a seaman. He seemed some recalcitrant to share with us his adventures from his time before the mast, but what little of his past we had gleaned made us thirst for more. I think he was disappointed that we had remained fast to the pier for so long. His whip-thin frame was topped with a long and quite narrow face, above which grew, in wild profusion, a mop of sand-colored hair over which the young man seemed to exert little control. He seemed overly serious and quite without a shred of humor from what I had so far observed. In fact, I could not recall seeing him even smile.

"I'd reckon we'll be getting underway once Cap'n Decatur thinks we're ready. He ain't one to go off at half-cock and so you can be right certain he'll be certain we know what we're about when he decides." Belcher smiled slightly at his own difficulty at saying what was in his head, then grew serious and looked around the table, concentrating his gaze on Taylor Scott and David Mosley.

I recalled the captain's intent to be underway within a fortnight of my return. Clearly, he had yet to determine that his crew and officers were sufficiently trained to avoid an embarrassment. Surely that was the case in the midshipmen's cockpit!

Belcher continued his admonishment to our junior messmates. "I would submit, gentlemen, that you might see to your studies and learn your duties right well, as it is my understanding that our captain does not suffer fools or their naval counterpart, ill-prepared midshipmen, gladly. Is that not so, Mister Baldwin?"

I nodded my agreement; saying more would have added nothing as all my fellows were well aware of my previous duty with Decatur.

And so the meal, and our days at the pier in Norfolk went; good-natured and sometimes, not so good-natured, bantering, joking, teasing, and second-guessing the officers. Training continued, including more exercising the great guns in dumb show, making and handing sail, and learning the use of hand weapons. Lieutenant Rowe had devised races to the maintop and back to the deck in an effort to give our lubberly crew, as well as the midshipmen, some confidence that would serve them well at sea. Of course, Mallory and I missed many of these events as we continued our efforts to enlist a sufficient number of sailors.

In mid-April a buzz started through the ship that the sentences of the Court Martial had been confirmed by the Secretary of the Navy, Robert Smith, and President Jefferson for each of the defendants: Commodore Barron was indeed suspended from the Navy without pay for five years, Master Commandant Gordon and Marine Captain Hall were reprimanded (they were carrying out orders of a superior officer) and Gunner Hook was cashiered for complete incompetency. Henry and I enjoyed a spate of good-natured I-told-you-so's for a day or two and then it was over, the effort to get our ship and crew ready to put to sea overshadowing most everything else.

And later that same month, with the promising breaths of spring warming the air, Decatur deemed his crew complete and ready and, for the first time since late June 1807, *Chesapeake* cast off her lines to the applause and cheers of a small, but enthusiastic, gathering on the pier, which included a makeshift band of musicians whose performance showed little evidence of rehearsal. Their cacophony inspired most of the hands to great alacrity in throwing off our bonds with shore and, with tops'ls, spanker, and jibs set and pulling in a freshening breeze, we headed down the river toward the Chesapeake Bay and ultimately, the Atlantic Ocean, retracing our course of the previous June, a course that then, had led us to disaster.

CHAPTER SEVEN

"My fellow Chesapeakes—and proud I am to call you that—we have been given an opportunity to right an injustice. To clear the good name of our fine and worthy ship and bring her reputation out of the cloud of doubt and the foul exhalation of those who would name her unlucky. . . or worse, jinxed." After uttering that last word as though it created a disagreeable taste in his mouth, Decatur paused and, for a moment, looked around the entire crew of his ship, making eye contact with many, as was his habit in times of high emotion.

"A ship is not lucky or unlucky. A ship is timbers and rope and canvas and iron. All inanimate and by themselves, incapable of being lucky or not. It is you, the men who breathe life into those inanimate parts that make up our ship, who determine her fortune. Should you . . . or I . . . fail in our tasks, others will say the ship was unlucky, or jinxed. Not so, I tell you; it will be you . . . and me . . . who should bear the burden of that guilt. For it would have been us who failed, not the ship.

"But we will not fail. None of us. Our commission is not of great moment. Surely not a cruise to glory. We are not going into battle against an adversary, worthy or not. Our country is at war with no one. We are not ordered to sail to the gates of Hell and face the ball and shot of an enemy, superior or otherwise. We will be on a routine patrol, seeing to it that the policies of our government as relate to trade are being followed, and should they not be, to take appropriate action."

Again, the captain paused, holding eye contact with several and, I am sure, noting those who seemed not of a serious bent. When a few murmurs and shuffling feet suggested he had remained mute long enough, he began again, raising his voice to encourage those laggards to sign on with his postulation.

"Those of you who have been chafing at your lines to be free of the shore with all its unsavory people, smells, and . . ." he hesitated for just a moment, as if seeking the right word, "temptations, now is your moment. I am told many of you tire of the drills and dumb-show exercises with the great guns. They are over; we will be exercising the great guns with shot and powder and firing at targets. We will drill at handing and making sail, reefing, furling, and shifting spars. If you thought those drills while we remained fast to the pier were dull and fruitless, you will soon discover they were not. You already know how to perform many of the tasks I . . . and Lieutenant Rowe and the other officers will demand of you. But in the space of thirty days, you will know many more and will be unflinching in their performance. Your shipmates will depend upon you to do your job quickly and correctly, as you will depend on them. I am sure you will all measure up to my demands and together will make our ship the envy of all who hear of our exploits, for in the same way as a ship is deemed unlucky, so may it be called favored and lucky."

Not a soul spoke or even moved for a space of several heartbeats. Then, from somewhere in the middle of the ranks of sailors, came a shout. "Three cheers for Cap'n Decatur!"

Lusty *huzzahs* rose to the heavens as the men and officers acknowledged our commander's prognostication.

And then, it might have been from the same voice, "Three cheers for *Chesapeake!*"

Without the same gusto, but nonetheless spirited, a further cheer resounded throughout the spardeck, evoking a genuine smile from our captain.

"Mister Rowe, dismiss the men to their watches and duties. We will go to quarters following the midday meal." Decatur nodded in response to the first lieutenant's salute, turned away from the rail and, with a look aloft ensuring himself that all sails were drawing perfectly, disappeared down the hatch to his cabin.

Lieutenant Allen and I were assigned to stand our watches together and now, clear of the confines of restricted and shoal waters, we took our positions on the quarterdeck, relieving the first lieutenant. After conferring briefly with the first lieutenant, Henry passed the word for our sailing master and bosun.

"We will be shaking out courses, and the for'ard stays'ls, Mister Cheever. Bosun Kelly, you will see to assisting him in that pursuit. Let us see just how competent, for all their training, is our crew."

A quick "Aye, sir." from each of them before they turned almost together and in one voice bellowed, "Sail handlers to stations. Topmen aloft. Look lively now. Stand by to make sail."

The bosun, a man given more to action than to instruction, appeared as if by magic on the spardeck, grabbing and shoving sailors to positions for loosing the big lower sails on the main and foremasts, while the sailing master exhorted the topmen aloft more quickly. These were supposed to be seasoned seamen, but in Cheever's mind, they were little better than farmhands who had never gone to sea. And he let them know it!

"Men at stations, sir." Cheever's voice carried clearly to the quarterdeck, and in response, Henry waved his arm. He turned to the two men at the big wheel, voicing a quiet order which would make the sails fill more quickly.

"Bring her head down a point, if you please, Quartermaster. Keep her at south, a quarter east."

As the frigate's bow bore away from the wind a few degrees, and to a great measure of shouting and calling, (I was able to hear distinctly only the command to "let loose the brails") the courses dropped from their spars almost at the same moment, billowing out in the cool breeze. And flapping madly in unrestrained freedom.

"Sheets and braces, haul. Look alive, you lubbers; it ain't no different than you done a hunnert times at the pier! Lay back on them sheets, for'ard, there." Between the bosun and Mister Cheever bellowing orders, shoving slow-to-react sailors to their tasks, and, in the case of the bosun, starting a few of the even slower ones with a sharp *whack* from the hempen quirt he seemed to have always at hand, the sails were successfully controlled and sheeted home. With a great *whoomp,* the forecourse caught the wind and filled. The main course followed a heartbeat later as the haulers on the main sheet seemed just a trifle slower than their mates forward. The maindeck watch, after securing them properly, dropped the sheets and ran across the deck. Then, picking up the braces, they heaved the yards around to properly position the sails for their best efficiency. It had not taken nearly as long as I had expected, in spite of the additional confusion created by the bellowing and physicality exhibited by both warrants.

Sailing Master Cheever announced his satisfaction with the way the sails were drawing as he yelled to his crew, "Tie off the clew lines and bunts. Make fast and coil 'em down. Secure your sheets and braces."

I had seen a great deal more confusion on *Argus* when we first attempted this and said as much to Henry.

"I reckon all that training Mister Rowe put us all through at the pier paid off. Doesn't appear any got hurt, and the courses are set! I 'spect some of it was just out of the fear of Kelly, but seemed like most had some idea of what they were about."

Henry, his face set in a frown at the sloppy execution of his order, merely glanced at me, deepened his frown and bellowed for Cheever to come to the quarterdeck.

"Mister Cheever, Mister Baldwin and I are of the opinion that we have yet to see a sloppier job of making sail than what we just witnessed. It might be understandable had the men not been drilled to death in the same task while secure in port. Even the topmen—experienced all, I recall?—seemed reluctant to act smartly. See to correcting that, if you please. And perhaps your topmen and haulers will do better with the stays'ls."

I was some surprised to be included in the aspersion Henry had cast; I had thought it went fairly well, considering.

"Mister Allen," I began when the sailing master had retreated to the safety of the waist, "was that not a trifle harsh? The men are mostly new to their tasks and will, I am sure, improve as they get more used to the ship being at sea."

"I am most surprised that you, of all people, would give voice to that opinion. Were you not aboard last June? I seem to recall you were. Being ill-prepared then cost us dearly." He paused, scowling as the memory of that frightful day flooded into both our heads. Then he went on. "I, for one, do not intend on that happening again. Neither, I suspect, does Cap'n Decatur." Henry's glare at my comment suppressed any further effort at conversation and I took myself away to stand by the quarter-masters handling the wheel and watched as Cheever directed the setting of the for'ard stays'ls. To my mind, successfully accomplished and, apparently even to the satisfaction of Lieutenant Allen, as the maneuver evoked no further comment from my watch officer.

The remainder of our watch went uneventfully, but quietly. Henry and I were both lost in our own thoughts. I suspected that those thoughts were not too far apart from each other. One could not sail this course without remembering our departure just ten months earlier. I noticed my watch lieutenant glassing the quite empty anchorage in Lynnhaven Bay as we drew near to it. I had thought of squinting through my own long glass too, until I remembered that Mister Jefferson's government had issued a prohibition against British ships using American waters. I wondered idly whether Henry might have hoped to see some foreign flags exhibited so as to have an opportunity to repay the kindness offered us by HMS *Leopard* last summer.

The embargo President Jefferson had designed was meant as a peaceful coercion of Britain into an admission of their guilt and responsibility for the unprovoked attack on our ship by denying them a market for their own manufactured goods. In turn, the order also denied them access to our American agricultural product, something Jefferson and his advisors evidently thought would bring to a speedy conclusion the languishing negotiations over what was now universally referred to as the *Chesapeake Leopard* Affair, so dubbed by the newspapers.

I had heard our first lieutenant discussing the result of the action with the captain only days before our departure. And both he and Decatur were confounded by the provisions of such a far-reaching law.

"Were they simply to close off trade with England, it might have made some sense, but I can not, for the life of me, understand why the president would shut off trade with *any* foreign country. Seems like Americans are likely to suffer the worst punishment on that score." Rowe's words echoed in my head as I took in the result of that edict in the quiet, undisturbed waters of Lynnhaven Bay.

Decatur's response was unemotional and characteristically pointed. "I imagine they'll get around to changing it soon's the merchants in Massachusetts, New York, and Charleston make a loud enough ruckus. But those same merchants'll try to figure a way around it afore they start howlin' and that's going to be why we're going to sea; to stop the violators. And that's what I intend to do, much as it pains me to intercept American ships. But there will be a spate of smuggling and similar nefarious practices all aimed at getting our cargoes out and theirs in; but it's against the law and they're further compounding the wrong by paying no customs duties."

After he started to walk away, the captain turned and said to Rowe, "I have a copy of the new Embargo Laws which I will see you get before we sail. I would suggest a thorough reading. Might as well have the officers read 'em too."

The laws Decatur mentioned had yet to find their way to the cockpit, but they had provoked any number of discussions among its residents, none of whom were in any way knowledgeable about the provisions our government had established. But that seemed not to limit any of us from expressing our views (or rather parroting the views offered both pro and con by the newspapers)!

"Mister Baldwin, I am your relief, sir." Silas Taggart's nasal voice brought me back to the quarterdeck and, turning, I saw his unruly sandy hair being blown about by the breeze as he stood, hat doffed, waiting for me to return his salute. Which I did.

Though Henry had said little to me following our disagreement on the abilities of our sail handlers, he now surprised me by suggesting I might join him in the gunroom for the midday dinner and a glass.

"That would be a pleasure, sir. And most appreciated." I responded, perhaps more formally than I might have, but I was still stinging from his earlier sharp rebuke.

"You're not still smarting over a bit of mild chastisement, are you, Oliver?" Henry actually looked surprised as he paused in his path to the hatch.

"I would have thought it to be unnecessary, Mister Allen. I would have maintained, given the opportunity, that encouragement was more likely to be effective with the men than invective." I was remembering words of Captain Decatur himself in *Argus*.

"As I mentioned then, Oliver, and will do so again, as perhaps you failed to understand me, we can not allow to happen again what happened in June. The men—and the officers, particularly that fool Gordon, not to mention the *commodore*—went to sea and got caught quite with their pants down and nothing to do about it. I was aboard and was partially responsible, as were you, I might offer. I, for one, will not be a party to anything of that stripe ever again. And if that means being a bit harder on the men and warrants, and yes, even the midshipmen, then so be it. Perhaps some time in the future, you might even thank me.

"Now, would you still care to join me for a glass and some dinner in the officers' mess?" He did not smile, but neither did he scowl at me.

"I would, sir. And thank you." I was still suffering slightly from previous wounds to my pride, a fact not lost on Henry.

"Oh, grow up, Oliver. You've been going to sea too long and experienced too much to be upset over a bit of chastisement. Now get yourself together and I shall expect you in the gunroom promptly at a half after one." My friend and mentor turned away and began to descend the ladder to the gundeck, effectively ending the discussion. I decided to stay topside for a bit, watching the shore slip past and collecting my thoughts, which seemed, unbidden, to turn to that dreadful June day and all that had occurred, and my, and Henry's, role in the horrific events then and after.

As two bells sounded the hour of one o'clock, I turned from the bulwark with a resolve to "grow up" as Henry had admonished me to and do my best to succeed in this commission without further antagonism, between Henry and me or anyone else.

My mates in the cockpit were already seated around our table laughing and chatting seemingly with nary a care in the world. None, I perceived had given a moment's thought to our previous departure through these waters; as for me, I could still hear the awful thump and crunch of *Leopard's* twenty-four-pound shot slamming into our sides and the cries and screams of my shipmates as they fell, some dying and some—perhaps the less fortunate ones—only wounded and facing the dubious skills of our surgeon, from the frightful splinters that flew indiscriminately from the ruined bulwarks and decks.

My arrival created a brief pause in the hilarity; Belcher, from his seat at the table's head inquired as to my wants and merely raised an eyebrow at my announcement of my dining plans. I noted that his participation in the jocularity of his mates seemed reserved and understood, without a word between us, that our passage evoked memories for him that were similar to mine. I smiled at him, shot a glance upward and received a confirming nod from him. He returned to the conversation at table and I stepped into my cubicle to change my uniform and wash my face.

Dinner in the gunroom was usually a most enjoyable experience; it also gave me a taste of my life after my promotion came through. Henry was welcoming with no hint of rancor or disapproval of my earlier comments. His mates were equally friendly and conversation centered on inane pleasantries as the food was served out. Henry poured me a glass of quite acceptable claret and standing, proposed a toast.

"To a successful commission and may we constantly be vigilant."

"Success and vigilance!"

"Aye, success and vigilance!"

His toast was echoed around the table by each of us and we drank in the hopes his prognostication would be true.

"Oliver. Did I not hear your father was ill? He is the cabinet maker what does the furnishings of some of our naval vessels, is he not? I trust his illness was none too serious or, God forbid, life-endangering." Lieutenant Dunne, next to the first lieutenant the most senior of our officers, spoke to me from across the table.

"Yes sir. That is, no, sir. He was not ill, but injured quite cruelly in an accident. And yes, sir; he is a cabinet maker who has done quite a measure of work for the Navy at the yard in Philadelphia. Thank you for asking."

"Well, I do hope the injury will not prevent him from continuing his craft. His work has always been of the first character. I had the pleasure of seeing some of it first hand in our Humphreys-built frigate *United States* when I sailed in her as a midshipman under Barry in the Indies. Back in '99, it was. As you are no doubt aware, she was laid down in Philadelphia and commissioned well before your time, in mid-'97, I recall. A fine ship she was. Too bad she is laid up in ordinary. A worthy vessel and sound, she is."

"Actually, sir, he is back at his bench now. I received a letter from my mother before we sailed which reported that he has built himself a chair with wheels under it to get around in his shop as he is unable to stand for any useful amount of time. And I know he was hoping for further orders from the Navy, but it would seem that President Jefferson has little use for . . ." I swallowed the end of my thought, realizing as I did so, that I had already done the damage expressing my views (and certainly, those of my brother) concerning the policy of gunboats which Edward, unhappily, was helping to build even now.

"You needn't concern yourself with *that* issue around me, Oliver. I quite agree. Those puny little harbor defense boats he has ordered built will never replace a frigate or, for that matter, even a brig or schooner. Can't go offshore and as far as chasing a smuggler, couldn't get after one if Jefferson himself ordered it! And God Himself couldn't help us if we ever went to war with them as our Navy!" Dunne gave me a crooked smile that seemed a bit wistful. Obviously he was a believer in fighting ships! I returned his smile, saying nothing, but noting that I had an ally.

"I say, Mister Baldwin." A booming voice from the other end of the table caused a pause in the conversation and me to turn toward its source. Lieutenant Peter Stoll, a newly acquired addition to our compliment and only barely senior to Henry Allen, was looking at me, quite unaware that his tone was over-loud.

"Sir?" I responded, quietly.

"Are you not soon to stand for your lieutenancy? I was of the impression that you would be joining our mess here in the gunroom imminently. Has something occurred, a transgression of some stripe, perhaps, to forestall that eventuality?" Stoll's voice dropped not a whit. And neither had the undercurrent of conversation begun again, so all heard—indeed they could not have missed—his interrogatory. Much to my chagrin. I thought for a moment before I responded.

"I would imagine my promotion will come when the Navy Department deems it appropriate, sir. As to the last, I have no idea of any crime I might have committed to change my seniority. Sir." My tone, I am sure, betrayed my distaste for his line of conversation.

"Well," he continued, paying little attention to any underlying meaning I might have had, "I am certain it can't be far off; I have it on quite good authority that you are a fine hand and ready for your rise in grade and responsibility."

How does he know anything about me? He only came aboard the ship a fortnight before we sailed. And why would he be concerned about a promotion that might or might not be coming to me in the future?

"Thank you, sir." I said, graciously. Ungraciously, I thought, *you are barely out of the cockpit your own self! How dare you patronize me?*

The meal continued with the usual buzz of several simultaneous conversations, none of which now included me. I had time to reflect on any number of things, including Stoll's remark. *Had I committed some sin that would delay—or even worse, preclude—my promotion?* I could think of nothing I had done, and certainly not here on *Chesapeake*.

"Baldwin. I say, Baldwin!" Stoll again. I jerked my head around to meet his gaze. Whereupon he put a half smile on his face, stopped chewing and, after tucking a mouthful of something into his cheek, asked, "What can you tell us about our captain? I know you sailed with him in the action against those heathens of the Barbary Coast. Anything to offer us about how he thinks or what we might expect from him on this commission?" Stoll finished by expanding his smile, allowing a goodly portion of whatever he had previously stowed in his cheek to make an appearance. I noticed that most of the conversation had ceased, as if all present were awaiting my response.

Why was he asking me? Aside from the fact that I had, as he knew, sailed with Decatur for a year and more in the Mediterranean, there were others among his brother officers who knew the man, who could answer as easily as I. Was he trying to make up for suggesting I had committed some transgression that would delay my promotion?

"Mister Stoll: Captain Decatur is perhaps the most honorable man I know. He is fair and even-handed with officer and seaman alike. But he will not tolerate slackers and blasphemers in his ship." I was pleased to note that the lieutenant seemed to blanch somewhat (he even stopped chewing for a moment) at this. I continued, "He has, to my knowledge, never asked any to do something he would not, nor has he ever taken some-one to task for being unable to do something beyond their capabilities.

"When there is fighting to be done, he has always been at the forefront, leading us and never hanging back to allow someone else to take a risk he would rather not. In fact, on two occasions, which I personally witnessed, he was first over the bulwark and onto the enemy's deck. I have nothing but admiration for the man."

"Hmm. Sounds like you think the chap is perfectly flawless." The sneer in Stoll's voice suggested that, while he seemingly had little knowledge of Decatur beyond his reputation (which admittedly, had grown with con-tinued telling of his exploits against the Tripolitan Corsairs), he had already made up his mind that no one could possibly be so grand.

"Few among us are perfect, sir. But I have found little flaw in Captain Decatur which would suggest we are not in the best of hands."

"Well, time will surely tell. Perhaps it is fortunate that we can experi-ence this *great* man's skills where there is little chance of confrontation with an enemy." Stoll offered with a sanctimonious smile.

Lieutenant Dunne pounced on this remark with a passion that sur-prised all present. "Mister Stoll. You are entirely too junior in your employment for such an observation. I would suggest to you, sir, that should this ship see action, action of any stripe, we could not be more ably led. And no, I have not sailed with our captain before this commis-sion, but I can think of few I would rather serve under. What Mister Baldwin has uttered is perfectly correct; in fact, I would venture that it expresses the opinion of most who know the man.

"You might bear in mind, sir, that the Congress of the United States felt sufficiently strong about him to not only award him a commemora-tive sword for his actions in the Mediterranean, but to promote him, over many senior to him, from lieutenant, not to master commandant, but directly to captain. That, in itself, should speak creditably to his skill and leadership.

"I would think that your ill-informed opinion and complete lack of experience, save in the coastal vessels you spent your midshipman years in, would quite disqualify you from even offering an opinion."

The silence that followed Dunne's rebuke was startlingly complete; no silverware clanked, no one coughed or even moved and, for several heart-beats, even the sounds of the ship itself seemed to stop. Stoll studied his senior from hooded eyes, determining what, or even whether, an answer might be appropriate. We all waited and watched; some, I am sure, hoped

Stoll would respond, while others, myself included, prayed that he would keep his peace.

After a moment or two, which seemed some longer than it actually was, Stoll smiled, picked up his fork, and continued eating. It was obvious to all that there would be more to this and that Dunne and his (very much) junior messmate would remain at odds.

"Mister Baldwin is likely the only one among us who is qualified from firsthand experience to opine on our commander. And I, for one, value his judgment. He is also one of the few aboard this vessel who has tasted the steel and grit of an enemy, save of course, those of us who were aboard last June. I would suggest, that despite his lowly status, you might accord him a level of respect just for that alone." Henry Allen could not resist the opportunity to add support for me—or perhaps it was more to line up against his boorish fellow officer. I smiled my thanks at Henry.

"Allen, you might consider our respective seniority. I would prefer you to show me the deference I am entitled to." Stoll spoke through clenched teeth, or perhaps just another mouthful. In either case, the rebuke to Allen provoked another, albeit shorter, silence, broken when Lieutenant Dunne spoke up again.

"Stoll, at your and Mister Allen's level of grade, seniority is much like virtue in a house of pleasure—non-existent. I would suggest you be mindful of that fact when you think to be lording it over anyone in the future."

This time, Stoll didn't even look up, causing him to miss the smiles that appeared on almost every face at the table. Including my own.

Quiet conversations ensued, just a buzz of mumbles from which I could distinguish little, save a word here and there. The disagreeable turn to the meal had extinguished most of the camaraderie and damped the usual good spirits common to both gunroom and cockpit, but the mood was broken by the call to arms.

Only a few minutes had passed before we were summoned from the last of our dinner by the insistent beating of a drum, sending the ship to quarters. While I did remember to ask permission to leave, it was not until I stood to take my departure. The others, recognizing the call as merely a drill, seemed more leisurely about going to their stations for fighting the ship, preferring instead to finish what food remained before them.

Lieutenant Allen was first out after me and caught up with me as I stepped off the ladder on the gundeck.

"That man is a fool, Oliver. Don't be troubled by his rudeness. What you just witnessed was a continuation of a festering feeling of hostility that has pervaded the gunroom since Stoll came into the ship. In fact Dunne and Joe Ripley have discussed within my earshot the possibility of asking the captain to put him ashore." Henry smiled at me, adding a friendly slap on my shoulder as punctuation to the comment. "His question about your promotion was simply an attempt to point up his obvious precedence over a midshipman and, more likely, remind you that even when you make the grade, he will still be senior to you." My friend's smile expanded and turned into a chortle.

"I thought Isaac Dunne did a splendid job of sorting him out on that point. Virtue in a house of pleasure, indeed!" Henry laughed at the memory.

I joined in with my own grin, relishing the momentary satisfaction at Mister Stoll being properly put in his place. My mirth faded as I realized I had most likely not made a friend in our new lieutenant and, recalled from my boyhood experiences in school that when others sided with an underdog, the underdog frequently suffered the consequences when the others were absent.

Oh well, I shall deal with that when I must. Can't think it would be much worse than facing some of the Tripolitan barbarians I did battle with!

As Henry and I arrived at our battery of eighteen-pounder long guns, we could feel the ship slowing as the topmen and deck crew shortened our sail to tops'ls, spanker, and jib, a usual procedure prior to going into an engagement. The gun captains were already organizing the men and clearing the tackles so the heavy cannon could be manhandled into position for firing. I noted, with some satisfaction, that our training while still at the dock had reaped some benefits; the men at each gun seemed to have a grasp of what they were about, requiring a minimum of pushing, shoving, and shouting from the petty officers.

What a difference from last June, I thought. *Too bad we don't have someone . . . no! Bad thought! We don't need any kind of hostile action now or later. We are not ready yet and the carnage, even were we to be ready, would be grave. Especially should the hostility come from a fifty-gun ship like* Leopard.

Henry was occupied with his six guns to starboard, so I took myself to the larboard side and ensured that the gun captains were as organized and prepared for our dumb show drills.

BOOM! From somewhere aft, a cannon fired. For a moment, everything and everyone stopped. Looks ranging from total confusion—I suspect my own mirrored the combination of dismay and bewilderment I saw on my superior's face—to horror and fear. Were we suddenly engaged again? Was this a repeat of last June? The smell of spent powder drifted forward, causing some who experienced their first encounter with a live firing to wrinkle their noses and make "smacking" noises with their mouths.

Then everyone began shouting and calling out at once. "What's going on?"

"Who fired?"

"Are we under attack?"

"Who ordered us to fire?"

"I thought this was to be dumb show!"

And finally, a voice boomed out above the others. "HOLD YOUR FIRE! BELAY THAT!"

I recognized Decatur's voice even tinged with anger and frustration as it was. Then the man himself appeared, thundering down the ladder from the spar deck, fire in his eyes.

"Who fired that gun? There was no order to fire." The captain stopped at the foot of the ladder, his eyes adjusting to the gloom and surveying the deck before him filled with sailors and officers quite as confused as he was.

"Sorry, sir. It was one of mine." The voice floated forward from one of the after batteries and, as I recognized its owner, I could not suppress a smile.

I shot a glance at Henry who obviously had recognized Stoll's tones even as I did, judging from the grin that wreathed his own face.

"Mister Stoll. Here, now!" Decatur stood where he had stopped but turned to face aft as he watched Lieutenant Stoll approach. Behind his back, sailors winked and grinned at each other as soon as he had passed their stations.

When the erring lieutenant arrived at the ladder, he was offering voluble excuses for his error, including something about a ". . . blasted gun captain." Decatur simply pointed up the ladder and then followed the officer up. The captain stopped about halfway up and, turning around and bending down to allow his voice to carry, called out, "For any of you that might not have understood, this drill is DUMB SHOW. There will be NO firing."

He did not wait to see nods of understanding and smiles of knowledge certain that Lieutenant Stoll would most likely be confined to his cabin for some period. It appeared that I was not the only person in the frigate who had no fondness for our newest officer!

"All right, you men. Take up those gun tackles and make ready." Henry's command was echoed up and down the gun deck. And the air was immediately filled with the rumble of heavy gun carriages being hauled back from the bulwark in preparation for mock loading. (The guns were, of course, already loaded with powder and shot as required when a ship was at sea.)

The exercise continued for several hours; the guns rolled in and out, spongers and loaders, powder monkeys, and gun captains all sweated with the effort and the officers in charge of the batteries yelled themselves hoarse with proper commands. But by the end of the afternoon, even the men felt as though they were comfortable with their employment and ready for the next phase which would include live firing, hopefully, at a target.

"Did you see Stoll's face when the captain sent him topside?" Joshua Belcher greeted me as I stepped into the cockpit. I shook my head in the negative; his back had been toward Henry and me. "Well, I did! He looked like a whipped puppy. All sorry and contrite, he was. And spouting a steady stream of excuses for why his battery let loose a shot! I'd wager a fair piece he done that on purpose to let us all know his guns were ready afore anyone else's."

"What did Decatur do to him? Do you know?" I couldn't help my curiosity and, I am shamed to admit, my hope that he was suitably punished. We all knew there was to be no live firing today.

"Aye. Dan Mallory told me—he was on the quarterdeck when Decatur came topside with Stoll—that the captain gave him a righteous tongue-lashing and sent him below. Couldn't hear all of it without appearing to eavesdrop, but he got enough to know the commander was hopping mad and Stoll's effort to defend himself and lay off the blame on his gun captain went for naught." Belcher's grin broadened as he recounted to me the event. I smiled in spite of myself at the thought of Stoll's career hitting some rough water. This was sure to do nothing to improve Mister Stoll's opinion of our captain and for the first time, I was glad not to be quartered in the Gunroom. I was sure Peter Stoll's messmates would bear the brunt of his bad humor.

During our evening meal of fresh vegetables and fresh, but quite tough, beef, the conversation seemed to revolve entirely around Lieutenant Stoll's behavior; his rude demeanor, overt hostility to his juniors, and his fawning subservience to his seniors, coupled with his crowning glory, the unauthorized firing of one of his guns, drew stories from all but young David Mosley who had no experience on which to draw. Mosley sat quietly and ate his supper, consuming his food with the same gusto as our tales.

Of course, I joined in the fray, recounting my confrontation with Stoll during my dinner in the Gunroom earlier that day. And while I had been taught not to speak ill of someone, especially behind their back, I must admit I took pleasure in being able to add my own offering to the stories of run-ins with the ill-tempered officer told by my mates.

Dan Mallory got all our attention when he quietly mentioned during a lull in the vituperous diatribe, "I sailed with Stoll in our small frigate *Adams* on my first cruise. He was one of the senior mids during our ought five and six coastal patrol cruise. And he was just as unbearable then!"

"Oh, Dan, do tell. We had no idea you knew the man." Silas Taggart begged in an uncharacteristic burst of enthusiasm.

"Not much to tell," Mallory said. "He was obnoxious and over-bearing then as now. Seemed something of a braggart to most of us. Played up to the officers and stepped on any of us who got in his way."

"But I'd wager you have some stories to share with us. Was he still aboard when *Adams* went into ordinary in oh-six? I collect that's when you were detached?" Belcher had joined the quest for what he had earlier in the meal termed "Stoll Tales."

"Mister Stoll spent some considerable time regaling us early in the cruise with tales of his exploits during that business with the French, back in ninety-eight. Said he was with Bainbridge in *Retaliation*—she was the schooner that Captain Decatur's daddy captured from the French, you may recall—when they were captured in the Caribbean. Told us horrifying stories of the prison where the crew was confined and the violent action that led to their capture. Held us quite in thrall with the wonders of his own heroic action and, of course, Lieutenant Bainbridge's faults. Turns out, he never left the Chesapeake all through that action nor saw a shot fired, save in training. We discovered *that* tidbit from one of the gun captains in *Adams* who had had the *good* fortune to sail with Stoll during their time in the Chesapeake." Dan was warming to his task. He paused, took a long swallow of his claret, and continued.

"Our senior mid, a grave sort of chap with a most dry sense of humor and a constantly dour expression, mentioned, quite indifferently, one night at supper in *Adams* during one of Mister Stoll's numerous recountings of the *Retaliation* story, that he had heard the only two mids with Bainbridge were boys called Samuels and O'Leary and one of them had expired during their captivity.

"Well, Mister Stoll about choked on his biscuit. His whole head turned scarlet, not just his face, and he turned on Jeffries—that was the midshipman's name, as I recall—sputtering and gasping for a moment before he could get out a single word. Finally, when he had caught his breath, he said, 'Sir. Are you accusing me as a liar?'" Mallory smiled broadly at the recollection, enjoying again Stoll's bluster.

"'No, sir. I have not mentioned the word, nor any like it. Merely mentioned what most have come to believe from the widely recounted reports of Bainbridge's capture. Never suggested anything that might confound your version.' Jeffries did not raise his voice—he never did, that I heard—or change his dour expression. Just stared at Stoll. Course, the silence in the cockpit was most complete. We had all stopped eating and I, for one, practically held my breath waiting for what would come next."

Mallory savored the moment, taking another swallow of his wine while we all waited for him to finish. After a suitable interval, he did.

"Stoll stood up from the table quite suddenly, giving us all the idea that he was about to go to fisticuffs, or worse, with Jeffries. He threw down his fork with such violence that he broke the plate and, without a glance at any among us, stormed out of the mess. It must have fueled his ire beyond measure when he heard us all burst out in laughter the moment his backside cleared the doorway. It was then that one of the lads came up with the nickname Retaliation for our messmate and a bit later that some of us began wondering what sort of *retaliation* Midshipman Stoll might have in store for us!" Again, Dan laughed, as did we all.

During the course of the meal and the "Stoll Tales," we were so captivated by our own merriment that not a soul among us noticed that the motion of our ship had changed; the earlier easy up-and-down movement had been replaced with a steady larboard heel augmented with the occasional sudden lurch that bespoke a gusting wind and greater seas. It was when a mostly empty bottle of not-bad wine tumbled and rolled across the table, spreading what remained of its contents on the unlucky diners to larboard, that Belcher called our attention to what should have been obvious.

"Seems like that bit of weather Mister Rowe was talkin' on earlier mighta begun to show itself. Mayhaps we might be of some use topside." He stood, pulling his napkin from his shirt collar, and made his way past those of us still at table, heading for the door. He grabbed his jacket from a peg and, turning his body while shoving his arms into their respective sleeves, donned it as he departed our midst.

It was at that precise moment when our steward chose to appear and the two collided with some force, sending them both sprawling. The event, in the context of our own mirth, caused us all to burst into gales of laughter which neither Joshua or nor the oft-put-upon steward saw fit to share. Both picked themselves up, offered their apologies, and the former continued on his way topside while the latter brought such a sour expression into the cockpit, it was as if he were daring any among us to comment further while he began to clear away the wreckage of our meal.

CHAPTER EIGHT

The scene that greeted us on deck as we stepped out of the companionway was quite different from what we had left only a short two hours earlier. The heavens and the sea seemed indistinguishable one from the other; the pewter sky matched the sea in hue and even the lighter gray clouds scudding across the heavenly dome had their counterparts in the white-topped waves that raced down on us from wind'ard.

The wind had not yet reached the point where it shrieked through the rigging, but the groan of its passage was constant; now a low moan, not unlike a man suffering the ill-effects of overindulgence, and then louder, stronger, his anguish having become barely tolerable. The whole of it, I suspect, was quite unsettling to some of our landsmen, especially when combined with the symphony coming from the creaking, snapping, and screeching of our blocks, yards, and canvas, and the complaints of our hull as the timbers worked and the seas slammed into *Chesapeake's* sides.

I stood with Joshua, watching the waves marching down on us from the east. His trousers were plastered by the wind to his legs and his jacket ballooned out behind him. His unfinished hair whipped around under his hat like a loose buntline caught in a squall and I put my hand on my own hat to ensure it would remain firmly in place. I turned to the west, hoping for a glimpse of the sun which might suggest how near complete darkness loomed, but was unable to determine even a brightness in the low, scudding clouds. I was equally incapable of discovering even where the sky met the sea; the whole of it was simply a heaving gray continuum stretching from the side of our ship to forever.

"This has the feeling of sticking around for a spell, Oliver. And I'd warrant it'll likely get worse before the middle watch." Joshua put his hand on my arm to pull me close to him and shouted into my ear. "We'll be down to reefed tops'ls by then, be my guess."

I had to agree, deferring to his opinion. We both had about the same time at sea, but Joshua had spent about all of his in these very waters while I remained in the more placid (though I didn't think so at the time!) Mediterranean. This developing storm called to mind the first bad weather I had ever experienced at sea, only a few days out of Boston in *Argus* while sailing east to join Commodore Preble's squadron in Gibraltar. And it was positively terrifying to a fourteen-year-old midshipman on his initial cruise!

"Aye. And I have the middle watch. With Lieutenant Dunne. I wonder what kind of a seaman he might be." I shouted back to him. Even though I was smiling in the darkness, it did occur to me that, with the exception of Henry Allen, I knew very little of the capabilities of any of our officers. And, of course, Captain Decatur; him I worried not a shred about. But the others? How would they handle this weather? I had seen others, granted, they were but midshipmen, who cowered in what shelter they might find during that storm and others, in *Argus*.

Wonder if we've got any like that aboard? Wager a month's earnings it'll be Stoll, if we do. I made a silent bet with myself, at the same time chastising myself for succumbing to the ease of naming him simply because I didn't like the man. But I shrugged it off as quickly as the feeling had appeared, and then gave thanks to the Almighty I didn't have to have him as my watch officer on the quarterdeck.

Dunne's got to be a good seaman; he's too senior to have never had to manage a ship in a blow. 'Sides, word has it, he's expecting to be posted to a first lieutenant's billet before too long. He'll likely do just fine.

Belcher had moved forward, staying on the lee side and resting his hand on the lifeline some thoughtful soul had rigged in the face of the building storm. I watched him as he made his way along the deck, his feet sometimes disappearing into a foaming froth as a wave lapped over the bulwark and rolled down the deck. He quickly vanished into the gloom and as I started forward my own self, I became aware that Silas Taggart had materialized from the companionway and stood next to me. I stopped.

"Looks like we're in for it, Baldwin. This ain't gonna ease up anytime soon. I expect I oughta round up a bunch of my sailors and get 'em ready to hand some of this canvas. Cap'n's gonna want us shortened down fair quick, I reckon, and he don't like to be kept waitin'." He squinted his eyes down and cast his glance aloft, quickly taking in the straining sails, bartaut sheets, bowlines, and braces. I doubted he could see further aloft than the lowers, but to judge from the bend in the fore spar, I could imagine what strain the higher, and lighter, yards must be suffering.

A faint shout drifted forward, most of it blown away by the now stronger wind and drowned out by the cacophony of the ship's struggles. I looked aft, peering through the dark and made out a figure alternately waving his arms and cupping his hands around his mouth. Clearly, he was shouting, but nary a word could I discern.

"That'll likely be Rowe," opined my colleague. "Wantin' to shorten her down a bit already. Perhaps I'd better get back there and find out what he's hollerin' about."

While my responsibilities in the ship were centered primarily on six of the long guns below, Taggart, in an acknowledgment of his years before the mast, was charged with the task of overseeing the men working aloft, an employment he welcomed (though I can not imagine that that work held great appeal in our current circumstances!). For want of gainful employment my own self, I followed him aft. Going for'ard with seas now breaking more frequently over the deck held little allure and, while I would likely be heading that way soon enough, why hasten the trip unnecessarily?

Barely had we gained the safer and surely drier quarterdeck than the heavens opened and poured forth rain in quantities sufficient to soak us through and through in only minutes. The heavenly offering was quickly accompanied by a resounding *craack* of thunder, then another, more sustained, rolling across the sky with the sound of dozens of eighteen-pounder gun carriages being rolled into battery all at once. All three of us, Rowe, Taggart, and I ducked instinctively and, having done so, straightened ourselves back up, each wearing a sheepish grin.

The smile quickly disappeared from Rowe's face as he grabbed Silas and me by the front of our now-sodden jackets and, pulling us close to him, shouted, "Get the topmen turned out along with Sailing Master Cheever and Bosun Kelly. Cap'n wants her shortened down to ease the strain on the rig."

"Aye, aye, sir." We shouted back in unison. "We'll see to it at once." This last added by Taggart even as we turned to make our way for'ard.

As I made to leave the quarterdeck, I noticed Daniel Mallory, who had the watch with Henry Allen, peeking out from behind the two quarter-masters as they struggled with the big wheel which bucked and fought their every effort at controlling the over-canvassed frigate. He looked as bedraggled, wet, and miserable as the rest of us, but there was something else there, too. Was it fear? I waved at him, quite casually, I thought, and received in return nothing, save the concerned expression on my friend's face. I smiled, hoping it might ease the obvious qualms of my less-experienced fellow midshipman. Henry stood at the rail, glancing from the rig to the raging seas beyond the bulwark, and quite oblivious to the rain pouring off the brim of his hat.

I caught up with Silas and shouted into his ear, "You find the bosun, Taggart, and I'll round up Cheever and some sailors." I saw the watch, sheltering by the mainmast and in the lee of the one of the boats; they would never answer for the task at hand in these conditions.

He nodded his understanding and ducked into a companionway to carry out my order. I continued forward, carefully, and with a firm grip on the lifeline. The footing was treacherous on the sharply canted and often inundated deck. And the darkness was now complete, broken only now and then by a brilliant flash of lightning which was followed by the crash of thunder, startling even when I knew it was coming after a bolt of lightning had brought a transient daylight to our surroundings.

I had made some progress for'ard when I sensed, rather than saw, a figure coming at me from the bow. Only when a hand touched mine on the safety line and followed my arm up to my chest, were we close enough that I could discern my stroke of good fortune; it was Cheever.

"I need you to gather your topmen, Mister Cheever, and stand by to hand courses and reef the tops'ls. Bosun Kelly ought to be along to help in a moment; Mister Taggart has been sent to fetch him." I relayed the first lieutenant's orders as though they came from me. (Lieutenant James Lawrence, First Lieutenant in *Enterprise,* had drilled into our heads that it was a sign of weakness to preface an order with "the cap'n said . . ." or the like. "Show that you are a leader," he often repeated, "and capable of giving orders yourself!")

"Aye, sir. I'll see to it." Cheever shouted into my face and, his hand still on the lifeline, turned to retrace his steps.

I waited in the lee of the upturned cutter, lashed to the grating near the foremast, for his return and then to oversee the operation of taking in some of our straining canvas. As a wave washed by me and the rain pelted down, a certain midshipman came to mind, cowering behind a ship's boat in *Argus* back in 1803. I stepped out from behind the shelter and, resting my hand on the weather shrouds, (gripping for dear life would be more apt!) assumed a pose of casual competence; this storm wasn't so bad, certainly not bad enough to warrant a seasoned and senior midshipman seeking shelter in the lee of the cutter! And I spat out the curious salty taste of the rain as it ran unimpeded down my face, the result of the wind-driven spume mixed with the still soaking, blowing rain, which assailed any who dared to venture topside. To any who might have noticed, the act likely added to the illusion of 'casual competence,' a sentiment quite remote from my, hopefully, well-hidden concern.

Forms began to materialize out of the gloom, each slowly taking the shape of a man in sodden coat and tarpaulin hat. Three, then five, then a half-dozen more, Sailing Master Cheever bringing up the rear like a shepherd encouraging his flock through a mountain pass. Though I suspect no shepherd ever sounded like Mister Cheever nor had the volume of voice he possessed!

A volume rivaled only by the stentorian tones of Bosun Kelly whose voice preceded him through the storm. He, too, had a 'flock' of sailors, heavers and pullers including the on-deck watch, who would remain on deck handling the sheets, braces, and clewlines, while the topmen worked aloft in the perilously pitching and bucking rigging. A quick conference between the two warrant officers, with Taggart and me standing by, but keeping our peace, determined a strategy for effecting the sail change, and I sent Silas to the quarterdeck to report our readiness.

"'Get it done,' Rowe said," Taggart reported upon his return and, with nothing but a touch on various shoulders and a few (likely unseen) nods, the topmen jumped to the weather ratlines and quickly disappeared into the maelstrom of wind-driven rain, spray, and inky blackness, pierced from time to time by the blinding intensity of the lightning.

Kelly's men, mostly trained, but surely not in these conditions, took more direction, most of which took the form of the bosun shouting, pushing, and half-dragging frightened landsmen to their positions. I turned in time to see Taggart, now hatless, heading aloft to oversee the topmen—it was his job, after all—while I stayed on deck to help with the heavers when the time came to ease sheets and work the braces around so the bulging courses might be clewed up. Taggart's comfort on the rope steps of the wildly bucking shrouds stemmed from his several years as an able seaman in the merchant service and he seemed to make even faster progress than did the sailors who preceded him. As he vanished into the night, I turned my attention to the instruction the bosun was shouting into the group of sailors, each of whom maintained a two-fisted grip on the fore sheet, the first of the several lines we would need to ease to enable the topmen to gather in the sail and secure it to the yard where they were, by now, perched, their feet on the wildly swaying footropes while their arms clung for dear life to the yard just above the straining canvas.

The thunder continued its ceaseless booming, now punctuated even more often with bolts of lightning so bright I could easily see all the way to the end of the gyrating jibboom as it dipped below the wave-tops then rose to an impossible angle, piercing the saturated night sky. And I could see, in the brighter flashes, the topmen at their posts, soaked, hanging on to the tenuous security offered by the yard itself as the wind buffeted them and tried, in concert with the violent motion of the mast, to dislodge each.

When Cheever's whistle sounded, Kelly shouted to the haulers and, with the care of men shown the fear of God and His tempest, the sailors gradually eased the straining sheet, allowing the foresail to billow out while another gang of sailors began to haul mightily on the clew lines. Kelly blew his own whistle as soon as the lower corners of the sail began to move inward and up, toward the yard itself. Against the backdrop of the storm and our own noises, I wondered whether any aloft could possibly have heard its shrill blast; standing only a few feet away, but admittedly to weather of its source, I could barely hear it myself.

But hear it they did—or at the least, *someone* at the top did—and, as the sail was drawn up toward the yard, flapping and snapping like some wild thing resisting its taming, the dozen men along the spar began to draw the sodden canvas to themselves, holding it to the yard with the weight of their individual bodies until a line could finally be passed around the restrained sail. All the while, the wind tore at their forms, working in concert with the seas and the pitching, rolling ship, to dislodge them and send any unfortunate who lost his grip to a certain death, either on the deck or overboard. The process was dangerous in a calm, but in these conditions, even the very act of going aloft required a courage possessed by few.

Finally the sail was contained and the topmen, on shouted orders from Taggart and Cheever, moved even further up the mast to begin the process of reefing the tops'l. A larger sail and thus more difficult to contain, it was also that much higher up the mast which exaggerated the motions they had suffered while on the fore yard. And I knew the wind was even stronger up there.

Hang on, Taggart! Even for an experienced hand, a single misstep or weakened grip might easily be your last.

I strained to see in the flashes of lightning what was happening up there, but the rain quite precluded any satisfaction. And between the often blinding strokes of lightning, the night seemed even darker; not even shapes distinguished themselves from the blackness.

Over the now shrieking wind and continued crashes, snaps, and screeches of blocks, sheets, and canvas, I heard the faint warble of Cheever's whistle and only slightly louder, the answering *tweet* from Kelly's as the heavers under his command took the strain on the tops'l halyard, sheet, and brace. Unlike the course, the tops'l yard was *lowered,* the topmen riding it down as they gathered up handfuls of the sail to tie in the reef. Kelly shouted at his men, his words whipped away from my own ears by the wind, but heard by those who needed to, and slowly, carefully, the heavers eased the halyard forward, letting down the tops'l yard and the topmen perched along its length. Another group of sailors eased the sheet and brace, providing some slack in the straining canvas for their colleagues aloft to gather into their bodies. When Cheever blew his whistle again, the reef was tied in to the sail, effectively reducing its size.

Already I could feel the struggles of the frigate ease and I knew that Captain Decatur's decision to reduce sail now, rather than after the weather worsened further—and surely it would do just that—was the right one. And as the topmen descended to the deck, obviously tired, muscle-sore, and soaked to the skin from their ordeal aloft, I shouted into the face of the tempest for Cheever and Taggart to get themselves and their men back to the mainmast so they could perform the same death-defying ballet on the higher and bigger main yard and main tops'l. Taggart looked at me and, in the flash of a bolt of lightning, his glance seemed baleful, perhaps even malignant.

He doesn't think I have ever been up there in such dreadful weather, I'll wager. Likely thinks I can send him and his men aloft but wouldn't do it myself! Well, little does he know; I did it all while I was still only a boy of fourteen.

I made a mental note to mention that to him, quite casually, of course, at some future opportunity. And then I did something I most likely should not have.

"Silas," I shouted through the storm to him. "You look beat. You stay with Kelly and the heavers here on deck. I'll go aloft with Cheever's men and oversee the work on the main."

Since I was significantly senior to him, he had little choice but to accede, but I think he might have smiled at me. Whether in relief at not having to fight his way aloft again, or at my bravado, or stupidity, I know not. But we both stepped aft, he to the waist where Kelly was organizing his men and I to the weather rail where I clapped onto the shrouds as the last of the topmen headed up the ratlines, prepared to follow them to the main top.

The wind, as I gained the first rope step rigged between the shrouds, plastered me against the rigging and required some considerable effort to gain each step. And, while I was not as fast going up as had been my colleague, I made it to the maintop with no misstep or delay. The topmen were moving out on each side of the long yard, carefully testing that each foot was secure in the footrope before moving further away from the relative safety offered by the railed platform at the junction of the lower and upper masts, just above the yard. Sailing Master Cheever stood on the top, as the platform is called, watching his men as a mother might watch a child taking his first tentative steps. The continued flashes of lightning aided his vision, though I am sure he was as blind as I between the bolts.

After what seemed like an hour but in reality was only a few minutes of balancing on the top (and clinging to the rail with one hand and a convenient halyard with the other), word was passed in to the center that the men had all reached their positions and were ready.

Cheever looked at me and shouted, "If you are ready, sir, the men are in position."

"Let's get it done, Sailing Master. No point in prolonging the joy more than necessary!" I hoped my glib response made it through the noise of the wind.

Without further comment, Cheever blew his whistle and I heard almost immediately the faint trill of Kelly's some sixty feet below us indicating his men were also ready. Barely a heartbeat later, I felt the mast tremble as the big sail was eased and the brace hauled around. The heavy sodden canvas began to shiver then luff in earnest. I knew the yard would be shaking as the canvas began to flap and, in addition to the already wild motion of the maintop, felt it shuddering as the yard transmitted its own motion to our lofty perch. I tightened my grip on the halyard.

Gradually, the sailors hanging over the yard bundled up almost all of the sail and were tying the sodden mass of canvas to the yard. In a flash of lightning—it seemed to be almost on top of us—I saw one of the men reaching over the yard to gain another handful of sail when one of his feet slipped off the gyrating footrope.

"Watch it! Hang on, there!" I yelled, quite unnecessarily. If he wasn't already hanging on with every fiber of his being, my shout (assuming he even heard me) would do little to help.

Cheever lurched toward the rail and before I could utter a word, dropped down onto the futtock shrouds, the almost vertical rope ladder which would take him to the lower shrouds and the yard. As his head disappeared from my view, I heard a shriek, decidedly not the wind, that was cut off almost before it started.

Panicked, I released my grip on the halyard and moved to the weather edge of the top, peering into the downpour and struggling to discover what might have happened.

What if Mister Cheever lost his own footing and slipped. No matter how the ship might be gyrating, he would most likely land at the foot of the mast in a broken heap ready only to be sewn into his hammock and . . .

The rain lashed at my eyes and blurred my vision, but I could make out the form of our sailing master as he stepped off the futtock shrouds onto the ratlines of the lowers some ten feet below me.

Thank God! Cheever did not fall. What, then made him scream like that?

"Mister Cheever. Are you alright? What has happened? What was that scream I heard?" I bellowed over the edge of the top.

A streak of fire lit the sodden sky and in its light I could see Cheever now on the mainyard, grappling with the sail. He did not even look up at my call but remained with this feet firmly on the swaying footrope and his body bent over the yard as he passed a length of line around the sail and the yard. The man who had slipped seemed no longer to be hanging onto the footrope; in fact, I saw no sign of him.

The motion of the ship had eased noticeably now with both the fore and main courses handed and a reef in the fore tops'l. The topmen were moving in from the mainyard and, without a word among them, climbing up to the top where they would continue to the main tops'l yard to reef that sail as they had the foretops'l.

Cheever appeared beside me on the top. Grabbing my arm, he shouted over the noise of the wind and groans of the ship, "Meyers musta fell. Time I got there, wasn't nothing I could do to stop him . . . already gone . . . reckon . . . goner."

"Overboard? Or on deck?" I screamed back, peering cautiously over the railing toward the deck. *Hope he hit the deck and was killed fast. Going into the sea in this weather would be dreadful!* It wasn't necessary to share my thought with Cheever; I am sure the same thing ran through his own mind.

"No idea. Didn't see much activity from the lads below in that last flash. Probably fell into the water." The sailing master shouted, his foot already on the ratlines as he headed further aloft to assist his men.

Mercy! What a horrible way to die. You hit the water and, if you still have your wits, you realize there is no way the ship can be turned about or a boat launched to save you. The huge seas toss you about like so much flotsam and it becomes a struggle just to stay afloat.

I reckon that after a while you realize you're dead and maybe stop struggling. I shuddered at the thought.

Whistles, luffing canvas, and muted shouts pierced my thoughts and then the men were passing by me on their way back to the safety of the spar deck. When Cheever went by, he gently took my arm and steered me to the ratlines of the futtock shrouds; I offered an unseen nod and made my own way down, stepping carefully through the howling madness lest I join our star-crossed topman.

CHAPTER NINE

. . . at last, dear Brother, I have found a few minutes to add to the scrib-
blings I started more than a week past.

My mind continues to reel, though it has been now more than a month
since our topman was lost. I am still bedeviled by dreams and even waking moments of consternation about the event. And not a soul on deck even
caught a glimpse of him falling! Of course, that would mean the poor devil
went into the sea and, assuming he was still alive when he came to the
surface after his plunge, he must have suffered an unimaginable horror,
first of watching his ship sail into the dark tempest away from him, and
then realizing he was as good as dead. I can not fathom what he must have
suffered, likely the reason for my continuing discomfort over it. That and
the torment of what I might have done to have prevented the tragedy.

The storm finally blew itself out two days—and dreadful ones they were,
indeed—later. During the day, the wind offered its range of shrieks and
screams; waves, their white-topped crests reaching often as high as the
mainyard, put me in mind of great dark horses with their white manes and
tails streaming out behind them. But at night, with nary the pinprick of a
star to light them, their enormity could only be imagined which, I think for
most of us, made them even more fearful. By the middle of the first watch
on the second day, the wind's shrieks had moderated to a hollow keening;
it penetrated to our very cores and there was no place on the ship where a
body could escape the sound.

With the wind easing, I knew the seas would settle, but until then we
had to endure the thrashing they provided. Mercifully, Capt. Decatur had
hove us to, a wonderful respite for the crew. Even some of the more seasoned hands had felt the effects of the storm, but, dear Brother, I am
proud to tell you, I was not among them! I continued, unlike several of my

mates in the cockpit, to stand my watches and perform what few duties I had and, several times, I took the employments of some too sick to work.

You will want to know also, that the gunroom suffered in similar fashion; some were overcome with more than simple queasiness and took to their cots, a modest dosage of laudanum providing some respite from their miseries. I am happy to report, Edward, that our nemesis, Lieutenant Peter Stoll, was, according to Henry Allen, among the worst stricken and, after the first night of the storm, appeared not once on deck, or elsewhere, save his cot. Even the mids too ill to leave their own were lifted by this bit of news.

I may have neglected to mention earlier in this missive (writing it, as I am, over a lengthy period of days and, as time permits) that during Taggart's and my travails the first night, Mister Stoll appeared as I stepped from the rigging having completed our tasks aloft and quite in shock over the loss over our sailor. He spent some considerable minutes shouting, into Taggart's face, instructions as to what the 1st lt. had in mind, quite unaware that the job was, in fact, done. Or that a seaman had fallen to his death. When I appeared, he had worked himself into a state or frenzy and launched his further criticisms into my face. For some reason, he had neglected to look aloft and, in my opinion, he was not enough of a sailor to recognize that the ship was managing easier under the reduced sail. In any event, my surmise about his seamanly skills was lent further credence when a wave washed down the deck and took him completely off his feet (he seemed to disdain holding the lifeline which allowed Taggart, Blanchard, who had returned to lend a hand to us, and me, as well as the others near at hand to maintain our own footing) and swept him right to the leeward scuppers! Mercifully, in the darkness and noise of the storm, he could have neither heard our laughter nor seen our amused expressions. He did not reappear to offer further instruction nor was his presence noted beyond the confines of his cabin for the next two days.

By the third day, the skies had cleared, the seas moderated to a manageable size and we made sail, continuing our patrol to the northward. Little of moment broke our routine and the days dragged on; gun drills, often with actual firing, filled our mornings, with ships work and assorted employments occupying us until the evening meal was piped. Nary a ship did we see, nor anything to arouse suspicion of nefarious activities, the reduction of which was our stated mission, as I am sure you recall. I am certain the Capt. and Lt. Rowe were disappointed and hoped for something with which they might justify our very existence! Especially, the Capt.

In early June, I think around the eighth or ninth, I had the watch with Lieutenant Allen (you must remember him from your visit to *Chesapeake* last spring) when a lookout cried from the foretop that he had espied a ship and she appeared to be on fire. As you may well imagine, Edward, after weeks of perfect weather, idleness and complete boredom, the entire crew was galvanized into action!

Many climbed to the tops—so many in fact that the 1ˢᵗ lt. had to call them down as it was fast becoming too crowded there!—just to catch a glimpse of the spectacle. Henry sent me to the maintop with a glass to determine what it was that the lookout had reported.

Indeed, it did appear that there was a ship, two masted she was, making great gouts of smoke, giving every appearance of being fully engulfed in fire. As I continued to glass her, I realized that she was making way in a perfectly regular fashion, but there were no sails set!

I duly reported this to all on the quarterdeck upon my return and the captain studied me as though I had quite lost my mind.

"How would you imagine, Mister Baldwin," he asked me, blinking in disbelief, "is a vessel able to make way with no sails set and fire consuming her?" He continued to study me closely as he waited for my response.

"I can not fathom that, Captain." I replied as calmly as I could manage. "But there is a white trail of wake astern and clearly, the ship is moving through the water."

"We will go and have a look. I can not have my midshipmen hallucinating. Mister Allen, you may bring her up a point."

By now, Edward, the vessel was plainly observed from our deck and, if she was not making way from her own efforts, she was drifting faster than we could sail in the very modest breeze. Decatur ordered us set to t'gallants and gradually, we overtook her.

We finally hove alongside of her close to shore at the mouth of the Delaware Bay where a strong tide was making. And to our absolute amazement, not only was she not on fire, she was indeed moving through the water quite handsomely without a shred of canvas aloft! A great plume of smoke, spotted with bits of burning embers, poured forth from a chimney amidships and, as we drew close alongside, we observed two large half rounds attached to her sides, starboard and larboard. None aboard seemed frenzied by the smoke and sparks; in fact, they acted more concerned over our proximity to them. I noticed she flew the Stars and Stripes from her taffrail.

Capt. Decatur stood on the bulwark and addressed their quarterdeck through his speaking trumpet. "What ship are you, sir? And by what means do you propel yourself at such a rate?"

The answer came back at once. "We are the steamboat *Phoenix*, sir. Colonel John Stevens commanding. We are nine days out of New York Bay and bound for Philadelphia!"

"Steam, then, she is. My stars! Small wonder you can sail . . . er . . . steam into the very eye of the wind! And what, sir, do you burn, wood?"

Again the tinny voice of Colonel Stevens shot back. "Aye. Wood it is, sir. And a fair bit of it! Three times we've had to put in along the New Jersey coast to take on more."

"Congratulations, to you sir. What a splendid accomplishment . . . and vessel. God speed to you!" Decatur had heard enough.

He climbed down from his perch at the mizzen shrouds, a quite disbelieving look upon his face. But he, nay, all of us (most of our crew lined our leeward rail, completely agog at the spectacle), saw the ship with our own eyes as she sailed directly up wind, a feat no sailing vessel, no matter how weatherly, could manage. And as I wondered about this smoke-belching vessel alongside of us, the Capt. spoke his own thoughts.

"Mister Rowe. Do you imagine that we have just been given a glimpse of the future or is it merely some lunatic's fancy that will die a-borning?"

And Mr. Rowe answered. "I can not believe, Cap'n, that such a vessel will ever replace the power and capabilities of a modern frigate. Just don't seem likely, I'd warrant! And besides, can you imagine the amount of wood she'd have to carry to go beyond the limits of a short coastal cruise! You heard Stevens mention he'd put in three times just from New York to take on more."

Brother, it was quite fantastic. Something none among us could fathom!

We tacked away to give her sea room to navigate the entrance to the Bay and because we were unable to place our bows in the eye of the wind (as *Phoenix* did so handily), we were, in fact, getting quite close alongside of her! I can assure you, the sighting and the ship itself were the center of conversation from the fo'c'sle to the Cabin for the remainder of the day and into the next. Not a man among us could comprehend such a remarkable and, according to some, ludicrous sight.

We now cruise with Block Island visible at the horizon and little but fishing smacks and the odd coastal trader to provide us opportunities to carry out our commission. We did manage to stop a fair-sized brig two days back as she seemed under a press of canvas in her haste to make her easting. At the instant, we were just to the east of the curve of Cape Cod.

The capt. was duly notified, quarters sounded, and we overhauled her quite handily. Hailing seemed fruitless when her watch appeared unwilling to heave to as we requested, but a single shot fired across her bow answered nicely and we quickly had a boat over and headed for her side.

Mr. Allen and I had the privilege of leading the boarding party to view her papers and cargo. It was most exciting and I was sure my colleagues in the cockpit were envious to a man that I got chosen to assist Henry.

A very angry man, we presumed him to be the capt. of the brig, greeted us at the bulwark, shouting all manner of epithets and decrying the fact that we were causing him delays. It turned out he was not only the capt., but also the owner of the ship, whose name was *General Washington*, and called himself Asa Rogers. Henry waited until he had spoken his piece and then explained our mission and the laws of the embargo precluding trade with foreign nations. At this, Mr. Rogers became further agitated and Henry's wink and nod to me said he believed, as I did, that we had finally caught a "runner," as those who sailed to foreign ports *in contra* to the embargo were being called.

Rogers told us to follow him to the cabin where he produced his papers indicating the ship's destination to be Charleston in the Carolinas and that he was carrying many puncheons of rum, woolen manufactured goods, and sugar in great hogsheads. A quick inspection of the hold confirmed his cargo and, after offering our apology, we collected our seamen and marines who had amused themselves by sharing stories with the men on the brig, and departed. I noted that Rogers got *General Washington* under-way even before we had covered half the distance to *Chesapeake!*

Our cruise seems quite pointless at times and I am sure that more than just the mids spend many waking hours discussing what we might prove out here, chasing mostly ourselves around the sea, with the occasional suspect vessel proving quite harmless to us or Mr. Jefferson's embargo. Either the shippers and customs officers are truly following the law or they are so clandestine in their commerce that we are unable to find them. And the fact that we are sailing off and on in the coastal waters seems little more than an annoyance to them. I wonder if the great Nelson felt as frustrated in his blockade of France some years ago!

I must close for now, brother, as I have been called for the watch. I am again standing with Lt. Dunne who seems a fine and competent sea officer. You will be no doubt pleased to know that I have learned much from his tutelage while on our watches. I shall send this off at the first opportunity.

Affectionately, I remain

Oliver Baldwin, Midshipman, U.S. Navy

CHAPTER TEN

"Oliver! Did you see that schooner alongside just this morning? I am told she was sent out to fetch us in! We are to have new orders, but first, it is rumored, we will have some time ashore. Perhaps our luck is changing! I, for one, can scarcely contain myself; an opportunity to go ashore and break this dull patrol!" Young David Mosley seemed to be fairly dancing in his exuberance.

The prospect of a run ashore, I knew, would be well received by all of us, officer, midshipman, and enlisted alike. And, should we actually receive a new commission, an opportunity to do something beyond this embargo patrol would be most welcome!

Of course, I was only assuming Mosley's information was accurate, but I surely hoped it was; he had been known to reach surprising conclusions quite unrelated to reality in the past. And I *had* seen a schooner making on us as I left the deck at the start of the forenoon watch. I recalled it had been shortly after the sun had burned off the early morning fog, an annoyance brought about by the cooler September nights in these latitudes. I knew we all shared the captain's frustration in finding and stopping embargo-runners as they likely sailed right past us in the mists. Our frustrations stemmed from continuing boredom; his, I am sure, from our failure to accomplish anything that might accrue to our, so far, unimpressive record.

We had been patrolling without stop from Charleston's entrance to Cape Cod for very nearly four months and had succeeded in catching not a single illegal trader. Indeed, we had stopped only a handful of vessels, hoping for a "runner," but sadly, each had turned out to be quite legitimate. The duty had been tedious beyond measure, making several of us pine for some of the excitement we had experienced in previous commissions. Or even some bad weather! But the weather, save for the single storm we encountered early in the cruise, had been splendid, clear blue skies, for the most part, with easy tops'l breezes that, while not always fair, were never overpowering. And when it had rained or squalled, the inclemency rarely lasted for more than a day or two. Captain Decatur trained us incessantly, ensuring, not only in his mind, but in the mind of each of us, that *Chesapeake* would never again be caught unawares by any, friend or foe.

We had early on exercised the great guns in dumb show; then, once the hands became accustomed to running the long eighteen-pounders in and out of battery while underway, just pretending to load and fire them, swab them out and repeat the process endlessly, we were allowed to graduate to live firing exercises. And still people got hurt; carriages rolled over a foot, crushing it, or the flash burned an unwary hand, or worse. The prospect of a port call, with the associated joys of being on shore for a period, however brief, along with the possibility (assuming David's surmise was correct) of a new and, hopefully, more exciting commission was most appealing to all of us.

The rumor remained exactly that until midway through the first dogwatch when Captain Decatur appeared on the quarterdeck where Lieutenant Keane and I held the watch.

"Mister Keane. Be so kind as to ease your sheets and bear off. Your course will west nor'west, a half west."

Without further comment, the captain turned to the weather rail and studied the sea through the deepening gloom of a September evening. Keane, for his part, shot me a glance, his faced wreathed in smiles, and stepped to the break of the quarterdeck, bawling for the sailing master.

The orders were given, men jumped to the sheets and braces with an enthusiasm inspired by the incipient rumor of change that had grown to maturity in the six or seven hours since it began. And, in the fresh easterly, we bore off and made for Castle Rock at the opening of Naragansett Bay, the site of Newport, Rhode Island. And a run ashore for all of us.

The light at the entrance to Naragansett Bay, perched on the top of Castle Rock, guided us into the narrow cut and we hardened up around the fort guarding the entrance to the harbor. Under tops'ls and mizzen, we set our best bower into the mud of Newport Harbor shortly before the middle watch would have commenced. And naturally, even though I had no official duties, I was on deck to watch; all of us were, being too excited about the likelihood of some shore time to even consider sleeping.

But no one would be going ashore then. Captain Decatur had indicated to Mister Rowe that liberty would be granted as soon as he had reported his arrival, in the morning, and discovered why *Chesapeake* had been summoned. This information was passed to the officers and mids and quickly circulated through the fo'c'sle in varying degrees of accuracy.

So the mids all gathered around our table sharing some claret which our senior Midshipman, Joshua Belcher, provided from his personal stores. Having never before been into this harbor, or the town, I listened attentively to those who had and their tales of grog shops, eating establishments, and, according to Silas Taggart, several houses of pleasure.

"You mean ladies to entertain us, Silas?" The innocence of David Mosley's query provoked great guffaws around the table, even from Taylor Scott who was barely a year older and, I am sure, no more knowledgeable than his junior messmate.

"What are you laughing at, Scott? You have experience in these things?" Mallory—his ability to change his mood quickly was well known by us all—challenged the youngster. Mallory's expression had gone from mirthful to harsh in a flash and, I think, caught poor Taylor all aback.

"Why . . . well . . . that is . . . yes, I think I understand. I am not as young as Mosley, you know." Scott blushed, stammered a bit, then became defensive.

"Well, then, Mister *experienced* Midshipman Scott, why don't you explain to young David here what Mister Taggart meant by 'houses of pleasure?'"

Silence. Taylor took a small swallow of his wine, gaining time to think, and turned to face his younger colleague.

"Since you obviously are not educated in these matters, David, what our messmates were discussing are simply places where a man, sailor or officer . . . or even a midshipman, can go to take a drink, make conversation with members of the fairer sex, and relax. They are not unlike public houses, but with a better quality of drink and décor. And generally, the ladies with whom one might engage in conversation are of a higher class than one might find in a waterfront tavern." He smiled, satisfied that he had scotched Mallory's attempt to ridicule him and educated his comrade all in one stroke.

Which provoked another gale of laughter from all of us. Poor Scott looked from one of us to the next, perplexed and blushing furiously.

"Wha . . . what's so funny? What did I say? Did I not get it right?"

Which only served to fuel the laughter to an even more raucous level.

"When you and young Mosley get a bit older, maybe grow some whiskers, Mister Scott, you will undoubtedly learn of the *pleasures* to be found in such an establishment. Until then, perhaps you might limit your travels ashore to eateries and maybe a library or two. I am sure there must be at least one here in Newport!" Daniel Mallory had enjoyed a laugh at his young messmates' expense and now was finished; he had no interest in educating either of them, nor in continuing the joke.

For my own part, I wondered if Mallory had any more firsthand knowledge of the subject than I, which was none. Of course, I had a pretty fair idea of what went on in those places, but only from comments I had heard from shipmates. And, I suppose, because I had been to war and 'seen the elephant,' no one challenged *my* experience!

Some hours later, after the second bottle of claret was exhausted, conversation reduced to mumbled slurs, and the two younger of our mates nodding off in exhaustion, we all stumbled into our cots for a few hours of sleep, dreaming (to judge others by my own lights) of the joys of moving about on stationary ground, dining on well-prepared fresh food, and enjoying the camaraderie of a public house. And mayhaps, for some, the joys of a house of pleasure.

When breakfast was served out and wolfed down, we tumbled out of our hatch to the spar deck, eagerly awaiting word that the captain had returned from his mission ashore. Alas! The boat was still absent and a scouring of the shoreline showed no sign of its imminent return. We milled about, watching listlessly as the crew finished holystoning the deck and beating it dry with swabs. Some of us chatted with officers, hoping to glean some worthy tidbit of information from them.

"Henry. You are quite sure you didn't catch any hint from Cap'n Decatur before he left of what he must suspect? Surely he said something that might have offered a clue as to what was happening." I kept my voice low, finding it less painful for my head to do so. And hoping that my conspiratorial tone might induce my friend to give up some intelligence that he felt he could trust me with.

All to no avail.

"We're all in the same boat, here, Oliver." (He didn't even smile at his play on words, giving me to suspect it was quite unintentional.) "I guess we'll all have to wait until he finishes and comes back aboard. But, were I a betting man, I would imagine we'll, at the very least, get a day or two to take a look around the town. You've not been in before, I collect?"

"No, I have not. When I left in oh three on *Argus*, it was from Boston that we sailed. And returned to after our commission in the Mediterranean. Actually, Boston, Washington, and Norfolk are the only ports I have made in the United States. Have you been here before?" I knew he had grown up not far from here and hoped he would agree to show me the sights!

"Oh yes. Several times in fact. You know I was raised just a few miles from this harbor and entered into the service right here—dreadful ship she was, a dull sailer named *George Washington*. Navy bought her as a merchant and converted her into a frigate. Gave her the name, I reckon, in the hopes that a lofty name might improve her abilities." He laughed at the memory, then continued. "I am sure I can remember a few of the better eating and drinking establishments here, even though I have not been back, except for a brief visit to my father's home, in three or four years. I'd be pleased to point out a few to you, if you like.

"And you might be interested to know there is a gunboat building yard here doing the same job as Commodore Chauncey and your brother are doing in New York."

"That would be most kind of you. Your mention of the gunboats reminded me that I have a letter to Edward to post while we're in. I must get it and put it somewhere where I will remember to take it with me. Assuming, of course, we do, in fact, get to go ashore."

"Boat approaching from the larboard quarter!" The cry from the mizzen top could not have been more galvanizing to us had it been announcing a ship sighting at sea. Any thought of my brother's letter vanished as all hands rushed to the larboard rail, craning and stretching their necks to determine if it might be our captain. Lieutenant Allen and I shared his glass and it was my friend who made out the straight form of Stephen Decatur sitting tall in the sternsheets.

"Won't be long now, Oliver. We'll find out everything in just a few minutes."

His words set off a buzz of excitement throughout the crew and, as Bosun Kelly piped the captain over the side, the hands were already lining up in their muster positions on deck. Some optimists were even in their dress uniforms, ready to ride the first liberty boat to the beach and, most likely, be drunk before the afternoon watch would start.

"What is all this about, Mister Rowe? Did a chaplain come aboard to hold services?" Decatur inquired of our first lieutenant in a voice loud enough to be heard by most of the hands.

Many of the more experienced men smiled, seeing the twinkle in the captain's eye and the hint of a smile forming on his lips; the rest remained mute and hopeful. Henry nudged me in the ribs, nodding and smiling.

"Seems in a good humor, Oliver. Must have some pleasing news to share out!"

"I would suggest you muster the crew, Mister Rowe, but it would appear you are well ahead of me on that score." Decatur continued walking aft, never breaking stride as the men in his way moved quickly to clear his path.

"No, sir!" Our humorless first lieutenant replied in great earnest. "I have not called the hands to muster at all. Seems they think your return might mean some news . . . and mayhaps, a run ashore for some. Terrible eager they are, sir."

"Well then, as long as they are all formed up, I might as well share the news I have with everyone at once." The captain mounted the three steps to the raised poop deck and, nodding at several of the officers who were also lined up right and proper, faced his crew.

"Men. I have just now come from meeting with the commander of this port and can tell you that, while we have little to claim to our credit from the past four and more months at sea, he is not disappointed in us. Seems much of the commerce has been already halted and little, save coastal shipping, is going out. He offers his thanks for your stalwart performance of your duty and has welcomed us to stay for a fortnight, or until some work I want accomplished in the frigate is done.

"Following that, we will return to the Chesapeake Bay and, I am told, a new commander will relieve me. I am to recommission the frigate *United States,* currently in ordinary at Washington, and man her sufficiently to sail. Without question, I will be choosing some of you to accompany me."

This caused quite a stir among, not only the seamen, but the officers and us midshipmen as well. An excited buzz began as a few whispered comments from one to another and then grew into an undercurrent of muted voices.

"Silence. Silence, fore an' aft!" Rowe's command lifted above the hum and brought the silence he ordered.

"Quite naturally, I will not be able to take all of you, or even all the officers. That decision will have to wait until such time as we are closer to our return to the Norfolk Navy Yard. But you should all be aware that I am most pleased with this crew, and would be proud to serve again with any of you."

"Will there be any shore leave, Cap'n?" Rowe's voice, even when he spoke quietly, was heard by all of the officers and midshipmen, as well as the first two or three ranks of the men. It started another rumble of conversation, some of which was clearly audible from my position.

"Aye, will we get ashore?"

"Shore leave? How could they not grant it?"

"Aye, been at sea too long to deny us a run ashore!"

"My goodness," Decatur managed with a perfectly straight face. "How could I forget? Of course, as the ship will be in for several weeks, liberty will be granted by watch commencing directly."

That loosed the pent-up excitement, which had brought the sailors to their muster stations in the first place. Men began slapping each other on the back, laughing and shouting over one another just to air their own plans for the next several hours. Some even began moving toward the ship's boats, obviously with a view toward helping ready them for lowering.

"Stand fast, there. You are not dismissed. Remain where you are." Rowe shouted above the enthusiastic voices.

As soon as they quieted down (and even some of the officers and all of the mids had added to the melee), the captain let his eyes rove over the group, clearly as pleased with his men as he had mentioned, then spoke quietly to his first lieutenant.

"You may dismiss the men to the care of the petty officers and warrants, Mister Rowe. I shall be below, should you have need of me." He then turned and, without another glance in our direction, disappeared into the scuttle leading to his Cabin.

Rowe shouted above the new and louder outburst, which had greeted the captain's words, and dismissed the men. There was a flurry of activity, laughing, and shouting, as three hundred and more sailors and Marines went into action, some racing to the fo'c'sle to change into shore-going attire, others making for the boats, removing their covers and rigging them to be lifted over the side, while still others, already dressed in dress uniforms, simply rushed to the break in the bulwark, hoping to make the first shore-bound boat.

And nobody had even mentioned which watch section would be granted liberty first!

"Oliver, get changed so we might visit the wonders of Newport!" Daniel Mallory grabbed my arm, moving me toward the hatch.

"Are you sure we will be in the first section, Daniel?" While both he and I stood watches together, I still did not know whether we would be allowed off the ship first.

"Aye, did you not hear Lieutenant Rowe? Just now he said to Mister Dunne and Mister Allen to let the larboard section have their leave. That includes us, I would think. We have stood most of our watches with the larboards. Now hurry, or we'll have to wait to get ashore." His eagerness was catching and I dropped down the hatch, my feet barely touching the steps of the ladder.

When Mallory and I returned to the deck, even though it had taken us barely ten minutes to put on proper uniforms, the bulwark was lined with sailors and I realized we would be unlikely to catch a ride on the waiting cutter.

"Here, now! Make way, you men. Officer coming through."

I recognized the voice instantly. Mister Peter Stoll, with whom I had had little truck since that day in the gunroom, strode through the throng of seamen, encouraging the slower among them to move with a push and a shove. The looks that followed him were surely not friendly or respectful!

"Mallory. Are you not the same Mallory who sailed in *Adams* back in aught-five or thereabouts? I have been quite racking my brain to recall your face. As we have not had the pleasure of holding a watch together, our paths seem not to cross that frequently and I have been meaning to inquire for more than a month now. Was it not you in the cockpit in *Adams*?"

"Yes sir. I sailed in the frigate then, two years, it was until she was put in ordinary." Mallory's tone gave no indication of the feelings he had shared with us some time ago, but I sensed a tension in him as the connection dawned on the unpleasant officer.

"Well, then. You and Mister Baldwin must ride ashore with me and we'll catch up on the past few years. A splendid idea, don't you agree?"

Silence. Mallory was quite at a loss to figure a way out of this. I saw the cutter making fast below us and the sailors beginning to clamber down the battens. The boat would be ready to leave in a trice.

I patted my jacket pocket quite obviously and said, "Dan. Will you wait for me while I fetch the letter I have waiting to post to my brother? I must have left it in my chest, such a hurry were we in to get ashore." I had felt the letter securely nestled in my pocket, but Stoll couldn't know that!

"Yes, of course, Oliver. How could I not wait, after the plans we have made?" The relief that flooded into his face—even if it meant missing the first boat—at not having to share company with Stoll was all the thanks I needed for my gesture. He turned to Stoll.

"You go ahead, sir. I must wait for Mister Baldwin to fetch his letter and wouldn't want to hold you, or the boat, up. Seems like it's ready for yourself to board even now. Perhaps we can meet at some place during the day."

Likely for that *to happen!* I thought as I heard my colleague's words.

"Ah, that will answer nicely, Mallory. Perhaps you and Baldwin would join me for dinner at the Jolly Anchor Tavern. Can't miss it; right on the main thoroughfare of the town and quite popular with naval men. Shall we say around two?"

"Aye, sir. I'll surely try to make it, but should I not, please do not wait."

Good job, Dan. 'Please do not wait,' indeed. Should have told him we'd be along and left him waiting all afternoon! I dropped down the hatch and lost Stoll's response, if he made one, in the general noise of the throng of excited men boarding the cutter.

By the time I returned, the cutter was a safe pistol shot away from *Chesapeake* and loaded to capacity with sailors, Peter Stoll slouching in the stern sheets. I noted he was the only officer aboard.

"Thanks for saving me, Oliver. I cannot imagine dining with that arrogant fool and having him dredge up all that bilge about *Retaliation* and our time in *Adams*. You have no idea the lengths I have gone to just to avoid him in this ship!"

"A pleasure, I'm sure, Dan. I have little desire to further my own relationship with the man. Once at dinner in the gunroom was a sufficiency in itself!

"Ah, here comes the other boat. . . and Henry Allen. Shall we invite him to join us?" I suggested to my colleague's obvious pleasure.

"Him I have no problem with. A decent fellow and a friend to midshipmen. Seems to not have forgotten his own time in the cockpit. He's been a great help to me. Hard, but fair and surely knows the ropes."

"All that is true. He's been enormous help to me, both before and after he left the cockpit." I offered my own agreement, though none was necessary, then turned to the lieutenant.

"Mister Allen . . . Henry. Daniel and I are going to take a look around in Newport. Would you care to join us? And perhaps share a glass or two later?" I smiled at my friend as he stepped into the queue next to me.

"I have a small errand to accomplish for the first lieutenant in town, Oliver, but then I should be pleased to meet you. Shall we say the Jolly Anchor around two bells in the afternoon watch? I should be done by then."

Mallory blanched at the name and began to make strange noises under his breath.

"Actually, Henry, I had heard of a place called Featherstone's which, according to Belcher, is quite nice and not as raucous as the Anchor. What say you to that?" I actually had no idea of what the establishment was like, this Featherstone's, but had indeed heard Joshua mention it several times during our run into the harbor. I hoped it would live up to my words.

"Not heard of it, my own self, Oliver. But sounds fine. Ah. Here's the boat. Step lively you two and leave me a space aft." Henry seemed quite indifferent to where we dined; a good thing, I thought. Certainly would do our future dealings with Mister Stoll no good at all should we show up with Henry at the Jolly Anchor!

Featherstone's was situated in a brick-fronted building above the town proper, but with a fine view of the harbor and an island named, for some reason, "Goat" Island. In hindsight, I recalled some curious glances sent our way when we inquired of passersby for directions. But find it handily we did and both Dan and I were pleased that it was nowhere near the Jolly Anchor, which we had noticed earlier, actually crossing the cobbled road so as not to pass too closely to it. Daniel and I opened the door at precisely one in the afternoon.

A dim parlor greeted us and, as our eyes adjusted to the gloom after the bright midday sun outside, we saw comfortable chairs, a small couch Daniel mentioned was called a "love seat," and, in the light of several oil lamps, any number of paintings adorning the walls. The drapes, dusty gold in color they were, were drawn, effectively shutting out the sparkling September day along with the noises of the street. The chairs were all covered in the same material and seemed, in the muted light, a bit threadbare. The scattered tables, however, were of a rich mahogany, gleaming with a deep patina that reflected the glow of the lamps. On the floor, a rug of many colors, all quite dark, softened our footsteps. In the far corner stood a staircase, complete with ornate balustrade and spindles supporting a well polished railing that disappeared aloft.

"Look at those paintings, Oliver." Mallory whispered to me, as he pointed with his chin. His wide-eyed stare gave credence to the awe—was it shock?—in his whisper.

In truth, I had not looked carefully at any of the artwork, too busy was I taking in the rich drapes, heavy furnishings, and beautiful lamps. I looked, at his suggestion. And was as shocked as he.

Women, ladies, I reckon, in varying stages of undress were depicted in a variety of poses; some reclined on couches, others stood by what could only be beds, while still others posed in traditional style with a large vase or urn on a pedestal.

"Well!" I whispered back when I had sufficiently regained the power of speech. "What do you make of that?"

We were discussing, in hushed tones, the titillating decorations when the door opened behind us and a soft voice, feminine, it was, interrupted our ruminations.

"Welcome, gentlemen. Welcome to Featherstone's. I am Missus Featherstone, the proprietress. What would be your pleasure today? It *is* a trifle early for our normal trade, but I am quite certain we can accommodate you . . . both."

I began to stammer, quite at a loss for words. It was Daniel who found his tongue first.

"Why thank you, Ma'am. We are meeting another gentleman here, directly I expect, and will be interested in partaking of dinner and perhaps a glass or two of some Madeira or mayhaps, a nice burgundy."

I could scarcely believe my ears! Daniel had put on the airs of a proper gentleman—he was a fine mimic, I knew—and seemed most credible. But did he realize where we were? It had finally dawned on me that this was not a tavern or eatery. At least not like any others I had occasioned.

"Excuse us for just a moment, Ma'am." I uttered, as I took my ship-mate by the arm and led him to a far corner of the room. Directly under, as it happened, one of the more graphic depictions of the female form. At which he stared with unabashed enthusiasm.

"Daniel! Do you not realize where we are? What are you thinking, man? We don't belong here. I am quite certain this is one of those *houses* we spoke of last night. They surely are not about to feed us, and the service they likely *do* render is not something we should be buying. Let's wait for Henry outside."

"Oh, Oliver. Don't be such a coward. I know exactly what this place is and, personally, would relish the opportunity to spend the afternoon in such delightful pursuits. Have you not, with all your wild travels all over the eastern world, partaken of similar such places?" He continued to use his "educated" accent, convinced, I assume, that a gentlemanly demeanor would hold more sway than his normal tone with any who might hear him. Which, in this case, was only Missus Featherstone and, of course, me.

"Well . . . I alm . . . I . . . can not . . . say . . . that . . . well, that is to say . . . Let's wait outside for Henry." I stammered, struggling with the sought-after admission of my naiveté and finally retreated to a safe repeat of my earlier plea.

Which fell on deaf ears. Daniel had turned and was addressing the quite attractive lady who had greeted us and now waited patiently, her hands folded in front of her and a half smile adorning her pretty face.

"I would be most interested, Ma'am, in having a glance at your . . . *bill of fare*, should such be forthcoming. My colleague seems a bit reluctant, but, I am sure, when he sees the fine offerings you must have available, he will become a willing participant."

I was beyond horrified! What was Daniel, who I thought I knew fairly well and thought of as my friend, getting me into? Well, I had pretty much figured *that* part out, but what was I to do? It appeared I was in a fine mess.

"I believe I shall wait for our colleague on the steps outside, Ma'am. Just in case he is not sure of the exact position of your establishment." I was making for the door as I spoke and, as I passed by Missus Featherstone, I could not help but catch a most pleasant whiff of her scent. I paused, enjoying the cloying fragrance of a wonderful tropical flower that seemed to have some sort of spice mingled with it.

"Why, sir, that would be just fine, if that is your want. I shall amuse your friend here until you and the third of you returns." Her smile was so genuine and warm, it almost caused me to linger just to enjoy this pleasant, and pleasant smelling, person. But the little voice within me urged me on, and, without looking, I put my hand out to open the door.

I was still two or more steps from my objective and felt quite the fool as I stood with outstretched arm and nothing to grab. Quickly returning the offending limb to my side, I mumbled something, likely silly, to cover my embarrassment, and hastened to the door, which, as my hand touched the ornate knob, opened.

I was momentarily blinded by the blast of daylight that flooded in and so, it seemed, was Henry Allen, whose eyes were equally slow to adjust to the darkness within. We collided and, only by grabbing each other's arms, did we manage not to land in an unceremonious heap in Missus Featherstone's parlor.

"Henry!" I gasped as I regained my senses. "You're here."

"Of course, I am here. Is this not the time and place we earlier agreed upon?" He released my arm, catching his balance, and closed the door behind him, once again surrounding us with the muted light of the oil lamps. My eyes adjusted more quickly this time.

I noticed, as we faced each other—me still toward the door and him looking into Missus Featherstone's parlor—that his gaze was focused over my shoulder, taking in the scene behind me. Shock registered briefly on his face as the realization of our whereabouts dawned on him. Much more quickly than it had dawned upon me.

"I was just going outside to wait for you, Henry, on the chance you might . . . er . . . uh . . . care to dine elsewhere. Perhaps the Jolly Anchor?" I stammered and uttered the first name that came to my addled brain. I hoped, after I offered the tavern as an alternative, that he might select yet another as I had no interest in a further encounter with Lieutenant Stoll.

"Aye, Oliver. A fine choice. I think our dining needs might be better served there. The Jolly Anchor it is!" As he spoke, he shot a glance at Dan, who was still examining a piece of vellum, presumably the *bill of fare* for the establishment.

"What say you, Mister Mallory? Will you join us at the Anchor?" Henry's voice left little doubt as to his meaning.

I waited, hoping Dan would come to his senses, but recognized that when confronted with the choice before him and a raucous tavern, there could be little doubt as to the winner.

"Perhaps I shall meet you there a bit later, gentlemen. For now, I am quite content with the offerings provided by Missus Featherstone's establishment. Please do not wait for me to begin your meal; I might be detained." Mallory was still putting on that ridiculous accent.

"Very well, then, *Midshipman* Mallory. Enjoy yourself." Henry's emphasis received not so much as a glance from Dan, who was now gazing at a female form descending the stair in a diaphanous wrap. I followed his gape toward the stair.

We might as well have been pieces of furniture for all the attention he paid us and Henry, sensing, perhaps, that I might become equally beguiled, took my arm and turned me toward the door.

"Well, then, Oliver. I reckon it will be just you and me for the Anchor. Let us waste not another minute; I am quite famished."

A moment later we were both on the street, blinking in the brilliance of the day, as Henry decided in which direction we should set our course.

I had no idea, nor did I care; all I could see was the vision of that dark-haired beauty on the stair.

The girl—or woman, possibly (I could see her neither clearly enough nor long enough to determine which)—filled my brain and, combined with the scent of Missus Featherstone, made a positively consuming image. And, with the passage of mere seconds, the vision, at first fuzzy and indistinct, took on a more defined form.

In a trice, I could see her lustrous dark mane held back with a long green ribbon and, below a smooth brow, her beautiful dark eyes. One delicate hand rested lightly on the handrail, as she paused to take in the scene below her. Her long, thin fingers gracefully assumed the curve of the wood and her fingernails reflected the glow of the lamps. A smile started, first on her full red lips, then moving to those captivating eyes, which seemed to dance at the sight of the three of us in her parlor. Her head moved slowly from one of us to the other, taking in each of us in careful study. Her smile dimmed nary a mite and she again started her descent, her white gown trailing behind her like a cloud. She stepped off the last step and floated towards us . . .

"Are you not interested in dining, Oliver? I had thought you were interested only in escaping from that place." Henry, unforgivably, intruded on my thoughts and the glorious image vanished before I determined the outcome.

I am afraid the look I shot him might have been a bit harsher than I had intended, but, after all, he did ruin my dream!

"Oh, aye. I guess. Which way do we go; I am a bit confused." From the glance I received, the last bit was quite unnecessary.

"You surely are! If you wish to go back with your friend, do so. I shall manage quite nicely on my own. I do not frequent establishments of that stripe. But I would suggest that your first choice was the right one and, while Mallory will no doubt have a salacious tale to share in the cockpit, he has done himself no good. Despite the ridiculous accent he was affecting, he is surely not of the first character! At least in my eyes."

Nor in Decatur's, should the tale reach his ears. He would most likely be uninspired by my colleague's behavior. Might even hold it against him, should he be told.

"No, Henry. I thank you for providing for my escape. A moment longer and I would undoubtedly have made the same mistake. So I am again in your debt. Let us get along to the Jolly Anchor. This way, I collect?"

Without waiting for an answer, I stepped off smartly, hoping I was heading in the right direction.

The noise of a busy waterfront tavern assaulted us as we entered. I cast a quick look around, peering through the gloom of the dim light given off by the lamps that lined three of the walls and the smoke of several dozen men puffing on pipes and cheroots. I noticed about half of the room's occupants wore naval uniforms, both officer and sailor.

Was Stoll here already? We had agreed to meet at two, but perhaps he is early. What will . . .

Henry interrupted my thought. "Well, lookee there; is that not your favorite inhabitant of the gunroom?"

I followed his outstretched arm and saw, to my horror, Peter Stoll sitting by himself at a table. A schooner of ale rested on the scarred surface before him and, mercifully, his head was turned away from the door. I took a second look, trying to determine a course of action and response that would excuse us from joining him. My addled brain was staggering under the weight of my confusion. I struggled to breathe the smoke laden air while I tried to regain some composure.

Out of the frying pan and into the fire!

Finally, after pretending not to see him at first and feigning a quiet coughing fit, I could delay no longer. "Aye, I think it might be Mister Stoll. Hard to tell in this light, but he does bear a resemblance to your colleague, Henry."

"In name only, and that only by virtue of his status as an officer." Henry's tone left no doubt that we would likely *not* be sitting with the aggravating officer. His next words confirmed my very thought: "We shall take a table over there . . ." He paused, then shot me a glance. "Unless, of course, you would prefer to join Peter."

He wouldn't! Henry likes that arrogant ignoramus no better than I.

In shock, I looked at my friend; the smile that wreathed his face and his outstretched arm pointing in quite another direction restored my sense of calm.

"Yes sir. I think that would be fine. A table over there, I mean." I agreed and, hoping we would remain unnoticed by our shipmate, moved in the direction of an empty table some distance away from him. Henry followed.

Hardly had we shouted our order for two tankards to the hard-faced maid who had inquired as to our pleasure, than I sensed a presence behind me. Henry's look, as his eyes rose above my head, confirmed my fear; the hand that landed heavily on my shoulder was connected to the arm and ultimately, the person of Peter Stoll.

"What a surprise to find you two in the Anchor." Even with his voice raised to ensure he would be heard over the din of the tavern, Stoll's tone sneered in derision.

I turned and found myself looking directly into the midsection of his waistcoat. By turning, I had caused the unwelcome hand to move, and so, out of a respect I surely did not feel, stood, a gesture called for by his uniform.

"Well, Mister Baldwin! Where is your colleague, my former shipmate, Mister Mallory? I was under the impression you two were thick as thieves and would dine with me here in . . ." Stoll paused and consulted a large gold watch with a studied arrogance. Then he raised his eyes back to mine and continued. " . . . in just short of half an hour. Surely he can not have found more agreeable entertainments?"

"I think Mister Mallory has been unavoidably detained in other pursuits, Peter. I doubt we will see him anytime soon." Henry jumped to my rescue, causing Stoll to shift his gaze.

I noticed that my friend did not stand. The conversation during the unpleasant meal in the Gunroom popped into my head, reminding me that Stoll was indeed senior to Henry, even if only by months, and was entitled to some show of respect. Regardless of Lieutenant Dunne's remark comparing seniority among junior lieutenants to chastity in a house of pleasure, it only took a moment for the obnoxious Lieutenant Stoll to call Henry on his slight.

"Mister Allen. May I remind you, sir, of our respective times in grade. Were you not taught to rise when approached by your senior?"

"Aye . . . sir. I was also taught that respect is earned and not to be given lightly." Allen remained seated.

"Well, then." Stoll's tone clearly suggested that more was coming and we—or at least I did—waited for the riposte he would surely deliver.

But the man, clearly incensed, could only stare at his messmate. His eyes became hard, his lips a thin white line across his face, and the muscles in his jaw worked as though he were chewing. No words, no sputters, no nothing. He simply stood there, glaring at Henry; I had ceased to exist. Finally, he just turned on his heel and left us.

"That man is a fart in a gale of wind! I can not, for the life of me, understand why somebody has not yet bludgeoned him to death!" Henry's anger was palpable.

"Well, Henry, just consider him a fool and be done with it. That's the advice my mother always gave me when confronted with a Peter Stoll and it oft times works." I tried to mollify him and, while I was irritated at Stoll's arrogance, I tried to overcome it by convincing myself the man was not capable of acting otherwise. And I tried to avoid him.

"Aye. But 'fool' is too kind. Did you know there was already a move by some of his fellow officers to have Decatur put him ashore? I can think of no one who would have any truck with him. But, here are our ales. Let us drink to better times. Perhaps to joining Decatur in his new assignment!"

Henry raised his brimming tankard and smiled. I did the same, saying, "Aye, better times . . . and perchance some action!"

We drank, talked, and eventually we enjoyed some quite non-descript food. The sun was low and more lamps had been lit in the tavern to counter the fast approaching darkness when we heard a commotion by the door to the establishment. Chairs scraped as people rose to see what the fuss was about and voices were raised both in query and anger.

"Out of my way! Can't you . . ."

Overridden by, "Here, now. Let go of me!" in a gruff voice.

Crash. And immediately following, more chairs scraping, feet on the hardwood floor, some quite rapid, while others seemed to move more leisurely. And a flow of men, Naval officers, sailors, and civilians of every stripe, pushing toward the growing hubbub.

Naturally, Henry and I stood, the better to see over the throng, and then, curiosity having won out, picked our way among patrons of the tavern and a few overturned chairs, in the direction of the clamor.

We were jostled and shoved and, at one point in our somewhat unsteady passage, I was almost knocked off my feet, saved from an ignominious pratfall by my friend's grabbing my arm.

"Well, there's a surprise!" Henry's voice was almost gleeful when we had maneuvered to a position where we could see the cause of the disturbance. "Never would have thought ol' Stoll would be rolling about on a tavern floor. Or engaging in fisticuffs, either, for that matter!"

And indeed, that is exactly what I saw when I got close enough to part the wave of humanity and pry myself into the group encircling two figures: one in the uniform of a navy lieutenant and the other, wearing most of the checked shirt and rough trousers of a drayman. The two figures, entwined in an embrace born of a surfeit of spirits, struggled on their knees to hit one another. Few of the thrown punches landed; Stoll's were ineffectual from the start and the drayman, bigger and surely stronger than his adversary, was frustrated in his attempts by what could only be an abundance of ale.

Suddenly, and no doubt thinking he had achieved a decisive advantage, Lieutenant Stoll stumbled to his feet and drew back a leg to deliver a kick toward his opponent's unprotected face.

As he did so, a roar went up from the spectators, voicing their disapproval of this tactic and caused the lieutenant to hesitate just long enough in his delivery to allow the drayman to clap onto the arriving foot, twist it, and, at the same time, lift it up, rising to his own feet as he did so. The result was unavoidable; Stoll went over backwards, describing a somersault as he rolled out the open door and down the two steps to the road.

Another roar from the crowd, only this time, it was mixed with laughter and applause. Somebody detached themselves from the throng and slammed the door shut, effectively cutting off our view of the loser before we determined whether he had survived his backwards tumble down the steps. But, for the men in the room, it put a period at the end of the sentence and, without a further glance at the door, those who had witnessed the fight were competing to clap the drayman on the back as they moved him back into the center of the tavern amid raucous and ribald congratulatory comments.

It is with some sense of shame that I admit Henry and I both joined in the applause, but we did move to the door, after the wave of celebrants flowed past us, to check on our shipmate.

Who, laying in a heap unbefitting his station in life, was already being administered to by a person, apparently a passerby, in naval uniform. As his back was to us, neither Henry nor I could identify the Samaritan who knelt over the prostrate lieutenant.

"What do you find, sir? Is our friend seriously wounded?" Henry inquired, drawing a glance from me at his choice of words.

The fellow started, focusing as he was on Peter's inert form, and rose. It was Dan Mallory!

"I was just about to see if you gents were still in residence here when a body fell backward out the door . . . almost knocked my own self down. Then we'd a both been lying there in the street!" Mallory laughed and I realized that, in addition to whatever had taken place at Missus Featherstone's, he had had more than a taste of spirits and was something less than sober.

"Well, how is he? Is he conscious, at least?" Henry's question hung for a moment, unanswered and then, before Dan could give voice to his, perhaps, muddled thoughts, the inert figure on the ground stirred, groaned, and, with some considerable effort, sat up.

Stoll shook his head and looked around, still unsure, it seemed, of how he had come to be sitting in the dirt street. His gaze finally focused and settled on the three of us.

"Wh . . . what . . . how . . . mercy! My head hurts! What happened?" He struggled to find his voice.

"Well, Peter, it appears as though you picked a bad time to start an argument with that wagoneer fellow. Seems he took some exception to you pushing him out of your way. Do you not remember the fight?" Henry was enjoying this. I could not help but smile my own self, though I did my best to hide it.

"Fight? Oh . . . yes. I do remember that rude fellow. Big, he was, as I recall. Wouldn't let me pass." His memory was improving with every passing moment.

"Aye. And you must have decided to give him a shove. A shove which, I reckon, he took some exception to." Allen continued to smile at his messmate.

"Then he just hauled off and punched me. I defended myself, I guess." Stoll rubbed his cheek where some lividity had already begun to show. "But not too well, I'd surmise from where I sit!" He even smiled as he looked about him, perhaps seeking the supine form of his adversary. "What happened to him? Did I do any damage to his person?"

"Not that we could tell, sir. Though we only caught a glimpse of the man in the throng that surrounded him after the . . . scuffle. And he is still within the tavern with his mates." I answered my superior and managed to hide the smile while I did so.

Henry offered a hand to his fellow officer and, after a moment's reflection, Stoll took it and, with help, managed to stagger to his feet. He swayed for a bit, whether from the excess of spirits or the effects of his most recent activities I could not discern.

"Are you alright, now, Peter?" Henry's question was less from concern, I thought, and more from a desire to move on.

Stoll was silent, shifting a bleary-eyed stare from Henry to Dan to me and then over our shoulders to the door of the Jolly Anchor.

Could he actually be considering going back in there? That big fellow would beat him senseless, given the opportunity. And Stoll surely needs nothing more to drink!

"Oliver: I have to talk to you. You won't believe . . ." A lurch and muffled cry cut off Dan's whispered entreaty.

I turned to the source of the cry and saw Peter Stoll, a stricken look on his face, bending double and clutching his stomach. Then he unceremoniously vomited his dinner and a great quantity of ale into the street. The three of us stepped back quickly and turned away.

"I think he will be able to navigate on his own; at least he is on his feet. We have little reason to remain with him." Henry spoke quietly to Dan and me, gesturing with his head that we should move down the street.

"Do you think he will be able to get back to the landing on his own, Henry? As much as I detest the man, I should not want us to be responsible for him coming to some further grief." I practically choked on the words, but, as I had been taught all my life, sometimes we have to do things we might not like.

"To the Devil with him! Perhaps he will fall into the harbor and drown. Or get himself run over by one of that drayman's colleagues. That would surely make the Gunroom a happier place!" Henry's vitriol surprised me, even knowing his feeling about Stoll. I guess my face showed it.

"Oh come now, Oliver. I am only teasing; I would not wish ill on a shipmate, even this one! We shall steer him to the landing as you wish . . . as soon as he finishes decorating the street." Henry's comment was born of guilt, not comradely responsibility. And it was punctuated with continued sounds of retching.

"All right, let us get this done. You two each take an arm and try to keep him from falling down again. The landing is not far." Lieutenant Allen took command and, assuming Dan and I would jump to carry out his order, stepped around the putrid puddle, and strode purposefully down the street.

"Oliver . . . Oliver!" Mallory's whisper, directed behind Stoll's lolling head, caused me to look at him and, in so doing, to stumble over a loose cobblestone. I relaxed my grip on Stoll's arm to catch my balance and, in so doing, removed my support from the larboard side of my barely conscious superior. Which created a pronounced list to larboard, which culminated in Stoll's landing in a heap on the street, Midshipman Dan Mallory on top of him.

"Look out, Oliver! Help me get him up. And watch where you're going!" Dan was scrambling to his feet, using the supine form of the lieutenant for leverage.

Together, we stood him up, shook him some to return him to wakefulness, and, half dragging, half guiding him, tried to hurry after Henry, who had not paused or even broken his stride one bit during our brief escapade.

God was smiling on us that night, as when we reached the landing, there was one of *Chesapeake's* boats waiting at the pier. We loaded our burden into the sternsheets while the cox'n and his crew looked on with bemused expressions.

"You may cast off, Cox'n. Have the watch on the frigate help you deliver Mister Stoll to the Gunroom, if you please." Lieutenant Allen issued terse orders, obviously eager to be shed of this unpleasant duty.

"Should you gentlemen wish to continue to enjoy your liberty, you are welcome to come along with me. Or not—suit yourselves." Henry shot us each an inquiring look, then turned and headed up the quay.

CHAPTER ELEVEN

"Gentlemen, when I tell you it was glorious, wondrous even, it does not begin to describe it. That lovely woman, Monica was her name, as I mentioned, was skilled beyond comprehension. She . . ."

My mind drifted away as I looked about our quarters, taking in the expressions of my friends, which ranged from mild interest to abject boredom. Dan had been holding forth for most of the morning, recounting of the events of his afternoon the day before and most of us had had our fill. I noticed that several of my messmates' eyes had glazed over, even the ones who initially had been nearly drooling at some of the details. Even I, who had seen the 'lovely woman', (and was captivated by my own enthusiastic imagination) had begun to lose interest. We had all heard his story start to finish at least once, and those with more patience, several times. Our cockpit Lothario had the unfortunate habit of restarting his tale each time one of his messmates stepped into the room. With little to do—and Dan knew it—few of us could dream up a credible excuse to leave and so were trapped to listen, once again, to the story of his amorous adventure.

It was a welcome relief, then, when Lieutenant Rowe stepped through the doorway, interrupting Mallory's third (or was it the fourth?) retelling of his tale, and causing all of us to leap to our feet.

"Lads, the officers of *Chesapeake* have been invited to a ball tonight. Of course, that will include you midshipmen. Uniform will be dress and you will be at the break in the bulwark at three bells in the first dogwatch to go ashore. Save the duty section, of course. Carry on." Rowe smiled at our reactions, turned, and left as quickly as he had arrived.

"A *ball?* I don't want to go to some ball; I want to pay Missus Featherstone a visit." David Mosley whined, causing a great round of guffaws.

"Missus Featherstone's? What would you do there, Mosley? I doubt she'd even let you in, save to cart out the rubbish or run some errands for her or the . . . em . . . gir . . . *ladies*." Silas Taggart, who, I noticed had not joined in the general merriment at Mosley's remark, merely smiling thinly, almost snarled at his shipmate.

The laughter stopped immediately, most of us staring slack-jawed at the normally taciturn Taggart.

"David, you might find the ball most enjoyable. I am sure the food will be good. There'll be music and, of course, there will be ladies there, too. Of a higher quality, I suspect than what you might discover at Missus Featherstone's. You'll have a fine time, I assure you." I tried to make the evening sound like fun to my younger colleague, but I fear it might have sounded a bit thin, to judge from the looks I received from our messmates.

I wasn't too keen on going my own self, but I would surely not admit that to young David. I did not fancy standing around watching my superiors dance and cavort with the ladies in attendance while I clearly, by my uniform, was insignificant and scarcely worthy of notice, let alone conversation or a dance. But the first lieutenant had said we would be there, so there we would be. Except the duty section, and I wasn't going to volunteer to take the watch on board *Chesapeake* when I could go ashore. Even to a *ball!* And who knows, I reminded myself, it might turn out to be better than I anticipated.

With Dan's story told and retold to the point of exhaustion, I brought up my encounter with Lieutenant Stoll, to the amused interest of my colleagues.

"When he landed in the street, in a heap and a most unfitting demeanor, Lieutenant Allen and I rushed out to determine his condition to find Dan, here, leaning over Stoll's prostrate form.

"At first we didn't smoke it was our shipmate—thought it just some Samaritan who happened by—but Stoll came to and Dan turned to us. You can imagine our surprise at the discovery! After all, a stranger wouldn't have known what a wretch Mister Stoll was, but a shipmate would surely have and might have just passed him by."

"Oh no, Oliver. Even I would not leave a mate, even Stoll, lying in the street. 'Sides, I was not quite on an even keel my own self, and in a fine mood, as you might imagine!" He leered suggestively drawing further comments from our audience.

"I saw Mister Stoll this morning; didn't look too good to me." Taylor Scott chimed in. "Had quite a mouse on his eye and a scab forming at the corner of his mouth. No one asked him, at least within my earshot, what might have brought such damage about, though. Can you imagine his reaction should one of the sailors have voiced such a thought? They surely noticed him, though; saw a bunch of topmen smirking behind his back. By their gestures, I suspect they likely figured he'd brought it about his own self!"

"I'd warrant the officers gave him a bit of grief in the gunroom at breakfast today." Taggart spoke for the first time since his earlier outburst, drawing laughs all around. "Wonder what tale he concocted to explain the wounds."

"Couldn't have been too far from the truth, you ask me," I offered. "Henry Allen was right there for the fight and his unceremonious landing in the street. In fact, it was Lieutenant Allen who insisted on our bringing him to the landing and getting him into the boat."

"Aye. Would have loved to be listening to *that* bit of chatter!" Mallory chortled. As did we all at the thought.

The balance of the day went by without further incident or argument. We did discover that Silas would be aboard the frigate for the night, having the misfortune to be in the duty section. And I discovered that he had, the night before, visited Missus Featherstone's emporium himself, though he chose not to share with us the details of his experience as had Dan Mallory. He likely would have not been comfortable at the ball in any case, having come from before the mast and more than likely, inexperienced in the ways of society.

Chatter at dinner in the cockpit—from the few of us aboard doing bits and snatches of work, studying, writing letters or reading—centered on the ball, our expectations, or lack thereof, and, as luck would have it, a mercifully shortened reprise of Dan's earlier tale, complete with ribald comments, jeers, and good natured chiding. And, it was noted with smirks and giggles, that no one had observed Lieutenant Stoll about the decks.

After the meal, we brushed our uniforms, blackened our boots, and polished our brass. It was important to make as good an impression on the fair damsels of Newport as we could, after all! And at the appointed hour, the four of us who would attend stood at the break in the bulwark waiting for the boat crew to pull around from the stern.

As midshipmen, we went ashore first, followed by the officers—they rode in the cutter—and last by Captain Decatur, who, of course, came into the quay in his gig. His crew put on a smart display of oarsmanship as they approached and his cox'n made a picture-perfect landing exactly at the stone steps where the captain alighted to join his officers for the short walk up the quay.

Two carriages were already in attendance for our transport to the ball. Each was dressed with banners in red, white, and blue, apparently in honor of our captain's reputation, won especially in the late trouble with the pirates of the Barbary Coast. It was common knowledge that he had distinguished himself in that conflict, but should any have been unaware, the decorations pinned to his jacket, even were one not aware of their specific significance, bore silent testimony to his deeds.

The matched pairs of horses—one pair was as white as the driven snow, while the other two were dappled grays with dark manes and tails—were pawing the ground, throwing their heads, and behaving in a most anxious manner. The skipper of each coach did his best to keep his chargers under control, as least while his passengers boarded. And, except for young David Mosley, all of us made it aboard our transport without incident; David chose the exact wrong moment to put his foot onto the step and, when the team—it was the grays—found some slack in their reins and lurched ahead, Midshipman Mosley made a most ungentlemanly remark and landed, seated, in the street.

His face turned scarlet as he realized that his words were uttered—shouted, actually—well within earshot of our captain, whose reputation for limited patience with such outbursts was of high renown. Whether more embarrassed over his pratfall or expletive is unclear, but he scrambled, more cautiously, I think, into our carriage, taking his seat next to his friend Taylor Scott, who covered his giggling with his hand, only to receive Mosley's elbow in his ribs. And off we went behind the spirited horses, which drew us at a fine pace away from the piers, through tree-lined streets, past stores, chandleries, taverns, and eating establishments, and finally, into an area of dwellings, some quite run-down, which I took as an indication of Newport's strained economic condition.

We turned sharply to starboard at a place called Washington Square and I heard our driver mention to us that we were now on Clarke Street, our destination just ahead. He slowed as we joined a queue of other carriages waiting to discharge their cargoes of ladies and gentlemen of Newport society. The horses stamped and snorted their displeasure at being reined in.

We mids craned our necks to watch the proceedings ahead of us as our carriage followed the line toward a large house, obviously the site of the ball, on the corner beyond us. Finally, about a pistol shot from the walk-way to the house, the officers' began to alight from their carriage, and we followed on directly, disembarking where we were, rather than waiting for the carriage to pull up to the walk.

I now had an unobstructed view of the grand dwelling where we would spend our evening. The building was stone of a pinkish hue; three stories tall, it boasted a railed flat area at its top, presumably where one could stand and watch the ships coming and going in the harbor below us. Two broad chimneys, one at each end of the structure, reached up higher still, giving the whole a most symmetrical and imposing appearance.

Following the line of gentry, we Chesapeakes gained the walkway and stood behind our officers, led by Captain Decatur, as they moved toward the gaping front door. There, I assumed, introductions were being made along with the social niceties to be expected in such an opulent setting.

"Oliver, who are the people what live here? I can't remember what Mister Rowe told us." Taylor Scott whispered to me.

"Vernon is their name, Taylor. He was a banker here in Newport, but left during the time the British occupied the city. Came back after the war. I think Rowe told us that he got heaved over the standing part of the foresheet a few years back and now his son—I can't remember his name—owns the house. I reckon we'll meet him directly."

More and more carriages, some quite grand, had pulled up in the street, discharging their cargoes of well-decorated gentlemen and ladies who, amid quietly dignified greetings to one another, strolled in our wake toward the house; unlike some of us, they all seemed quite comfortable in this elegant setting. We surely were going to mix with the cream of Newport society!

The Chesapeakes followed astern of our captain, who, I must say, looked as splendid as any in his full-dress uniform, complete with the sword awarded him by the Congress of the United States for his brilliant and heroic action in the Tripoli Wars. Our officers were next, in line by seniority, and we midshipmen brought up the rear of the flotilla. We maintained a sense of decorum, having been admonished by Mister Rowe that unseemly behavior would be dealt with harshly.

A polite burst of applause greeted Decatur as he approached the entry-way, obviously recognized by the ladies and gentlemen in attendance. I craned my neck, peering around my colleagues, to watch what would happen and to see how the captain greeted the beautifully decorated civil-ians in the doorway, whom I took for our hosts. While I certainly expected no applause to greet me, or any other of us, I wanted to watch what he did so as not to embarrass myself when introduced to the fine folks of Newport. He bowed to the ladies and shook the hand of several men as, I assumed, they were introduced to each other. Captain Decatur lingered in his handclasp with an older gentleman who wore a colorful sash of some type across his chest. The captain spent considerable time talking with this chap, clearly more than a simple greeting would consume, and then stepped back into the doorway. He drew Rowe aside and spoke to him.

My interest in the goings on ahead of me waned, and Mallory and I were engaged in quiet conversation as we waited in the queue for entry. Imagine my surprise when Lieutenant Rowe stepped back along our ranks and stopped where Mallory and I stood.

"Mister Baldwin. The captain would like you to attend him, if you please." Rowe spoke quietly and more formally than he might have on shipboard.

I looked again at the doorway for some sign that Mister Rowe was serious and saw Decatur catch my glance, smile, and motion for me to come to the front of the line. Which, of course, I did, noticing the curious glances from my messmates, officer and midshipman alike.

As I made my way up the walk and ascended the four steps to the front door, the captain turned to the white-haired man standing next to him and spoke.

"Mister Little, may I present Midshipman Oliver Baldwin, the young man of whom I spoke. He was with me in *Enterprise* and quite distinguished himself against the corsairs."

The older fellow, the one with the scarlet sash, smiled warmly, and stuck out his hand in greeting. I felt the color rise up my neck and right on up to the top of my, now uncovered, head.

"Oh, uh, sir." I stammered. "It is a pleasure to meet you."

I had been holding my hat in my right hand and, seeing Mister Little's hand suspended between us, waiting for me to take it, shifted the hat to my other so I could accept his greeting. And managed to drop it in the process. It bounced down the first step, where it sat, balanced precariously on the edge of the stone steps just below the doorway. I remembered with a shudder the first time I had met Captain Decatur in Boston and experienced a similar mishap with my hat, though with potentially more disastrous results.

Do I pick it up first, or shake his hand first?

I bent to grab the elusive hat and, upon straightening (to the amusement of my colleagues) took the proffered hand. Mister Little smiled, but in greeting, not amusement.

"It is truly a pleasure to meet another hero of that brilliant campaign, sir. Your captain told me, all too briefly, of your exploits in the matter of the *Philadelphia* frigate. He also mentioned that your own brother was held captive by those . . . people. I look forward to hearing more about that affair, just as soon as I complete my duties here. My daughters would be most unforgiving should I absent myself from my post while our guests are still arriving." His voice was surprisingly strong for a man bearing the weight of age. Deep and resonant, I knew instinctively Mister Little's voice could be heard when needed.

"Oh thank you, sir. But I surely was not a hero—of any stripe. Captain Decatur was the true hero of that business." I had never been called a hero before, and hardly thought of myself as one. I remembered all too clearly how terrified I was as we approached and boarded the ship in Tripoli Harbor. *Hero* indeed! "But I would be delighted, sir, to tell you what I can at your convenience." I smiled and let go of his hand, the image of that huge, black-bearded Arab waving his scimitar with the intent of splitting me stem to stern, still lingering in my brain.

In an effort to dispel it, I focused my eyes upon the gentleman and gave him a more careful scrutiny. He was old, into his sixties, mayhaps more. The skin of his face seemed transparent, parchment-like, where it stretched over his cheekbones. His hair—what there was of it—was totally white and wispy. He wore a most luxurious, also snowy white, mustache, droopy, but turned up at the ends, and a significant dewlap under his chin swayed noticeably when he moved his head. I had the fleeting thought that the weight of his dewlap had pulled the skin on his face down, stretching it over his skull, and managed successfully to restrain the smile the image provoked.

But it was his deep-set eyes that held my attention and I found myself quite unable to tear my gaze away from them; pale blue, they were, and as bright as a September sky. They seemed to sparkle when he spoke and, when he was listening, focused on the speaker with the same intensity a thirsty man might cast upon a tall tankard of ale. I had the feeling that he really wanted to hear my story of the *Philadelphia* raid though he was well aware, I suspected, of most of the details. And in spite of the fact that I was, I am sure, in his eyes, a mere boy, he seemed genuinely interested in what I might offer. I made a mental note to seek him out later.

An attractive young lady stepped to where we stood and spoke briefly to Mister Little, who acknowledged her with a nod. He smiled an apology to me and returned his attention to greeting the arriving guests, which still included my shipmates. I stepped aside to await my peers and watch the procession of guests make their way into the house.

"What was *that* all about, Oliver?" Mallory's insistent whisper made me turn my gaze from the gaily decorated guests as they passed into the house. As if he were unsure that his voice would attract my attention, he plucked at my sleeve as well.

"Just a chap the captain wanted me to meet. Has an interest in that business in Tripoli some years back. I think he might be . . . no, he must be father-in-law to our host, Mister Vernon."

"Oh. I thought perhaps you might have . . . oh well. Never mind. Let us follow the others and see what might be in store for us. I noticed some appealing young women ahead of us earlier, though I doubt I will find them as appealing as the lovely daughters of Eve at Missus Featherstone's." Mallory grinned lasciviously, took my elbow, and propelled me further into the broad central hall.

Rooms, two on each side of the hallway, were empty of people, but decorated tastefully. Dark furniture—even from the hall I could see it was well made and of a pleasing design—gleamed dully in the waning light of the late day sun. Some portraits of distinguished looking, stern-faced men hung on the paneled walls, separating brass sconces, each holding long, unlit tapers.

We moved slowly down the hall toward an ornately detailed archway, beyond which were stairs leading up and, beyond them, another door, also open. I could not help but notice the beautifully carved balusters adorning the wide staircase; I am sure that even my father, a well-respected cabinetmaker in his own right, would have thought them magnificent.

"Where are we going, Baldwin? Doesn't look much like this place is rigged up for fancy ball." Why Mallory thought I might know the answer to that was quite beyond me.

"How would I know, Dan? I've been here as many times as you have!"

He looked at me strangely, started to say something and thought better of it.

Following the line of guests, including our officers, with Decatur in the van, we passed through the open door beyond the stair and found ourselves, surprisingly, once again outside. A short walkway led us to another building almost as large as the house we had just left. Though built of the same pink-colored stone, the structure was less splendid and not as tall as the house. A pair of steps led us within and immediately, we found ourselves in what could only be the Grand Ballroom.

Longer than it was wide by about twice, the room seemed to swallow the people that flowed into its maw. Chandeliers of gleaming brass—I think there were at least eight of them—hung from the high ceiling on great lengths of chain. Each of them held more candles than I could easily count; I could only imagine what a task it must be to light them! But lit they were, even though the waning rays of the sun shone through the west-facing windows and a pair of doors open to a garden beyond. Strung between the windows and the door were chains of greenery interwoven with delicate flowers, giving a most festive air to the room. Someone, it appeared, had gone to considerable ends to show off this grand room.

Along the paneled walls, fixtures, also of brass, appeared about every five steps, and each held four candles. I noticed several of them had burned down and watched as a servant, dressed smartly in some form of livery, replaced and relit each of them. What opulence! He continued to maintain a watch over his charges, (apparently, he was responsible for only one portion of the room; there were several others who managed the problem further into the room) moving quickly to remove a guttering taper and put in its place a fresh one. Their efforts maintained the room in brightness, allowing the fine colors of the ladies' costumes and the decorations throughout to show brilliantly, an artist's pallet of every imaginable hue. Looking glasses on the wall opposite the windows reflected the swirling colors and threw the dazzling radiance back into the room. A fireplace was fitted at either end of the hall, each displaying a perfectly laid fire, not so large as to be overly warm, but surely adding to the charm of the room. The marble floor tiles, alternating gray and black squares, ended before each fireplace at what appeared to be a rough hewn stone hearth. Ladies and gentlemen filed into this opulence, seeking friends and calling greetings to one another as they espied their associates.

Mallory and I moved cautiously through this elegant setting, nodding politely to well turned out gentlemen when they noticed us. Tailed coats, mostly brown or dark gray, over high-collared ruffled shirts and waistcoats complete with stocks seemed the order of the evening. Each wore closely fitted knee-britches, stockings, of course, and low shoes. I noticed that some of their costumes seemed a bit worn while others seemed to have come directly from the tailor.

They stood in groups of four or five, some smoking cigars, chatting, and all holding glasses of amber-colored liquid which I took for rum, or perhaps American whiskey, similar to that which was served on *Chesapeake* when "spirits up" was piped.

The ladies of the gathering also stood in small groups, but none smoked a cigar and the glasses they held were tall slender affairs and seemed to contain wine, perhaps Champagne. A few held round glass cups, ornately carved, that called to my mind some of the glasses that, in the past, I knew were for a punch. I noticed that each of the ladies took very small sips of their beverage, and some appeared to cover their mouths as they swallowed. Others giggled. Their dresses were of the finest material, brightly decorated with beads and other sparkling doodads that caught the light. Bare necks were adorned with jeweled necklaces and, should there be any expanse of skin below the neck, it was decorated with a pendant of prodigious size effectively maintaining a level of modesty suitable to the gathering. Some of their sleeves ended above the elbow, but, in the interest of modesty, their arms were covered in white gloves, which left very little skin exposed. Their hair was coiffed in different ways, but the vast bulk of them seemed to favor piling the hair in masses of curls on top of their heads, leaving a few strands to fall down alongside their faces. Tall feathers had been employed to top off this arrangement, adding, in some cases, as much as a foot to the height of the lady so decorated. I found it somewhat unsettling, this feat of balance, and Mallory and I enjoyed wagering on which arrangement might fall over first. How they held those seemingly precarious hairdos in place without the pine tar favored by sailors seemed to us a great mystery!

A small assemblage of musicians perched in the corner and, on a signal from a person unseen, picked up their instruments, those with violins or violas tucked them under their chins, and their leader took his place in front. He also held a violin, but his was tucked under his arm rather than his chin. He held his bow up and in front of him, and then suddenly pointed with it at one chap seated at a pianoforte.

The piano-player began to move his hands over the keys before him, but I heard not a sound come from the instrument. People in the room paid the musicians no heed whatever, continuing talking among themselves, each a bit louder than the other so as to be heard over the competing voices. Gradually, as the stringed instruments joined in, I began to hear the music; so must have others, as the conversations died down much as a tumbling stream quiets as it flows into the millpond.

The young lady whom I had noticed at the door took to the floor in the center of the room, joined by a rather dull looking fellow who, to judge by his face, would rather have been elsewhere. And they began to dance.

Others joined in, and soon, Mallory and I, along with a number of others moved to the side of the room to allow the dancers the space to perform their steps.

"Goodness, Baldwin! Have a look at that one. No, you dolt, not *that* one! *That* one, with the crimson gown. What a beauty! I believe I shall have to make her acquaintance."

I shot my messmate a look that clearly indicated what I thought of his chances of success.

"You just wait and see if I don't, Baldwin, you doubter!" He laughed, still convinced of his ability to dazzle the ladies with his wit and sophistication. "You'll still be standing here, looking about and feeling awkward while I am . . . well, you'll see. Might even learn something, were you to keep me in your sights." He laughed again, and accepted a glass from a passing servant.

I took one as well, and sipped it tentatively. It was indeed whiskey, as I had earlier surmised, but clearly not of the same stripe as that served on *Chesapeake;* this was exceedingly smooth and had no burn at all when swallowed.

What a pity the Navy doesn't carry this type! I thought. And took another, less cautious taste.

"You must be off the frigate recently come into the harbor." A well turned out fellow, who had taken station to my right, spoke.

I looked at him and, in an effort to achieve more sophistication than surely I felt right now, paused to take another swallow from my whiskey.

"Aye, I am from *Chesapeake.*" I responded after what I thought a suitable interval.

"Must be quite a life in the Navy. Out on the deeps, chasing pirates and living with all that excitement! Storms, battles, guns blazing, sails straining. Goodness! What a grand existence. Never been to sea my own self, save once when my father sent me to Virginia on business. Hated every minute of it. Dreadful sick I was! Took a stagecoach back. Took less time and was surely more steady. I do admire you for the life you chose. Couldn't possibly do it myself, though!" He smiled.

"I never thought of it as particularly exciting, over all," I answered. "Though it does have its moments."

"Never seen action, then, I'd reckon. Looking forward to your first real sea battle, are you?" His grin grew wider.

The chap was about my age, maybe a trifle older. He was dressed in the same fancy clothes most of the other men wore, and his face was round, almost doughy. Which also described his complexion.

This fellow has never done a day's work outside, I'd wager! Must work in a counting house somewhere, likely for his father. That's what I would look like had I not gone to sea six years ago. Poor chap!

"Well, sir. I cannot say that. I have indeed experienced the horrors of war, and can honestly say I do not relish experiencing more of it." I said quietly and turned back to watch the dancers pirouetting around the floor.

"Couldn't have been much of a war. Our country has not been engaged in a real war since we won our independence. And you appear too young to have fought in that one." His smile was gone, replaced by a look that was both challenging and, I thought, sneering, which certainly fit the tone he used.

I fought the urge to respond sharply by taking a breath. My mother's words about thinking before you speak floated through my head and, remembering occasions where I had not, and regretted it, took another before I answered his challenge.

"Actually, sir, I was with Captain Decatur on the Barbary Coast in ought three and four. You must have read about that conflict with the Bashaw of Tripoli; I am sure it was in all the newspapers."

I did not think that adding my participation in the incident with HMS *Leopard* would signify to him.

"You must have been merely a boy then," he said. "Did you actually see action yourself then?"

"Aye, I did indeed. My name is Oliver Baldwin." I stuck out my hand in an effort to be friendly and, hopefully, change the subject.

"Josiah Tibbets, is mine. Pleasure to make your acquaintance. Born and raised right here in Newport."

"You know what I do, Mister Tibbets. What is it that you make your living at?"

"Please call me Josiah, and I shall call you Oliver. I clerk at my father's bank, right down the street."

Hah! I was right! Spends all his time pouring over ledgers, counting currency, and other such similarly boring entertainments.

"That must be most interesting," I offered, not meaning a word of it.

"Oh, I find it quite dull, to be honest. But it gives me an income, paltry though it might be, and, I'd reckon to take over the bank, once my father has either tired of it or passed on. Then I shall gain the respect of these people."

Hmmm. I wonder if he really thinks that people respect someone based on how they earn their keep.

As our conversation drifted to a halt—I think we both realized we had little in common and less to share—I became aware of the music stopping and the dancers all moving to the sides of the ballroom.

The dull-looking fellow I had noticed dancing with our hostess earlier now stood in the center of the room by himself. His face was now smiling and animated; he was the center of attention.

"Ladies and gentlemen. May I have your attention, if you please?" His voice was tinny sounding, almost as if he spoke through a speaking trumpet, which, of course, he was not.

The conversations and laughter of the gathering quieted and he beamed as he continued in the same high-pitched voice.

"I want to welcome you to our home and take this moment to introduce to you our most special guests: Captain Stephen Decatur and his officers of the frigate *Chesapeake,* which has graced our harbor for the past several days."

So that is our host. Vernon, as I recall from what Rowe mentioned. So I wonder who Mister Little might be. Perhaps his father-in-law?

An enthusiastic round of applause greeted his introduction and I watched Captain Decatur detach himself from a small group of men and ladies and make his way to the center of the room, next to our host.

"As some of you are no doubt aware, the captain and his officers distinguished themselves off the coast of North Africa some four or five years back, fighting the corsairs of Tripoli and helping to regain for our splendid country the rights to trade in the Mediterranean Sea. Something I know that is near and dear to many of our hearts." Mister Vernon extended his hand to Decatur and smiled.

The captain muttered something to his host as he took the proffered hand, smiled, took a breath, and spoke.

"My officers, midshipmen and I are most pleased to be included in your grand ball. What a marvelous welcome to Newport! I thank you, Mister Vernon, for your most kind words of recognition. Indeed, I, along with many others, did see some action with the corsairs of the Barbary Coast, an event that came to a thankfully favorable conclusion. While none of the officers presently with me served in my command in that theater, one of my midshipmen did, and with notable courage." He looked around the room, obviously seeking me.

Oh no! What is he doing? I have no interest in this, whatever. I could feel the color rising up my neck.

"There you are, Oliver. Friends, may I present to you Midshipman Oliver Baldwin."

Another round of applause greeted his words and I could feel heads turning as the guests sought me out. My companion, the bank clerk, smiled broadly, shook my hand again, and spoke to a few around us, acknowledging their glances of respect with nods and smiles. For my own self, I wished I could have taken my crimson face and crawled into a hole! But I smiled manfully, and bowed my head, respectful of the recognition.

Decatur continued speaking after a brief interval and, once again, the crowd hushed.

"*Chesapeake* has been on an extended embargo patrol for the past four and more months, ranging from the Carolinas to Cape Cod. You can imagine our joy at coming ashore, and especially, to this wonderful town. I trust that my crew will do nothing to embarrass us or abuse your welcome. We thank you for your hospitality and look forward to enjoying it for a few more days before we will weigh anchor and return to our home waters of Norfolk." He bowed, hand on his sword, and received more applause, though this time, I noticed several men who did not join in the adulation.

In fact, while I could not hear the words they muttered to one another, their hard expressions were clear indicators that they did not appreciate our assignment.

Must be ship owners, angry about Mister Jefferson's embargo. Likely got ships either endeavoring to slip through or rotting at the docks.

At a nod from Mister Vernon, the musicians went back to work and couples immediately took to the dance floor, forcing our host and Decatur to make their way by a circuitous route to the outboard side of the room. I noticed several guests, including a number of the ladies, at once surround the captain.

" . . . see some action. Sorry to have doubted you, sir."

I realized that Josiah Tibbets had spoken to me, but, intent on watching the proceedings across the room, I had missed most of what he said.

"I'm sorry, Josiah. What was that? I did not realize you were speaking to me."

"I was apologizing for making light of your war experience, sir. I hope you will forgive me. I imagine that it must have been horrific to be there, but you must have distinguished yourself, given the accolade you just received from your captain."

"I did my job, sir." If he was going to be formal with me, I would not be outdone either.

He pressed. "But had what you did not been of some note, I doubt that a man of Captain Decatur's renown would have taken the trouble to single out a mere midshipman. After all, there are, what, half a dozen officers senior to you, in attendance. Would it not have been more fitting to introduce at least some of them over a midshipman?"

"I have no inkling of why the captain chose to single me out. I did nothing that any other would not have done in my place. It could have been only that I am the only one aboard *Chesapeake* to have sailed with him, as he said, to the Barbary Coast. Will you excuse me, please? I would like to have a look outside before the darkness is complete." I was most uncomfortable with the seemingly belligerent nature of his questions.

I smiled, nodded, and, without waiting for an answer, stepped off toward the open doors across the room and, hopefully, some respite from the interrogation. I could feel his eyes on my back as I took my leave.

CHAPTER TWELVE

The daylight outside was fast waning; in fact, there seemed more shadows than light, but the nearly full moon had shown itself above the horizon and augmented the afterglow of the sunset. The garden was laid out with paths between flowerbeds, which contained a variety of blooming plants and shrubs. A large tree, set away from the house, cast long shadows over the whole of the garden, its branches swaying gently in the easy breeze. A bench, carved from stone, sat in a small opening at the end of one path, not far from the tree.

I strolled casually in its general direction, my choices limited by the available paths. The sounds of the party dimmed as I moved further from the open doors; voices and music mingled together to become a dull buzz. The sounds of the night insects chirping, the birds twittering, and the rustle of the breeze in the tree, instead filled the air. I found it quite refreshing.

Reaching the bench, I stepped beyond it and saw before me the harbor, the path of the moon reflected quite clearly in the ripples of its dark surface. Ships, including *Chesapeake,* swung to their anchors, some facing the gentle breeze, others pointing their bows into the ebbing tide. Several, perhaps a dozen, more lay at the various piers, which poked out into the harbor, a clear indication that at least some of the citizens of Newport were observing the embargo.

Likely owned by those unhappy gentlemen at the ball. I thought, recalling the angry looks Decatur's remarks received from some.

"What a perfectly lovely evening." A feminine voice from behind me startled me out of my reverie. So caught up in the view and the night sounds that I had heard naught of her approach. I turned.

Before me, bathed from the front in the moonlight and lit from behind by the lights of the ballroom, was a young woman of astounding beauty.

She was smiling, seemingly amused by my slack-jawed gape. With considerable effort, and hopefully, before the passage of too much time, I collected my wits.

"Aye, ma'am. Indeed it is. And what a lovely . . . uh, home and . . . uh, view of the harbor. Do you live here?"

Oliver! Try to act less the bumpkin and more like a seasoned officer of the Navy. My goodness, what a beauty!

"Oh no." She giggled. And it sounded like distant bells tinkling. "I am here with my family, sir, and just a guest of the Vernon's. Like you."

"Oh dear," I exclaimed, extending my hand and bowing from the waist. "Where are my manners? I am Oliver Baldwin, Midshipman in the *Chesapeake* frigate. But I guess you know that. The part about being a midshipman in *Chesapeake*, I mean."

You sound the perfect fool, Oliver. Get yourself together. You have spoken with pretty girls before.

"Well, surely I knew you were from the ship. Goodness, I think everyone knows that! And I was in the ballroom when your captain introduced you, so, since I did not get the chance to speak with you before you left the room, I followed you out here." She smiled again and I felt my knees go weak.

Her voice was soft, gentle like an easy breeze, and as musical as the wind in the rigging. Long dark hair, gently teased by the light wind, and haloed by the light from the ballroom, framed her face and fell to her shoulders, unlike the style worn by some of the other ladies at the ball. A flower was tucked into a strand of hair on her left side and in the dim light, seemed to perfectly match the color of her gown.

Her face, oh my goodness, her face. It was perfect. Eyes set exactly the right distance apart and exactly the right distance below her hair, a small nose, which turned up a bit at the end, and a mouth that was surrounded by full lips, which apparently were set in a perpetual smile. I was captivated. I was staring.

"Sir, you are staring at me. Is something wrong?" That musical voice was edged with a touch of concern.

"Oh, no, Ma'am. Nothing, nothing at all. I apologize. It's just . . . well, it's simply . . . I have never . . ."

Get ahold of yourself, you dolt!

"No, Ma'am. Nothing at all is wrong." I repeated.

"Oh, I am so glad. The way you were looking at me, I thought . . . well, never mind what I thought!" She smiled again, only this time, her eyes danced in merriment.

"Where are my manners?" She took my hand, still extended between us. "My name is Ann. Ann Perry. A pleasure, Mister Baldwin, to make your acquaintance, I'm sure."

Either she was still holding my hand, or I hers, but neither of us let go for a moment longer than might have been normal for a handshake. My head was swimming. Her hand, so soft in mine, so small and feminine, made me forget anything else: the garden, the bench, the tree, the harbor, the ship, the moonlight, the ball, that I was a midshipman in the Navy and serving under the most famous captain ever to hold the rank. I could scarcely catch my breath.

"Are you enjoying the ball, Midshipman Baldwin? It is certainly a festive affair, but it is not every day we have the pleasure of such distinguished guests!"

"Oh, yes, Ma'am. It does seem festive and most pleasant."

Oliver, you fool! Think of something intelligent to say.

"Do you live here, in Newport, Miss Perry?" Finally, words came to me that seemed to make sense.

"Quite near here, actually. South Kingstown." she replied, letting go of my hand, which, of course, forced me to let go of hers, reluctantly. "One of my brothers, the eldest of us, whose name is also Oliver, is in the Navy, too. His ship is normally berthed here in Newport, but he is presently at sea. My family has lived here, or near here, for several generations."

"How interesting. What ship would he be in, if I may be so bold as to inquire?"

"She is a schooner, named *Revenge.* He just took command of her this summer. They are, as I mentioned, at sea now. About a month into their cruise, I believe."

In command? Lieutenant or master commandant, I wonder.

"Did he see action anywhere yet? Perhaps in that business with France in ninety-eight? Or perhaps in the Mediterranean?" I was trying to determine how long he had been in the Navy, and hoped I was not being too obvious.

"Oh, he had just received his warrant near the end of the unpleasantness with France and saw only brief service in the Caribbean during that time. However, he did experience service in the war with the Barbary corsairs, as you did, but sadly—at least from *his* point of view—saw none of the actual fighting. When he returned from his service in the Mediterranean, he received his commission, but was put on extended leave for most of the next two years, a circumstance we thought would drive him mad! Like a caged beast he was, frustrated and writing weekly letters to the Navy for an assignment.

"When he finally received orders, we were all relieved, but Oliver felt he should have been at sea."

My expression must have told my thoughts, because she quickly continued.

"He was assigned right here in Newport, superintending the construction of a flotilla of gunboats. Here and in Connecticut. He absolutely hated it. Considered it far too tedious and not at all how he wished to spend his time. He continued to write his letters and after a long, very long, year, was most pleased that the Navy Department finally saw fit to send him to sea . . . and in command." She smiled in the dark, lighting up her entire face again.

"Well, Miss Perry, it would appear we have something beyond names in common then. I, too, have a brother, also older, named Edward, who is presently doing the same chore in New York, under Commodore Chauncey. He, like your own brother, finds it equally tedious and has petitioned for a seagoing ship repeatedly, but to no avail."

"Had he been to sea or seen some action, as you would call it, prior to his current assignment?"

"Indeed, he had. He was third lieutenant in *Philadelphia* in eighteen three."

"Oh goodness!" Her hand flew to her breast. "Was not that the ship taken by those dreadful pirates on the Barbary Coast? I seem to recall hearing about that from my brother. Was he aboard then?"

I heard genuine concern in her voice.

"Aye, Ma'am, he was that. Spent nearly two years in the Bashaw's dungeon, until the treaty was signed in the year ought five. Terrible time it was for me and our parents, but I reckon it was the worst for him!"

I was pleased to notice that I could carry on a conversation with this beauty now without stumbling over my tongue. She was so easy to talk to!

"I am becoming a bit chilled, Mister Baldwin. Would you mind escorting me back into the party? Perhaps a dance would warm me up." As if to add some emphasis to her words, she shivered delicately as she looked up and into my eyes expectantly.

I could stand here with this lovely woman for the rest of my life, cold, hot, or anything else!

"Of course, Ma'am. It would be an honor." I stepped toward her, but she didn't move as I expected her to and I inadvertently brushed . . . well, more than brushed, against her.

"Oh my, Miss Perry. Please excuse me. I thought . . . that is, I expected you . . ."

"Oh my goodness," she laughed. "It was my fault entirely." She laughed again, that wonderful tinkling sound, and took my arm to walk toward the lights of the house.

It was about halfway to our destination that she stumbled, whether on purpose or by accident I do not know. But she clung tighter to my arm and brought her other arm across her body to ensure her security, intertwining now both arms in mine. Which, of course, required that her body be touching my own. It was glorious and, using her misstep as the excuse, I slowed my pace to extend this moment.

The path, which earlier had presented a quite modest walk to its terminus, now seemed barely a few steps, so quickly did the time pass, even at our reduced pace. We reached the door and were immediately assailed by the cacophony of sounds from within. Laughter, voices raised in conversation, and the music of the orchestra providing a lively dance tune seemed overwhelming after the quiet of the garden, when all I could hear was the sweet sound of her voice and my own blood rushing through my body.

"I would be honored should you wish to accompany me onto the dance floor, Miss Perry." To ensure that she heard me, I leaned close to her head, placing my mouth in proximity to her ear.

And inhaled the glorious fragrance of her scent. Once again, my knees turned to rubber and I wondered if I would be able to manage the steps called for in the dance.

"Oh, Mister Baldwin, how lovely. I should be enchanted to dance with you. It is surely one of my favorite pursuits. Let me just report my return to my mother and I shall meet you right here, by the door." She smiled radiantly at me, slowly released my arm from hers, and moved with astonishing grace away from me.

After a few steps, she turned her head toward me, as if to ascertain I remained in place. Seeing me unmoving, she rewarded my immobility with another smile, and continued on her mission. What she could not have known was that I would have been unable to move had the building been on fire!

So intent on watching her progress as she made her way across the dance floor, avoiding swirling couples, smiling brilliantly at some and merely nodding at others, that I was quite unaware of a presence at my side.

"Mister Baldwin. How nice to finally catch up with you." Even without turning in his direction, I knew at once that the voice could only belong to Mister Little, the elderly gentleman I had met earlier. "I do want to hear your tale of the *Philadelphia* affair. While I am quite aware of the broad strokes of the story, it would be an honor, sir, to hear a firsthand account of that extraordinary business."

He extended his hand, which held one of those round glasses, filled nearly to the brim with a tea-colored liquid. A piece of an orange floated in it. It was the same glass I had earlier noticed the women enjoying. To be polite, I took the proffered glass, wondering what I would do with it.

"I have brought you a glass of punch to wet your whistle and ease the telling of your tale. Quite tasty it is, as you will see." He smiled as I accepted his offering.

I took a tentative sip, determined to at least look as if I enjoyed it. To my delight, it was, as Mister Little had put it, "quite tasty" and seemed liberally laced with rum. I took another sample, just to be sure, and tried to figure a way to forestall my recounting of that dreadful memory.

I cannot do this now. She will be back in a moment and I have promised to dance with her, something I would surely rather do than spend the evening talking with this old bird.

I turned to Mister Little and, smiling in what I hoped was a disarming way, said, "I would be most pleased to describe that event, sir, but would you mind waiting just a bit? I am currently engaged with a young lady who has promised me a dance. She should be returning in only a moment."

He must have noticed me glancing around the room, seeking her out of the throng and, hopefully, heading this way.

With a broad smile and a bow, he acceded to my request. "Of course, lad. I should never put myself in the way of one enjoying the company of the fairer among us. When you are free, then. Perhaps when we sup, or after?"

He stepped away, exchanged his now empty glass for a full one from a passing waiter, and melted into the guests watching the dancers as they twirled and laughed to the music.

His place was immediately taken by Josiah Tibbets, the bank clerk in the employ of his father. He touched my sleeve, causing me to turn and thus, acknowledge his presence.

"Hello again, Mister Tibbets." I offered, hoping he would merely respond in kind and follow in Mister Little's footsteps. Which, of course, he did not.

"You departed quite suddenly, earlier, Oliver. I thought perhaps I might have offended you in some manner." He held a glass of whiskey, which he raised to his lips as he waited for me to respond. I let him wait while I took a swallow from my own glass.

"Not at all, sir. I believe I mentioned I wanted to have a look around outside before it became full dark." As I spoke, I again cast my gaze around the room, hoping for a glimpse of the fair Miss Perry.

"Well, I am glad for that. I seem to have a talent for unwittingly affronting people." He waited until I turned to face him again, and smiled broadly before continuing.

"I assume you have read the report on Meriwether Lewis' grand expedition of discovery to the far Pacific. I would be most interested in your assessment of their discoveries. I think everyone must have read that extraordinary account, even a Naval officer." He paused, looking inquiringly at me for some sign that I had. And proved his earlier statement about affronting people unwittingly.

"Actually, I have little knowledge of it beyond what I have read in the newspapers. Is there a published paper describing their trek?" I hoped not to show my ignorance, but equally, did not want to encourage his continued attendance at my side.

"Oh my, yes. Indeed there is. Came out just this year, it did, and is quite brilliant. Gives a firsthand accounting of the whole of their three year odyssey, and describes in some detail the heathens they encountered as well as the vast stretches of land their band marched through. I found it to be riveting. You really should clap onto a copy of it; I think it would be most revealing to someone such as yourself."

"Such as myself?" What does he mean by that? Presumably, in his opinion, I am a hide-bound Naval officer with no interest beyond the coastline. Indeed!

I nodded in agreement, wishing not to prolong our one-sided conversation and, raising my glass again to my lips, glanced hopefully around the room.

Where is she? It could not take this long simply to report her presence to her mother. Why does she not come back?

Then I saw her, making her way across the dance floor, again smiling and nodding to other guests as she passed. I could not help but smile.

Thinking I was smiling at something clever my unwanted companion had said, Josiah again launched into a further description of the "wonderful adventure" of Messers Clark and Meriwether Lewis, something about camping on the banks of some river through the winter while hordes of hostiles beleaguered them. I heard little of it and cared even less!

"Well," he interrupted himself. "Here is Ann Perry. What a pleasant surprise. I did not know you were here, Ann. Are you seeking me, perchance for a twirl about the dance floor?"

Miss Perry had taken a position by *my* side, linking her arm through my own, a posture greatly pleasing to me. She looked at Tibbets, almost as though she had not before noticed him.

"Why no, Josiah. I am not. I have found what I am seeking, and intend to enjoy the dance Mister Baldwin earlier promised me." She did not smile at him, nor give any indication that he held any significance to her whatever.

Then she turned her glorious face to me and smiled as radiantly as I had earlier witnessed. "Would you care to make good on that promise, now, Mister Baldwin? I believe they are playing that new dance, the waltz. Are you familiar with it?"

She had already begun to move toward the dance floor and, since she still had her arm linked to my own, I had little choice but to accompany her; doing otherwise would never have occurred to me in any event! Quickly, I thrust my now nearly empty glass into Josiah's hand, hoping he would not drop it.

I had a fleeting glimpse of Tibbets standing where we had left him, holding both his and my glasses, and wearing an expression of stunned incredulity, a fact that augmented my already towering joy at being in the company of this lovely woman.

"I am not very experienced at this dance, I am afraid. There have been so few opportunities to practice it since it came to America, what with my being at sea so much. But we shall find our way, I am sure!" I smiled hopefully at her, already laying excuses for my natural ineptness.

Of course, just the thought of holding her in my arms for the duration of the dance made my legs turn to jelly and I hoped that my plea of inexperience would cover any clumsiness that I was quite sure would rear its ugly head. The fact was, that I had learned the dance while at the Academy, in Philadelphia, before winning my Warrant as a midshipman.

She reached a spot she deemed suitable for us to start and turned to me expectantly, her arms raised to a position that invited me to close with her. Which, of course, I did, unhesitatingly. We listened to the music for a moment and began to dance.

Move your legs, Oliver. Hear the music and try not to embarrass yourself!

She was light in my arms; it seemed her feet barely touched the floor as she floated effortlessly through the intricate steps of Vienna's wonderful contribution to dance. The rest of the couples disappeared; it was just Ann Perry and Midshipman Oliver Baldwin floating along to the music. Her fragrance filled my nostrils each time her hair brushed my face. Her hand on my arm barely touched me, but, though light as a feather, I could feel it burning its impression into my flesh right through my jacket and shirt. Her other hand, more tightly gripping my own, seemed to join us as one in our movements, and I realized she was helping me guide her through the turns and moves of the dance. And I was grateful.

All too soon, the music ended and, reluctantly, I stopped. I did not at once release her, a fact that prompted a smile and a brief—oh! How fleeting it was—hug from my partner. Then she stepped back and looked at me appraisingly.

"For one who has been at sea, Mister Baldwin, you managed that most elegantly! I thank you, and look forward to repeating it soon, very soon."

"Oh my, Miss Perry. It is I who should be thanking you; you are truly a splendid dancer, perhaps the best I have ever known. I enjoyed that more than ever I could relate to you. Simply delightful, it was."

Oliver, you imbecile. You are running out words like a loose sheet on a flogging sail! Grow up!

Her smile was all the thanks I needed, but the words that followed made my heart soar like a sea bird riding a gale.

"Mister Baldwin. It appears that the orchestra has stopped so we might partake of some supper. It would be an honor were you to join my family and me, should you not be otherwise engaged. And you could meet one of my brothers as well. My father was a navy man also." She looked expectantly at me, the smile gracing her radiant face broadening.

I quickly agreed to her request—it was not as if I could have even uttered the word "no"—and followed her off the dance floor and to one of many tables which had appeared along the opposite wall, set out by the servants while the guests were dancing.

Already seated there were a handsome older couple who I took to be Mister Perry and his wife, Ann's mother. In addition, a brace of young men—they looked to be about my age, so must be Ann's brothers—stood nearby, engaged in conversation.

"Ah, here you are, dear Ann. We were wondering what had become of you. Please take your seat. They will be serving out the meal directly, I should think." Mister Perry stood to welcome his daughter, all the while casting an appraising glance at me.

"Father, Mother, may I present to you Midshipman Oliver Baldwin. He is with Captain Decatur on . . . I mean, *in,* the frigate *Chesapeake.*" When she corrected herself, she smiled at me.

"Yes, dear. We heard the captain introduce him earlier." Mister Perry spoke to his daughter, then turned to me.

"A pleasure to meet you, sir. It would appear your captain thinks most highly of your abilities." He smiled at me, extended his hand, which I took, and went on. "I would presume that Ann has brought you here to join us for supper. We would be delighted if you would be so kind."

"Thank you, sir. It would be a great pleasure to join you and your family." I, too smiled, partly out of relief at not stumbling over my tongue, but mostly out of anticipation of remaining in Miss Perry's company.

"This is Ann's mother, Sarah Wallace Alexander Perry. You may take the seat next to her, if you please." Mister Perry pointed at the empty chair next to the smiling woman with the four names.

How strange he should introduce his wife that way. I must remember to ask Miss Perry about that.

"A pleasure, Madam." I said as I moved to the assigned seat, and stuck out my hand, bowing from the waist as I did so.

A soft, but warm and moist, hand took my own, and immediately released it. Missus Perry smiled at me and watched as I sat down.

"Have you been a midshipman long, Mister Baldwin?" She asked in a delightfully musical voice.

That's where her *voice comes from! Small wonder.*

I remembered the gentle sound of Miss Perry's laugh; the memory provoked a secret smile.

"I received my Warrant in eighteen three, Madam. Sailed immediately with Captain Decatur in *Argus* from Boston. September, it was; right about this time, I recall." I looked at her with a smile, taking in her attractive features, stylish hair (to judge from what I had seen other ladies sporting), and lively eyes.

I think Miss Perry got more than her voice from her mother!

"My first born is also in the Navy, Mister Baldwin, as was his father."
She shot a glance at her husband before she continued.

"Oliver Hazard, my eldest, began his career in the spring of ninety and
nine as a midshipman sailing in *General Greene,* under his father's command. I would presume you will be passing for lieutenant soon?"

"Oh, Madam. I hope so. I have only to take the examination and wait
for an opening. It is six years since my Warrant, so it should not be overly
presumptuous of me to assume it likely." I spoke earnestly, hopefully.

"Oh my! I should think so. Oliver received his promotion in . . ." She
stopped, thought for a moment, then turned to her husband.

"Christopher, pardon me, Dear. When was it Oliver was granted his
lieutenancy? Do you recall?"

"Of course I recall. It was in June of ought five, just after he returned
from that business against the Bashaw." He paused, and scowled. "And
just before the Navy put him ashore for two years!"

I knew how long Henry Allen had waited for the opening, carried as
he was as a 'passed midshipman' for some months after he had passed
both the oral and written testing required for the promotion. I hoped I
would not have to wait as long. And I certainly did not want to be "put
ashore" after I won the promotion!

"Hello, sir. I am Matthew." A fine looking young man, perhaps fifteen
or sixteen years of age seated himself to my left. I recalled that he was one
of the two I had earlier noticed chatting before supper; of the other lad,
there was no sign, so my surmise that both had been Perry brothers was
in error.

When I turned to him, he was extending his hand in greeting which,
of course, I took.

"A pleasure to meet you, Matthew. I am Oliver Baldwin."

"Have you been in the Navy long, Mister Baldwin? I hope to gain a
Warrant my own self soon."

"I was fourteen, Matthew, and Captain Decatur secured for me a
Warrant. I should think your older brother, or perhaps your father, could
be of help to you in that."

"I will be fourteen on my next birthday, sir. Did you find it exciting? I
mean, going to sea?"

Goodness, he appears some older than his years!

"It was quite overwhelming, at first. But there was little time to be
overwhelmed; we sailed from Boston shortly after I reported into *Argus*
for the Mediterranean. And then we were engaged with the corsairs of

the Barbary Coast. I am sure you would find it exhilarating, and not a little scarifying, as did I."

"I hope I can fight, too, sir. Not likely I'd be scared; I come from a long line of fighters! Ain't that so, Mama?"

The matriarch of the Perry family laughed that same musical laugh and looked at me, then her youngest son, the sparkle never leaving her eyes.

"'*Isn't* that so', Matthew, is what I am sure you meant to say." Her expression changed not a whit, but Matthew's did at being chastised in front of a stranger. The matter of her son's grammar dealt with, she looked directly at me.

"What my son refers to, Mister Baldwin, is my descendancy from the thirteenth century Scot, William Wallace. Some thought him an outlaw, but we prefer to think of him as a revolutionary, not unlike our own countrymen here in America. He, too, fought the English for the sovereignty of his country. Unfortunately, he lost his quest and his life, but not until he had brought the English to heel, ruled his country for a time and established its independence. Sadly, he was betrayed—it was in thirteen and five, I believe—and executed most cruelly by Edward the First. I was raised on the story, and have ensured that my children will pass it on through future generations." Surprisingly, she smiled so sweetly I could scarcely believe the heroic and warlike tale she had just related to me.

So that's why she carries all the names! William Wallace; haven't heard that name since I left the Academy.

"He was drawn and quartered, Mister Baldwin. And his parts were displayed in four parts of the country! To be a lesson to those who might take up the cause. Can you believe it?" Matthew chimed in with youthful exuberance.

"Matthew! That will do! Mister Baldwin is not interested in the details of the story, and certainly not at the supper table!" Ann Perry, for the first time, had joined the conversation.

I looked at her and smiled to show her brother's sense of drama had bothered me not a whit. What *did* bother me was to have her sitting several chairs away from me, where I was unable to speak to her without all hearing my words. But I was rewarded with her own brilliant smile, and my heart beat a bit faster.

The conversation at the table was light and generally insignificant. Servants brought successive dishes of food, each more elegant and delicious than its predecessor: cold meats, a cornucopia of vegetables, breads of every imaginable stripe, and each with a different wine. I followed the chatter, answered young Matthew's endless questions about the Navy, my experiences in Tripoli, and his father's questions concerning the incident with HMS *Leopard*. Between my discourse and eating a bit of the supper, I tried to catch Miss Perry's eye when I could. Each time I succeeded, I was rewarded with a marvelous smile, sometimes a wink or a nod, and the promise, unspoken, of more. I barely tasted the meal, pushing my food around the plates as they appeared and were cleared, to be replaced with more.

From time to time, Captain or Missus Perry would query me on some detail of my past, from whence did I come, family connections, and my father's business.

"Your father, young man: is he—or was he—a Navy man, perchance?" My host at the head of the table asked me quite suddenly during a lull in the conversation.

"Oh no, Mister . . . uh, excuse me, sir . . . Captain Perry. But he does have business with the Navy, building the fittings for officers' quarters in some of our ships."

"A cabinetmaker? How wonderful!" Missus Perry exclaimed at my response. "And yet you decided to take up the sea as *your* trade, surely, a wise choice."

She smiled sweetly at me. "I have always admired a clever craftsman. I would assume him to be quite skilled, as you mentioned that he fits furnishings to our government's seagoing vessels."

"Thank you, Madam. I have heard only reports of a positive nature concerning his work. And yes, he has, in the past, fitted the Cabin and wardrooms on several frigates and at least one brig that I know of. Captain Decatur, also a Philadelphia man, has often complimented my father's craftsmanship." I chose not to comment on my "choice of trade," but was a trifle put out by what I took be a certain aloofness in her comment about my father.

Any number of retorts had flashed through my mind, but one look at the lady's daughter sitting across from me as she watched the interaction between her parents and me stifled all thoughts of remarking. Instead, I simply smiled, and lifted a morsel of cold beef to my mouth.

Toward the end of the repast, I noticed Miss Perry's eyes shift to a point over my head and, immediately felt a hand on my shoulder.

Oh no! Not Tibbets again. Can he not just leave me alone? Does he think he has a claim on the attention of Miss Perry? I surely hope not!

I turned and looked into a midsection bisected by a scarlet sash. And stood.

"Ah, Mister Baldwin. I have finally tracked you down." Mister Little beamed into my face. I noticed his was some flushed, the color high in his cheeks more obvious on account of the thinness of his skin.

"As you appear to have finished your supper, Christopher, might I borrow this young man for a few moments. He has promised to relate to me—and now I have discovered two others as well who wish to hear—the tale of his derring-do in Decatur's brilliant . . .ummm . . . *burning* of the *Philadelphia* frigate."

"Without question, William. And I myself would be interested in hearing a firsthand report of that splendid job. Haven't been able to corner Decatur yet to tell me about it, so the midshipman's recounting will have to answer." Captain Perry stood, stepped to where Mister Little stood, took his arm and together, they marched off toward one end of the ballroom. It was assumed that I would follow.

Which, of course, I did, but not before I threw a long face at Miss Perry. I received, in return, a wink and a smile. I had hardly taken two steps before I remembered my manners and tacked sharply, reversing my course back to the table.

"Missus Perry. I greatly enjoyed supping with your family and I thank you for allowing me the privilege. I hope I shall be able to visit with you again." Only the last part did I really mean. And then, my hope was centered directly on her beautiful and charming daughter.

"Indeed, Oliver. We enjoyed your company. I hope my son's constant torrent of questions was not a bother for you; he misses his older brother dreadfully. As to visiting with us again, I will assume you mean to visit with Ann again and, I suspect, were I to judge from the expressions I saw pass between you, there is every likelihood of that eventuality."

I shot a glance at Miss Perry who, I saw, had colored visibly, but smiled at me, offering a barely perceptible nod of concurrence. Then I hurried off to catch up to Mister Little and Captain Perry.

CHAPTER THIRTEEN

I described to the four gentlemen, Mister Little, Captain Perry and two others—I never did get their names—in some detail, the attack on the frigate *Philadelphia,* answering their questions and repeating several times a description of the display of cannonading the dying ship put on as we left the harbor.

"Mister Baldwin. I assume, from the detailed recitation you have offered, that you were in attendance for this performance, and are not simply re-telling the tale of others." Captain Perry looked at me, quite sharply, I thought.

"Aye, sir. I was that—there, that is." I tried to smile and keep at bay the image of that huge "piratical bastard" (as Mister Tarbox, Gunner on *Enterprise,* would have called him) wielding his scimitar at my head.

Mister Little jumped to my assistance. "For the love of God, Christopher! Of course he was there and, from what Decatur indicated, acquitted himself with honor. His own brother was an officer—third lieutenant in the frigate, if I recall correctly, and a captive of that piratical collection of rogues." Little shot a glance at me for confirmation, which I gladly gave with a nod of my head. Then he continued.

"How, or perhaps more aptly, why, would he ever imply his attendance at the 'performance', as you put it so keenly, with his shipmates involved in such a scrap and his own brother languishing in the Bashaw's dungeon? Come now, sir!"

Mister Little had actually become somewhat red in the face from his outburst, or perhaps it was the alcohol he had consumed. Either way, it had the desired effect.

"I do apologize for doubting you, sir. Obviously your captain thinks most highly of you and, upon some reflection, that should be quite enough for me. I have nothing but respect for Decatur and his brilliant accomplishments." Captain Perry bowed slightly from the waist, a further indication of his apology.

"Tell me, Mister Baldwin: were you scared in your foray against the enemy?" Mister Little, satisfied that Captain Perry had paid for his earlier insult, studied me closely.

"Aye, sir. Quite so . . . terrified in fact." I answered with complete honesty, recalling easily how frightening the whole experience was for me. Large, angry corsairs with scimitars flashed through my brain once again.

"Good, good! A bit of fear sharpens the senses. Makes one more aware. You must, of course, be able to continue to navigate in spite of it, though. Very important, that." Mister Little smiled quickly, then became quite stern once more. He continued.

"Courage, bravery, lad, is seeing it through—keeping your head and doing your job—in spite of your fear. Few possess the trait, but those who do, often rise to glory. It would appear that your Captain Decatur is blessed with a large dollop of courage as well."

"Yes, sir. I would say he is. I never saw him show anything but bravery in the face of battle."

"Here now. What are you gentlemen up to? Cooking up some grand scheme to break the embargo and sail for profit?" Mister Vernon, who I had only seen from a distance, joined the group, offering his words with a smile.

"Well, you have no need to scheme and plot; the embargo has been lifted. I just now received word from the captain of a coastwise schooner in from the Chesapeake Bay. Apparently, our pleas to Jefferson's administration bore fruit. That, or those fools in Washington finally realized that their idiotic policy has done more damage to us, America, than ever it could to England or France. But we can return to sea . . . legally." At this, Vernon shot a knowing look at one of the men whose name I did not know. Perhaps a "runner."

"And you must be Oliver Baldwin. The midshipman who Decatur thinks so highly of." Vernon turned to me and stuck out his hand. "I am Sam Vernon."

"Very pleased to meet you, sir." I smiled and took his hand. Quite small, it was, almost feminine in its size, but the grip was deceivingly strong. This, then, was our host.

"Thank you for including us in your grand ball, sir. You home is beautiful." I looked around the room as I spoke, obviously including it in the praise of his home.

"Thank you, sir. How could we not include you? You and your gallant shipmates are our guests of honor! As to the house, at least the part you walked through when you arrived, was built by my father, well before the Revolution. 1760, it was. After the house was built, he purchased the land next door, in fact where we now stand, to use as a garden.

"When the war started, my father left, taking all of us with him as he felt it unsafe for a patriot to remain in Newport under British occupation. Subsequently, after the British left the area, General Rochambeau, the Frenchy, took the house as his headquarters and, without so much as a 'by your leave,' constructed this ballroom where my father's garden had stood. It has been reported that he and General Washington designed the victory at Yorktown, here, in this very building.

"After the war ended, my family returned to claim our property and here was this magnificent grand ballroom. At least, my mother and I thought it magnificent; my father complained bitterly about the loss of his garden. Said more than once, I recall, 'I can not think it polite of Rochambeau to build such an assembly room in my garden without my leave.' But here it is, and well-used." Vernon smiled at the recollection of his father's grousing at the French general's temerity.

"Well, sir," I said. "I think it most grand and am enjoying myself."

Vernon smiled and the other four men nodded and smiled, whether at my naiveté or in agreement, I know not. Then Mister Little changed the subject—something about the abandonment of the embargo—and with nothing to offer, I waited for a lull and begged their permission to depart.

I set a course across the dance floor to where I had supped with Miss Perry and her family, hoping to find them, or at least her, still at table. I consulted my watch and discovered to my horror that I had been absent for over an hour while Captain Perry and his colleagues questioned my attendance at the 'performance' in Tripoli Harbor.

She will surely not still be sitting idly by, waiting for my return. She is too pretty by half and will have been besieged by invitations to dance.

My disappointment was realized as I caught sight of the table; only Missus Perry remained and she was deep in conversation with another woman of similar vintage. I stood nearby, not wishing to interrupt, but hoping she would notice me and perhaps, direct me toward her daughter.

Which, after what seemed an eternity, she did, exactly.

"Oh, Oliver. Have you been standing there long? I must try to be more aware! I would assume you are seeking Ann. I believe she is dancing . . . with Mister Tibbets, I recall. At least, it was he who appeared seeking her for a waltz, directly after you left the table with Captain Perry. Perhaps they are still dancing, though I think the waltz ended quite some time ago." She laughed delicately and returned her attention to the lady seated next to her. I was dismissed.

She's been with that buffoon for over an hour! What am I to do? What if they are no longer on the dance floor? Perhaps he took her outside to steal a kiss. Oh my heavens!

Rooted to the spot, I frantically scanned the dancing couples, seeking the woman who had stolen my heart. I saw Captain Decatur dancing with a matronly lady in whom he seemed less than interested. I saw Mallory and smiled in spite of myself when I saw he was dancing with the young woman we had both admired earlier. I recognized one of the men who had listened to my story of the *Philadelphia* attack. But not a glimpse of Ann Perry or Josiah Tibbets did I catch.

Where have they gone?

Carefully, I made my way back across the dance floor, weaving through the gyrating dancers while I maintained a weather eye for the interloping Tibbets and Miss Perry.

But my search bore no fruit. They were nowhere to be seen.

Perhaps outside? Oh, goodness, I hope not.

I made my way with increasing haste toward the doors—knowing now the history of the room, I assumed they were *French* doors—and finding them still open, stepped outside.

The cool air was refreshing after the close atmosphere of the ballroom and I breathed deeply of it in an effort to calm myself. The light spilling out of the brightly lit room illuminated several couples nearby to the entry, but beyond that, it was impossibly dark. The moon had either set or nearly so and I could barely discern the dim outline of the big tree where Miss Perry and I had first met. I moved cautiously in its direction.

"Oh! Excuse me, please." I had bumped into a couple—they were startled from their embrace—and pressed on, my eyes gradually becoming accustomed to the gloom.

"Please unhand me, sir!"

The female voice could only be Miss Perry's. Ahead of me, I picked out a couple standing a bit apart, engaged in conversation, or was it an argument?

"Oh come now, Ann. Surely you can't be serious. Is it that midshipman . . . what's his name? Baldwin! Yes, Baldwin. Is it he you would rather be with? I am a much-preferred choice. And someday I will be as well set as the Vernon's. He will never have anything. You know well that a Naval officer rarely makes a living wage in peacetime. And besides, you only just met him!" Tibbets words were some slurred; he was obviously feeling the effects of the several glasses of spirits he had consumed, perhaps along with several of that strong punch.

I stepped more quickly toward their dim outlines, focusing on the sound of their voices. And tripped.

Over what I have no idea, but stick or rock in the path, I struck my foot and stumbled, only catching myself at the last moment to avoid falling full length. As it was, I was off-balance and bumped quite solidly into Tibbets.

"What the . . ? Here, sir! Be more careful. You very nearly knocked me down. Have you no courtesy, heading down a dark path at such a rate?" Tibbets, catching his own balance, had not seen who had run into him.

"Sorry, Josiah. Didn't mean to knock you." I quickly apologized and turned to Miss Perry. "Miss Perry, are you alright? I thought I heard sounds of an argument. I . . . well, that is . . ." I ran out of words.

"Oliver! How timely! Mister Tibbets was just about to return to the party. Perhaps you would not mind lingering a moment or two while I collect myself."

Before I could respond, Tibbets, now recognizing his antagonist, grabbed my arm.

"I was no such a thing, Ann. And Baldwin should know better than to interrupt our conversation. Be off with you, Baldwin, and leave us be before I do something we'll both likely regret in the morning."

"He'll do no such a thing. Oliver, please stay right here. Josiah, our conversation is finished, clearly. You really should return to the party. I am sure your father or mother is wondering where you have wandered off to!" Miss Perry's voice, no longer the lovely musical sound I had enjoyed earlier, was firm, almost rancorous.

Tibbets recoiled visibly, offered a "humph," added something about "damn midshipmen," and stepped away. I was overjoyed!

"Miss Perry," I began, when I found my voice. "Are you alright? When I returned to find you after the inquisition I received from Mister Little and your father, your mother mentioned you were dancing with Josiah. But I couldn't find you on the dance floor." I stopped, realizing I was spilling out words and likely sounded the fool.

"Well, we did dance a waltz, but he was stumbling all over me and suggested the cool air might help him to clear his head. Then he took me out here, beyond the spill of light, and was trying to convince me he could become a suitor. Something I have absolutely no interest in! And please, call me Ann."

My joy knew no bounds! I wanted to reach out, grab her and pull her to my embrace and, quite possibly, even kiss her. But I restrained, not wanting to act like the besotted Tibbets.

"Thank you, Miss . . . Ann." I could barely speak.

"I would enjoy another dance with you, Oliver, should you be willing. Now that I have calmed down, I notice that it is some cool out here. Shall we?" She smiled in the darkness and I heard the wonderful, soft, musical sound back in her voice.

"It would be entirely my pleasure." I offered her my arm, which she took, it seemed, with some enthusiasm and we walked slowly back down the path, for the second time that evening. And I was careful to avoid whatever it was I had so fortuitously tripped over earlier!

The rest of the evening went by in a blur; Ann and I danced, sipped some punch, and reveled in each other's company—at least, I reveled in hers and she seemed quite comfortable in being with me.

When I took her back, finally, to the table where I had last seen her family, she clutched my arm a bit tighter and turned her head so her lips were close to my ear.

"I hope your ship will remain a while longer, Oliver. I would dearly love to see you again." She whispered her sentiment, but even over the noise of the waning party, I heard every word as though she had shouted to me.

And then, just as she turned her head, her lips brushed the side of my cheek. I had never experienced such rapture! I wanted, once again, to embrace her in my arms and kiss her and never let go. But that would most likely have been most unseemly and ungentlemanly. I restrained myself, looking at her beauty with a silly smile plastered across my face and stammered.

"Oh, my, Miss. . . Ann, I mean. Thank you. That would be wonderful, indeed. Perhaps . . ."

Her brother Matthew chose that moment to rush up to us, words tumbling out of his mouth in a torrent.

"Mister Baldwin! Father has given me permission to come out to *Chesapeake* on the morrow, should that be acceptable to you. I have never been in a frigate, and would dearly love to see one, especially one as famous as yours. May I, sir, please?" He stopped as suddenly as he had started and studied me with wide eyes.

"I, uh, well, that is." I stopped, drew a breath, and realized here was opportunity come a-knocking. "Yes, Matthew, that would be fine. Perhaps your sister might bring you out during the afternoon watch. I can have a boat sent in for you." I shot a glance at Ann; she smiled at me then looked at her brother.

"You have to promise to behave yourself, Matthew. No nonsense like you did on your brother's ship before he sailed."

"Oh, no, Ann. I would not do that. Besides, I expect I will be getting my midshipman's warrant before long—Father has said it would be permissible—and so I would have no need to hide." He stopped, looked at me, and added, "Besides, I don't believe Mister Baldwin's ship is about to sail. Father said Captain Decatur told him there was work needed doin' and they would be in the harbor for several more days, at least."

"The little rascal disappeared in *Revenge* and Oliver and one of his officers spent nearly an hour, scouring the ship, before they turned him up, hiding in a stores room. He was actually trying to stow away!" Ann laughed her delightful laugh as she told me of Matthew's antics.

Missus Perry appeared, on the arm of Captain Perry. She smiled at me and spoke to her children.

"Our carriage is waiting. Say good evening to Mister Baldwin and come along." Then she turned to me. "A pleasure to make your acquaintance, Mister Baldwin. I trust I shall see you again before long."

"Oh yes, I certainly hope so. And it was a great pleasure to meet both of you and your family. I shall look forward to meeting Ann's older brother at some time in the future." I bowed to Ann's mother and extended my hand to the captain. He took it, looking me in the eyes.

"I enjoyed your tale of the attack on *Philadelphia*, young man. And I am sorry to have insulted you with my earlier remark. You are the type of lad I would wish to have under my command, were I still thought useful by our Navy. A good evening to you, sir."

And they left. Ann turned once, looking back at me, and smiled. I grinned back at her, feeling foolish, but was quite unable to help myself.

CHAPTER FOURTEEN

Henry Allen and I had the watch, midnight until four in the morning. The ship was under easy sail, riding pleasantly to the long swell of the Atlantic, as we made our way down the coast of Long Island. Stars lit the heavens, and the moon, now on the wane, added its gentle glow to night, making it not difficult at all to see all the way to the bowsprit as it described its arc across the sky. Neither of us had spoken in some time, not out of any animus, but simply as there was nothing much to talk about. And we were enjoying the peace and quiet of the night, listening to the whisper of the wind through the rig and the gentle burbling of the water as *Chesapeake's* bow parted the seas. A cluster of men, the sail-handlers of our watch section, sat or leaned on the spardeck gun carriages, smoking and yarning quietly. Their cheroots and pipes glowed briefly in the darkness and, from time to time, described a bright arc over the side as one or another finished his cigar.

After a lengthy silence, Henry spoke. "I have been meaning to ask you, Oliver, who was that most attractive young lady I noticed in your company aboard last week? I keep meaning to bring it up, but have either not had the chance, or in the press of getting the repairs done and getting the ship underway, quite forgot. You seemed most attentive to her."

I had taken some good natured teasing in the cockpit about Ann's visit to the ship after the ball, as well as my reluctance to participate ashore in the adventures my colleagues from my mess enjoyed, preferring, instead, to hire a horse and ride to South Kingstown. Of course, I also had to work on the ship, overseeing some modifications to the great guns and the magazine, as well as stand my watches on board.

But Henry's question was not asked in the spirit of making sport of me and I answered it earnestly.

"Oh, Henry! Isn't she wonderful? I met her at the ball and am quite smitten by her. She is so charming and warm, and interested in what I have to say. She has a brother, also named Oliver, who is lieutenant and commands the schooner *Revenge*. A fourteen gunner, she is. Her father was a captain during that business with France in the last century."

I knew my enthusiasm had gotten the best of me, but it seemed I had no control over it when speaking—or thinking—of Ann. Which I had done almost nonstop since we won our anchor from the mud of Newport Harbor. Everywhere I went on the ship made me think of her visit; walking through the gun deck would bring back our conversation (how much she—and I—enjoyed the dances we shared the night before) and a visit to the galley made me recall that she had taken my hand as we stepped into the space. That her brother had been present barely signified in my memory.

"Well! Sounds to me like you are some taken with the young lady. But you have not told me her name, Oliver. Her brother's, certainly, but not her Christian name, nor her family name. Is it something you wish kept secret?" Henry's tone had a smile in it. A glance at him, lit by the reflection of the binnacle, confirmed it.

"Oh my goodness, not a bit! Her name is Ann . . . Ann Perry. And her brother is Oliver Hazard—Perry, of course."

"I know Oliver Hazard! A fine officer and well qualified to command that schooner. Sailed with him in the Mediterranean with Bainbridge. During that unpleasant time the Dey of Algiers forced us to carry his tribute to the pasha in Constantinople. Dreadful humiliating, it was. Perry was a midshipman in *George Washington,* same as me, then. We was too young and inexperienced to say much, but I can tell you, we spent a lot of breath talking among ourselves in the cockpit about what a disgrace it was, both for the Navy and the United States.

"Course, he was some senior to me, but we got on famously. Very pleasant chap, but terrible prone to getting seasick.

"I had heard he was ashore after the trouble with the Barbary corsairs ended, right about when he passed for lieutenant. I remember thinking what a blessing it was for him."

Recalling Ann's description of her brother's restiveness during his sojourn ashore, I replied, "Well, according to Ann, he hated it. And then he was assigned building gunboats, same as Edward was. Hated that too. Finally got to sea and got his own ship. Couldn't have been bothered much by the seasickness; he spent the years ashore writing the Navy for a ship. Right pleased, he was, according to his family, when he was assigned in *Revenge.*"

"It surely appears you have spent some considerable time with Miss Perry. I assume you didn't spend all of it discussing her brother's naval career!"

I noted his good humor and chose not to answer his statement. Instead, I simply smiled in the darkness, my mind once again enjoying our bittersweet visit in South Kingstown the day before *Chesapeake* left Newport. I glanced aloft, seeing her face in the sky and hearing her musical laugh in the breeze.

"Sail! Sail broad on the larboard bow. Appears to be ship-rigged, sir."

The lookout's hail to the quarterdeck stopped our conversation and jerked me out of my reverie about Ann Perry. Shattered were the images of the lady and the sounds of her voice. For several heartbeats, not a soul made a sound; only the groans and squeaks made by a ship underway broke the sudden silence and added emphasis to the man's cry.

"Aloft with you, Oliver. See what you make of her, and back as quick as ever possible, if you please." Henry handed me his night glass as he spoke.

Who could that be? Well, likely not a concern as we aren't at war with any country.

I glassed the ship from the main fighting top. Indeed she was ship-rigged. What the lookout had not included in his report was that she was making a course that would cross us, and close aboard. It appeared she was perhaps a league away and making a fair turn of speed, to judge from the ghostly white bone in her teeth. And she looked to be under a greater press of canvas than *Chesapeake* carried. I slung the glass over my shoulder and hurried back to the quarterdeck to make my report. I noted that several of the watch standers, earlier taking their ease, were now lining the bulwark trying to catch a glimpse of the approaching ship, and no doubt recalling another encounter in peacetime with another ship.

"Jump down, if you please, Oliver, and inform Cap'n Decatur I intend to beat to quarters directly. If this turns out to be nothing, so be it; it will be good training for the men. However, I'll not be caught short again, not ever. We will be prepared should this vessel have some mischief in mind." Henry's tone would brook no delay and I obeyed his order with alacrity.

By the time I returned to the quarterdeck, our commander close in my wake, the Marine was well into the drum call for quarters and I could hear running footsteps pounding on the decks and ladders as men, still groggy from sleep, moved to the battle stations. Gunports were heaved up, clattering against the side of the ship and topmen swarmed aloft, under the direction of the sailing master and bosun, to await the order to reduce our spread of canvas to battle sail.

"What is *this* about, Allen? Sometimes I think you would do anything to disrupt my slumber. Can you not simply stand a watch, quietly, peacefully, and let those of us below remain at rest?" Peter Stoll's nasal voice was raised beyond what might have been necessary; I suspect he was aware of Decatur's presence and hoped that he might curry some favor with him.

"Mister Stoll: had you ever seen action, real action, I mean, you might understand that it is better to be prepared than caught sleeping." Henry fairly snarled at his colleague.

"To my knowledge, Henry, we are not at war with any at the moment, unless some disaster has recently occurred while I was below." Stoll answered the snarl with a patronizing tone suitable for a none-too-bright student.

"Aye, Mister Stoll. And in June of ought seven we were at war with none, either. Had you been aboard this vessel then, you might even thank me for going to quarters. Are you prepared to relieve Mister Baldwin of his responsibilities? I see that Mister Rowe is here to assume the deck." Henry addressed his comment to Stoll but had turned to the first lieutenant as he approached, ready to be relieved.

I noticed that Captain Decatur had missed most of the exchange between Henry and Stoll; he had taken a glass and was midway up the mizzen ratlines studying the approaching vessel.

He returned as Allen and I headed below to the gundeck and our own battle stations. But I did hear him remark to Mister Rowe that the vessel was showing the Cross of Saint George, making her British.

Well then. Most likely, we're not going to fight tonight. Course, Leopard *was British as well and we weren't at war then, either.*

My brain continued to argue with itself as I mechanically went through the process of getting my guns, three on either side of the ship, ready to fire. Matches were lit and stuck in buckets of sand, another of my crew spread sand liberally around the deck to provide traction for us should the deck become slippery with blood, and several others stacked cartridges by each cannon, ready for instant use. Of course, the guns were already loaded, their breeching tackles uncoiled and laid out alongside. Gun captains at each gun used their awls to puncture the powder cartridge already residing in each barrel, and have at hand a quantity of powder with which they would prime the guns.

"Mister Baldwin. Are you ready and is your battery ready?" Henry Allen called to me, his voice carrying easily over the cacophony of the gun deck.

"Aye, sir. Ready in all respects. Sir."

"Then make your report to the first lieutenant, if you please, and do it personally. I am sending Mister Mosley along with you."

I saw David Mosley scampering toward me, presumably with the report that the entire battery on the gundeck was prepared, manned, and ready.

When we arrived on the quarterdeck, First Lieutenant Rowe was in conversation with the captain while Peter Stoll stood at the windward rail glassing the approaching vessel. I stepped up to the two seniors and, keeping a respectful distance so as not to intrude in their conversation, waited. Decatur took notice of our arrival—it might have been that Mosley was virtually dancing a jig, so palpable was his excitement at what might develop into his first action—and turned to me.

"Yes, Mister Baldwin?"

"Cap'n, the battery is ready in all respects, sir." I doffed my hat in a salute as I made my report.

"Mister Allen's compliments, sir. The battery is ready in all respects, sir." Mosley doffed his own hat as he repeated my report as Henry had instructed him.

Decatur smiled thinly at the young man's enthusiasm. "Thank you, gentlemen. I am hopeful our preparedness will be unnecessary. You may return to your duties."

"Aye, sir." We replied, almost as one.

Mosley seemed reluctant to return to the gundeck, apparently wishing to linger and watch the developing situation from topside. I saw his glance move upwards, where the shadowy figures of our Marines lined the fighting top, their muskets glinting dully in the moonlight. With a gentle touch on his arm, I steered him toward the companionway. But not before I heard Stoll's nasal whine announce that the British ship was standing on, unwavering in her course which would likely intersect our own in short order.

"Sailing Master: we'll reduce to battle sail, if you please." Rowe's shouted order carried well forward and was answered with a faint "aye" and the clomping of leather-clad feet as the topmen headed for the rigging.

By the time I arrived at my post, the forward battery on the gundeck, I could feel the ship beginning to slow as she responded to the reduction in canvas. I peered out the open gunport of the forward-most gun. There she was, the bone in her teeth clearly visible in the moonlight, and now not even a mile distant. Her course seemed unchanged. To my mind, unless one of us veered, we would collide.

With our reduced speed, she should have passed clear ahead with little problem. But she must have altered to weather to ensure a confrontation! Why would they do that?

My mind churned with the conundrum, unable to come to grips with the fact that this British vessel seemed bent on ramming us. We were not at war, there was, as yet, no trading between our countries thanks to Jefferson's embargo, and no reason for this behavior. I looked again through the port. Still she came on, with no slackening of her pace judging from her frothing white bow wave.

"Mister Allen: fire a leeward gun, if you please. NOW." Rowe's voice left no doubt in any mind that trouble was definitely afoot, and Decatur was doing his best to avoid a confrontation.

"Mister Baldwin, stand to your gun. You may fire number one. Quickly, please." Allen's voice rumbled up the gundeck.

With a nod to my gun captain for both forward-most thirty-two-pounders, already standing by his charge, I relayed Henry's order to fire.

I watched as he poured a charge of powder into the pan on top of the barrel and jammed a brightly glowing slowmatch, held securely in the linstock, into the puddle of powder. It sparkled brightly, sizzling as it consumed itself, and burned down the touch hole and into the flannel-wrapped charge of powder tucked securely in the barrel. A split second later the cannon roared out, shooting a blinding tongue of orange flame a dozen feet into the night.

After the huge gun had come to rest in its breeching tackles, the crew jumped into action, swabbing out the barrel to rid it of any burning embers from the powder, and ramming home a fresh bag of powder and a ball. Finally, the crew heaved around on the side tackles and dragged the dead weight of the wheeled carriage back into its firing position with the muzzle poking out through the gunport.

I watched the process long enough to be certain that the gun captain had everything well in hand, then turned my attention to the open port opposite the just-fired gun. I could barely believe my eyes. There she was, barely a pistol shot distant, bearing down on us under a huge press of canvas. I knew every man not otherwise engaged would be watching her progress and wondering, as I was, why she did not alter her course to avoid the almost certain collision that would occur if one of us did not. With the ship headed fair for our larboard bow (which also happened to be on the weather side), he was forcing Decatur to tack to avoid a collision. Wearing or even bearing off would not answer at this point; there simply was not time.

"Topmen aloft! Line handlers to stations for tacking the ship. Lively now, lads. Look alive, there." The sailing master's voice carried with it all the urgency needed to inspire the sailors to alacrity. And the sight of the British frigate full and by, heading right for us, surely added to the enthusiasm felt by the topmen and haulers!

I followed a clutch of sailors up the ladder to the spar deck as my sail handling position was aft, supervising the men on the mizzen. By the time I arrived, sheets and braces were in hand, men were almost to the cro'jack yard and I heard the order to "put over your helm, quartermaster."

Slowly, the bow came up, led by our rakish jibboom, as it described an agonizingly slow arc across the star-filled sky. I shot a glance at the Brit; still coming on. She sailed as though there was not another soul on the sea. I could not help but wonder, as I am sure Decatur and Rowe were wondering, what on earth the captain of that ship was thinking. They could not miss seeing us, and our leeward cannon, had their lookouts been asleep, would have surely called attention to our presence.

"Tops'ls in hand, sir." Came the faint cry from aloft, relayed aft by the bosun.

"Back the jibs and stays'ls, if you please, Sailing Master." Decatur's voice carried clearly over the noise of a ship tacking, slapping lines, flogging canvas, shouted orders. "Keep your helm over, Quartermaster. Should we miss stays, we will surely be in jeopardy."

I looked forward again; the jibboom still swung, but more slowly. I saw that if we completed our turn without missing stays, we would escape being hit by the British ship, but only by a whisker. If we missed stays and hung in irons, it was clear to anyone, even a landsman, that we would be struck. And still the Brit came on. I don't believe there was a man aboard *Chesapeake* who was not praying, with every fiber of his being, that our ship would complete the tack!

Gradually, *Chesapeake* followed her bowsprit through the eye of the wind. I could feel the breeze as it now blew over the starboard bow and the ship as she responded to it. Square sails filled, one after the other, with a loud *whooomph*, and voices were raised, giving orders to sheet them in. I could sense that every man topside finally released the breath he had held, waiting for the inevitable crash; some men I could see were clapping each other on the backs and shouting epithets at the British ship as she sailed by.

"A pleasant good evening to you, *Jonathans!*" The strong English voice that floated down to us from the deck of the Royal Navy frigate sounded scornful, chiding, almost as if we had passed one another on a clear day with ample sea room.

I glanced at the quarterdeck to see what reaction might come from Decatur and Rowe. I certainly knew what I would do, and likely, what my friend Henry Allen would do as well. But I had no idea what our captain might do.

As I watched, the captain leaped onto the bulwark just forward of where I stood, a speaking trumpet in hand.

"You, sir, are as ignorant of the rules of navigation as you are arrogant! And a dull sailer as well." Decatur's voice carried easily across the water and I saw a jaunty wave offered in response.

"Mister Rowe: you may stand down from quarters and set a normal at-sea watch. And maintain vigilance; should that . . . *fool* return, he may get a taste of my iron!" Decatur was angry, in a rare black humor, and I had little doubt that were the Brit to reappear, shots might well be exchanged.

Henry appeared on deck when the ship secured from quarters. Even in the darkness, I could see the anger, frustration, and hate etched into his face. Lines around his mouth—his lips formed a thin straight line—told me he was clenching his teeth, perhaps to avoid saying what he thought.

Do I still have the watch? What time is it?

I fished my watch out of my pocket and, holding it in the glow of the binnacle, was surprised to see that barely an hour had passed since the lookout's cry had galvanized the ship and crew into the frenzy just ended. I still had the watch, as did Henry.

"Mister Rowe: I am here to relieve you, sir." Allen spoke sharply, his tone provoking a look from the first lieutenant.

"Very well, Mister Allen. You may resume our earlier course. The hands are still at sheets and braces, the tops manned. As you know, we are secured from quarters." Rowe stated the facts and the condition of the ship in a flat, unemotional voice. He made no reference to the British frigate or our encounter.

I relieved Lieutenant Stoll who took the opportunity to glare at Henry as he left the quarterdeck to return to his "slumber"; he had another hour before he would be back to take the watch over from Henry, Silas Taggart with him to relieve me.

The ship quieted down after we tacked her back to our earlier course following the coastline of Long Island in a generally sou'westerly direction. The night was as clear and star-filled, the sea as gently rolling, and the breeze as pleasant as before our encounter; to the forces of nature, it was as though nothing had changed. But to the men, especially Henry Allen, much had changed.

Memories of past meetings with ships of the Royal Navy, most notably HMS *Leopard* occupied our thoughts and, more than likely, the thoughts of every man still aboard who experienced that horrifying day in June of ought seven. This time we had escaped without exchanging iron; who knew what might happen when next we crossed tacks with one of His Majesty's warships?

"You know, that arrogant bastard was no different from the one what chased us in *George Washington* when I was with Bainbridge. *Dragon* it was. I recall it like it happened yesterday." Henry's cryptic remark broke into my own thoughts.

"I don't believe you've mentioned that before, Henry. You have told me of the pasha in Algiers commandeering *George Washington* to deliver his own tribute to the Turks, but I have not heard about a British ship chasing you." I glanced aloft to ensure that our sails were all satisfactorily filled as I spoke.

"We were about three weeks out from the Delaware Cape. A calm passage with fine weather and the rare contact. *George Washington* was a purchased vessel and a dull sailer; Bainbridge hated her for that reason. But we had enjoyed a reasonable cruise to that point. One morning the lookouts espied several ships, frigates and brigs, as I recall. None showed any colors.

"As we drew nearer to the ships—they were well to our north—one of them hauled her wind and headed for us. Shortly, they fired a gun to leeward and showed their colors: Brit, as you might expect. We answered her gun with our own and hoisted our own colors. But Bainbridge was in a rage.

"He stormed around the quarterdeck, smacking his fist into his hand. Kept up a steady stream of blasphemies, all aimed at the Brits, he did.

"I remember the first lieutenant asked him if we should heave to as the signal requested; Bainbridge flew into a rage and ordered more sail set." Henry stopped, his face contorted with the same anger I had witnessed earlier.

"But if your ship was such a dull sailer, he couldn't expect to outrun the Brit. Why not just heave to and find out what they wanted?" I asked in all innocence.

And got a fierce look from my friend.

"Oliver, they had no right then, nor did they in ought seven, to order a warship from another country, a friendly nation at that, to heave to. We were not at war with England then any more that we were when *Leopard* stopped this ship. But what happened next defies all understanding; they fired another gun, this time *loaded*. Of course, they were well out of range, but we clearly saw the shot land a half musket shot astern. I thought then that, had we been more heavily armed, Bainbridge would have rounded up and returned their fire. Instead, he crowded on as much sail as the old bucket would handle and bore off a trifle to increase our speed.

"The Brits responded to that with another gun, also loaded, which again fell short. They were still well out of range. But they set more sail and came after us. We went to quarters, I reckon, expecting we would have to fight. I think every man-Jack aboard knew that should it come to that, we would suffer cruelly. But there were no shirkers.

"For seven hours, Oliver, they chased us across the sea. Finally, even I knew they were within range of their bow-chaser and they fired another shot close on board of us. Bainbridge had no choice but to heave to as ordered; their firepower was simply overwhelming and we stood not a chance in a hundred of coming through an engagement, or even an exchange of iron, without being turned into matchwood.

"The Brits came within hailing distance, identified themselves as HMS *Dragon* and bore off after wishing us a pleasant cruise. Never have I seen anyone, before or since, as angry as Bainbridge was that day. I am quite convinced that should we have had sufficient weight of iron, he would have engaged them, friendly relations to the devil!"

He stopped and the sounds of the ship, the creaking of the hull, the gentle song of the wind through our rigging, and the music of the water against our sides, filled the night. Henry was lost in his own thoughts, no doubt recalling that day, our meeting with HMS *Leopard,* and our recent encounter with the unknown Royal Navy ship. The arrogance and degrading behavior of the Royal Navy toward us was clearly weighing heavily on him. His mouth was screwed tight shut, like he had bitten into something sour.

No wonder he holds such animus toward the Royal Navy! I thought as I watched his face gradually relax and return to its normal expression.

There was nothing to say further. I left Henry to his recollections of unpleasant encounters with the Royal Navy and I spent the remainder of our watch seeing to the needs of the ship and thinking about Ann Perry. Peter Stoll was, for a change, on time to relieve Henry, and Silas took over for me with barely a comment.

CHAPTER FIFTEEN

November 20th 1809

My dear Brother:

It is with great joy that I announce my wonderful good news to you. I have passed for lieutenant! Just this morning I have been informed by Capt. Decatur that my examinations, both the oral part and the written navigation section were satisfactory and, as he is taking me with him and Henry Allen (I am sure you remember him from when you visited the ship in Norfolk) to his new command, USS *United States*, there is an immediate opening for me to serve in my new rank. I needn't wait for a suitable position to occur here in Chesapeake, an unlikely event with our present officer complement.

We set our anchor in the Bay nearly a month back, in from a long cruise that was mostly frustrating—training and more training in every aspect of our lives from sail handling to the firing of the great guns. We midshipmen were schooled constantly in navigation and mathematics, as well as gentlemanly behavior. Few port visits were allowed, but I must tell you about our visit to Newport, in Rhode Island.

The officers and mids were invited to a ball at a grand house. At the start of it, I felt somewhat out of place. All these grand people cavorting about, dancing and visiting while we—the mids especially—simple stood by and watched. Then, quite without warning, I met a young woman who has, to put it most simply, stolen my heart. She is most beautiful, Edward, and seems equally smitten with me. We danced and I was invited to sup with her family. Her father, a capt. during the French war, was some brusque, but her mother seemed very pleasant. She has several brothers— I met one, a young man called Matthew, who aspires to the navy life. Another you may have encountered—Oliver Hazard Perry is his name—and he currently commands the schooner Revenge. He was at sea during my time in Newport so I did not meet him. Ann—that is her name—and I spent much of my off-duty time enjoying each other's company, both in Newport and in South Kingstown, in her family's home. Truly a wonderful time and sad—for both of us, I believe—when our frigate won her anchor from the mud of Newport and returned us Chesapeakes to our life at sea.

A close encounter with a frigate of the Royal Navy during our passage to the Bay, designed to embarrass and humiliate a vessel of the United States Navy, was our only diversion during our run south. With the provocative attitude those people possess, I shouldn't wonder if we will once again do battle with them.

I trust your employment continues as you stated in your last letter. I share in your joy at being assigned in *Constitution*. She is reputed to be a fine vessel, well built, well gunned, and with competent management. And now, Brother, you are part of the management which would bear testimony to the fact that she is indeed well staffed! You may recall that while you were languishing in the Bashaw's prison, *Constitution* was standing offshore and in the harbor, pounding the fortifications along with many other vessels of the Mediterranean Squadron. I am sure you remember she was Preble's flagship while I sailed with Decatur in *Enterprise*. I look forward to hearing more of your adventures in that fine ship. Perhaps, once Capt. Decatur gets *United States* to sea, we might even sail in company some day. Would that not be splendid?

"Oliver! Are you coming? Our boat is waiting." Henry's insistent shout down the companionway signaled the end of my correspondence with my brother and I hastily scribbled a closing.

I must post this quickly as my time on Chesapeake has come to an end and I, along with Henry, am heading for the Washington Navy Yard this very afternoon. He is to be first lieutenant on the frigate—did I mention she is *Constitution*'s sister ship?—and I will be fourth lieutenant, or perhaps fifth depending on what other officers Decatur can gather. I suspect our work will be rigorous as we shall have to bring the frigate to life from her several years in ordinary. But we shall manage, and what a wonderful opportunity for yours truly.

God speed to you, Edward. Please write when you can spare a line or two for your brother,

Oliver Baldwin

4th Lieutenant, United States frigate *United States*.

Quickly, I sprinkled some sand over the wet ink, wiped my quill, and jammed it into the leather writing case which my parents had given me when I left their home on Held Street to sail with Decatur in *Argus*. Blowing the sand onto the deck, I folded the letter into an envelope and dashed up the ladder to find Henry pacing the deck by the break in the bulwark, a look of consternation on his face.

"About time, Lieutenant! You may step into the boat, if you please."

The tone he used suggested nothing beyond a desire to get on with moving bag and baggage to Washington Navy Yard and our new responsibilities. Besides, hearing him refer to me as "lieutenant," made me smile regardless of any tone he might have used.

With our sea chests and belongings already in the boat, we both climbed in and set out for shore, propelled by the strong arms of four sailors on the oars. Once there, a waiting carriage would carry us to Washington and our new assignment. Despite the bleak November weather, I was ebullient with anticipation, whether because of my new status or the new assignment, continuing to serve with both Henry Allen and Captain Decatur in a wonderful heavy frigate, I knew, nor cared, not a whit. I was quite in thrall regardless!

"It is too bad that Cap'n Decatur will not be aboard when we get there, Oliver. I could do with his guidance. Never have I brought a ship into commission before, save *Chesapeake* under Gordon. And *that* was surely not a teaching experience, except perhaps in what *not* to do!" Henry chuckled at his remark, but I suspected both the remark and his laugh covered a bout of nerves brought about by his, and my, new assignments. We continued to talk about what we might find, as we bounced along in the coach, and compared our conjecture to what we had experienced in *Chesapeake*.

"At least *United States* isn't burdened with the reputation of being a 'bad-luck-ship' as far as I have heard. Should make it easier to find some willing hands. I will, of course, want you to oversee that process, Oliver. Set up some rendezvous under whatever warrants or midshipmen we might have available and try to sign a crew." Henry's tone had qualities I would expect in the first lieutenant. Perhaps he was simply 'trying it on for size.'

"Aye, sir. Do you have information on any of our officers or mids, sir?" I wondered, at the same time acknowledging his role as second in command of the ship.

"Only that we will have a clutch of midshipmen and another officer who calls himself Devon; I know not whether that is a Christian name or surname. According to what little intelligence I have gathered in my talks with the cap'n, this Devon fellow claims to have been involved in some of the scrap with the pirates in North Africa. And I believe Decatur mentioned he either knew him or had met him." He shrugged and finished, "I reckon we'll both find out when we get aboard."

Devon! Could that be Judd Devon? *Senior midshipman in* Argus *and* Enterprise? *He participated in the 'scrap' with those pirates as surely as I did. And, of course, Captain Decatur would have known him. Perchance he even requested him! Wouldn't that be a grand thing? And he would be a lieutenant by now also. Senior to me, of course. Oh! I hope it is Judd; it will be good to see him again. And won't he be surprised to see me, especially with my new swab!*

"I knew a man called Devon—Judd Devon it was—and should it be the same man, he surely did fight the corsairs in Barbary. He was a midshipman then, but a good deal senior to me . . . as was everyone else in the cockpit, save one. A good man, Devon, and you would be lucky to have him in the Gunroom, should it turn out to be the self-same Judd Devon I knew some four or five years back. Sir." I offered what intelligence I had more as conversation than real wisdom, and added the 'sir' because Lieutenant Allen seemed to have fit himself quite nicely into the role of first lieutenant already.

"Well, we'll have to wait and see who it might be. Perhaps you are right and it is your former shipmate. Perhaps not.

"And you may continue to call me Henry when we are alone. We go back too far and have seen too much together to do otherwise." He smiled warmly—the old Henry was back—and, putting his head back against the jouncing seat, closed his eyes, making it quite clear he was finished with our chatter.

For a while, I watched out the window as the trees lining the road gradually gave way to a few shops, taverns, and inns and then, with equal reluctance, the buildings surrendered their claim to more trees. It was fast becoming full dark, so I followed Henry's lead and closed my eyes as well.

My beloved Ann, was leaning towards me, intent on kissing me yet again as we stood on a bluff overlooking the sea somewhere. The kisses were her way of congratulating me on my promotion to lieutenant. As her lips neared mine, I closed my eyes.

She spoke. "Time to heave out and trice up, Lieutenant." But her accent was not the wonderful, sweet tones I recalled; it was a man's voice. Startled, both at her words and her tenor, I opened my eyes and looked straight into the eyes of my traveling companion and new first lieutenant, Henry Allen.

He smiled, almost as if he was aware that he had, once again, spoiled a wonderful dream.

I struggled up from the depths of my slumber, gradually acknowledging that my dear Ann was not about to kiss me.

"Aye, sir. I'm awake. We are arrived, I collect?"

"We are indeed, Lieutenant. And, as I am famished, I submit we see our gear aboard and find some supper. What say you to that?"

As I heaved myself out of the coach, I realized that my belly growled in protest at not having been fed since well earlier in the day and smiled my agreement. Our chests and associated paraphernalia were mostly on the ground aside the coach, having been thrown down by the coachman to his associate. Henry was already heading for the ship, or what I took to be our ship.

A more forlorn sight I could not imagine. Before me, tied to a decrepit pier, was a large frigate—or what I took to be a frigate, based mainly on Henry's announcement that we had arrived. Three masts, lowers only, stood with slack shrouds, and poked through a wooden roof which had been constructed over the spardeck. Paint seemed to be falling off of everything I could see, from the masts to the bulwarks. Some of the gunports stood open and latched up; other were adrift, neither open nor closed, and still more seemed to be secured in their closed position. That is, until I looked more closely and discovered that what I had taken for gunports were, in fact, several boards simply nailed over the openings in both the spardeck and the gundeck.

As I drew closer to the vessel, I could see garbage and other jetsam jamming the water between the hull and the pier. A gangway extended from the deck to the pier and, seeing that Henry had already stepped over it and onto the deck of the ship, I followed, casting my glance aloft. My brain reeled at the sorry sight of the mainmast, complete with a skewed fighting top and a passel of ropes hanging down. I moved my eyes forward and kept walking, astonished at the horror spread out before me. And stopped when I bumped squarely into my superior's back.

"Here, Baldwin. Mind your step." Henry caught himself (fortunately I did not hit him hard enough to knock him over) by grabbing my outstretched arm. "Have you ever seen such a wreck? And they expect *me* to put this . . . this *ship* . . . into useable condition, let alone make her capable of sailing? Oh my goodness! What have I gotten myself into!"

I had not experienced this part of my friend, mentor, and now, first lieutenant. His shoulders slumped; his whole demeanor seemed . . . well, beaten. He wore the mantle of his newfound responsibility uncomfortably, much like a man in coat and trousers several sizes too large for him. He was nothing like the angry, outraged Henry Allen I had known throughout the entire *Chesapeake Leopard* affair, including the courts martial of Baron, Gordon, and the others. Then he was undaunted by man or event, and confident.

I hesitated, not knowing how to respond to his outburst.

Finally, I tried something my mother used to say to make me feel better. "Things will look better in the light of a new day, Henry." Then I added, for good measure, "And on a full belly."

"Aye, I suppose you might be right. Besides, what choice do I have? I wonder if there are any aboard." He stepped forward toward a companionway, picking his way through coils of line (rotten), blocks (split and broken), and casks (mostly sprung) that littered the deck.

"Halllooo! Anyone below?" Henry shouted down the ladder, his voice echoing with a hollow eeriness into the void below. Silence responded to him.

He tried again, a bit louder.

Still nothing.

"Very well, Oliver. Apparently we are the first to arrive. Let us find a pursers' glim and move our chests below."

They had been somewhat unceremoniously dropped on deck, just at the end of the gangway.

"And then we shall find a suitable place to feed us." He slapped me on the arm in a most jovial manner.

At least he is back to his old self, again. But what a daunting task lies ahead. How ever will we manage it? Heave to there, Oliver. You're sounding just like Henry a short while ago.

He started down the ladder, cautiously, feeling for each step in the Stygian blackness of the companionway. I waited until I heard him sufficiently below me that I would not again run into him and then started my own self down into the lower level. As I reached the bottom of the ladder, I put out my hand and felt Henry's back in front of me. We both waited, listening.

All we heard was the scrabble of little clawed feet scampering away from the intruders.

"I'd reckon we might have some company tonight." Henry said softly.

"Would it not make some sense to find a suitable lodging ashore for tonight, Henry?" I, quite frankly, did not care a bit for sharing my accommodations, no matter how rude they might be, with the owners of the feet I heard running about the deck.

"You are not afraid of the dark, are you, Oliver?" Without waiting for an answer, he stepped forward, then stopped.

More scampering sounds reached our ears. Then he fished in his pocket and produced a phosphorus match, which, bending down to the deck, he struck.

We both blinked in the bright flare of the match. Dozens of rats scurried around before us, and the disarray of the gundeck was, if anything, worse than we had encountered topside. Piles of canvas, cordage, and casks littered the decks, each one a suitable hiding place for an entire colony of the furry rodents.

Then the all too brief flame burned down to his fingers and, with an exclamation, he shook it out and once again, plunged us into an even darker environment.

"You might be right, Oliver. Step back to the ladder and let us return topside. At least then we won't be falling all over each other!" He did not mention that it was I who had fallen all over him, for which I was grateful, and I turned, stuck out my hand, and happily, felt the side of the ladder. Which I climbed back up into the dim light of the spardeck.

A chill November breeze greeted us and stirred the dirt on the deck, swirling it into little clouds, lit by the watery glow of the moon. I pulled my great coat tighter around me, and in spite of myself, shivered in the cold. I could imagine how cold it would become later, in the darkness of the lower decks.

Our possessions were exactly where our coachman and his assistant had left them, though why they should be otherwise—or gone—was too silly to contemplate; there simply was no one around to disturb them.

"I don't fancy hauling those chests anywhere, Oliver. I propose we tuck them away out of sight and leave them for morning when, as you suggested, this will all look less daunting." He stood by the small pile, his foot resting on my sea chest, and glanced about, as if looking for someone to find fault with his suggestion.

"I would imagine, Henry, that no one has been aboard this vessel in weeks, maybe months. Ain't likely to come aboard tonight, just as we leave our belongings here." And I certainly did not have any more wish to carry my own chest somewhere than did my superior.

We pushed them behind some casks, threw a scrap of canvas over them, and retraced our steps over the gangway to the pier.

"You were still snoring, Oliver, but when we arrived here, I noticed a tavern just outside the Navy Yard . . ." He hesitated, looking about to get his bearings, then pointed. "That way, I believe, and not terribly far. Perhaps a rifle shot or two should see us there." And off he went, following his outstretched arm.

It happened that his instinct was right. And we both recognized the establishment from our time spent putting *Chesapeake* to rights several years ago. Not a bad place, with palatable vittles and unwatered spirits. We found a clutch of officers sitting 'round a large table laughing and yarning, the ruins of a meal distributed across its scarred surface, unnoticed, in the light of tankards of ale and rum before each. On their invitation, we joined them.

CHAPTER SIXTEEN

"Those fellows certainly seemed to know the ropes last night, I'd warrant. And their faint praise for the craftsmen here did little to bolster my confidence in getting this barky back to sea, Oliver." Henry shared his feelings as we approached the pier to which was secured our "barky."

There was little I could say; he was quite right on both counts. I simply nodded as I continued to stride forward, trying to show a confidence I myself doubted.

We both stopped to study the United States frigate *United States* from halfway down the long pier. In the emaciated morning light of mid-November our ship looked little better than she had last night; paint still peeled, gunports were cocked, hanging, or missing, and the rigging was as slack as I had imagined it to be last night. There was nothing rigged above the lower masts, no yards were slung in their ties, and two of the three fighting tops seemed to be balanced precariously on top of the stubby spars. She floated high; obviously her ballast had been removed along with her guns.

"Hello. Who do you suppose that might be?" Henry pointed to a disreputable looking wharf-rat leaning on a piling of the pier, his foot on a broken cask. He wore a slouch hat pulled low over his face, a patched and dirty greatcoat that appeared to have once belonged to an officer, and trousers of filthy canvas. But what drew our attention was the singularly large pistol, stuck in a wide leather belt cinched around his waist, in full view of any. His gaze, from under the brim of his hat, was focused on us.

"Surely not a seaman, I'd warrant." I offered the comment under my breath more to cover my discomfort at the specter before us than to add any information to our store of knowledge.

Another image from some years ago jumped into my brain: that of Edward Langford, former sailor and wharf-rat who had robbed me in

Boston. He was easily as disreputable in appearance as the gent now blocking our way into the frigate and most likely, they were brothers in arms, though I doubted either knew the other. We approached him, albeit a trifle cautiously.

"I'd reckon you two fine lookin' gents come to do sompin' on the ship? That be about right, then?" His voice was a deep, resonant rumbling sound, and seemed to come from the bottom of a barrel.

Henry took a step forward, preparing to answer the man's query as I studied him. He was quite tall, and if one were to judge from his face, remarkably thin; I could see little of his body, wrapped as he was in the greatcoat. His mouth, when it opened, was little more than a hole in the scraggily beard that covered his face from ears to chin and up to his nose that stuck out like an island from the fur surrounding it. A nose, I thought, suppressing a giggle, more appropriate to the face of a hawk than a man. Two teeth, that I could see, were prominent in the front of his mouth, one pointing north, the other pointing south. His hands remained hidden from our view, stuck as they were in the pockets of his coat. I was relieved to note that the enormous pistol remained where it had been, secured in the front of the moldy leather belt, apparently unnoticed (at least by him). Or perhaps, he thought us no threat to whatever he guarded.

"Aye, sir. That would be a correct assumption." Henry asserted, his authority over the ship and all that attached to her in plain evidence. "And what would be your interest in the vessel?"

"What do ye have in mind to be doin' to her?" He asked, quite ignoring Henry's own question.

"We will be restoring the vessel to active duty, taking her out of ordinary and returning her to a condition acceptable to the Navy." He paused, momentarily, studying his inquisitor who still had moved nothing but his mouth. "And what matter would that be to you, sir?" He repeated.

"It's my home. Been livin' here nigh on to two years, now. Don't take it lightly you boys're takin' my home away. Where do you propose I am to go?" The hollow rumble seemed to echo in the air as his deep-set eyes narrowed, shifting between Henry and me. The effect was singularly startling, emphasized by the bushiness of his brows.

"Well, surely you can not remain aboard as the ship is part of the Navy and only my sailors and officers and the craftsmen from the Navy Yard will be allowed in her. So where you go to live, sir, is not my concern. Anywhere but here would be quite satisfactory to me and, I am sure, my colleague." Henry shot a glance at me and I nodded my concurrence, as expected.

"I know ever' board and line in that there barky, lad. I been ever'where in her; top o' the lowers to the bottom o' the bilge. I know where things is you'll be needin' and you'd be right silly you throw that help by the boards. Aye, you surely would. You make it worth my while an' I'll see to it you get whatever it is you be needin'." As he spoke, he withdrew his right hand from the pocket where it had rested since we arrived.

Though he made no move toward the pistol (which, now upon closer inspection, I noticed was covered in rust and decay and, I surmised, most likely could not be fired), but Henry seemed to keep a close eye on both the man's gnarled and dirty hand, and the gun.

"I'd reckon the workers from the Navy Yard would be well-versed in such information, as well, sir. And how do I know you have this knowledge you claim?"

"Them yardbirds be lucky to find they's own arses with both hands, they would. Ain't like the old days when ships like this was a- buildin' here. No sir. These boys now too busy buildin' them little skiffs they put a gun or two in and *row*." His disdain for Mister Jefferson's gunboats was palpable and something I knew both Henry and I agreed with.

"We fully expect to have a Navy crew aboard, sir. I am sure there will be skilled craftsmen in that group, even should the 'yardbirds' be incapable." Henry seemed to be wavering in his resolve. Besides, we had both heard from the officers in the tavern last night about the capabilities of the craftsmen employed by the Navy Yard.

"Aye. A Navy crew. Seen them. Ye'll open a rendezvous or two and manage to scrounge the dregs o' the waterfront scum. Ne'er do-wells, drunks, rascals, and scoundrels, all the leavin's of them what come afore ye." He turned and spat a glob of something into the water.

And got me to thinking about the sailors we had recruited both in Norfolk and Washington for *Chesapeake*. 'Scoundrels, rascals, and drunks' seemed close to the mark. I nudged Henry.

"Why not see what he can offer, Henry? Might be helpful, at least at first, to have him—and his knowledge of the ship—around." I whispered to my superior.

"Aye, you'd do well to listen to yer young friend . . . *Henry*. Seems like he might be on to sompin'." The wharf-rat poked a long finger first in my direction, then at Henry. And he smiled. Then he added, "Sides, you two boys gonna need help in setting the barky to rights. I don't see a passel of Navy sailors standin' 'round. Yardbirds, neither."

"Oh they'll be along quick as ever you please. But perchance there's something to what you say." Henry paused, glanced at me with an inquiring look. I nodded.

After a moment, he stuck out his hand. "All right, Mister . . . what do they call you, sir? I am Mister Allen, assigned as First Lieutenant in *United States*. Captain Decatur will be along in a day or two."

"That'd be the Decatur what did all them heroics over yonder 'gainst them corsairs?"

"The very one, sir. And will suffer no skylarking, blaspheming, or insolence from any. And you have yet to tell me your name, sir."

"Halethorpe be the name. Arbutus Halethorpe, *Henry*. Ever'one just call me Billy, though, when they call me anyt'ing." He smiled as he used Henry's Christian name, noting the reaction it drew.

"As I said, Billy, my name is *Mister* Allen. You may as well get used to using it if you plan on staying in the ship. Of course, you may always just collect whatever belongings you might have hidden away and find new lodgings . . . should you find it inconvenient to refer to me properly." Henry didn't raise his voice or change his tone a bit. And I think that made it all the more forceful.

Halethorpe took his foot off the cask where it had been resting throughout our conversation, pulled himself away from the piling, standing erect. And saluted by doffing his slouch hat. A great thatch of unruly hair, mostly black, but shot through and through with white, tumbled out and fell to his shoulders.

"Oh my!" he said, as he saw my eyes dart to his head. "Must've forgot to dress me hair when I rose this mornin'. How careless of me." The sarcasm fairly dripped from his words as he reacted to Henry's rebuke. "May I be permitted to show you young gentlemen into my home, since we're now great and good friends?" He bowed from the waist and brought his hat from aloft where he had held it briefly sweeping it across his midsection in a grand gesture toward the ship.

Assuming we would follow, he stepped off in a manner sprightlier than I would have thought from a man of his years and condition. And follow we did, right up to the gangplank and onto the deck, where our new guide, Arbutus Halethorpe, *Billy,* stopped, turned, and spoke again.

"You lads oughter be aware some folks thinks I ain't got a full seabag. Some even calls me crazy. Most o' the time, I ain't so crazy; lived here without getting' caught over two years now. Know ever' inch o' this floatin' rat's nest and most o' where they stow things—things you lads gonna need for puttin' the ship to rights."

Billy stopped, took off his hat again, and scratched his head enthusiastically. He got a wild look in his eyes—it *did* make him seem a bit off-center to me—and, in a move most sudden, withdrew the horse-pistol from his belt.

Henry backed up a step, right into me, and put his hands up in front of his body.

"Here now. What's the meaning of that? There's no call for waving that gun about." Henry's voice remained calm, quiet in an effort, I assumed, not to further rile Billy.

And waving the gun about was exactly what Billy was doing. He pointed it aloft, then toward the poop deck, the pier, and briefly, us. I withdrew a step further, wishing there were others about who might be of help.

"Ain't gonna shoot you lads. Just like to hold her ever' so often. Makes me remember the good times. Calms me feelin's, it does."

He chortled at our obvious relief, and returned the pistol to its resting place in his belt.

"Well, whether or not you intend to shoot us or any other, it would be assuredly *calming* to us if you would just leave it be, tucked there in your belt." I spoke to the man for the first time and received a nod of approval from my superior.

I cast a look about the disreputable, cluttered, and most un-Navy-like spardeck. And noticed at once that our chests no longer rested where we had secured them the night previous. I quietly mentioned my discovery to Henry.

He took a few steps forward, to confirm my observation, I assumed, and gave our guide a hard look.

"Last night we left our chests here, secured under a bit of canvas to make them less visible to prying eyes. As you were here, *Billy,* perhaps you might shed some light on what might have befallen them?" It was obvious to any that he was clearly of the opinion that Billy Halethorpe had made off with our possessions.

"Aye, I seen 'em right yonder, there. Not hid too good, you ask me. Seen 'em right off, I done, soon's I come back aboard. Knew quick as a cat someone been here, pokin' around in *my* home with not so much as a 'by yer leave.' Then I seen yer names on 'em and figgered the Navy wanted their barky back. So I put 'em somewhere safe for ye."

"And that would be exactly where?" Henry was becoming less patient with our new friend.

"Well, Henry," Halethorpe grinned maliciously at his intentional gaffe, "like I jus' tol' ye: somewhere they'd be safe from the prying eyes and grabbin' paws of them what didn't have no business pokin' around in 'em."

"So you said. And I say, *again*, where might that 'safe place' be?" Henry seemed quite exasperated now, though I found myself smiling at the exchange; if Billy was crazy as he had mentioned, he, for the moment, seemed to be getting the better of my colleague in spite of it.

"A bit testy, Henry. Perchance a bit of yer breakfast might be troublin' ye, I'd warrant." Without waiting for an answer, and likely in response to the black look that had taken residence on Henry's face, he immediately added, "Well, follow me, lads, and ye'll soon be seein' just what good care I took of yer belongin's."

Billy turned and, moving around the detritus that lumbered the deck, made his way quickly to the quarterdeck, where he stopped at the hatch which, I assumed, led to the gundeck, most likely just forward of the Great Cabin. He paused long enough to ensure we had followed, then stepped into the hatch, his lanky frame moving with a speed and grace that surprised me.

"If that refugee from Bedlam has pilfered our belongings, Oliver, I believe I shall do bodily damage to him. Moving our chests, indeed! What right had he to do that? Likely thought he'd get away with taking them and be able to refresh his wardrobe, I'm thinking." Henry's whisper and reference to the famous British insane asylum told me he had second thoughts about his decision to allow Mister Halethorpe to remain aboard.

Down the ladder we went to discover Mister Halethorpe waiting for us, a purser's glim glowing weakly in his hand and a mischievous grin distorting his face.

"There ye be, lads; safe an' sound, jut like I told ye." He pointed into the open door of the Cabin, and, there, we could see, in the weak light struggling into the room through the filthy glass windows, were our chests. Side by side they sat, lined up square on a deck seam with the precision of a squad of Marines. Unlocked.

"You have apparently been through our possessions, Mister Halethorpe. I hope, for your own sake, there is nothing gone missing from either chest." Henry's tone, as he stepped to the front of his sea chest, held enough malice that even I wondered if he would actually carry out his earlier threat.

"Well, not knowin' whose belongin's they was, I had me a look-see in 'em. Never know what might come in handy to a fellow what's livin' in such precarious times. Didn't find much of use, 'ceptin' these." He had stepped to a small writing desk attached to the inboard wall of the room and, with a flourish, opened it to produce and display for us to see, a brace of pistols. Henry's.

Henry stepped forward, his face changing with alarming speed from horror to anger, to satisfaction in his earlier prediction.

"I'll have them, Billy." He stuck out his hand to take the weapons. "Is there anything else you found that 'might come in handy to a fellow'—something perhaps from my colleague's chest? Hmmm?"

"Not so much as ye'd be thinkin', I reckon. Just this wee sticker was all I found in the lad's chest."

He placed the pistols in Henry's hand, carefully, then released the belt from around his middle, laying his own pistol carefully on the desk, and opened the ragged coat to reveal the "wee sticker" stuck into the top of his trousers.

"My dirk!" Suddenly the events seemed less amusing. Even though, since winning my commission, I no longer needed it (its place now taken by a sword), my dirk had been through much with me and was one of my very few cherished possessions. I would have been saddened by its loss.

"Here! Give me that you . . . rascal!" I poked my hand in his direction, taking a step towards him.

He withdrew the "sticker" from his waist, turned it handle first, and returned my stolen property with a rueful grin, again distorting his face. But his eyes, earlier some scarifying, now glistened in mirth.

"And welcome to it, ye are, lad. Reckon me own sticker's a more useful blade anyway." From behind his back he produced the largest dagger I had ever seen, including even the ones carried by the Corsairs of the Barbary Coast. And, so quickly I almost missed it, flung it across the Cabin where, with a resounding *thunk*, it found its mark in the center of the door leading to the captain's sleeping quarters, some six or seven paces distant.

Neither Henry nor I spoke for a moment or two, taking in the quivering blade and Billy's back as he strode over to retrieve it. We looked at each other, both clearly impressed by the demonstration. It gave new significance to his earlier brandishing of the pistol.

Maybe he really is crazy. Maybe Henry should invite him to leave, regardless of his "vast knowledge" of the ship and ability to 'find' things.

I suspected, from his astonished look, Henry had similar misgivings.

"Now that you lads're satisfied I took good care of yer possessions, maybe ye'll let me give you a look-see 'round my home. Ain't no one better to do it." He now faced us, speaking while he restored his enormous knife to its sheath on his stern. His demeanor was quite calm, as though brandishing a huge dagger at two naval officers and then throwing it into the door of the captain's bed chamber was an ordinary occurrence.

"Henry. Should we not check to see what else he might have lifted from our chests? Maybe our weapons are only what he chose to mention." My urgent whisper fell on deaf ears, dismissed with a casual wave of Henry's hand.

"Aye, Billy. Let us have our look around, then I think Mister Baldwin and I must determine what is to be done to the vessel, find a crew, establish a schedule with the Navy yard superintendent, procure supplies, our battery, cordage . . . oh my! There is just too much to list." Henry seemed momentarily overwhelmed with the tasks ahead of us.

With some effort, he straightened his shoulders, looked our guide in the eye and smiled, a bit ruefully, I thought. Then he added, "Let us see what you will show us. Lead the way, sir!"

He stepped aside to let Halethorpe pass, nodded to me to follow, and stepped into the gundeck passage with all the authority of the first lieutenant, once again restoring my confidence in his ability and leadership.

CHAPTER SEVENTEEN

By mid-December, the U.S.F. *United States* had changed as dramatically as anything I had ever observed. While we were still a long way from being ready for sea, no longer was the ship a near-derelict; the wooden roof over the spardeck was gone, as were most of the rats. Heavy wagons laden with supplies and equipment had deposited all manner of necessaries at the pier head, much of which had been manhandled aboard by our newly recruited crew. Now, instead of being covered in filth, broken casks, rotten spars and cordage, our deck was littered in great coils of hempen rope, barrels of tar, neat stacks of canvas sails, blocks of every size and shape, and newly shaped spars.

Below, a seemingly never-ending supply of paint had appeared through the magic of Mister Halethorpe's vast store of knowledge about "where things was kept" and sailors worked side by side with the less-skilled men of the Navy Yard spreading it liberally over anything that would stand still long enough to receive a coating. Carpenters had re-hung the gunports, replacing those that were beyond repair while Mister Perkins, our new gunner, oversaw a complete rehabilitation of the magazine and shot locker.

Our crew had begun trickling in about a week after Henry and I first came aboard the frigate. Reassigned from other ships, pulled from duty on Mister Jefferson's gunboats, and recruited at two rendezvous I had established with a pair of "borrowed" midshipmen near the Navy Yard, we had, by mid-December, some two hundred souls, about half of the number we would ultimately need, many of whom were seasoned hands. Officers, too, had reported for duty, including, to my great joy, Judd Devon, my old mate from our days on the Barbary Coast.

He was assigned as third lieutenant and we spent several evenings catching up on each other's experiences since we had parted company after our return to Boston in 1805. Henry had joined us for a few of these

evenings and seemed to enjoy Judd's company and stories, most of which
dove-tailed perfectly with my own. I noticed Henry nodding from time
to time at this or that detail Judd mentioned, acknowledging that he had
heard it before, quite obviously, from me.

Captain Decatur had been aboard several times, first appearing some
two weeks after Henry and I had.

Not an hour after his first arrival, a sailor sought me out (I had been
overseeing some work on the orlop deck) and indicated that the captain
would have me attend him in the Cabin. As I hurried up the ladders to
the gundeck, I tried to brush myself off as best as I could; the work below
was dirty and, while I surely did not wear my best uniform, all were so
new that any could have passed inspection. Except today working in the
bowels of the ship. Of course, that would be the day Captain Decatur
would wish me to "attend him."

I knocked on the bulkhead outside his open Cabin door and was
called in.

"Ah, Mister Baldwin. Sorry to have bothered you, but I thought you
might have an interest in this. Look around you. What do you see?"
Decatur asked me as I stepped in.

"Sir?" I was confused. What I saw was what I would see in any Great
Cabin on any frigate: writing desk, dark wood paneling on the walls, several chairs (some the worse for wear, or perhaps, Billy's usage), a carved
seat built in under the sternlights, now cleaned of their earlier grime, and
a large table which could serve as a dining table or work table. There was
a mahogany sideboard built into the bulkhead next to the long side of
the table. And a fancy-carved door leading to the sleeping chamber,
still bearing the scar from a knife wound. In the corner rested a large chest
bearing the name of our captain, unopened, in a stark contrast to the way
Henry and I had found our chests when we came aboard!

"What do you see, here, in the Cabin, Oliver?" He repeated, a smile now
crossing his face. "Perhaps something familiar?" The smile broadened.

I still wasn't getting whatever it was he wanted me to see. And my
mind was still working on the job I supervised below. This wasn't like
Captain Decatur: playing guessing games was something I had never witnessed before, but then, *before,* I had been only a midshipman. Perhaps
he reserved the game for his officers?

When I remained mute, Decatur said quietly, "Do you recall, Mister
Baldwin, where this ship was built?"

"Yes, sir. Of course. She was built in Philadelphia and launched in May of seventeen-ninety-seven. Her first in command was Cap'n Barry. Sir."

Why was he asking me for information pretty near every midshipman had studied and learned by rote?

"What you might not have known, Mister Baldwin, was that this was the very ship in which I first sailed as midshipman, back in seventeen-ninety-eight under Cap'n Barry. We sailed immediately following her commissioning for the West Indies to fight the French." Decatur was smiling; I could hear it in his voice, even though my eyes were fixed on the finely crafted sideboard.

And, as he spoke, the dawn broke and, finally, I realized what he had been getting at earlier. I looked around the Cabin again, this time with a more knowing eye. And now, I smiled too.

"Sir. I see it now. Thank you for pointing out my father's work. I should have recognized it at once. I recall, now, when he told me about the work he did for Cap'n Truxtun at the Philadelphia Navy Yard, and especially on this vessel. She was one of his favorites and he felt honored to work on a Humphries ship. And now that I think about it, I believe he took me to see her during the spring of ninety-eight, while she was fitting out. Just before she went to sea for the first time. And no, sir; I did not know you had been a midshipman in her. This must be a bit of a homecoming for you, then."

It had all come flooding back to me: Father's joy first at being commissioned to do the finishing work in the Cabin and gunroom of this great ship, his unflagging enthusiasm during the process, and his delight at taking me, a youngster of eight or nine years, aboard this great warship, the largest in our Navy. I offered the captain an acknowledgement of his first warship a bit absently; my mind was completely focused on the graceful curves of mahogany just across the room.

Carefully, I stepped to the sideboard, cast a questioning glance at the captain, who nodded his acquiescence. I ran my hand across the top, noting a few scratches in the finish, but nothing that had damaged the fine inlay work just inboard of the edge, a trademark with which my father had been particularly pleased. And when I opened the center drawer, there on the left side, carefully done and clearly visible, was his plate, showing his name and Philadelphia as his place of business. I smiled again.

"Yes, sir. This is surely his work; his stamp is just there, in the drawer."

"Yes, Oliver. I found it also. I had thought this . . . all . . . was your father's fine craftsmanship, but that plate confirmed it for me. That is when I sent for you. It must be a special treat for a son to sail in a ship his own father had a hand in building!"

"It surely will be that, sir. I can only imagine how surprised he will be when I tell him I have discovered . . . well, *you* have discovered . . . his work. I have already written to him and Edward that I am assigned in the frigate, but I had quite forgotten that Father had a hand in her building. Thank you again, sir, for showing me. If there is nothing further, sir, I shall return to my duties."

"By all means, Mister Baldwin, by all means. And thank you for responding to my summons so quickly; I was most excited anticipating your reaction to all of this. You have not disappointed!" Decatur turned back to whatever it was he had been doing before my arrival and, I assumed, immediately put me out of his mind. I left.

The captain had been aboard only a week, exerting his influence into every area of the ship and Navy Yard, when he received word that his mother was severely ill and not expected to live. He immediately hired a coach and departed for Philadelphia, where he arrived in time for a final good-bye. Another week to bury her, deal with family matters, and make arrangements for the disposition of her estate (his father had passed a year or so earlier), and he was back among us, driving himself unceasingly in, I assumed, an effort to overcome his grief. And he brought greetings from my own mother and father. He learned that my cabinetmaker father had secured some fine work in the Navy Yard at Philadelphia restoring several ships to their original condition. A joy it was for me to hear and, I am sure, for my father to carry out.

Decatur had accepted Billy's presence with reluctance, bowing to Henry's argument that the strange, off-center wharf-rat had been most helpful and would speed the tasks ahead with his unerring sense of avoiding the pitfalls of Navy Yard bureaucracy. The captain did, however, impose a condition on Billy's continued presence: he must be cleaned up and made to look presentable. The patched and dirty greatcoat vanished, the horse pistol as well, and, with a shave and a proper haircut, the man became, of a sudden, a different person.

Without the beard, his hawk-like nose was even more pronounced and emphasized his sunken eyes. Eyes which he could change moment to moment as the mood struck him; they could be flat and apparently unseeing one instant and then, in a flash (should something have provoked or amused him), those same eyes would sparkle, almost *glow*, in a wild demonic way that was reminiscent of old Seth himself. And of course, he still had the heavy brows, which he oft times used most expressively, and the paucity of teeth, but with clean trousers and coat, he seemed a good bit less scarifying, especially to the younger lads in our crew. And he still called our first lieutenant by his Christian name.

Gradually the ship was taking shape; with the gunports restored, the hull could be painted and the landsmen among our crew, under the watchful eye of our bosun, Jack Comstock, a Nantucket man who had been to sea since a boy, stages were rigged over the side and a fresh coat of black paint applied to the sides. Decks were holystoned, the stores and furniture scattered about being moved as necessary, and by late January, *United States* looked almost presentable.

Still needing attention were the rig and the hull below the waterline. The rig needed new hempen shrouds and stays, topmasts and t'gallants fitted, and yards crossed; the hull needed recoppering. This latter would demand that the ship be moved and heaved down to allow the yard workers to pry off the old sheets of copper (what was left of them) and apply new sheets of the thin metal to protect us from the ravages of worms and other sea creatures that would, in the course of time, eat the wooden bottom right out from under us. And the masts would receive their due attention when the frigate was moved to a berth alongside the shear hulk that could lift and place our masts. To my knowledge, no decision had been reached by either the yard superintendent or Captain Decatur as to whether new masts would be stepped or the old ones spruced up and left in place.

Of major concern to the captain and, I should add, Henry Allen, was still the matter of our guns; the frigate was designed to carry a main battery of twenty-four pounders—thirty-two of them mounted in carriages on the gundeck—and twenty-four forty-two pounder carronades with their slides, both on the spardeck and below on the gundeck. Additionally, Captain Decatur wanted half a dozen eighteen-pounder long guns set forward on the fo'c'sle deck and aft on the poop as, respectively, bow and stern chasers.

He personally had visited the civilian foundry under contract with the Navy, which would cast the barrels, and had spent considerable time overseeing their construction. There seemed no detail too petty for his attention when it came to our guns; he eyed the molds, watched as the iron was melted down to a flaming, white-hot liquid, and poured into the form, which ultimately would produce the armament we would need. Each evening, on those days he visited the foundry, he returned to the

68

ship exhausted, his uniform filthy, and frequently, his skin red or blistered from the heat of the process.

Some days, when Captain Decatur was involved in another aspect of our re-commissioning or attending the Secretary of the Navy with another of the endless reports the Secretary required, Henry Allen would take his place at the foundry, sometimes including me in an effort to "expand my education."

I can only imagine what the netherworld is like from the preachers and elders I have heard propounding on its miseries, but short of watching the frigate *Philadelphia* burn in February 1804, I suspect that the foundry was as close as anything that exists in our world. The heat assaulted us from the moment we entered the establishment; the air was choked with smoke—smoke laden with sparkling embers and bits of ash. The combination made it impossible to breathe without a wet kerchief tied across one's nose and mouth and I quickly discovered how the captain's uniform became so soiled and his face reddened and blistered.

Men moved about in this hellish atmosphere like spirits, the clothes and faces coated in white ash, heavy leather gloves protecting their hands, kerchiefs tied about their mouths. They seemed to drift through the building, materializing suddenly from the thick fog of smoke, soot, and ash. At times the noise all but precluded talk, and from time to time, one or another of the men would give an order in a voice loud enough to be heard over the din, when suddenly the racket stopped, leaving his voice unnaturally loud and, sometimes, provoking a wry comment from another. I was awestruck.

"We surely are not going to spend the entire day here, are we, Henry?" I sputtered out the question that had been in my brain for the entire time since we entered the building: about ten minutes.

"We will be here until I am able to report to the captain that the work on our battery is progressing to my satisfaction, Oliver. I will not, nay, I *can* not, risk an improperly cast barrel should we have to confront an enemy. We must have the best there is and be well prepared to take full advantage of the moment without the worry of a poorly-cast gun exploding." Henry had to shout his answer over the noise of molten iron being poured not ten feet in front of us. I nodded.

And stay we did; Henry's attention never wavered from the task at hand. As new forms were built, he checked each carefully, running his hand over the surface. He examined the iron before it was delivered into the maw of the furnace, ensuring that there was no contaminating element that might somehow escape the heat of the smelter and wind up in our new cannon. When the mold was sufficiently cooled to allow its removal from the newly cast gun barrel, Lieutenant Allen ran his hand over each surface of the still hot iron, pointing out areas that would require additional attention, both to me and to the put-upon overseer, who dutifully noted, with the stub of a well-chewed pencil, each comment on a scrap of paper, sometimes shooting an unseen glance at Henry which clearly conveyed his thoughts on whatever criticism had been offered.

Even I thought some of his complaints a bit petty, but held my tongue in the belief that *United States* must have the best castings possible, and be able to take full advantage of their quality.

But, we aren't at war with any. Why would we be worried about facing an enemy with inferior barrels? We haven't any enemies! I thought more than once during my long day at the foundry, but answered myself each time the same way: *We weren't at war with any in June of ought seven, either. Henry and the captain are absolutely right.*

With the casting of our cannon and carronades well in hand, Henry directed me to oversee the construction of their carriages and slides, a task underway within the confines of the Navy Yard and managed by a team of civilian carpenters. Each day, when I left the lodgings ashore where several of us had procured quarters, I made my way directly to the shed housing the carpenters and their task, without first visiting the frigate.

I was surely looking forward to spending time in the carpenter's shop after the few days I spent at the foundry. It would be more temperate in every way, quieter, and something I had grown up around.

On the first day Lieutenant Allen had asked me to "look in on the progress those rascals are making on the carriages," I thought that here was a place I could at least act knowledgeably about and imagined knowing conversations with the master carpenter, who would surely be surprised at a naval officer so versed in his craft.

Instead, I embarrassed myself to the fullest. I quite forgot about the reason I had gone to sea instead of becoming the cabinetmaker my father had wished for me: I was prone to violent attacks of sneezing, choking, wheezing, and running eyes in the presence of sawdust.

And here was no exception. I smiled to myself as quick as I entered the shop, enjoying seeing the men busy with sawing great oaken logs, then squaring them and shaping them with broadaxes and adzes. Sawdust and chips flew everywhere and lay in great profusion about the floor at each work area. It took bare minutes for my smile to dissolve into bouts of sneezing complete with running eyes and nose, and great gaspings for air. I beat a hasty retreat to the unsullied air of the out-of-doors.

When I had caught my breath and found my composure once again, I re-entered the shop with a kerchief over my nose and mouth, much in the same manner as I had in the foundry.

"Have you a touch of ague, Lieutenant?" A man, dressed in homespun shirt, the sleeves rolled up his massive forearms, and canvas trousers, smiled at me when I re-entered his shop. Obviously he had witnessed my initial arrival.

"I seem ill-affected by the sawdust and chips, sir. My father is a cabinetmaker in Philadelphia and I am well familiar with the symptoms." I choked out a response which, I am certain, sounded as muffled from the kerchief covering my nose and mouth as it did from my seeming inability to draw a full breath.

"Oh thank the stars; I had thought you might be a highwayman what lost his way!" He laughed uproariously at his attempt at humor, his eyes crinkling up at the effort.

Then the carpenter clapped me on the shoulder in show of comradely good nature and said in a more serious tone, "Well, son, just you keep that bandanna tied there 'round your face and I am sure you'll manage just fine."

He looked hard at me, his smile now gone, and inquired, "What is it brings you here? Is there something we can do for you?"

"Sir. I am Lieutenant Baldwin, fourth lieutenant in the *United States* frigate. I have come to determine the progress you are making with our gun carriages and carronade slides. The barrels are being forged as we speak and we will need the carriages and slides as quick as ever you please." I thought *that* sounded better and had convinced the man that I was not to be taken lightly.

"Aye," he answered, apparently not impressed. "That would be Cap'n Decatur's ship, would it not? Reckon he sent you to find out what was actin'. Well, we have the project well in hand, lad. See for yourself." He pointed to a further area of the shop where, in the gloom of dusty light that filtered in, I could make out several men working on what could only be gun carriages.

"May I go there and have a look, for my own self? It would be helpful for me to have firsthand knowledge of your progress when I report to Cap'n Decatur." In fact, I had already started moving in the direction he had pointed and was pleased to see he stepped right along in my wake.

"You'll want to be careful, moving about in here, lad. They's dangerous machines and a body might get hisself hurt, he's not careful."

"You must recall I mentioned having grown up around my father's cabinet shop, sir. I know well the hazards associated with this type of work." And so saying, I let forth a great sneeze, one that seemed to originate in my feet, it came out with such force.

The foreman was still chuckling when we reached the area where our carriages were taking shape. He pointed out several in varying stages of completion, making comments about each as we examined them.

Before I could give voice to my dismay at seeing only four or five in varying stages of completion, he spoke again.

"Outside are the ones we've completed, Lieutenant. You'll be wantin' to see them, I'm certain. And I 'spect the air yonder will be less troubling to you." He grinned at my obvious discomfort and seemed to make a point of stirring up as much sawdust with his feet as he could as we made our way to doors I had not previously noticed.

And there, lined up with the precision of Marines, were a dozen and more heavy carronade slides and at least that many carriages, complete with iron-bound wheels, for the long guns.

"We was fixin' to have these drug over to the ship by the end of the week. Thought we might get a few more done by then." He seemed quite pleased with himself at his accomplishment. Then added, "If you approve of they's construction, of course, sir."

I thought this last a bit caustic and several replies sprang to my mind, replies which would surely put him in his place. But recognizing that we still needed many more carriages and slides from him, I held my tongue. Instead I looked them over carefully, running my hands over the wood, checking the iron fittings, and noting that the wheels on the carriages were well greased.

"A fine job, these are, sir. And should answer nicely." I smiled at him, hoping the praise—and, I meant every word—would soften his demeanor a trifle.

Of course, I still had the kerchief tied across my face, rendering my smile, broad though it was, quite invisible to him. Quickly I drew the cloth down, letting it fall to my neck, all the while maintaining my expansive smile.

He visibly brightened at the acknowledgement of his craftsmanship and pointed out several features I might have overlooked in my initial examination. At each, though I had missed none, I nodded appreciatively and uttered some unintelligible exclamation of delight.

Well, now I can tell Henry what a fine job the Yard is doing. And won't he be thrilled to learn we will be receiving perhaps half our carriages this week!

I lingered throughout the remainder of the day, watching the craftsmen work (through the open door!) and, from time to time, chatting amiably with my new friend about my father's work for the Navy and my own experiences with Captain Decatur. At the end of the day, to my great pleasure, he invited me to return at any time, by now, calling me "Lieutenant Baldwin" instead of "lad." And there were no further comments about my reaction to the wood chips and sawdust.

As I made my way down the pier, admiring the improvement to our, now, fine-looking frigate, which sat high against the pilings, I was smiling at my experience in the carpenters' shop and enjoying being able to take a breath without the sneezing and weeping brought about by the wood dust.

I reckon when the battery is in place along with the ballast, she'll look even more regal, floating to her lines again. And of course, get her masts topped up with the uppers. Pretty as Constitution, *I'll warrant!*

"May I help you, sir?" A young sounding voice interrupted my thoughts as I stepped aboard.

Standing before me was a cherubic face I had not before seen; a midshipman's uniform, complete with dirk, seemed to be draped over his thin frame which, combined with his narrow features, gave him the appearance of a scarecrow. To complete the image, a shock of unfinished hair spilled from beneath his hat, which he was holding aloft in salute, presumably to me.

Being saluted by midshipmen was not something I had yet become accustomed to, and it took me a moment to react, returning his salute with a smile.

"And who might you be, Mister Midshipman? I am Oliver Baldwin, fourth lieutenant in this ship." I continued to smile at him, recalling my own terrifying first encounters with officers in the brig *Argus*.

"Oh, sir. My goodness. I didn't . . . that is, sir, no one told me. . . Well, sir, you would be coming aboard. Guess it slipped Mister Devon's mind." He stammered a bit, but managed finally to limber up his tongue and speak coherently. But he still had not mentioned his own name.

"And you are . . ?" I repeated.

"Oh sir. Beggin' your pardon, sir. I am William O'Donahue, sir, from Boston . . . in Massachusetts. Just came here yesterday." He smiled tentatively, gauging my reaction.

"This would be your first ship, then, Mister O'Donahue?"

"Yes sir. And most pleased I am indeed to be sailing with Capt'n Decatur. His feats are legendary where I come from."

While I uttered not a word, I must have made some facial response to this, which Midshipman O'Donahue took as encouragement to continue in his faintly Irish lilt.

"You see, Lieutenant Baldwin, when he went off to accomplish those wondrous acts against the pirates of Barbary, he sailed from Boston, on the ship *Argus*. I remember me da' taking me to the harbor to watch 'em sail out. Da' said even though the captain hails from somewhere else, we should always consider him a "son of Boston" as that is where he started." He beamed at me, obviously delighted to have shared the story of his "Da's" hero.

I refrained from telling him just yet of my and Judd Devon's participation in that very departure. There would be ample time for that later, and likely better it should come from others. I also refrained from correcting his use of "on the ship" remembering my own rough treatment by Edward Langford on the docks of Boston when I had misspoken at about the same point in my own Navy career, and about the same vessel.

Instead I simply wished him good luck, and welcome aboard, at which he brightened even further.

"Oh Oliver! You are back. And what of our carpenters? Have they accomplished anything of note? That you could tell?" Henry was just emerging from the companionway as I was about to go below to find him.

"You will be most pleased, Henry. Not only are they hard at work on the carriages and slides, but the foreman mentioned that he would have more than a dozen of each brought to the pier by week's end." I announced my news with enthusiasm and won a smile from the first lieutenant.

So I added, "And they look grand, truly. Fine, solid construction of prime woods bound with iron straps. They will serve well, I believe."

The smile expanded and he turned around to accompany me below.

As we reached the gunroom, Henry said, "I would reckon you met our newest, Midshipman O'Donahue? Seems harmless enough, and a pleasant fellow as well. Can you remember those days on your first ship, Oliver? I surely can, and terrifying they were. Had it not been for a couple of officers, the acting commander—a man named Jacobs, I recall—and

Sailing Master Hallowell, who took me in tow, I might have jumped before even we sailed from Newport! And then Bainbridge and that dull sailer, *George Washington*. Oh my goodness, what memories. I'd reckon young O'Donahue is making those memories right now, though I doubt he'd be aware of it if you told him! And I'd warrant he's likely as frightened as we were." Henry laughed at the recollection.

"I can remember Oliver's first days aboard. And I can tell you, he might not have been terrified, Henry, but he surely was a landsman! Came aboard falling all over himself and everything on deck. Didn't know the jib boom from the mizzenmast. Remember, Oliver?" Judd Devon sat at the table, a huge grin lighting his face.

Oh my! I surely hope he doesn't go into all that business with my encounter with the wharf rat and arriving aboard with nary a penny in my pocket!

I looked searchingly at Judd, who continued to smile, but mercifully, said nothing further.

"Gentlemen, I propose a glass or two ashore and perhaps, some supper. What say you?" Henry seemed in fine humor and I think, we were all ready for a small celebration; events had been running in our favor for several days now.

"Give me a moment to clean myself up a bit and I am with you." I answered, grateful that Judd's recollection had received no encouragement.

"We'll meet you at the gangway, Oliver. Don't dally." Henry tossed over his shoulder as he and Judd headed for the ladder.

Even before I arrived at the gangway, where my friends waited, I could see some kind of a confrontation taking place. A civilian, who was unfamiliar to me, seemed most angry with someone and was speaking loudly, right into Henry's face. He gesticulated and pointed about the ship, waving his arms and giving our first lieutenant no chance to get a single word out. As I drew closer, I heard mention of paint and our civilian overseer, Billy Halethorpe, and realized that this gentleman must be the Superintendent of the Navy Yard.

"Oh, Lieutenant Baldwin. Good you have joined us. Mister Johnson, here, is the headman of the Navy Yard and seems to have a problem with some missing paint. For some reason, he believes it to be in the frigate. Do you have any thoughts on that?" Henry Allen kept a perfectly straight face.

"You're damn right it's here in this old bucket! I know that scoundrel Halethorpe took it sure as we're standin' here. Done it before, he has, but never so much. The rogue knows where everything is and feels it's his right, *his right,* by the Almighty, to just help himself whenever the mood strikes him. And I know he's still aboard; seen him with my own eyes, I have. And just a'cause you people cleaned him up some, don't you think I wouldn't recognize that scalawag!" The Superintendent was spitting with nearly every other word, and I stepped back a step to avoid most of the spray.

"Yes, Mister Johnson. Billy Halethorpe is surely aboard—though I am not sure he is right at this moment—but I have no knowledge of your paint. You can see we have been painting *United States*—she surely needed it after being in ordinary with nary a soul even checking on her—but since *your* men were working with our own to get the job done, we all assumed the Navy Yard had provided the paint." This was not a lie; we knew Billy had provided much of it, but we also knew he got it from the Navy Yard. I smiled as warmly as I could, trying to pacify his rage.

"What do you mean, no one was checking on the ship; our watchman checked her as part of his regular rounds." Johnson had worked himself up to a point where he picked up on just what I hoped he would, quite forgetting the paint issue, at least for the moment.

"Well, I can tell you she was quite infested with rats, and, of course, Billy was living on board. Had been for several years, he said. Doesn't sound to me like your watchman was doing much of a job!" Henry jumped back into the fray, eager to keep his antagonist a bit off-balance.

"I knew that crazy fool was living in the ship. And it was his choice to live with the rats. Liked it, I'd reckon, or he wouldn't have stood it. Hope he got hisself bit, crazy old fool." Then, under his breath, he added something that sounded a bit like, "birds of a feather, I'd say, him living with the rats!"

"Well, I reckon that would be his own choice, then would it not?" Henry, ignoring the last mutterings of Mister Johnson, spoke calmly, and even smiled.

Midshipman O'Donahue returned, having earlier been sent to find Billy. He was empty-handed, of course, a concerned look at having failed at his first assignment on his first ship, creasing his face.

"He's no' aboard, sir. I checked everywhere and even asked several sailors. Nary a one offered so much as a hint of his whereabouts. I am sorry, sir."

"That's quite alright, Midshipman. We will manage just fine without him. You may return to your post at the gangway." Judd spoke for the first time.

O'Donahue's relief was visible, and he stepped away a few feet to the head of the gangway to resume his watch.

The distraction, and perhaps, Billy's absence, seemed to end the discussion about the paint, and more lately about Billy's mentals, and Mister Johnson muttered something about "seeing where this might go," turned abruptly and stalked down the gangway after physically moving the midshipman to the side.

We watched in silence as he continued his march down the pier. When he was about a half-pistol shot distant, Henry and Judd started laughing and I joined in.

"I'd reckon we made the right choice, keeping that 'crazy rascal' aboard to help us out. Seems he has done exactly that!" Henry struggled to get the words out around his mirth.

"Might be we should tell him to lay low for a bit. I'd warrant that yard fellow is going to be keeping a weather eye out for our friend, at least for a while." Judd, who had had several dealings with Billy, suggested, sagely.

"Oliver, why not let him know what's acting here. We'll wait for you." Henry had gained control of his senses.

"Did not O'Donahue say he was not in the ship?"

"Oh, he's here. You know he can disappear almost at will when he's of a mind. I am most sure he knew Mister Johnson was aboard and it might answer best were he out of sight. You know where to look, Oliver." Henry winked at me as he spoke.

And indeed I did. I found him almost at once, lounging on a pile of new canvas that had provided Billy with a bed for the past fortnight and more in the sail locker. He seemed unmoved by my announcement, merely nodding at my recounting of Mister Johnson's dismay. He offered no acknowledgment of his deeds, nor was any sought.

"He'll stay put for bit, I think, Henry." I offered in response to Henry's inquiring look as I rejoined my colleagues and left the ship.

Not a month had passed before Billy's charitable instincts bubbled again to the surface. The early-morning darkness had just given way to the yellow ball of a late-March sun, as it began to warm everything it touched, a true harbinger of springtime, when a large wagon lumbered to a halt alongside the frigate, just back at her original pier from having been heaved down while her bottom got a shiny new coat of copper sheets. I still had the watch at the gangway, and observed with interest as the drayman stepped on the front wheel and then jumped to the ground. A slouch hat hid his face, but the build was familiar.

Jack Comstock, our Bosun, and Mister Worth, the new Sailing Master, also saw the wagon pull up and, with barely a "by yer leave," to me, the officer of the watch, were down the gangway and pulling the canvas tarpaulin off the bed of the wagon. I was reminded of children receiving the visit, and obligatory gifts, of a favorite uncle. And then I recognized the drayman; Billy Halethorpe had been visiting the stores shed, apparently during the dark hours.

I craned my neck to see what it had been that so delighted both the bosun and the sailing master, a dour fellow not given to jollity. The bed of the wagon was piled high with blocks, large and small, some with iron hooks and some with rope straps affixed to them. Most appeared new or nearly so, the wood bright and the iron well blackened. The wagon appeared to hold enough to finish restoring our rig, and about time!

"Billy, you old scoundrel, you: you done it, by the Almighty! And them riggers told me, an' you, John, they wasn't a block to be had!" Comstock was fairly jumping for joy. Even John Worth was clapping Billy on the back.

Billy, for his part, just smiled, the hole in his whiskers growing bigger, while his remaining teeth interrupted the symmetry. His eyes, deep-set though they were, twinkled.

"Mister Baldwin, sir. Would you mind calling out a work party to get this bounty aboard the ship? Likely oughter get it did sooner 'an later." Comstock shouted up to the deck.

I acknowledged his request with a wave, agreeing silently that, considering who delivered the 'bounty,' getting it out of sight was likely a fine idea, and sent my messenger to roust a handful of seamen from their morning meal.

Very quickly, the dozen or so sailors who showed up in response to my summons, had the wagon emptied and the blocks struck below, all under the watchful eyes of our bosun and sailing master, one at the wagon, the other on deck ensuring that Billy's surprise was cached safely below.

The remainder of the day passed uneventfully, much of the crew readying our spar deck for the carronade slides we expected now that we had received almost all of the long gun carriages. The remainder of the sailors, under the supervision of Judd and the sailing master, worked aloft, reeving running rigging—it seemed like miles of it—through our newly acquired blocks. Halyards, sheets, braces, clew lines, and other tackles all had to be rigged before we could bend on a shred of canvas, canvas which had been aboard for several months, keeping our sailmakers busy as ever could be.

The crew's evening supper and spirits had just been piped when the first lieutenant and I, talking about our great good fortune in being assigned to this wonderful ship, espied Mister Johnson marching purposefully down the pier. Captain Decatur was ashore on another summons from the Secretary of the Navy, presumably reporting on our progress, so Henry was the senior officer aboard.

"Well, lookee there! Do you s'pose our eagle-eyed Yard Superintendent noticed he was missing some blocks, Oliver?" Henry's tone was more bemused than concerned, and I took my cue from him.

"I would have thought he might not have noticed at all, Henry. After all, look at how long it took him to discover we had gotten ahold of his precious paint!"

We watched in silence, both smiling, as Mister Johnson stormed down the pier and noticed that he kept casting his gaze aloft. With our topmasts up, I am sure he found the frigate an impressive sight, but didn't for a moment believe he was coming to pay us a compliment!

"You people have allowed that lunatic to rob me again!" He started his rant even before he stepped aboard.

"Excuse me, sir. I am afraid you have the advantage over us; whatever are you referring to?" Henry's innocence might have convinced a more rational sort, but clearly, Mister Johnson was neither rational nor convinced.

"That rascal, Halethorpe, has stolen all my blocks. I know he has, sure as we're standin' here. I demand you produce the thief and make him answer for his crimes." Johnson was standing almost toe to toe with Henry and, on every "s" word, he sent forth a shower of spittle, making Henry retreat a step, and then another.

"Mister Johnson: the last time you were aboard my ship, you accused us of stealing your paint, though you had absolutely no proof whatever of the act. Now, here you are yet again, accusing us of more mischief. Do you have some proof this time that your blocks are indeed in the ship? And you mention Billy, who admittedly is not quite right aloft, as the culprit. Have you any witnesses or are you merely assuming that, because our man is a bit simple, he would be the easiest to persecute?" Lieutenant Allen put a bit of an edge to his voice which brought the Superintendent up short.

"Witnesses? By Jove, man, of course not. I don't need any witnesses; I can see the blocks hanging right yonder in your rig. All you have to do is look." Now his tone was incredulous, as if he thought Henry was a simpleton, too.

"Yes, I know we have blocks rigged aloft. Have you, in your long career as a civilian employee of the Navy Yard, ever seen a ship put to sea without blocks? My goodness, man. Think about it: how would we hoist our sails, adjust their set, reef or hand them, or anything else without blocks? Couldn't be done! Why would you expect us to be any different? We are trying to put *United States* into service and get her, and us, out of your Yard; without our rig complete, we clearly would be unable to accomplish that. And *that,* my friend, is something that both the Secretary and Cap'n Decatur are most keen on." Henry spoke quietly and slowly, as though he were talking to someone who might be a bit slow.

"Those blocks are mine, damn all! They were all stowed in my rigging shed and earmarked for other vessels. Now I am going to be behind on those, while you sit here, fat and fancy, almost ready to sail. I demand you produce that scalawag, Halethorpe, and let us see what he might have to say about this." Johnson might have taken umbrage at Henry's earlier tone.

I noticed, behind Mister Johnson, that our night-time supplier was ambling aft, perhaps heading for the gangway and a run ashore. I gently nudged my colleague who followed my glance.

"Well, Mister Johnson, this would appear to be a lucky day for you; Mister Halethorpe is aboard and, in fact, about to join us." Henry waved to Billy who smiled broadly and waved back.

"Hullo there, Jeremy. What brings you out this evening?" Billy greeted Johnson as though the two were old shipmates, not antagonists in an ongoing confrontation over Billy's habits. And I smiled as I heard his use of Johnson's given name; apparently no one, save Cap'n Decatur, was immune from that.

"You rascal, you. You are a thief, Halethorpe. And I have told you hundreds of times, damn all, do not call me *Jeremy*. You ain't got the right!" Johnson's demeanor was quite a contrast to Billy's.

To his credit, our civilian crewman never changed his pleasant expression. He continued to smile and held his hand out, waiting for Mister Johnson, a very riled up Mister Johnson, to shake it. Which was surely not about to happen. Henry and I made every effort to suppress our own feelings of mirth, deciding to let Billy handle this and see how he did.

"Why, Jeremy, whatever has got you so riled up? Couldn't be good for yer constitution. Look at me; I don't let meself get so worked up and likely accounts for my years." Billy's smile never wavered.

"You *stole* my entire supply of blocks, you scoundrel. I can see them all over your rig. I don't know how you done it, but I got no doubt it was you. Sure as I'm standin' here."

Henry's nudge caused me to notice that the raised voices and unbecoming language had begun to draw an audience, Bosun Comstock and Sailing Master Worth prominent among them.

"*Stole?*" Billy's innocence was clear; it couldn't have been him! "How could you say such a thing? Oh, I know; my memory ain't so good as it useter be—since I got hit by the lightning back in ought six. Sometimes makes me take on the craziness, time to time. Some o' my old shipmates useter call me flat-out crazy after that. And they sent me ashore on account o' it. But stealin' from the Navy? Ain't in me to do *that*. And struck crazy by that bolt o' lightning or no, I'da likely 'membered I done that! When'd you say this happened?" Billy was carrying off his act with brilliance!

"Hadda been last night . . . or this morning. This ship wasn't rigged out with her runnin' riggin' last week, and here you are, lookin' damn near ready for sea—and all of a sudden. Hadda be you; ain't no one else woulda dared steal from me."

Jack Comstock chose that moment to join the group. A large man by anyone's standards, he towered over Mister Johnson and used his bulk and height to intimidating advantage.

"You seem some riled up over our bein' part-rigged, sir. Why is that a problem? You sent them blocks and the runnin' rigging over by dray more'n a month ago. As we was heaved down in the gravin' yard at the time, we couldn't put 'em to use then. Matter of fact, when we received our gun carriages, we had the devil's own time getting' 'em aboard without our rig done. So, as the bosun of this fine vessel, I personally am glad to have the chance to thank you for seein' to it we had our rope and blocks in jig time!" Comstock stuck out his massive paw, which Johnson simply gaped at for a long moment, before allowing the bosun to pump his hand enthusiastically.

"Over a month ago?" The Superintendent asked. "There's nothing wrong with *my* memory, sir. And I would have had to personally order that material to be sent round to this ship. Which I clearly did not. Halethorpe stole it! And last night, it was."

Billy beamed at this, his head cocked to one side as though hearing something distant. And then he began to shuffle his feet, dancing to a tune only he could hear. Johnson stared at him, shook his own head and turned to leave.

"You people ain't heard the end of this. No siree. I *know* what happened." Then he shook his finger at Billy.

"You can't get away from me, you rascally thief. I know you been stealin' me blind over these past years and I aim to see you stand for your crimes!" With an angry look at, first Billy, who simply continued to shuffle his feet with a far-off look in his eyes, then at Henry and me, he left, marching down the gangway as angry as when he had marched up it.

We watched in amused silence, the four of us. Then Comstock took Billy by the arm.

"Come on, Billy. We'll fix you up with some spirits and a bit of supper."

For his part, Billy just looked at the bosun as though he had just noticed him, and continued to dance. Suddenly he stood stock-still, fixing his gaze on something aloft.

"Lookee there, Jack. We got some o' the rig up! You lads musta found them blocks an' rope I had stowed below!" He smiled, toothlessly, and added, "You say something about spirits, Jack? I could use me a dram."

Comstock shot Henry and me a befuddled look, though he knew well about Billy's fits of the "mentals," shook his head and guided our benefactor toward the scuttle to the gundeck.

CHAPTER EIGHTEEN

Six weeks later saw us swinging to our best bower in Hampton Roads. The rain dappled the water of the harbor, falling straight down on this windless morning. Each drop, generous in size, left a momentary scar where it landed, marking the surface like the face of a survivor of the pox. Even with the rain, this dreary May morning bore the promise of being hot with little hope of a cooling breeze, according to Gunner Perkins.

"On deck, there. Boat approachin' from shore. Looks like the cap'n." The hail from the lookout inspired the deck watch to action, rain or no.

"Boat ahoy!" I had heard both the lookout's cry and the hail from the watch officer—I saw it was Midshipman O'Donahue and was pleased that he had responded correctly—and started aft from where I had been overseeing, along with the gunner, the mounting of firing locks on our new bow chasers. And I heard the reply from the boat.

"*United States!*" The cox'n's shout would serve to alert the watch that Captain Decatur was in the boat and headed for us.

Henry and Judd arrived at the break in the bulwark just after I did, O'Donahue having sent his messenger for the first lieutenant as soon as he heard the boat cox'n announce his passenger. Squinting through the rain, I could see another man, an officer who appeared to keep a sodden boat cloak wrapped tightly around him, sitting in the sternsheets with the captain. Silently we all watched the boat's approach and smart, seaman-like landing directly at the boarding battens below us. The watch threw down a line and Decatur and his passenger started up the battens holding the manropes that hung from the deck. To my eye, the passenger seemed less than accomplished at scaling the side of a warship.

"Welcome back, Cap'n. I presume you enjoyed some success in your errand ashore?" Lieutenant Allen was first among us, as appropriate to his position in the ship, to greet the captain.

"Indeed I did, Mister Allen. Give me half an hour to change out of these soaked garments and then please have the officers assemble . . ." He stopped, thinking.

After a quick look aloft, seeing, I am sure, the unbroken, heavy, gray clouds that still sent their offerings down on us, he finished. "Have them come to the Cabin, if you please. I expect we'll all be more comfortable there. I have some news to share out with you." He returned our salutes and started to head for the companionway to his quarters, then stopped abruptly and turned about.

"I very nearly forgot. Gentlemen, may I introduce to you Lieutenant Peter Cochran? Mister Cochran has been assigned in the frigate as our second lieutenant. I am sure you gentlemen will make him comfortable." Decatur finished the introductions by announcing our names and our respective assignments, Henry first, then Judd, then me, to our newest officer.

After salutes and handshakes as appropriate were exchanged, and Henry and Mister Cochran exchanged some pleasantries, I took the opportunity to study my new superior.

He had a weak jaw, seeming not to have a chin worth mentioning. His side-whiskers were sparse, though black, which made his skin appear even more pallid than I am sure it actually was. His eyes were wide-set, giving the impression that he could look to both sides at once. I also took note that his hand, when proffered during his introduction was as soft as a lady's. I made his age somewhere greater than any of us there, perhaps twenty-eight or so.

This fellow has not been doing much in the way of work, I'd warrant! And if he has, it surely was not outside. Hasn't been in the sun in quite some time. I compared his complexion to Judd's, who happened to stand close by his new shipmate.

His frame was slight and he stood, I'd guess, something over five and a half feet tall. And his voice was, in keeping with his soft hands and pale skin, quiet; in fact, even to hear him, as close as we stood, over the sound of the rain, I had to attend closely. I noticed my colleagues seemed to strain to catch his words, as well.

But he stood straight, and had had a firm grip; he also looked into the eyes of whoever had engaged him in conversation, most particularly, Henry. His uniform, though wet in spite of the boat cloak, was well fitted to his modest build and had been properly brushed.

"Mister Baldwin: you will show Mister Cochran to the gunroom, if you please." Henry ended the pleasantries and turned to O'Donahue who was close at hand. "Mister O'Donahue: please see that Mister Cochran's chest and anything else he brought are sent below promptly."

"Have you much time at sea, Mister Cochran?" I inquired as I showed him into the gunroom and noted his seeming chagrin at the accommodations.

"Not since I was a midshipman, Lieutenant. And *that* was a long time ago . . . during that business with France in the last century." Cochran did not look at me as he spoke, unlike his direct gaze earlier.

I was right on the edge of asking where he had been for the past ten years when he continued.

"I was quite young at the time and did not take well to the sea-going life. Suffered dreadfully when the weather was up, you know. Sailed with a compassionate—well, after a while he *became* compassionate, at least—captain—Morris, it was—who sent me ashore. Called in a favor, I think, to find me a position in Washington. Working with the secretary of the navy. Lasted through three of them, I did, Stoddart, Smith, and, until just last week, Hamilton." He finally graced me with a look, haughty and self-important, I thought.

"Can't, for the life of me, imagine why Decatur would want me as his lieutenant in this vessel, grand though she is. I am sure he knows my history, as inglorious as it may be." He did not speak directly to me, merely voiced the thought as though he were talking to himself.

Suddenly he turned to face me. "Have you a full complement recruited, Baldwin?"

I thought for a moment about why he might ask this, deciding finally he was trying to determine when we might be sailing. "No, sir. We were able to fill something more than half our requirement in Washington and expect to find the rest of our men here, in Norfolk. I have established three rendezvous at local taverns and rooming houses and we have enjoyed some success so far."

"Hmmm. Then it must have been a bit of a trial bringing the ship down from the Navy Yard with only half of your crew, I would reckon?"

The trip down the Potomac in *Chesapeake* immediately jumped into my mind; *that* was a trial! In *United States,* we had no such difficulties. We stopped in Alexandria to take on the gun and carronade barrels we had not loaded in Washington, so as to be able to get over the bar, and the rest of our ballast and stores. We fired our salute at Mount Vernon without incident, had no bad weather and fair winds all the way. No one took ill, and no one expired. No indeed, this trip most certainly was not a trial. I said as much.

Before we could converse further, two sailors entered the gunroom staggering under the weight of Cochran's chest, followed by another with a bulging seabag.

"Ah, my trappings!" You may put them there, in that cabin." Cochran acknowledged their arrival without a word of thanks, but, to my chagrin, had directed that they deposit his belongings in *my* cabin.

"Uh . . . sir? I, uh . . . that cabin is already taken." I stammered, a bit confused over the protocol of giving up the little cubbyhole I had called home for nearly six months.

"Oh, indeed? Would it be Mister Allen's cabin, then?" He asked, offering me a sideways look.

"Uh . . . no, sir. That one is where I have been sleeping."

"Oh, well, in that case." He turned again to the three sailors still toting his chest and bag. "You may leave my luggage right here then, and I will move it into the cabin once Mister Baldwin has vacated it."

The sailors set their burden down and beat a hasty retreat from the gunroom. For my own part, I was stunned! He was aboard the ship barely fifteen minutes and had already thrown me out of my quarters. I must have shown my dismay.

"I am sure, Baldwin, the little cabin, there," he pointed to the smallest and, as yet, unoccupied space opening off the gunroom, as he spoke, "will be more than suitable for our fourth lieutenant. I expect you can move your belongings directly after we meet with Decatur. You wouldn't mind doing that, would you?" The smile he offered was in no way friendly.

I had no choice, nor apparently, any consideration. "Uh . . . no, sir. I will take care of it directly."

"Well, then, Baldwin. Let us see what news our esteemed commander has to share out. Though I suspect I know what it will be. News from the secretary, I expect. Likely something I copied for Hamilton my own self. He had me copy, in a fair hand, most of what he wrote; man has dreadful handwriting, for a fact." He puffed up a bit at his self-importance.

We'll see how self-important you are once we get to sea, Mister "I-copied-for-Hamilton!" Maybe you'll wish you had stayed in Washington then!

Without further comment, my new superior walked out of our quarters, heading aft for the Cabin. I followed, seething at this interloper's arrogance.

Henry was already there, seated in a round-backed chair opposite the captain's desk. Judd walked in immediately after we did. I stole a look at my father's handiwork throughout the room, smiling inwardly as I recognized again the graceful symmetry of the sideboard and desk, the several chairs, and the ornately carved window seat under the quarter-gallery. Where I sat. Cochran took, appropriately, the other chair in front of the desk, while Judd joined me on the window-seat.

Captain Decatur picked up a thin sheaf of papers, stood, and stepped to the side of the room in front of the sideboard—my father's sideboard. He looked at each of us in turn, as was his custom before uttering anything of consequence.

"Gentlemen: I have a letter from Secretary Hamilton which he handed me only yesterday. Copies of this have been sent to each commander capable of getting his ship to sea, something not all of us can manage just yet. But I expect the efforts to that end will increase directly, as a result of the opportunity offered by this letter."

I noticed that Cochran smiled slightly, preening at Decatur's words, and obviously pleased that his earlier prediction to me had borne fruit.

The captain continued. "I am sure you have all heard that our government continues to be frustrated in resolving the difficulties that exist between America and Great Britain. The newspapers have daily reported on public outcries and printed editorial condemnations, both of England and our own government. Most claim it is high time something is done to resolve the matter once and for all.

"Still, ships of the Royal Navy continue to stop our vessels and remove seamen from them, claiming them to be British subjects. They have virtually blockaded the entrance to New York, allowing no American ship to depart or enter without first being subjected to the scrutiny of a boarding party. That Britain continues to impose these outrages on us, a free and independent nation, is nothing more than a continuation of the insult . . . the *inhuman and dastardly* insult, which occurred almost four years back, not far from this very spot." Decatur paused, glancing for a long moment at each of us, but his eyes lingered on Henry and me.

I wondered if the haughty Mister Cochran even knew what the captain referred to. Surely it was unlikely that he knew of our participation in that dreadful experience.

Decatur resumed his monologue. "Secretary Hamilton calls on his captains to be prepared and determined while at sea. And to vindicate, at every hazard, the injured honor of our Navy. He also suggests, and I quite agree, that restoring our honor will go far in reviving the drooping spirits of our nation. I am sure that, these difficulties once resolved, our merchants will again enjoy a brisk trade with every nation they choose to trade with, and that alone should lift their spirits." He stopped, again searching our faces for agreement.

For my own part, I could not agree more with the sentiments he expressed; they were long past due. And though, as a participant in a few hostile actions and well aware of the toll of such, I would not select an armed response as my first course of action; but I knew that there had been no retribution for the injustice of Britain's policies which had inspired the monstrous insult of eighteen ought seven. I noticed from Henry's expression that he was of a like mind.

A glance at Cochran confirmed my earlier thought: he had no connection with the *Chesapeake/Leopard* affair in spite of his position in the secretary's office. Decatur's remark, save the part about the blockade of New York, seemed not to register with him and his expression remained blank.

Captain Decatur now addressed our first lieutenant. "Mister Allen, we will be preparing for sea as quickly as ever possible. I . . . *we* can ill-afford to miss this opportunity to forestall further indignity or injustice. Unless I am deceived by the feelings of all to whom I have talked since receiving this missive, I suspect there will be no reluctance in any quarter to carry out these instructions. Nor do I have any doubt whatsoever of the outcome, should a contest take place!"

"Sir. We are not fully manned as yet, nor are the men we have trained beyond the basics. There are myriad details, not the least of which are the loading out of the rest of our munitions and the upgrading of the remainder of our battery, which must be attended to before I can report to you we are ready for sea. And whatever we may find once there." Henry stood to apprise our commander of the situation.

I am sure the recollection of *Chesapeake's* departure, unprepared and lumbered, was in the forefront of his mind. Unlike Captain Gordon, *he* would not report "ready for sea" until we were well and truly ready, in all respects.

"Very well, then. I would expect you to continue, apace, those things necessary to achieve my intent. I am sure Mister Cochran will be of great assistance in procuring anything we might need and not yet have aboard. And perhaps it would be prudent to establish another rendezvous for bolstering our crew. Have you any thoughts as to when you might be ready?"

"Sir. I cannot imagine it would require more than a few more months to bring aboard supplies, ordinance, and seamen. In the meantime, of course, we will continue to attend to the rig, the battery, and those projects not completed by the Navy Yard. Pressed, I can assert to you, sir, a sailing in the early fall." Henry was hesitant, I could plainly see, to commit to a time prediction; there simply were too many variables.

I also noted Cochran's smug response to Decatur's mention of his being of help to Henry.

Judd, obviously, did as well, and whispered, "I'd warrant Billy will be of more *real* help than ever that pop-in-jay might be!"

"Very well, Mister Allen. I shall let the secretary know of our condition and, while I loathe personally anything that might extend that schedule, I will hope that we might, with fortune, improve on it."

The meeting was concluded and we were dismissed.

"Mister Cochran: please attend me, if you would, sir. I have a task for which I suspect you will be well-suited." Henry, wearing his role as first lieutenant like a well-fitted coat, established quickly his position relative to our newest member of the gunroom. Cochran, for his part, made his way to the door smiling, sure, I suspected, that he was about to be given a lofty assignment suitable to his own lofty opinion of his abilities. He had been employed by *three* Navy Secretaries, after all.

I lingered for a moment, hoping to hear what the assignment might be, but Allen and Cochran stepped forward, deeper into the gundeck and I could not easily remain within earshot.

"What do you think of our new second, Oliver?" Judd spoke softly to me as our superiors moved away. "Reckon a few days with us on the coast of Tripoli might have changed his attitude some!"

"He threw me out of my cabin, Judd. Just decided he should have it on account of it being a trifle bigger than the empty one. Not so much as a 'by your leave'; just said 'I'll take this one.' Reckon he thinks his fancy assignment in the secretary's office makes him better 'an us." I was still furious over his preempting my cabin, the one I had lived in almost since Henry and I came aboard.

"Well, Oliver, he *is* senior to you. Me too. So I reckon he likely feels that entitles him to live where he wants, save, of course, in Henry's cabin." He winked at me, easing the pain of reality. Then went on.

"But I would not count on his being much of a help in getting the barky ready for sea. I have little idea of what Henry has in mind for him, but I would think, as I mentioned before, Halethorpe would be more help in securing a few of the items we still lack. Especially now since the cap'n's signed him officially into the crew."

I still marveled that Decatur had agreed to Henry's request that Billy sign our articles, making him a full-fledged member of the crew, and that he gave him the rating of petty-officer assigned to the bosun. And a welcome addition to the crew he was, in spite of his occasional offbeat behavior. He had demonstrated, quite ably, his abilities in the bosun's department during our preparations for the trip here and during the weeklong run to the Roads. The issue of the purloined blocks, rope and paint from the Navy Yard was long forgotten, though I suspect not by Mister Johnson, the Yard Superintendent.

And Billy still addressed the first lieutenant by his given name; something that Henry had long since given up trying to stop. He now simply avoided personal contact with the man, preferring to direct his actions through the bosun or the sailing master.

Judd and I were still discussing Peter Cochran at the foot of the ladder leading to the spardeck when an outburst from the darker recesses of the gundeck caught our attention.

"A RENDEZVOUS? You want *me* to run a rendezvous?"

Judd and I shared a knowing look and moved a bit closer to hear what might follow. Cochran's voice became higher as his agitation rose.

"Sir: may I remind you I have spent many years in the office of the Secretary of the Navy, handling matters most sensitive and important. Surely having me sit in some drinking establishment, frequented by seamen, wharf-rats, and other lowlifes, trying, with spirits and tales of heroics, to attract them to join the Navy, is a less than perfect use of my many talents. Further, I am assigned as second lieutenant in this ship; I had been led to believe that that assignment held more. . . responsibility than merely operating a rendezvous. Is it not usually the job of midshipmen and junior lieutenants to manage such duties?"

"It is. And they are. Midshipmen O'Donahue and Holt, who you have yet to meet, are both running recruitment desks. Our sailing master, when he can be spared, also helps with the recruitment duties. You heard the captain mention he would like another rendezvous opened to speed the process. As you have little knowledge of the ship, but are well versed in the . . . *political* aspects of the Navy, you are my choice for that chore."

"But what about that fellow Baldwin? Well junior to me, I am sure, and this task would certainly be more suited to him than me, I think." Cochran whined, though his voice had returned to a more normal volume, causing Judd and me to inch forward a few steps.

"As I mentioned, Mister Cochran, with your fine knowledge of the politics of the Navy and, I am sure your ability to get on with most, you are my choice for the job. And I think the Horn and Thistle would be an appropriate establishment for your endeavor; it is just beyond the gates to the Navy Yard and a fine place to find seamen. You will see to it, if you please, with no further comment."

Judd and I fell into paroxysms of choking at Henry's mention of the 'political aspects of the Navy,' and had to turn away so as not to reveal our eavesdropping. Political, indeed! As to Peter's ability to 'get on with most,' we had seen little indication of that to this point.

"Oliver: isn't that tavern the worst in the city? I've not been within the walls of the place my own self, but I've heard nothing but waterfront toughs, 'longshoremen, and ne'er-do-wells occupy the place." Judd asked, a smile creasing his face.

"Aye, Judd. I've heard the same tales, but, like you, have avoided any attendance of my own. Should make our second lieutenant take notice that the seagoing navy might be a bit different from the one he has enjoyed in the secretary's office!" Thoughts of Peter Cochran spending time in that nefarious establishment made me smile as broadly as my friend.

Discretion being the better part of eavesdropping, Devon and I headed topside. We heard no more of the conversation, and Henry, having settled the matter in his own mind, appeared on deck shortly after Judd and I did.

It was still raining. The heavy air seemed to instill a sense of lethargy in all hands. The work being done on our topside long guns, I noticed, was either completed or the gunner had moved his men to the more sheltered gundeck. Certainly, there was no paucity of work for the gun crews. And after the captain's remarks, I expected Henry to begin a more ambitious training schedule, not unlike the efforts put forth in *Chesapeake* prior to our departure from this very harbor after the court martial.

It was during dinner that day that Lieutenant Peter Cochran managed to solidify his future in *United States*—at least in the gunroom. Without the smallest bit of encouragement, he began to hold forth about his previous employment, not at sea, but in the office of the Secretary of the Navy. Actually, he was talking directly to Judd, but with only four of us present (we still hoped for one more lieutenant—I hoped he would be junior to me!), there was little chance for a private conversation. I am not sure it would have been Cochran's choice in the event. And Judd, sitting next to me, on Henry's left, was directly across the table from his tormentor. Each time Peter made some self-serving observation about how important his work had been, Judd's elbow found its way into my ribs, below the level of the table, of course.

Henry, sitting at the head of the table, as befitted his position as the senior among us, seemed oblivious to the one-sided conversation, apparently deep in thought over the tasks remaining to carry out the captain's orders. He scribbled furiously with the stub of a pencil on a bit of foolscap; whether writing notes to himself or simply enumerating the tasks that lay ahead, I knew not. From time to time he would look at Cochran and, should Peter notice it, our newest shipmate would then redirect his self-aggrandizing diatribe to the first lieutenant. On the third occasion, Henry responded.

"Peter: I am sure you will find your previous chores unlike anything required of you in this ship. While at the moment we are burdened with petty details rivaling, I am sure, those with which you have experience, once we actually make sail and leave the hallowed shores of Virginia in our wake, you will find the experience harkens back to your midshipman days. It is my hope that you will be up to the task." Henry, having had enough of our newest member's puffery, effectively ended it.

Peter seemed momentarily confused at the reference to his midshipman days. "I fail to see, sir, what the experiences I . . . *enjoyed* during my midshipman time would bring to bear on performing adequately as second lieutenant in this ship. Seems unrelated to me. I have my greatest strengths developed during the nearly ten years I spent in the office of the secretary. Lasted through three of them, you know. Couldn't have been too unsuccessful with *that* to my credit!"

"Mister Cochran: I repeat, if I may, sir, that managing the day to day chores in this vessel will be most distinct from your ten years in Washington. Here, sir, should you not do your job properly, men could die. And if this country heads in the direction Cap'n Decatur, and, I might add, I as well, think it will, we will again be at war against what some have called the finest navy in the world; surely the largest and most powerful. God knows we fared poorly enough the last time we fought 'em! As you have never experienced the horror of close-in ship-to-ship combat, it will be a revelation to you, I am certain." Henry's look, as he spoke, held not a hint of friendliness.

"Should you wish to know more of what you might encounter, I am sure that Mister Baldwin, the junior among us in rank only, would be pleased to offer some of his wisdom. Or perhaps Mister Devon; he, like Baldwin, spent a year and more sorting out the corsairs of Tripoli and both have ample bits of wisdom to offer on the sundry pleasures of naval combat, should you require it."

I thought Cochran would choke. The claret he had just swallowed seemed unwilling to make the journey through his throat, preferring instead to linger somewhere short of its destination. Peter looked at Judd then me; that Devon, and especially I, should have actual battle experience was quite beyond his ability to grasp. His face grew scarlet at his effort to swallow the wine, breathe, and deal with this new, and most unsettling, information about his shipmates. Of course, with the wine filling his mouth, he was unable to utter a sound beyond the gurgling caused by the struggle within. Finally, he did manage to complete the task and, after drawing several breaths, found his voice.

"I had no idea that I served with such. . . combat-experienced officers. I am sure you both will regale me with tales of your derring-do at some point. I shall be agog, I assure you." The sarcasm dripped from every word, ensuring, at least in *my* mind, that nary a word of my past experiences would be shared out with this pompous buffoon!

Judd seemed of like mind. "Mister Cochran, I am sure, that once we join an engagement, you will discover, quick as ever you please, the true joys of naval combat. It can be exhilarating, ain't that so, Oliver?" He winked at me, the jocularity of his tone quite missed by our antagonist.

"Oh my, yes, Mister Devon. Rarely have I felt so *exhilarated* as the night we boarded *Philadelphia*. Inspirational, it was!" This was the first time I had ever spoken of that horrifying night with anything other than reverence.

"You lads are obviously having me on. And I will not tolerate . . . such . . . such insulting behavior from my subordinates. I insist on the respect due my office . . . at least in my presence." Cochran spoke with unexpected ferocity, a hard scowl pasted on his face that was designed, I am sure, to intimidate both of us.

Judd had been looking at Henry, enjoying our bit of jocularity with him when Peter spoke. Devon's head snapped around toward his superior, his face darkening with anger.

Henry broke the momentary tension. "Mister Cochran, you have barely been aboard four hours and already you seem to have antagonized your shipmates. Not a good beginning, I'd warrant. As to the respect you feel is due you: I would again remind you, sir, this is not the secretary's office in Washington. On ships, respect is earned. I am sure, once you become more comfortable in your surroundings, you will discover, or perhaps, recall, that in the fleet, both the sailors and junior officers will respect and follow an officer who leads them by example; one who knows, not only *his* employment, but also that of those beneath him. That, sir, is what you must strive for.

"Now, if you gentlemen will excuse me, I have much to do." Henry stood, nodded to Judd and me, and walked behind Cochran heading for the door.

Cochran said nothing further; in fact, no one did, and soon, Judd and I excused ourselves and left the wardroom to Mister Cochran.

That one meal seemed to set the tone for our future dealings with the second lieutenant; he never missed an opportunity to exercise his position over both Judd and me, and we, for our part, never missed an opportunity to antagonize the man, within the bounds of our junior-senior relationship. When he was aboard the ship and not sitting in the Horn and Thistle, encouraging the dregs of the Norfolk waterfront to join the Navy, and specifically, the frigate *United States*, Lieutenant Peter Cochran kept to himself. He was quiet, save for ship-related matters, during meals, and, during the day, should he not be at the rendezvous, he prowled the ship, watching my gunners at work fitting firing locks to the battery or shooting baleful stares aloft as the bosun's men bent on sails, adjusted rigging, or sent up yards.

And so went the spring and summer. Until one day, shortly after the crew had been piped to breakfast, when Arbutus 'Billy' Halethorpe appeared alongside in a longboat—not one of ours—towing a small barge.

I had the watch on the quarterdeck and Mister Cochran, always the early riser, had appeared, for the second time, to ensure I was acting the proper watch officer. My anchor watch hailed the quarterdeck, announcing a boat approaching from the bow.

"Is he making for us?" I shouted back, mostly into Cochran's face.

"Aye, sir. Appears to be Billy. And he's towing a barge."

Before the passage of five minutes, Billy was clambering up the battens, directing the messenger, whom I had sent to fetch him aft, to call out some hands to bring aboard the contents of the lighter.

"Halethorpe!" I shouted. "What mischief have you gotten into now?"

"Nary a thing, lad. Nary a thing. Just found us some supplies the barky'll be needin' once we win our hook. Something to wash away the stink of this place."

The requested sailors appeared and I watched, rapt, with our second lieutenant, as four hogsheads without markings, were swung by tackles from the mainyard onto the deck, and thence into the hold.

"Halethorpe: step aft here, if you please." Cochran's tone would brook no nonsense.

After a pause, during which a few words passed between Billy and the boat crew, our scavenger made his way, quite deliberately, to the quarterdeck.

"What, pray, was in those barrels you just put into the ship?" Cochran began before Billy could offer a word.

"Well, sir. I reckon it's sompin' we'll be needin' afore long. And I ain't seen much brung aboard yet." Billy smiled.

"I asked you, Halethorpe, *what was in those barrels?* You will render me a straight answer to the question. Shouldn't tax even a man of your capacity." Cochran struggled to maintain his Washington demeanor.

And Billy just smiled and, cocking his head to one side, began to hum quietly and shuffle his feet to a tune only he could hear. His dance grew stronger and soon his arms were swinging in time to his music, his smile broadened, and gradually, he moved away from the lieutenant.

"Halethorpe, damn it!" Peter was losing his bearing; his face contorted and the pitch of his voice went up.

And still, Billy just smiled, danced, and moved forward, away from the quarterdeck.

"Mister Baldwin. Have that man arrested. Call out the master at arms and seize him up. I will not be ignored that way by anyone, let alone a sailor." Cochran had turned about and used the same voice he had just used to blaspheme Billy.

"Mister Cochran. I fail to see the need to holler at me; I am barely a foot away from you. As to seizing Billy and clapping him in irons, there is no need for that either. The man is not right in the head. It would be most cruel to lock him away merely on account of him being a bit simple. I know him; he will settle down soon . . . perhaps after he's breakfasted, and then we'll find out what he has brought aboard. I would venture, though, that it is something we'll likely find useful, as he mentioned." I knew I risked censure by refusing his order, but I could not let him lock up Billy purely out of vexation. I also had a fair idea as to what the barrels might contain.

"We'll see about that! And we'll see what happens to junior lieutenants who refuse an order from their superiors." He stormed off the deck, heading for the companionway, hoping, I thought, to fill Henry's ear with the twin tales of his frustration.

As fervently as Cochran hoped to land Billy in irons and me in hot water with our first lieutenant, I hoped Henry would stand up for the both of us, given Mister Cochran's ignorance of our ship and people. I waited on the quarterdeck, idly watching the boat drag the now empty lighter back toward the shore.

"Mister Baldwin, sir, I am your relief." Midshipman Harold Holt had approached me from astern unseen.

So deep in daydreaming, I had no inkling he was there until he spoke, causing me to start visibly.

"Blast it, Holt! You snuck up on me without a sound!" I must have sounded irate, as he took a step backwards.

"Sorry, sir. Didn't mean to startle you. You seemed so intent on something ashore that I hesitated to disturb you, but I figured you'd want your breakfast on time and wouldn't mind. Sorry."

"Oh no, Holt. You've done nothing wrong. Indeed, you are right on time to relieve me. There is nothing actin' aboard at the moment. The captain's ashore, as usual, but will be back directly, I should imagine. You may take over the watch."

That encounter with Cochran must have stirred me up a trifle. I never snap at midshipmen like that.

I smiled at Holt, returned his salute and walked calmly forward to the companionway.

CHAPTER NINETEEN

The following two months passed quickly, so busy were we with the captain's demanding schedule: finishing the work on the battery; loading powder and shot, stores; recruiting the remainder of the crew; bending on sails and making spares; tightening the rig; testing the running rigging; and throughout it all, maintaining the ship in the spotless condition expected by both the captain and the first lieutenant.

And training. We trained the crew, about half of whom were landsmen, in everything from working aloft to managing the great guns (in dumb show, of course), use of the cutlass, and the "hauley-pulley" deck work necessary to the making and handing of sails. The watch, quarter, and station bill was drawn and the men gradually grew accustomed to getting to their assigned places without getting lost in the bowels of the frigate. Officers, especially Peter Cochran, and our midshipmen gained insight into the use of the pistol, cutlass, and navigation. Interestingly, Cochran, despite his claims to the contrary, was a poor shot with the pistol and complained the weapons we had were best used as cudgels.

The only sour note among all the hustle and bustle of our daily lives sounded one morning when Henry asked me if I knew the whereabouts of our lightning-struck bosun's mate.

It occurred to me that I had neither seen the man nor thought about him in quite a few days, being busy as I was with overseeing the employment of my division. I said as much.

"Well, he seems to have jumped ship. No one claims any knowledge of his whereabouts and it would appear he is not aboard." Henry's tone seemed a bit sad.

I assumed that, in spite of Halethorpe's casual attitude about most things in the ship, especially the protocol of titles, the first lieutenant had developed a fondness for the man and found, as I did, his eccentric behavior amusing and refreshing.

"Should I send out a few men to see if they might turn him up, Henry? I'd warrant he might have felt a need for more spirits than were available aboard and is likely sleeping off a drunk somewhere."

"A good idea, Oliver. See what you can find. And send O'Donahue as officer in charge. Won't need more than three or four, I imagine." Henry smiled, but his heart wasn't in it.

For two days, Midshipman O'Donahue scoured the waterfront taverns, pubs, houses of ill repute, and eating establishments searching, but also, asking about our scavenging crewman. But to no avail; if any had seen him, he was long gone. My thought about him sleeping off the effects of a surfeit of spirits proved fruitless and the search party returned each day empty-handed. Finally, Henry, in the face of more pressing matters, gave up. I would miss Billy's antics and his cleverness in avoiding those officers he chose not to see. And him calling our first lieutenant by his Christian name.

In late July, a freshly minted lieutenant (and so, happily junior to me) reported to the ship. Thomas Goodwater seemed a fine fellow of about my age; his experience, while including no actual fighting, held sea time on several vessels, including the frigates *Constellation* and *Essex*. We got on famously right from the start, and he quickly won over all the occupants of the gunroom save Mister Cochran, a fact that the others of us applauded. Goodwater hailed from Boston and had sailed as a lad with his father in several merchants, something, along with his vastly superior experience in the Navy, which put him squarely on our side of the rift, Cochran being on the other.

The second lieutenant had won my continuing enmity about a month after taking my quarters when I came into the wardroom and noticed him reading several sheets of foolscap, which, as I came closer, I saw were written in a decidedly familiar hand.

"Oh, Baldwin! I didn't hear you come in." He hastily folded the papers, laying them on the table to one side.

"Mister Cochran: I could not help but notice the writing there." I nodded at the papers he had just dropped. "That wouldn't be something of mine, would it?"

"Hmmm? Oh this?" He picked up the small sheaf and pretended to look at it as if just noticing it for the first time. "Let me see, now. Hmm. Yes, it would appear that . . . well, that is to say, it could be yours. I see no address on it. But it does begin with your name—unless there are other Olivers aboard—and an endearing notation." He handed the letter to me.

Of course, it was the most recent of the several dear missives I had received from Ann Perry.

"Where did you get this, sir, if I may ask?" I was seething, barely under control.

"Oh my. You must have left it lying about on the table, I'd reckon. Just picked it up to pass the time. Shouldn't get yourself all in a dither over it. No harm done, I'd warrant."

I knew quite well the letter had been in my writing desk, not left lying about the wardroom. I could feel my face reddening from the anger welling up within.

"Sir: I do not know the word *dither*, but I am sure that even in Washington, reading another's personal mail might be cause for concern. I should not think a gentleman would even consider such a violation of propriety."

"Well, Oliver. *Dither* means simply getting yourself worked up, just as you are now. Heard it all the time in the secretary's office. Seems everyone there was constantly getting their selves into a dither. And I did, in fact, read almost all the mail in the secretary's office, personal or otherwise." He stopped his prattling, and suddenly looked at me, as though he had just heard my words.

"Mister Baldwin: are you, perchance, calling me out? Suggesting that I am other than a gentleman would seem to imply a challenge. I assure you, sir, I am an accomplished marksman. And regardless of your vaunted *combat* experience, I submit to you, you would likely fare poorly were we to face each other at four, or even ten paces. If you are calling me out, you have only a moment to change your mind. I encourage you to reconsider, as I have no wish to kill you. Which, were we to duel, I surely would."

A duel? I find it pleasing to contemplate killing the man, but I never mentioned the word. It never even entered my mind until he said it. A duel? Pistols? Surely he can't think I was challenging him!

Memories of Judd and Thomas Wheatley's experience in the Mediterranean flashed into my mind; Wheatley wounded and an innocent murdered, though quite by accident. No, there would be no duels for Oliver Baldwin!

"No, sir. It never entered my mind. I have no wish to fight you. I would simply appreciate the return of my letter and your forbearance in rummaging through my possessions." So wrought up was I that I had quite forgotten that I held the letter in my own hand.

A point that Cochran smugly pointed out to me. "Now take your letter and run along, Oliver. You must learn to control your temper. Others might not demonstrate the same patience—nor might they give you the chance to withdraw from a challenge." He stood, picked his hat off the peg and left the room without a backward glance.

Suddenly the gunroom had become quite close and, desperate for fresh, if damp and warm, air, I stuffed the letter in my pocket and followed shortly behind him.

By early August of eighteen and ten, Lieutenant Allen reported us ready for sea to Captain Decatur, who promptly called for his gig and went ashore, a small canvas-wrapped packet tucked firmly under his arm. When he returned two days later, he repeated his call for the officers to assemble in his Cabin.

"Gentlemen, as you are aware, the first lieutenant has reported us ready to sail. From my own observation, it would seem so. I have just returned from Secretary Hamilton's office with orders to proceed at once to sea, joining up with *Essex, Hornet,* and for some, an old friend, the brig *Argus.* In addition to commanding this vessel, I shall also be responsible for the squadron. Commodore Rodgers will handle similar duties to the north." Decatur's smile spread quickly to each of us as we anticipated our return to open water.

That we had been landlocked for too long had become apparent to all of us, perhaps with the exception of Lieutenant Cochran. But even with his lack of experience, he was as aware as all of us were of the frustration the men and officers alike felt at being trapped in Hampton Roads; fights had broken out, sailors, in varying stages of drunkenness and disarray, were routinely returned to the ship by the local constabulary, and, in a few cases, there were desertions. This last was particularly vexing as we had yet to fill our complement. But we would sail!

"When do you anticipate sailing, Cap'n? We are still a score and more short of crew, but I suspect we will manage nicely with what we have, for now. And the men need to. . ." Henry stopped mid-sentence, noting that the captain was well aware of our condition.

"If you have stores aboard for two months, Mister Allen, we can win our anchor in two days. That will give any of you time to conclude any business you might have ashore. I have already bid farewell to Susan who will do nicely here in our Norfolk home without me. So I will be remaining aboard the frigate preparing to carry out our mission."

"Sir. You have yet to state what that mission might be." Cochran gave voice to the thoughts running through each of our minds.

"We will be enforcing President Madison's recent proclamation of the embargo with Great Britain." He looked at Henry, then shifted his gaze to me. "Much the same as some of us did in *Chesapeake* in ought eight."

I thought I heard Henry stifle a quiet groan.

What dreary duty! Near enough as dull as what we had been doing for nearly a year between Washington and here in Hampton Roads. But at sea, finally!

Dismissed to go about our duties, Thomas Goodwater caught up to me as I gained the spardeck.

"Mister Baldwin," he said earnestly. "I thought all that embargo business was through a year back. Madison opened trade again with England right after he took the office, did he not?"

Goodwater was from New England. It was an area sorely affected by Jefferson's embargoes, causing all manner of "runners" to operate clandestinely and one of the reasons *Chesapeake* had been assigned to patrol those waters. Of course he would be acutely aware of the trade difficulties his father and other traders had experienced, as well as be enormously relieved when Madison lifted Jefferson's trading prohibition.

"I learned just this week, Tom, that the British ambassador has been recalled as he did not have the authority of the foreign secretary to treat with our administration, offering to have the orders in council—the ones about stopping our ships and impressing Americans—revoked in exchange for re-opening trade. As soon as Madison learned that, he revived the Non-intercourse act and now we can go out and enforce it. And given my scant seniority, I would suspect 'Oliver' would do better than 'Mister Baldwin'."

"Well! I'd reckon my father and his associates will take to smuggling again. A sorry situation, indeed. This business with Great Britain is heading down a tortuous path. Seems like neither them nor us want to live and let live. I fear for the future, Oliver." Tom's sincerity was heartfelt; he had lived—or his family had—both with British domination and with American anti-trade laws.

There was little I could say to salve his concern, either for his family or our country. I hurried off to talk with the gunner and then retire to a quiet place and write to Ann and share the good news of our imminent departure with her.

As I wrote, describing recent goings-on aboard the ship and waxing joyfully about our plans, it dawned on me that she might not share my delight at returning to sea. But I had been almost a full year ashore—being harbor-bound, though in a ship, was just as bad as remaining on the beach—and could barely contain my joy at the prospect of clean air, rolling seas, and star-filled nights. Her last letter, subsequent to the one Mister Cochran had purloined, expressed her dismay at the recent difficulties Oliver Hazard, her brother, had experienced when his schooner, *Revenge,* had been ordered south to take station off the Charleston, South Carolina, coast. The ship had been badly damaged in a storm, losing several spars and two men to the tempest. And after repairs had been carried out and the little ship made her southing, Perry had become plagued by illness, being unable to tolerate the heat and damps of the southern climate.

According to Ann, he had requested that his assignment be restored to New England. The letter did not mention whether his request had been granted, so it was possible that *United States* and the schooner could cross tacks at sea, even though the captain had yet to mention where we would be headed. But Decatur was put in command of the Southern Squadron and, should Oliver Hazard still be in those waters, I might at least *see* his ship. I said as much in my letter, mentioning also that the captain expected us to be at sea for some two months and not to be concerned should she not hear from me in that time.

The following day, as might be expected, was a blur; final stores were loaded, sailors who had been ashore were rounded up, and everything was checked any number of times. Henry would take no chances of being caught ill prepared, no matter the circumstances.

We also discovered, or rather Peter Cochran did, the contents of the hogsheads Billy Halethorpe had stowed away prior to his departure: whiskey. The fact that Cochran did not know had consumed him to the point where he ordered the bosun to find and open one. And he became incensed over his discovery until Henry, one evening, suggested he might be better employed by "learning the skills he lacked instead of caterwauling about a few extra barrels of spirits," apparently a parting gift from the strange man.

And finally, on a bright August morning and with a fair breeze for our departure, *United States* won her anchor, set in the muddy bottom of

Hampton Roads for nearly four months, spread tops'ls and stays'ls, and pointed her bow to the southeast.

Captain Decatur stood on the quarterdeck, watching as it became evident that the training Henry had undertaken for the crew was paying off. As the tops'l yards were hauled up to their full height, he turned to me.

"Mister Baldwin, you may take her out!"

I had been watching the men on deck heaving on the halyards under the watchful eye of the sailing master and bosun, praying that nothing would go awry. I was caught all aback and was unable to respond at once, as I should have.

He wants me to conn the ship out of the anchorage! I am to be the officer of the deck, responsible for the whole ship! What if I make a mistake? I wish Henry were here instead of up forward overseeing the anchor. Oh my.

All manner of thoughts flashed through my brain; conflict and uncertainty momentarily held sway, but I put them away and, after Decatur repeated his order, I acknowledged it, properly and with a salute, and tried to show a confidence I surely did not feel.

"Anchor's in sight, sir!" Came the call from the fo'c'sle.

"Very well, Bosun." I cried out, in response. "Sailing Master: see to your tops'l sheets and braces. Stand by the stays'l halyards."

I smiled in spite of myself as I saw men scurrying to do my bidding.

"Lay in and down from aloft!" I shouted into the wind. Then, "Starboard head braces: brace around the foretops'l. Sheet home the main tops'l. Lively, now."

I heard my commands echoed by the sailing master and felt the thrill of knowing I had given the proper commands.

"On the quarterdeck: anchor's clear, sir."

"Aye, clear it is. Rig out the cat and ring up the anchor!" I was gaining confidence now with every command I uttered.

United States paid off on the larboard tack, her head bearing off as the backed foretops'l caught the breeze. When I was certain we were off the wind enough to make headway, I cupped my hands to my mouth and shouted forward again.

"Haul your braces, Mister Worth. Set the foretops'l for a larboard tack. Man the jib halyards and heave away!"

The sailing master gave me a wave of acknowledgment even as I heard him echo my orders.

The jibs climbed smartly up their stays and were sheeted home. They filled with a quiet thump, unlike the foretops'l, which, as the heavers on deck strained at the braces, shook briefly, then shivered violently as the sail's edge caught the eye of the wind, finally filling on the larboard tack with a mighty *woomph*.

We are sailing! And I did it, my own self!

I was delighted. This was as exhilarating as when I first felt *Argus* stir to life beneath my feet in Boston almost seven years ago. I am sure the smile (outright grin might be more accurate) I wore gave any who noticed it a fine reading of my joy.

"Quartermaster, make your course south by east, if you please." I remembered to give the final order necessary for the ship to make the Capes, passing Lynnhaven Bay to starboard.

"Nicely executed, Mister Baldwin. I am sure that neither Mister Allen nor I would have done it differently. You may continue to see us out of the Bay. Set your courses when you wish. Please call me when we clear Cape Henry; I am anxious to see how she goes." Decatur's compliment would live with me forever and I know my smile grew even broader.

"Aye, sir. And thank you, sir." I doffed my hat in salute.

"Should you encounter any of our consorts, please send for me at once." Decatur smiled at me again and stepped off the quarterdeck, heading forward.

"I've seen midshipmen do a more seamanlike job of sailing, Baldwin. I'd reckon you still have a good deal to learn."

Peter Cochran had come forward to stand on the quarterdeck near at hand. Earlier I had noticed him standing at the rail near the mizzen shrouds; now he was next to me. And offering insults to boot.

I whipped about, not believing my ears, sure that he was chiding me, but the disdain on his face was clear.

"Oh Mister Cochran, sir. I am sorry I did not measure up to your own standards, sir. It appeared to me that Cap'n Decatur seemed pleased enough with my seamanship." I uttered, still in some shock.

"Well, what did you expect him to say? He chose you to get the ship off her anchor. A man like Decatur does not admit easily that he has made a poor choice."

"I do not think that was the case, sir, with all due respect. He complimented me on the job I did."

"We'll see about that, I'd warrant. Perhaps I should have a word about your skills, or, more properly, *lack* of skills, with Mister Allen." He left me frowning at his parting shot.

During the next several hours, while I superintended the ship through the Chesapeake, past Lynnhaven Bay, the same body of water that had harbored the British ships, including HMS *Leopard,* back in eighteen seven, I thought of many different ripostes that I might have made to Cochran's comment. But it was clearly too late for any.

I set courses and stays'ls in an effort to, not only make the frigate look smart and seamanlike, but also to try and get a few more knots out of her. She seemed a bit sluggish, even with the nice breeze we now held off our larboard quarter.

With Cape Henry off our starboard side, I sent my midshipman, Willy (as he informed us he preferred to William) O'Donahue to inform Captain Decatur of our position, as he had instructed me. The midshipman blanched at being sent to the Cabin.

"Really, sir. I . . . uh . . . well, I wouldn't know what to say to him."

"Simply say, 'Mister Baldwin's compliments, sir, and we're passing Cape Henry. He thought you'd want to know.' Just that simple, Willy. Then listen to what he tells you. It will only be that he will be right up or that he will be along presently. I don't think that even John Thayer could make a hash of *this* job!"

I referred to our newest midshipman, a young man who had never seen salt water until he arrived at the pier in Norfolk. Straight from a Pennsylvania farm, his father had found a bit of interest with a local politician who gained for his tenth, and youngest, child, a Warrant. More to ease the burden of feeding and educating such a brood, we suspected, than to find the boy a worthy career in the service of his country. John had attained the age of thirteen years just the day before he showed up on the pier begging a ride to the ship in one of our boats. But he looked about eight and, of course, drew the appropriate comments from his messmates. The officers spoke of his youthful appearance, but only among ourselves.

He was quite without guile and, naturally, knew nothing of the Navy or the workings of a ship. I thought of my own journey to manhood and felt some measure of pity for the lad, but none-the-less, participated in a few of the pranks the officers (except for Lieutenant Cochran) enjoyed at his expense. The lad took them in stride, having been, I suspected, the butt of many such during his earlier years. And he learned quickly and seemed afraid of nothing. Henry had asked Jack Comstock, our Bosun, to "bring the lad along" and, like Bosun Anderson in *Argus,* Comstock seemed to thrive on teaching the youngster.

I think my reference to Thayer might have stung Willy a bit and, while I noticed him stiffen at my remark, he made no further complaint, doffed his hat in perfect salute to me and turned about to carry out his errand.

When the captain appeared moments later, and on the heels of my midshipman, he seemed in a fine humor. He looked about a bit, checked the set of the sails, and studied the shoreline at the southern cape for a moment.

"Well, Mister Baldwin. You have done well; here we are abeam of Henry's Cape, just as Mister O'Donahue mentioned. And nary a problem, I collect."

He stepped to the leeward rail and watched the water churn past us as we lifted on the rollers coming in from the sea. Then he cast his eyes to the heavens and studied the set of our sails for a long minute. When he turned back to face me, his easy smile was gone; in its place was a frown.

What have I done? I simply acknowledged his earlier comment. Have I forgotten something?

"The frigate seems some sluggish, Mister Baldwin. I have sailed in her near sister, *Constitution,* and found her a great deal more lively than this. Even *Congress* showed more appetite for a turn of speed."

Uh oh. Have I got the sails set improperly? Surely Sailing Master Worth would not have allowed such a blunder. Is Decatur blaming me for the poor speed we are making?

"Oh, sir," I offered quickly. "I have not yet set the t'gallants, as you can see. Perhaps with some more sail aloft, she will become more lively."

"No, Oliver. I don't think that will answer. Pass the word for Mister Worth and the bosun, if you please."

I nodded at O'Donahue who fairly leapt at the opportunity to escape the quarterdeck now that the captain trod its planks. I could hear his call for the two warrant officers echoing throughout the ship.

"Mister Worth," Decatur began as the sailing master stepped onto the quarterdeck, knuckling his forehead as he did so. "What do you think of the sailing ability of our vessel; how does she swim, hmmm?"

"Not a bit what I might have expected, Cap'n. Thought she'd be a bit more eager. Perhaps a bit of touching up on the shrouds might improve her . . . give her a knot more, possibly." Worth rarely looked at whomever he spoke to, and even the captain gained no exception to his habit; the man's eyes jumped from masthead to shrouds and back again.

I watched as the two of them, and then, when Comstock appeared, the three of them, certainly the three most experienced hands aboard in such matters, as they discussed, pointed, nodded, and gestured, as the ideas for improving our speed flew. Finally, they agreed on a course of action and, immediately, the pair of warrants left, bellowing for their seamen.

"Bring her up a couple of points, Mister Baldwin, if you please. We'll need to ease the sheets and luff her a bit so as to even the strain on the shrouds. Worth will take care of that, soon as you bring her head up." Decatur was watching carefully as the topmen scrambled up the weather ratlines and the heavers rigged purchases from the shrouds to the capstan.

While *United States* shuffled along, her sails luffing in a most unprofessional manner, the deck crew and topmen, under the direction of Comstock and Worth, heaved and hauled, marched around the capstan, and suffered the abuse of their superiors. With each change to the standing rigging, the sails would be sheeted home to draw efficiently. As soon as he was satisfied with the set of the sails, the captain would peer over the side, watch the water for a moment, and shake his head. The frigate still suffered her sluggish ways and it was beginning to look as if there was little our officers and sailors could do for it. Worth, it was, who finally became exasperated.

"She's just an old wagon, Cap'n. Ain't gonna show her heels to much of anything. Hope our lads can shoot, on account of we ain't likely to outrun any trouble we might happen across!"

Decatur whirled to face the frustrated sailing master.

"Mister Worth. You will not refer to my vessel as an 'old wagon.' She is as fine a ship as ever was built and will bring us to glory, should we have occasion to see her into action. And you may rest assured that Gunner Perkins and Mister Allen will see to it that her guns will more than make up for any shortcoming in her sailing ability. But, we will continue to make adjustments, modifications, and changes to her tophamper so she might ultimately sail as well as she will fight!

"Perhaps if we give her a trifle more rake, she will favor us with a trifle more speed. But tomorrow, Mister Worth. I fear you have fairly worn out our men today, so order an extra ration for your lads and let us try again on the morrow."

Worth saluted and left the quarterdeck, the thought of extra spirits lighting his face. Decatur's exasperation and rebuke about the "old wagon" remark seemed not to burden him a whit.

Indeed, the remark had been heard by several sailors and made the rounds of the ship as fast as the announcement of the extra ration; I heard it repeated often during the ensuing days and, while I am ashamed to admit to it, each time it caused me to smile. *United States* had become *Old Wagon,* at least when out of earshot of Captain Decatur.

We caught up with our consorts—or more aptly, they caught up with us. *Argus,* always a sprightly vessel, showed her upper works first, coming down hard from the north. Quickly hull up, she drew alongside to leeward, luffed her tops'ls, and matched our stately pace. *Essex* and *Hornet* remained a half cannon shot astern, but the former soon drew up to our windward side.

"Thank you for waiting for us, Commodore. We had a spot of difficulty two days ago with *Hornet's* rig and that slowed us considerably. But here we are now and ready for whatever lies ahead." The commander of *Essex* stood on his leeward bulwark at the mizzen shrouds and shouted to us through a speaking trumpet, giving his voice a curiously tinny quality.

"Glad you have joined us, Captain. Let us proceed and see what mischief we might thwart to the south!" Decatur had jumped onto our bulwark, but eschewed the trumpet in favor of simply cupping his hands around his mouth.

"Mister Allen: you may make your course south a quarter east and set t'gallants." Our captain spoke to the first lieutenant, who had assumed the watch from me earlier, even as he leaped from the bulwark.

The order produced a flurry of activity as topmen swarmed aloft and heavers on deck stood ready to take in hand the sheets, braces, and halyards. Even Peter Cochran, Henry's junior officer of the watch, seemed caught up in the excitement of the moment as he tried to give orders (unnecessarily) and act as though he knew what he was about.

I stood amidships, currently unemployed, and watched our consorts as they, too, set t'gallants and hauled their wind to make a course to the southern reaches of our patrol area. Sadly, before the watch had ended, they were well ahead of us; *Argus,* the stately little brig that had carried me, Judd Devon, and Captain Decatur across the sea to the Barbary War, had soon outstripped us, a fact that was surely not lost on our increasingly frustrated captain. I knew what would be coming and was not disappointed.

"Pass the word for Mister Worth and Mister Comstock."

And once again, the efforts of the previous days were played out and, to our chagrin, with little better result. And once again, I heard continuing references to the *Old Wagon.* The epithet had grown to the point where the men now referred to themselves as Wagoneers, but only when our perplexed commander was out of sight.

On the third day after joining us, *Essex* handed her t'gallants and fore-tops'l, allowing us gradually to overtake her. When we drew alongside, her captain once again took up his position on the bulwark, speaking trumpet in hand.

"Commodore: are you experiencing some difficulty? May we be of any assistance to you?"

Decatur fumed. His lips grew white with the effort at controlling his oft-spoken feelings on the sailing qualities of his ship. His glance jumped from our sails—they were set and drawing perfectly—to *Essex*, and then to the water passing by our leeward side. Finally, he climbed slowly onto our own bulwark, again cupping his hands around his mouth.

"Thank you, sir, for the offer. But no. We have no difficulty save getting a significant turn of speed out of the old girl. She seems unwilling and appears to prefer a more stately pace. You will adjust your own speed accordingly, if you please."

Without a further look at our consort, smaller, older, and apparently a good deal livelier, he instructed Judd, who had the watch, to maintain his sails as set, and retired to his cabin, still fuming over the humiliation.

Gunnery practice, both in dumb show and in live firing of the great guns, resumed the next day and continued daily for some weeks. During our first day of shooting while in company with the others, Decatur suggested in clear terms to Henry Allen that, as we were unable to outsail even *Hornet*, we had better perform up to *his* expectations during the firing exercise.

Of course, this sentiment was passed throughout the gundeck in a somewhat different form than was initially offered by the captain. Each gun crew who hit the floating targets set out, in turn by *Argus* and *Hornet*, and did it smartly, would receive an extra ration of spirits that evening. Even the carronade crews on the spardeck received the incentive.

Our long guns fired at a rate not before attained in the ship, and with startling accuracy. *Hornet* finally showed a signal indicating her captain's lack of humor at having to replace the barrels that served as targets after each salvo. And it was nearly impossible to determine which gun had actually fired the ball that struck—and often obliterated—the target, so much water was thrown up around each. But after each broadside, the target was gone, only splinters left floating in the wake of our devastating fire. Neither *Essex* nor *Argus*, for all their fine sailing qualities, could match our accuracy or rate of fire. The smile on Decatur's face broadened with each of their misses as he compared the time between broadsides to our own. At the conclusion of the exercise, *Essex* again drew alongside.

"Your gunnery is most impressive, Commodore. I salute your fine crew," came the now familiar tinny voice.

And our captain, his delight clear, both at the performance and its recognition, shot back immediately, "Thank you, sir. You may rest assured that, should we encounter any mischief abroad, we will engage whilst you make your escape. But until that day, we will continue to practice in live firing as I signal."

A silent salute acknowledged the commodore's words. There was little doubt in any who heard them that, while jocular initially, Decatur not only took most seriously our charge to assist American interests being harassed by either British or French vessels, but in fact hungered for the opportunity.

CHAPTER TWENTY

The balance of eighteen-ten passed shrouded in boredom; *United States* (or *Old Wagon*, as our stately frigate was now known, at least by her crew) completed her first cruise in the company of *Essex*, *Hornet* and *Argus* in November and with precious little to show for it. Cochran remained at odds with most of the officers; the midshipmen were learning their trade at speeds determined by their native intelligence, and our gunnery improved even over the superior level we had demonstrated to our consorts early in the cruise. Tom Goodwater and I became fast friends, sharing stories about our pasts with laughter and a spirit of camaraderie I had not enjoyed with any save Henry Allen and, of course, Judd.

Another succession of patrols were, as expected, all to the south and each lasted from one to three months, taking us into late spring of eighteen eleven. Some were with the entire squadron and others with just one or another of the brigs, but nary a one produced any opportunity for providing assistance to a beleaguered American vessel. In fact, we saw only a small handful of Royal Navy vessels, no French, and one Spanish ship. Our commission continued as before: assist American vessels which had run afoul of British or French warships, enforce the embargo as President Madison had reconstituted it, and curtail ships of any nation engaged in the slave trade. Our gunnery and seamanship continued to improve with each commission, but sadly, especially for Captain Decatur, our only targets were jetsam and rafts put overboard by our colleagues. And our frigate continued to live up to the sobriquet she had earned on her first commission, to the captain's growing consternation.

Other ships, often commanded by friends of our captain, had experienced contact with ships of the Royal Navy, a fact that ate at Decatur every time he learned of one or another. He often shared incidents with those officers invited to dine or sup with him.

"Oliver," he started one evening after the light meal had been cleared away and some claret shared out. "You remember Trippe? Served in *Vixen* during that business with the corsairs?"

"Yes, sir. A fine officer, as I recall."

Judd, who sat to my right, nodded, adding, "A splendid fighter as well. I recall the day we engaged the polaccas with the borrowed gunboats. Trippe was right in the thick of it. Never blanched in the face of fire."

"Yes, that would be the same Trippe. Well, he's been named as commander of *Vixen* now and, from what I hear, doing a right fine job of it. Faced off with a Royal Navy brig off Havana not long ago. Brits fired off a shot to bring him to and then another into him. Took the main boom with the shot, I'm told.

"Trippe responded, but with little success, and brought his ship to. When the commander of the British brig sent his boat on board *Vixen* to apologize for his error—he claimed not to be aware of *Vixen's* national character—Trippe sent the officer packing. Told him he would accept nothing short of a *written* apology. And he got it!"

"Bravo for Captain Trippe, sir." I actually clapped my hands together, but only once, so caught up was I in the splendid tale of our besting the Royal Navy.

"Yes. Well done, indeed. It sounds as if Trippe exercised fine judgment and succeeded in embarrassing the brig's commander." Devon added, again nodding his approval.

"Aye, he practiced moderation, something clearly not called for, gentlemen. Trippe missed an opportunity to remove the blot under which our flag continues to suffer and bring himself and his vessel to honor for doing so. We must not, nay, we *cannot* allow those . . . those arrogant . . . commanders of the Royal Navy to take any advantage of our ships. At some point, they must be taught that we will suffer their indignities no longer." Decatur's face was hard, his eyes gleaming in the light produced by the whale oil lamps and candles. He had placed both hands flat on the table, as though preparing to rise, but remained in his seat, his shoulders hunched up, and his mouth a thin white line.

"Sir. I wonder whether little *Vixen* might not have come to grief against the firepower of a brig. As I recall, she carried only a dozen six-pounders against the corsairs. Would that not have been a somewhat uneven matchup? And had he had his ship shot to matchwood . . . well . . ." I hesitated, realizing I was on a course set for thin water and dangerous reefs.

"I know what you are saying, Baldwin. But nonetheless, we cannot allow this provocative behavior to continue at their will. And you surely must feel, as I do, that the humiliation of Barron's meeting with *Leopard* stands like a festering wound in the breast of our nation." The captain had relaxed his posture slightly but remained agitated.

"Cap'n, do you not think that President Madison and his politicos in Washington City are endeavoring to bring about a peaceful solution to that problem? I keep reading in the press that envoys are being sent to England as well as France for that very purpose." Judd offered, obviously in an attempt to restore the peaceful atmosphere we had previously enjoyed.

"Not likely to happen by that means, Mister Devon. Those politicos will get all the agreement and platitudes the Brits can scare up, but in the end, it will have to be a hard lesson for them, if they are to learn from it. Recall, if you please, we managed, barely, to overcome them thirty years ago. And, while our Navy fared poorly in most contests with the Royal Navy, our country did manage to throw off the yoke of colonialism, thanks be to a merciful Lord and General Washington.

"Yet, in spite of that lesson, here they are again; they continue to harass our ships, board and strip crew on the flimsiest of reason, and, above all, gentlemen, let us hold in the forefront of our memories that day in June of eighteen and seven, surely the greatest blot on our national honor this country has experienced. And still the politicians wrangle over some form of restitution or compensation; I fear it is all nothing but persiflage at its finest. How do you suppose they plan to compensate Commodore Barron, not to mention Gordon and the others, for the sentences they received from the courts martial? Or those poor devils who had the misfortune to lose their lives during the contest, such as it was.

"The answer is very simple: they don't plan to do anything! I suppose, eventually, there will be some form of treaty or other device signed that will satisfy the politicos, who will then slap themselves on the back at doing such a splendid job. But the harassment will not stop, not until we show them we will no longer allow it. You gentlemen mark my words well: we will have to fight the British again."

Decatur's angry words cast a pall over the balance of the evening and, scarifying as they were, Judd and I both knew he was most likely right; there would be another war.

It was during the early morning hours a day or two later when Ben Reynolds, who now shared the watch with me, mentioned, quite casually, an incident that had occurred some months back. At the time, we were sailing in solitary splendor some fifty or sixty miles off the coast of South Carolina in our continuing quest for trouble.

"Sir: did you hear that we lost a ship off Rhode Island? Last January, it was I recall."

I had heard. Indeed, it was Oliver Hazard Perry's little schooner *Revenge* that had managed to strike the reef guarding the western reaches of Block Island Sound. The ship was lost and several hands had succumbed in the frigid waters of a New England winter. Ann had written a vivid accounting of the tragedy just weeks after it had happened. To her infinite joy, her brother had been unharmed by the loss, but, as might be expected, would face a court martial or at the minimum, a court of inquiry, just as Barron and Gordon had four years earlier. Needless to say, she felt the weight of his travail and spared little detail of it in her letter as well as in subsequent correspondence.

After several months of expressing her concern for her brother, to which I could respond only lamely, she quit the subject, dwelling on more mundane subjects instead. I had heard no more from her on the court martial and assumed it was still in the offing. I questioned my midshipman for any new details.

"I read just last week, sir, in the paper in Charleston while we were there, that Cap'n Perry had faced a court martial to determine his guilt in the loss of the schooner. The article mentioned they had exon . . . exc . . ."

I cut him off, eager to hear the finding. "*Exonerated* him, Mister Reynolds?"

"Oh, aye, sir. That's the one I was trying to recollect. I reckon it means he was not guilty, right, sir?" He smiled hopefully.

"Yes, it means exactly that. I would imagine on account of he likely carried a pilot who likely ran the vessel onto the hard. Is that what it said?"

"You must have seen the same article, sir. That is exactly what it said. The pilot had assured Cap'n Perry he would have no difficulty navigatin' them waters, even in the fog they was in. Seems right stupid to me."

"What seems stupid, Reynolds? That they exonerated Perry or that the pilot received the blame for the mess he created?" I noticed there had appeared an edge in my voice that surprised me, as well as young Midshipman Reynolds, who recoiled a bit when I confronted him.

"Oh, sir. Not a bit. I meant no disrespect to Cap'n Perry, sir. I meant just that the pilot seemed stupid to be sailing so close to a reef he should have known was there and in the fog. Don't sound like much of pilot to me, leastways."

"Aye. I quite agree with that! Likely got what he deserved for losing the ship and sure as not, damaging a fine man's reputation."

I had never met Ann's brother, but as far as I was concerned, he must be a fine man, coming from such a wonderful seafaring family. And having a sister like my Ann.

We stood our watch in silence for a while longer, the midshipman recording the casts of the chip log and taking his regular turns around the deck to ensure all was well. When he returned from one such ramble, he stood close to me, his earnest face reflected in the feeble light of the binnacle, and spoke quietly, almost timidly. Perhaps he was afraid I might again take some exception to questions about Hazard Perry.

"Sir. Why would they court martial a captain when it was the pilot what ran the ship onto the hard? Don't quite seem right. After all, ain't a pilot s'posed to know his own waters? It's what makes him a pilot, I thought. And the account of the court martial in the paper mentioned that the cap'n wasn't even on the quarterdeck."

"Ben, the captain is always responsible for his ship. Were I to run afoul of something out here and cause the ship to sink, you may be assured that our own Cap'n Decatur would be facing a court of inquiry and mayhaps, a court martial as well. Course, so would I, and you, too, more than likely." I chuckled some halfheartedly at the thought. But, in spite of my jocularity, a chill ran down my back.

"But the cap'n's asleep, sir. Down in the Cabin. Why would they court martial him?"

I resisted the sarcasm that leaped into my head and replied simply, "On account of the fact that he *is* the captain, Ben. Just like in Haz. . . Cap'n Perry's situation. Cap'n's always responsible for what happens in his ship, no matter where he is or what he might be undertaking at the moment. Just the way it works. So if you want to help keep the cap'n from facing a court martial, do your job and stay alert. "

Satisfied with that answer, and perhaps, as a response to my admonition, Reynolds nodded, and stepped into the darkness at the leeward rail, watching the moonlit water pass down the side until it was time to once again, cast the chip log.

When *United States* returned to our homeport of Norfolk at the end of May in the year eighteen and eleven, we were greeted with some bad news about yet more Royal Navy interference with American ships; news that seemed to speak directly to the captain's prognostication of looming war.

The Royal frigate *Guerriere* had stopped and boarded the American brig *Spitfire* at the entrance to New York, taking off a clearly native-born American for service in the British Navy. Newspapers devoted huge amounts of ink to the task of voicing the people's outrage at this continuing practice, made all the more disagreeable by the fact that the impressed seaman was vouched for as an American and indeed, had carried a legal protection, signed by the collector of customs in New York, proclaiming him as such. Decatur, and all of us, reacted with similar anger and heated talk of retribution.

What we learned several days later, touched off the captain like a flame to the powder hole of a thirty-two-pounder; Rodgers, in Annapolis with *President* at the time, had sailed to avenge the deed.

"We were at sea and could have been after those rascals in no time at all, had they sent a schooner out with orders! Why would Rodgers be sent? His cruising grounds are well to the north of here!" Decatur vented his spleen to any of us within earshot.

We agreed quite readily, all of us spoiling for a fight as much as the captain. And not one among us dared voice the thought that the incident that prompted some form of retaliation occurred off the entrance to New York Harbor, clearly well within Rodgers' cruising grounds. It was our— or perhaps Decatur's—bad luck that put Commodore Rodgers in the Chesapeake Bay at the time.

The captain was chafing to get his ship underway and be after "those royal rascals" to teach them a lesson they would not soon forget. Never mind that we had only just returned from nearly three months at sea and our frigate needed a few of the usual repairs, victualling, and powder to replace that which we had expended for our great gun drills.

Not two weeks later word came into the Roads that *President* had indeed engaged a Royal Navy ship. The story went that while the British ship had been seen and chased during the daylight hours, darkness had fallen before they were close enough for a hail. When Rodgers hailed, he was greeted with the roar of a pair of long guns and, of course, responded in kind. And then both ships exchanged broadsides. After several, Rodgers realized he was not engaged with *Guerriere,* the ship he had been sent out to find; the other vessel turned out to be the small, formerly Danish, frigate, *Little Belt,* mounting but twenty-two twelve-pounders. And he ceased firing. Even after such a short combat, the lightly armed Brit was no match for *President's* twenty-four pounders; *Little Belt* suffered eleven killed and twenty-one wounded.

"Mister Baldwin: Cap'n wants all officers and mids to attend him in the Cabin, sir." The message came by way of our youngest midshipman, John Thayer, who currently presided over the quarterdeck.

"Thank you, Thayer. I shall go at once."

When I knocked on the open door, I was waived in by none other than Peter Cochran who was standing next to my father's sideboard, his hand resting on it, and his posture such that he seemed more the inhabitant of the Cabin than did its proper occupant. Henry sat opposite Decatur, both deeply involved in quiet conversation. As I stepped around and past Cochran, he neither moved nor made any indication that he even saw me.

I took a seat below the quarter gallery next to Judd and watched as Lieutenant Cochran directed his juniors, most particularly the midshipmen (who would dare to say nothing to him), to seats around the Cabin. He, of course, remained standing; Henry kept his seat in front of the captain's desk. Finally it appeared as though all of us were in attendance and Captain Decatur stood and, in the silence the act promoted, looked at each us of in turn.

"Gentlemen: I have received a letter just this hour from Secretary Hamilton." Decatur brandished the missive aloft in case any of us doubted him. Cochran smirked as he looked toward Judd and me.

"As you know, Rodgers has mistakenly engaged a little twenty-two gun frigate with results that could have been easily predicted. The secretary seems to think that *President* might be marked for vengeance by our British friends and has ordered us to proceed at once to New York to join his squadron. Additionally, he has ordered a court martial for Commodore Rodgers and named me to preside over it." The look on the captain's face made it quite clear that he agreed with Rodgers' actions and presiding over the trial of his friend was distasteful to the utmost.

"To my mind, gentlemen, the unfortunate incident with *Leopard* some four years ago has been avenged. My only sorrow is that it was *President* and not our *United States* that achieved the honor."

"Oh Glory, Oliver." Judd whispered to me as soon as we had departed the Cabin, "the Cap'n was right; there's likely to be another war. They ain't about to sit still and let us shoot up some little pipsqueak ship like that. Hamilton's right; Brits are apt to be huntin' Rodgers and his squadron already. Won't they be surprised when they find a pair of heavy forty-fours as well as the others 'stead of just *President*!" Devon laughed joyfully at the thought that we might actually find the opportunity for some glory.

We sailed two days later.

The court martial was called to order a day after *United States* set her anchor in the mud of New York Harbor and, in addition to Decatur, included Captains Charles Stewart and Isaac Chauncey. Having experienced only one such event in my past, I was surprised at the small number who sat on the court, but was delighted that, after a most thorough examination of the facts surrounding the incident, including interviews and testimony of many of the officers and crew who had sailed with Rodgers, the three men exonerated Rodgers of all blame. Indeed, they commended him for his vigorous defense of the flag.

As soon as the court adjourned, we sailed, in company with *President, Essex, Hornet,* and *Argus* on a patrol designed more to show the British that the rumors of retaliation would do little to keep us harbor-bound than to actively seek out runners or slavers. We saw no other ships during the month we were out save one Spanish trader in which we had no interest whatever.

And in October, eighteen eleven, we were ordered back to Hampton Roads along with our consorts. We spent a month and more in the yard at Gosport getting the ship's bottom re-coppered while *Essex, Nautilus,* and *Wasp* sailed to interdict embargo runners, and slavers, and offer assistance to any American flag vessel being harassed by the Royal Navy.

Christmas and the new year came and went with many of us officers and a few midshipmen being allowed leave to pursue our own plans. I managed to get myself to Philadelphia for a most pleasant visit with my family which, with *Constitution* also undergoing some much needed repairs in Boston, included my older brother, Edward.

Thinking it unlikely that he would be able to make it all the way to Boston in the short time allotted to us, I prevailed upon Henry to allow Tom Goodwater to join me at my parents' home on Held Street in Philadelphia, something my friend enjoyed, though I suspect he pined for his own parents.

Needless to say, much of the discussion, particularly between Edward and myself, centered on the increased American hostility directed at England in the light of her continuing practice of impressments and persecution of our merchant ships and the likelihood of it leading to further confrontations, or even another war. I voiced our captain's sentiment, so oft expressed of late, and Edward mentioned that Isaac Hull, commanding *Constitution,* felt similarly inclined. Our parents, though outraged at the British actions and clearly pleased that Rodgers had fired at *Little Belt,* were inclined to a more moderate stance, preferring that the politicians be given more time to sort out the differences that had, for a dozen and more years, troubled our two nations.

"Don't you understand, Mother," Edward had remarked one evening at supper, "that the English will continue to stop our ships, strip crew from them, and try to suppress our trade until such time as they are made to stop. Even the latest embargo President Madison put in place last March has not made sufficient impression on them—though I hear in some quarters they are suffering—to promote sincere talks with any from Washington City. The reality is that they have over one thousand sail in their Navy and, even while occupied with the French, they have sufficient strength to completely overpower our little Navy of a mere handful of vessels. They feel that this superiority of numbers gives them the right to do what they will on the seas."

Father, hearing this, spoke up. "Would that not speak quite eloquently to trying to avoid an armed confrontation, Edward? I know I am not a naval officer and privy to much of the talk you lads hear, whether in Boston or," here he nodded at me, "Norfolk, but my simple craftsman's mind says that the fleet of ships under the British flag could make short work of anything we sent out against them."

"Father," I offered. "Most of the opinion in the Navy seems to offer that our heavy forty-fours could make short work of virtually any of their frigates, even were they to array several at once against us. *Constitution*, *President*, and my ship, *United States* are solid-built and well armed with a heavier weight of metal than the British frigates. We are closer in strength to one of their seventy-fours than a frigate. I have heard Cap'n Decatur say any number of times that there is not a Royal Navy frigate he could not take in only one hour. He only pines for the opportunity!"

The conversation continued sporadically in different forms for the ten days Edward, Tom, and I were allowed leave and, when we ultimately left for our respective duties, both our parents offered the admonition not to further stir up the enmity that might, should the politicians have their way, die off simply from lack of interest. None of us felt that outcome likely, especially since it was widely known that the British had not been satisfied with the outcome of Rodgers' court martial and continued to seek redress.

Tom, while he shared our concern over a looming war, had a different perspective on the situation, hailing from New England as he did. While he did not give voice to his convictions publicly, he did mention to me on several occasions his concern about the paucity of trade in New England

and the difficulty his family and friends experienced on account of it. A war, he claimed, might finally put under those who had been struggling with the embargoes for so many years. Though he did not include them by name, I knew he was thinking of his own seafaring family.

Wonder at British intentions peaked when, in February of eighteen twelve, HMS *Macedonian* appeared in Hampton Roads. While trade was still cut off with England, Madison's embargo did not go so far as to prevent their ships from entering our waters and, indeed, seeking refuge in any of our ports.

Captain Decatur, quite in thrall with the Royal Navy frigate, invited her captain, John Carden, into *United States* as a gesture of friendship, mutual respect, and, I am most certain, with the hope of being invited for a look at the visitor. In this he was successful and, with Henry ashore on some business, he invited Judd and myself to accompany him.

Macedonian was a fine looking ship, her paint bright, her cannon well blackened, and her decks spotless.

"Oliver, take a look at her long guns. Eighteen-pounders, they are! Surely too light for any serious fight. I wonder how she might fare against a battery of twenty-fours." Judd spoke quietly to me as we toured the gun deck with Captain Carden and his first lieutenant, a disagreeable fellow named David Hope. I noted that many of the younger sailors seemed some afraid of Lieutenant Hope.

"Aye, Judd." I responded. "And I'd warrant they favor close-in fighting; heavy in carronades, she seems; I counted sixteen of them. Thirty-two-pounders, I'd reckon, but fewer and lighter of weight than our forty-two's. On just this quick look, I'd say our weight of metal might be half again theirs. Goodness me!"

"Seems some smaller than us on top of it. Course, she'd have to be or she'd be carryin' closer to our own broadside weight." Judd shook his head and smiled.

It was not only interesting, but also educational to see the ships of other countries and how they compared to our own.

The same conversation was revisited several days later, but by the two captains. Decatur had invited Carden and his officers, as well as our officers, to a dinner party at his home in Norfolk. A most pleasant event it was, well enjoyed by all of us, English and American both. After the meal, when Susan Decatur and a few of her lady-friends, invited to add the softness of the feminine touch to the affair, had left our company, Captain Carden, perhaps in the flush of the fine spirits that had flowed most liberally, pointed out to our captain in a voice easily heard by all, the shortcomings of *United States.*

"You know, my friend," he offered, "*Macedonian* is considered, by those who know, to be the finest frigate in the Royal Navy. Fast, weatherly, and renowned for our gunnery. Even though only two years have passed since her launching, she has already established quite a fine record for success against the French. It is indeed too bad your Navy Department saw fit to provide you with twenty-fours; not nearly as efficient as our eighteens. Too difficult, by half, they are, to manhandle into battery, and demand too many men to train 'em. I'd warrant your crews tire more quickly than were they handling an eighteen."

I watched as Decatur smiled at his opposite number; we all knew he was of a quite different opinion, but a well-developed sense of propriety denied him the luxury of hostility toward a guest in his home. The only indication that his smile belied his thoughts was the two bright blotches of color that had appeared on his cheeks. Then Carden went on.

"You know, old fellow, should our ships ever meet in combat, I suspect there would be little doubt as to the outcome. After all, what practice have you lads had with war? Very little, I think. At least since that business in the late century, and as I remember it, you chaps did not fare all that well. There is the rub. Of course, we meet now as friends, and may God grant that we never meet as enemies, but, as officers of our navies, we must follow the orders of our governments. I would surely regret having to destroy that fine looking frigate of yours!" Carden smiled ingratiatingly.

Henry Allen, standing next to me and well within earshot of the conversation, nudged me with his elbow.

"*That* ought to provoke the cap'n. And he never mentioned how *well* we fared against the corsairs. I can't wait to hear how Decatur responds to that bit of bluster!"

We had barely the time to draw a breath before Captain Decatur smiled pleasantly at Carden.

"I surely reciprocate your sentiment, Captain, about our meeting as enemies and offer that we may never do so. But, should our governments order us to war, and were we to meet with equal forces, you may rest assured that it would be a most severe conflict, as the flag of my nation will never again be lowered as long as there is a hull for it to wave from!"

A profound silence filled the room and a look of surprise flashed across Carden's face. Decatur's veiled reference to Baron's surrender had struck home.

In the moment, the British captain regained his serene expression, smiled and proposed, "Captain: I would, in light of your considered opinion, offer you a wager. Should we ever meet in battle, though my hope, as yours, is that our two countries return to amity, and quickly, I will purchase for you a new beaver hat, should they still be in fashion, were you to prevail in a contest between our two ships. And I would expect that you would reciprocate, should the outcome be as I predict. What say you to that, my friend?"

"Would not the outcome of such a meeting provide sufficient reward to the victor without the added inducement of a new hat? But, should you desire to buy me one, were our paths to cross with hostile intent, I shall be most pleased to wear it with pride." Decatur's smile had faded, leaving not a trace of jocularity in its place. Indeed, both his grave look and his tone suggested he held no doubt about the accuracy of his words.

The story of the wager made the rounds of the ship within a day or two and Decatur's fervent belief in the ultimate outcome surely added to the loyalty and confidence his men enjoyed. The *Old Wagon* would never be beat!

CHAPTER TWENTY-ONE

The remainder of the winter and spring passed without incident. *United States* made several cruises which provided little opportunity for action, but the time surely was not wasted; Decatur and Henry Allen saw to it that the guns were exercised regularly, providing a level of competence that we felt was the equal of any and better than most. The midshipmen gradually learned their trade, even young John Thayer proving his grasp of the mathematics involved in the astronomical determination of the ship's position on the earth. Judd and I went through each day overseeing our divisions, supervising the training of the mids, and avoiding Peter Cochran, who continued to remain aloof and distant and, clearly, was still uncomfortable with life aboard a ship. To our great joy, he still suffered mightily from seasickness and each time we sallied forth from the relative comforts of Hampton Roads, we entreated the deity for unseemly weather.

In early June, we received orders that took us to New York once again. Only this time, there would be no courts martial or a need to bolster John Rodgers' squadron. Talk of imminent war was everywhere; newspapers ran a steady stream of editorials, either urging action or decrying the War Hawk posture, depending on which region of the country one happened to occupy. The New England states, clearly starving for trade and concerned that war would end once and for all any chance for a return to affluence, were exceedingly vocal in their condemnation of the possibility. Elsewhere, New York and Norfolk particularly, the papers were equally adamant that a "second War of Independence to prove the first" was unavoidable. In the ships of John Rodgers and Stephen Decatur, sentiment clearly favored this latter view.

I knew that my friend, Tom Goodwater, shared the sentiment of the New England journals, but equally, as a naval officer, felt that war with

England was inevitable and likely justified, and as such, he welcomed the opportunity. His private comments to me churned with consternation at the split loyalties that confronted him and I felt sorry that he could not simply share our eager anticipation of action.

That the Royal Navy was, in just the waters between the West Indies and Halifax, over seven times more powerful than our own held little sway; we Americans were defending our nation, our sailors were, for the most part, not pressed into service, and our frigates, while less numerous, were clearly superior. So too, in our considered opinion, were the little brigs and schooners that filled out our fleet.

Commodore Rodgers held the opinion that not only was war a certainty, but that it would come sooner than any expected. He had made his plans accordingly and, immediately we received word from Secretary Hamilton that President Madison had declared war on Great Britain, set out from New York Harbor in his flagship, *President,* accompanied by two frigates, *United States,* mounting forty four long guns, and *Congress,* mounting thirty-six. Two brigs, *Hornet* (eighteen guns) and *Argus* (sixteen) filled out the squadron. Our commission centered on intercepting a large convoy of British merchantmen, which had left Jamaica for England about a month earlier. Four days out, we received word from a passing American merchantman, a brig, that the slow moving convoy was some three hundred miles ahead of us.

Only a single day later, in the final hours of the afternoon watch, the lookout's cry of "Sail ho!" galvanized the ship's company with the hope of action and the resultant honor and glory that would derive from being the first to engage. That we might suffer defeat was never a consideration.

Even before the Marine drummer had sounded the beat to quarters on his drumhead, sailors were at their stations, unlimbering our guns, wetting sponges, and beginning to spread the sand that would soak up any blood that spilled on the decks. Marines ran up the ratlines to the fighting tops, muskets and swivel guns at the ready. Topmen, eschewing temporarily their positions on the gundeck, stood by the ratlines awaiting the order that would send them aloft to clew up courses for the coming fight. The drum, when it ultimately rolled, was mostly unnecessary, a mere formality.

I ran to the mizzentop with my long glass slung over my back. As the officer of the watch, it was my responsibility to confirm the sighting. And indeed, there were sails, tops'ls and t'gallants, I assumed, showing above the rim of the horizon. I studied them carefully, steadying the glass on the shrouds to keep the image still.

When I returned to the quarterdeck, the captain was waiting, his face taut with anticipation as he paced the windward side. Immediately I stepped off the bulwark, he turned to me and stopped his pacing.

"Well, Mister Baldwin? What have we found? I suspect it might be a day or two early for the convoy to appear, but perhaps a straggler, hmm?"

"A single ship, sir, it is. Full rigged and still hull-down to her tops'ls. No flag that I could make out. Possibly a warship, to judge by the set of her sails. All taut and pulling. I would reckon a merchant might be a bit sloppy in that." I doffed my hat as I made the report.

"Very well, then. Let us find out who she might be. Crack on every stitch of canvas Mister Worth might find and be after her."

I acknowledged his order and bellowed for the sailing master, who, as it turned out, was standing but three steps away from me. My embarrassment faded as quickly as it had appeared, and I gave him the captain's instructions.

"Mister Reynolds," Decatur ordered my midshipman, "show a signal to the flagship that we have sighted a ship and will investigate."

It was unnecessary to tell Rodgers, sailing in *President* some half a league to our weather, about the sighting; his own lookouts had also spotted the ship. Even as our hoist, hastily prepared, was climbing to the cro'-jack yard, a bright string of flags broke out from *President's* main yard telling the others and us essentially the same thing; we would all pursue the unknown vessel.

President and *Congress* quickly took the lead in the chase, our *Old Wagon* living up to her nickname. Even *Argus* had no difficulty in keeping up. But regardless, we inexorably all drew closer to the ship. She was indeed a frigate and broke the British ensign as quickly as her captain determined he was being pursued. Rodgers bore down from time to time to offer his iron to the Royal Navy vessel, but each time, his shot fell short and, by bearing off from the course, he lost ground, not only to the chase, but also to us. And each time *President* fired, the British frigate returned the fire with her stern chasers, equally ineffectively, but she maintained her course, crowding on sail to make good her escape. While this dance was progressing, *United States* continued to hold her course, advancing on the flagship and the chase. Soon we had caught up to the fleet, now outstripping the brigs as we pulled ahead of *President*. Decatur got himself into the mizzentop with his glass.

"You had better get yourself down to the gundeck, Oliver. I will relieve you here." Henry spoke quietly to me, sending me to oversee the battery below.

Earlier in our training, I had been assigned the spardeck guns, bow-chasers and quarterdeck guns and carronades, assisted in my duties by Midshipmen O'Donahue and Ben Reynolds. Peter Cochran, after some instruction from Henry Allen, won the main battery, a result of his seniority, according to Henry. With him on the gundeck were Tom Goodwater and Midshipman Harold Holt. I sensed that the first lieutenant, realizing that we were about to fight, had changed his mind, preferring to have Cochran on the spardeck where Henry might oversee his actions. Shooting at floating targets was one thing, shooting at an enemy ship who would be shooting back, quite another.

As I ran below, I expected the order to open fire at any moment; the British frigate had already offered a dozen rounds from her own stern-chasers, though we had been unable to tell at which of us she might be firing, so poor was her aim. I moved among the gun crews, each chafing to join the fray. Tom Goodwater, in charge of the after larboard and starboard long guns, six to a side, grinned nervously at me, while words of good cheer, confidence, and eager anticipation from the men greeted me at each gun. I smiled, clapped a few of the men on the back, and continued my tour of the gundeck, ensuring that each of the long twenty-fours were fully manned, stocked with ample powder and ball, and had slow matches lit to back up the sometimes balky firing locks. When I arrived at the forward-most guns and saw the look on Holt's face, I grew concerned; the young man was ashen, withdrawn, and oblivious to the swirl of activity about him.

Few of these lads have ever seen a shot fired in anger, much less had someone shooting back at them! I wonder how much enthusiasm they'll be showing when the first British ball crashes through our side and they see their mate skewered by a splinter!

I admonished myself for my doubt, thinking *that's* your *job, Oliver. Keeping them in their employment regardless of what's happening down here. Besides, Henry and I trained them; they'll be as good as ever they might. And remember, there is none in the American fleet who can match our gunnery for speed or accuracy.*

A bit of self-doubt crept into my thoughts. *But no one has ever shot at them before! No way to train 'em for that. But just the same, I reckon I had better stay close to Holt. Looks as if he might be about to jump out of skin.*

The Lord alone knows how he'll react when we start taking enemy ball into our hull.

But the excitement and joy they felt at now being able to put two years of training to practical use was contagious and, in spite of my own experiences, I became infused with their confidence. But why were we not bearing off some to open our larboard battery?

Clearly, I could not simply step up to the quarterdeck and inquire of Captain Decatur why he had not ordered us to fire. Instead, I made my way back to the forward battery on the gundeck and peered out one of the larboard gunports, listening to the gun crew voice my own concerns as I did so.

"What's happening out there, Mister Baldwin?"

"Why ain't we goin' at 'em?"

"Looks like they's in range, least of the bowchasers. We gonna shoot them Brits?"

Of course, I had no answers for any. I continued to crane my neck around the barrel of the cannon. Then I saw all manner of jetsam floating towards us; barrels, spars, and even two boats drifted by, one swamped and on its side, the other looking ready for use, its painter dangling uselessly from the ring on the boat's bow. The British commander was jettisoning unneeded equipment to lighten his ship! Would it make a difference? Would one of us (unlikely now to be *United States!*) be able still to catch up to him? Why hadn't Decatur fired when we had the chance?

All manner of questions raced through my mind like leaves in a fast running stream, tumbling over each other in their haste to be answered. In the midst of this chaos, it occurred to me that outside it was becoming darker.

We hadn't been at quarters long enough for it to be getting on towards dark.

I pulled my silver watch from my waistcoat and saw that indeed, it would not be dark for at least another three hours; the weather was taking a fast turn for the worse.

Just what we need now! That Brit will run into a squall and disappear. Hope we can close with him right quick!

Thunder, mistaken for gunfire and causing some to duck involuntarily, followed close behind the darkening sky, and then came the rain. Still watching out the gunport, I watched as the force of the rain beat the easy sea into a calm, the surface no longer white-capped, but now, dappled with deep pockmarks surrounded by overlapping rings where each teacup-sized drop landed. It would not last that way, I knew.

The wind increased—I could feel the frigate leaning to starboard as the force of the gale pushed her tophamper toward the sea. A bucket slid across the deck, joined by an unsecured ramrod and sponge. A cry from a gun captain sent a sailor scurrying after them as more items necessary for our employment slid down to the starboard side, drawing a laugh from the gunners who had had the foresight to keep control of their own equipment.

We remained at our stations for another two hours by my watch, until it was apparent to even the most unskilled of us that we would not engage in combat today. As if in confirmation of the muted complaints from the men, we heard, over the continuing sounds of the storm, the Marine's drum beating out the roll that would secure us from quarters and send the men to their supper, a meal they would gladly have forsaken in favor of joining into a contest with a British frigate.

As I made my way to the gunroom for our own supper, I wondered what had caused us to abandon the chase. I knew the captain would not give in except in extraordinary circumstances; he was spoiling for a fight more than any aboard. The storm, while surely unpleasant, was not suffi-cient to break off the chase. Had Rodgers and the others continued, but our stately *Old Wagon* was simply unable to keep up? Goodwater had joined me as I made my way aft down the length of the gundeck.

"I thought we had him, Oliver! What happened? Why did we stand down? Was it the storm? I wouldn't have thought the cap'n would let that stand in his way of engaging." Tom's anxious look betrayed a new feeling in him. The conflict he had earlier felt about the war when it loomed was gone and in its place was a naval officer's spark and hunger to meet the enemy face-on.

"I have little more idea than you, Tom. Henry had the quarterdeck during the chase; perhaps he can illuminate us. I am sure the cap'n must have offered him *something* by way of explanation." My confusion matched that of my junior colleague. Why indeed?

Cochran sat at his customary place and in solitary splendor at our mess table. Haskins, the gunroom steward, had yet to set out places or any food and Peter's hands gripped the edge of the table, his knuckles white from the effort. From the hunch of his shoulders, I could see he was uncomfort-able in the motion of the ship; he did not sway with it, as would a sailor, but instead, fought to remain in one position, tensing his arms and shoul-ders to counteract the movement of the ship around him. His color was, while not quite gray, surely not normal and when we first entered the space, his eyes were closed.

"Mister Cochran, sir. Are you quite all right? You look a bit peaked." Tom spoke, his amusement at the second lieutenant's obvious distress barely contained.

Peter opened his eyes and peered at us, trying to determine who had violated the tranquility of his misery.

"Oh, my God, Goodwater! Of course I am not all right! Here we are, first wallowing and then being bounced about by this dreadful weather; enough, it is, to put anyone out of sorts, and you ask if I am all right. Look at me, hanging on for dear life just to keep from being tossed about this miserable little closet we are forced to endure!" The plaintive tone was a far cry from the imperious, haughty one we had so often heard.

"Oh, sorry sir. I hadn't noticed the weather was so bad. We've certainly seen worse!"

"Aye, worse indeed, but this is bad enough. Would that I had never let the Secretary talk me into going back to sea! I thought the change would be salubrious to both my career and me. Oh, how wrong I was! Oh, how wrong. I cannot do this; I must return to Washington City. For all the annoyances there, at least the land stays still under one's feet. Those things I complained about there were petty indeed, compared to being thrown about in the belly of this infernal vessel!" Cochran dropped his head into his hands, releasing his grip on the table to do so, but as quickly as he found some solace in the position, the ship lurched and he returned them to their relentless grip on the security of the fixed table.

He closed his eyes, his position now returned to what it was when first we entered. Clearly, the conversation was over!

But not for long; our first lieutenant strode into the wardroom wearing a frown most foreboding. But when he noticed Cochran and his condition, the frown vanished like a puff of smoke in a fresh breeze.

"Hullo! What have we here? Peter, are you not well? You seem . . . well, a bit under the weather." Henry glanced at us, a smile playing at the corners of his mouth.

"Oh my God! Can't you people just leave me alone? I am wretched. And yes, the weather is the cause of my misery. The weather and this wallowing hulk of a ship! Beyond human endurance it is to be trapped in such desperate conditions!" Cochran's voice was now more a moan than anything we had heard before.

"Well, do not worry yourself about it; I am quite certain this little bit of weather will not last beyond three days. Rarely does, at any rate." Henry's solicitous tone did little to eclipse his words, and the wink he offered Tom and me caused us to look away, hiding our smiles.

Cochran noticed none of it and merely groaned, repeating how miserable he felt.

"Maybe, Peter, when we return to port you might ask Cap'n Decatur for leave, or a transfer back to Washington City. I'd wager he'd be agreeable to such a request."

"I may not last that long, Henry. I am feeling worse with every passing moment."

At that moment, Haskins entered the wardroom with a steaming tureen of fragrant fish chowder. Fragrant to all of us save Peter, who opened his eyes as the smell registered and, covering his mouth with both hands, ran from the room, nearly knocking Tom Goodwater into my sleeping quarters as he passed.

"Well, Haskins! What delectable treat have you found for us this evening, hmmm?" Henry winked again at Tom and me, this time, provoking a laugh from both of us.

"Grand timing, I'd warrant! Listening to him moan throughout the meal would have been insufferable for all of us." I offered through my laughter, then grew serious as I turned to face my superior. "Henry, what was it you were so angry about when you first came below? You looked ready to take off someone's head, you did!"

"I am as frustrated with this unfortunate weather as Peter, just for a different reason. That little frigate we were chasing just disappeared into the squall. I'd wager a month's pay he tacked or wore immediately he could no longer see us and neither the cap'n nor Rodgers has any clue as to where he might have run to. Plus, with his heaving overboard all his spare yards, boats, and, I am certain we saw him jettison at least two of his anchors, he has lightened his ship so we, most certainly, have no chance of overtaking him. *President* might, if Rodgers can find him, but we've lost time already trying to guess where he's gotten himself to." Henry emphasized his words and frustration at missing out on what might have turned out to be the first action of the war by pounding his fist into his open palm.

"Why did we not fire when we had the chance, Henry? It looked from the gundeck that we were in range of him at least for a while." I had to know. Henry seemed more likely to share out the answer than would the captain.

"You saw what happened to Rodgers when he fired. He bore off to open more of his broadside and each time, lost more ground to the chase. The commander didn't want to engage until we could range alongside and give him the whole battery. Would have made short work of that little Brit, had Decatur managed to get us up there, but when the chase started heaving over everything that wasn't nailed down, he began to pull ahead and then that squall came in. Guess it wasn't meant to be for us today." Henry sounded a bit wistful, to me. "They'll be others, I assure you. Plenty of opportunity for a good fight, before this is done!" He finished.

As we sat at the table, absent of course our second lieutenant, Henry suddenly looked up. "In case anyone cares, it was *Belvidera*."

"What was *Belvidera*?" Tom asked in all innocence.

Henry simply looked at him for a moment. As the silence grew heavy, Tom seemed to become a bit uncomfortable, as though he had made some serious gaffe.

"The frigate we chased, I'd reckon, Tom." I offered, guessing correctly what Henry had had in mind.

"Oh."

To Lieutenant Cochran's great relief, the weather moderated before the next day dawned and, realizing we had been drawn far from our intended course by the chase, Rodgers made the correction and the squadron once again headed to the northeast, still hoping to catch up with the British convoy.

It was several days later that we passed another returning American ship and learned that the convoy had been spotted off the coast of Newfoundland. Immediately, the signal went up turning the squadron in that direction.

A day and a half later, we began encountering garbage in the water; the coconut shells and orange peels we saw littering the surface gave us a visible indication that we were indeed on the right track and, most likely, gaining on our quarry.

And the next day, *President* took, without a shot fired, the British armed merchant brig *Dolphin* and learned that the convoy, consisting of eighty-five merchant sail and escorted by a single two-decker, a frigate, sloop of war, and a brig, had been sighted only the evening before still on course for the English Channel.

Rodgers took the squadron to within a day's sail of the Channel before he wisely decided that our relatively light force would be no match for the Royal Navy, should they be tipped to our presence. We tacked about, heading south for the Canary Islands and the Azores, hoping to encounter a few lone merchants or warships we might take.

We all knew the captain was less than happy when we reached Boston on the last of August. We had, as a squadron, managed to capture just six British merchant vessels and one American ship, which was under a British prize crew. We arrived in Boston to discover great celebrations in progress along the waterfront, which, at first, we thought might have been in recognition of our limited success. They were not.

Edward's ship, United States Frigate *Constitution*, had returned to Boston only hours before we did, victorious after a single ship engagement with HMS *Guerriere,* during which Captain Hull's gunners pounded the Royal Navy frigate into matchwood, leaving not even enough to sail in as a prize; the hulk was burned and sunk. I could scarcely wait to get myself over to Long Wharf, find my brother, and hear of his marvelous victory.

That night, I found Edward with some of his messmates in a waterfront eating establishment, surrounded by a large number of the good citizens of Boston, all as eager as I to hear their tale. Immediately he spotted me, Edward left his group, pushing through the raucous throng, and steered me to a table a bit away from the celebration.

"It must have been thrilling, Edward," I began. "I cannot imagine what a duel between two equals like that must have been! Please, tell me all. I can barely contain myself with envy over your brilliant victory." As I spoke, the publican placed two brimming tankards in front of us, indicating over the noise that they were free of charge, as would our meal, should we wish to eat.

"Oliver, you are quite right! I have never before experienced such a thrilling adventure! And the outcome was so much more desirable than when *Philadelphia* encountered the enemy." He smiled ruefully, recalling that dreadful day which began his nearly two years of captivity in the bashaw's prison.

Then he continued. "But before I tell you of our most lively battle, I must tell you of our narrow escape from an entire squadron—the New York squadron, we assumed—off the coast of New Jersey. In July, it was, and we were just underway from Annapolis and heading for New York.

Hull's plan was to meet up with Rodgers' squadron and add our guns to those you already had with you.

"Well, we got ourselves tied up in a southerly current and were making only very slow progress toward our destination. Cap'n Hull offered one night at table that he hoped you gentlemen had managed to get yourselves out of New York and might be heading south to find us.

"The very next evening, just at the start of the first dogwatch, we spotted a sail to the Northeast and, from the masthead, we could see the ship was under all sail, and in shore of her, we spotted four more, also under a press of canvas. They all continued that way until sundown, but even the closest was still too far in the offing to recognize any signals we might show. We continued on, still in the grip of the southerly current and suffering from a failing breeze.

"At about ten that night, we were near enough to the first vessel, now clearly distinguishable as a warship, to make the night recognition signal, which we did. Hull kept it up for a full hour and, receiving no response, he concluded that they must belong to the enemy. With such a large force against us, the cap'n wisely decided to haul his wind and we bore away to the south and east, crowding on all the sail we might manage." He paused in his narrative and took a long swallow from his tankard.

I followed suit and waited impatiently for him to finish his tale and get on to the one I really wanted to hear, about smashing the British frigate into matchwood.

"The enemy gave chase, signaling with lights aloft to her consorts. Soon we had the whole squadron after us. The daylight, when it came, showed us a frigate belonging to the enemy some five or six miles astern and behind him, a line-of-battle ship, another frigate, and brig and a schooner, all dashing after us in a decent breeze. The breeze where we were, unfortunately, had about quit and we realized they would be on us sooner than later. Two ships under our lee seemed to be making good progress and showing weatherliness quite beyond our own grasp.

"Instantly, Hull ordered the boats hoisted out and, as the ship's head had drifted around in the calm, had them pull us back toward the seaward. By now, the enemy had also suffered the absence of any breeze, and followed our lead by hoisting out their own boats.

"And at us they came! With the last remnants of the breeze and the boats towing, they came up very fast and Hull ordered a fo'c'sle gun brought aft along with a long twenty-four-pounder from the gundeck. We also dragged two of the twenty-fours aft to Hull's own sleeping cabin, poking them through the portlights in the gallery. We cleared for action, sending all the hands to their quarters station, but did not shorten to battle sail. Those men in the boats were kept there, pulling for their lives.

"We fired one of the stern guns—I thought the range might be a bit far—but Hull wanted to see if we might reach them. The shot fell short and he ceased firing as a waste of shot and powder. And the enemy had put six or eight boats to the task of pulling. With their sails furled to the yards to reduce their drag, they were fast gaining on us.

"Lieutenant Morris—I think you may have met him during that business with the corsairs, Charles Morris?—discovered we were in only twenty-four fathoms of water and Hull instantly brought up two anchors along with three or four hundred fathoms of rope and thought to warp us ahead with the boats. He mentioned it would be faster than simply pulling the ship with the boats. A look astern at the enemy making ground on us was all the inspiration we needed and all hands turned to with a will to get the anchors rigged and into the two boats.

"Each time the boats ran out the cables and dropped the anchors, the hands would heave around on the capstan and haul the ship ahead. It proved to be faster by half than rowing the ship and with a dozen and more such maneuvers, we pulled well ahead of our pursuers."

He stopped again to swallow more ale and, when I picked up my own, I realized I had been holding my breath, so in thrall with his story was I.

"I would imagine you escaped, Edward, as you're here, sharing out this tale with you little brother rather than languishing in a British prison somewhere." I still wanted the other story.

"Patience, little brother! I will get to the end quickly, but first, I must see about another tankard. Are you ready for more?" Without waiting for an answer, he picked up my pewter and pushed through the crowd of onlookers to refresh our drinks.

"Now, where was I?" He sat down, pushed mine to me, and took a drink from his own. "Oh yes, we were kedging *Constitution* away from the enemy. Well, let me tell you; those Brits didn't miss a trick! They saw what we were doing, and at once followed suit. That brought them some closer and they thought, apparently, they might be in range and opened a lively fire with their bow chasers.

"Hull, of course, fired back, and with not just the quarterdeck guns, but with the twenty-fours in the Cabin as well. Not a single British shot came aboard of us, but I believe (and so do the others) that at least *some* of our shots found their mark, as we were unable to observe splashes from many. Later that morning, one of the frigates had managed to haul himself under our lee and offered us his entire broadside; not a shot found us; they were still a bit too far for their eighteen-pounders.

"We continued to kedge the ship, quite eagerly, I thought, and we were then blessed with a light breeze from the west which helped keep us ahead of our pursuers. The line-of-battle ship broke off the chase, sending all her boats to aid with towing the frigate closest to us, but as they were towing to wind'ard and still had their sails furled, they were unable to take advantage of the breeze we had found. Or rather, had found us! But still we kept the boats working to aid the breeze.

"By dark, the wind had picked up a bit more, and the boats could no longer keep ahead of us so we picked them up. You have never seen a more exhausted pair of boats crews, Oliver. Those lads were quite spent, but an extra ration of spirits brought them around quick as ever you please!

"During the night, those determined souls chasing us lost not a bit of interest in the game and kept right on us, never in range, but threatening all the time. Of course, they had hoisted in their own boats and set their sails too.

"By morning, our fickle breeze had again died to barely a whisper, and Hull order the hands to wet down all our canvas from the royals down. Buckets and the fire engine did the job well and we soon found ourselves pulling well ahead of our enemy. They finally gave off the chase, perhaps in the realization that they would be unlikely to catch us that day or the next. It was quite tense for those days, I assure you, Brother, and few of us slept more than a bare wink at a time!" He stopped, smiled, and rewarded himself with a long pull on the pewter.

"I reckon Cap'n Hull had given over any thought of meeting Rodgers' squadron by that time, right, Edward? We had left and were well at sea in chase of a large convoy of merchants heading for England." I offered. "We did encounter a Royal Navy frigate, but she escaped us in a bit of nasty weather, so we were unable to engage. And speaking of engaging, how about the tale that brought you all this fame and celebrity?" I swallowed some ale, watching him over the rim of my tankard for some indication he might be ready to share out the story I wanted so desperately to hear.

"Oh! Yes, our second cruise, the one out of Boston. That's where we went after that harrowing experience with half the Royal Navy chasing us, you know. Not to New York. Hull must have known Rodgers' lads had already departed, assuming you made it through the British blockade stationed off . . . th' port." He looked at me, his eyes a bit bleary from the surfeit of ale he had consumed in the telling of his tale.

I nodded, absently.

"Hull had waited in Boston for some word, either from the Secretary or Rodgers, giving him instructions on where to cruise. Unfortunately, either those lads di'n't know where we were or somethin' else happened, but none found us and the cap'n determined to sail eastward toward Georges Bank and work the water between there and Cape Sable and on to Newfoundland with the hope of intercepting some small convoys we had heard were makin' up to leave Halifax for England." He was slurring more of his words and, as he paused, he took another long pull on his tankard.

"We had been out about ten days—we did take a small naval brig and the merchant under her care early on—when we espied a single sail to our southeast. From the distance between us, we could make out no details of the vessel and Hull ordered all sail and make chase.

"As we drew nearer, we saw she was a warship, a frigate, under easy sail and as we drew closer, he showed his colors and backed his maintops'l, clearly waiting for us and with the intention of engaging.

"We took in all our light sails, sent down the royal yards and poles, and reefed our tops'ls. A bit . . . later, when we were a bit closer, we hauled up our main and fores'l and cleared for action. When Hull announced his intentions to the crew, they gave three cheers and asked to be laid alongside the chase so they might board and take her without a shot fired! Hull rewarded their spirit with some spirits," he laughed at his drunken play on words, smiling at his cleverness and waiting for me to join in. He took another deep drought of his ale.

Finally, he went on. "Of course, Hull was not about to board staightaway, but instead, bore down on her weather quarter. Our quarry put an English ensign in the mizzen shrouds, in addition to the one at his gaff. Then we watched him add a Jack to his foretop and yet another at his mizzentop. He wanted to make sure, I reckon, that his flag would not be struck by any of our shot.

"Then he offered us his broadside—not a shot had the range—and wore around to fire the other. Two of these struck our side, but with no injury. All the while the Brits were firing at us, Cap'n Hull was having our own colors raised up to the mizzen t'gallant masthead, the mizzen peak, and the fore t'gallant. We had discovered that we had found HMS *Guerriere*, the ver' same ship Rodgers had been sent out to find when he shot up that little frigate back a year and more ago.

"*Guerriere* started maneuvering, trying to get the wind on us, but he could not. Finally, he managed to get himself across our bow and fire into us. Except for a couple of bowchasers, we were unable to return the fire, so Hull ordered the main t'gallant set to get a bit of speed from his ship and told the helm to run up alongside her. Which we did." He stopped again, looked around the room, which had become darker as the filtered light of the sun showing through the dirty windows waned, and took another drink.

I could not contain myself. "Edward," I said. "You must go on. I have to hear the whole tale. Don't torment me with any more interruptions."

I wanted to suggest he stop the ale until he finished, but, recognizing that he was my elder, held my tongue.

"Be patient, Brother. I have little more to tell, especially as you already know the outcome. But tell you I will." He smiled, wiped his mouth with the palm of his hand, blinked several times, and continued.

"Well, there we were, barely a rifle-shot distant from a British frigate, broadside to broadside. I needn't tell *you* what happened next." He paused again, took another taste of his ale, and smiled at my obvious frustration.

"But I will; we fired the entire broadside into her. Both round shot and grape. They fired back, but as some of our lads noted, their lighter shot simply bounced off our sides. One of the sailors called out, 'Lookee, lads. Their shot bounces off us. Our sides must be made of iron!'

"We kep' firin' with great execution and in no time . . . well, of course it took time—about fifteen minutes, I recall—his mizzen went by the boards and his mainyard hung in the slings. His hull . . . not *our* Hull," he laughed again, drunkenly, at his little joke, "was very much damaged and his sails torn up bad."

I had never seen my brother so much affected by spirits and hoped he would remain conscious long enough to finish his story. But who was I to offer a criticism? He had participated in the greatest victory our nation had experienced and was surely entitled to celebrate!

"Well, Hull realized we would pass the enemy and put his helm over which forced *Guerriere* to do the same or suffer bein' raked. But we got 'em anyway! Poured several broadsides into his larboard bow, all loaded with grape and canister. Terrible, the carnage it caused to his fo'c'sle hands and sails. Tore up the rig pretty bad on top of it. See, Oliver, with his mizzen over the side, he couldn't get the ship around and was forced to endure our raking fire." He grinned drunkenly at me, recalling the thrill of the event and forgetting that I, too, had experience at sea.

"He took more punishment, he did, as Hull continued rakin' him. Then we bore up and came around his stern, preparing to board 'em. I called away the boarding party, but afore they might even draw their weapons, the Brits foremast and mainmast went down, and took with 'em the jibboom and every other spar, save the bowsprit.

"Didn't seem much point in boardin' at that point, but we couldn't see if they'd struck, it now being full dark. Hull ordered us off a mile or two to see to our own knottin' and splicin' and wait for what might happen.

"After a while, we went back, but they seemed to have jury-rigged some kind of staff with their colors nailed to it. Hull ordered a boat rigged out and sent me over to see what was actin', which o' course, I did. Flew a truce flag so as not to draw their fire, in case you were wondering.

"Oliver, I couldn't believe the carnage and chaos I saw when I went on board that ship! Bodies and cruel wounded sailors and officers layin' about, blood and pieces of flesh everywhere, an' the medicos workin' tryin' to save who they might. Rig was down, spars and masts hangin' over the side, holes in the spar deck as well as 'tween wind and water. A mess, it was an' dreadful to behold. I thought I might be ill from the sight and the smells that greeted me. And the sounds: groans of the wounded an' dyin' souls, screams of them under the surgeon's care, and pitiful cries for everything from their mothers to spirits. But Cap'n Dacres—he was the commander there—said he'd struck and asked me to take him back to Hull so as to surrender. Which, of course, I did." He stopped again, shaking his head at the recollection of the devastation he had witnessed. He did not, however, raise his tankard, but stared at me with red-rimmed eyes, moist, I assumed, from the fearful memories.

"Hull accepted his surrender, heard of the condition of *Guerriere*, and determined he would take off the wounded and others, then burn the ship as we would be unable to sail her in as a prize." Again, he stopped, studying me for some reaction, and lifted his tankard in a silent salute either to his ship or her conquest.

I followed suit, impressed by his story, but more impressed with the splendid victory our ship had won.

"Well, hullo! You two seem right depressed amid all this gaiety and celebrating! What ho? I might have thought you gentlemen would be celebratin' your own selves, bein' brothers an' all! May I join you?" Judd Devon was standing between us, a pewter of rum held before him and a questioning look on his face.

"Of course, Judd. Edward was just telling me of their splendid victory against the British frigate *Guerriere*. That's what those others, yonder, are celebrating as well. All of Boston likely is, I'd reckon!" I smiled and stood to make room for my friend and messmate.

"Edward, you recollect my friend Judd Devon? Sailed with me and Cap'n Decatur in Tripoli and joined *United States* in back in Washington Navy Yard."

My brother stood, unsteadily, I noticed with little surprise, and stuck out his hand.

"Please' to meetcha. Don't recall having had the pleasure, though I may have forgot it. Couldna been in the Mediterranean; I di'n't even see Oliver there. I was otherwise engaged most o' the time I spent in those waters!" Edward pumped Judd's hand.

It appeared that I was the only one in the room not taking advantage of the host's largesse; Judd obviously had been enjoying a bit of rum and Edward . . . well, Edward could barely stand! I resolved to maintain some level of sobriety, if only to see my brother back to Long Wharf.

"Did *Constitution* suffer many casualties, Edward? I have only heard the tale of her glorious victory, and that already too many times to count! No one seems to have mentioned any of her souls being lost or hurt. Or the ship, for that matter. I had a look at her as we came in and she looked quite healthy." Judd sat down.

"We lost seven men killed, including Lieutenant Bush, our Marine officer. Poor sod took a ball right in the head as he was preparing to board. And the tragedy was, we never even boarded! Bloody shame, it was. He was a fine fellow and a good officer. Had seven wounded, only a few cruelly, and unless one or another of them succumb to the medico's ministrations, they'll likely all be back to duty in a fortnight.

"The Brit was a different story. I couldn't count the numbers of dead and wounded I saw when I went aboard her, but Cap'n Dacres—he was commander of the frigate—told me he'd had twenty-three killed by our shot and fifty-six wounded. Our surgeon helped him out with them, so maybe some of them will live! Or not. Dreadful sight it was to see the carnage we created! Hope never to see that again!" He shook his head sadly, and again, raised his tankard in a salute to his fallen comrades.

"Our ship was barely scratched. Biggest mess was in the Cabin when *Guerriere* got behind us after we exchanged broadsides. No holes through the hull, though the rig got some shot up; halyards, braces, a pair of shear ties, and both the fore and main masts got wounded some in their lower portions. Reckon the only reason they didn't come down was on account of their girth. Cro'jack and the mizzen gaff got shattered and a couple of boats. But considering the damage we did to the Brit, what we suffered was minor. She's a fine ship!" Again, up with the tankards, this time, to the frigate.

"Here, you heroes! Why not join us? We'd much like to hear yer tale of derring-do 'gainst that Brit! 'Specially after that fool. . . wha's his name, John? You know, that old buzzard what surrendered the whole damn army out to Detroit. Hall, or Hull—no, he's the hero of *Constitution*. Something like that, though. Right depressing it was to hear. The victory you lads brung us give us a bit o' hope that we might not get stomped inta the ground by them self-rightous Brits. Aye, a right bit o' stirrin' news it was to hear. Ha! The mighty Royal Navy whipped by a bunch o' upstarts. Reckon that smarts some!" A none-too-steady patron, a local citizen caught up in the citywide celebration of Hull's victory had staggered over to our table.

"Aye, you lads come over yonder. No point in settin' here by yerselves! 'Sides, be an honor to buy you a drink . . . or two. Right, Bill?"

"'At's what I just said, you old fool! What'd you think I was talkin' 'bout?" Bill looked drunkenly at his companion who decided to retire to another table.

"We're not in *Constitution*, sir. *United States* is our ship." Judd smiled at the new arrival, now left to his own devices by his earlier companion.

I suspected he was hoping that by mentioning we were not part of the victorious crew we might be left alone to talk among ourselves.

"No matter! Yer Navy, ain't ya? Don't matter what ship you sail; yer welcome to join us." Bill nodded at the table where his friend now slumped, and turned to join him.

We did not.

The night passed quickly, drinks, some food, and many tales of exploits shared eagerly with Edward and several others from the now famous frigate. Local folks, denizens of public houses along the waterfront, bought us vast quantities of liquor in exchange for repeated stories of *Constitution's* triumph. With little for Judd and I to boast about, we enjoyed the hospitality until we could no longer hear the story one more time, then left to find other entertainments.

Constitution's commander, Isaac Hull, remained aboard his ship for two full days without setting foot on the soil of Boston. Many invitations were sent out to the frigate, but he remained steadfast in his reluctance to bask in the adoration of a grateful public. Finally, some invitation or another—or perhaps it was just the need to feel solid ground underfoot—caused him to order his gig and appear on Long Wharf. I happened to be there to witness the throngs of people who greeted the great man.

There was scarcely room for him to set foot on the stone pier, so crowded was it with well-wishers. Salutes resounded across the harbor as cannon roared out a greeting from shore side batteries and were answered by the frigate, all doing homage to his valor. In adjacent buildings, ladies waved handkerchiefs and cast flowers on the great man as he made his way along the roadway. The city was in the same state of turmoil as it had been when first the frigate set her anchor in the harbor. Music played, cannon roared out, and people shouted praise at their hero, rejoicing over one of the most brilliant naval victories ever achieved. During his reluctant acceptance of the crowd's tumultuous welcome, Hull remained almost Stoic: his face wore a smile, he shook the proffered hands thrust toward him, and accepted the thumps on his back by the overzealous men who greeted him, but clearly, he would have rather remained aboard his ship.

And through it all, Captain Decatur churned; outwardly, his face was a mask of joy at the splendid victory won by his friend and colleague while, inwardly (and visible only to those of us who knew him well) he pined for an even greater glory than achieved by Captain Hull. We knew he would never be satisfied with a simple victory; that had been done. For Decatur and *United States,* only something even more spectacular would answer.

After *United States* had made her stately way up the harbor to the Navy Yard, Decatur badgered the civilian personnel to work quickly, "there was a war to be fought and won which can ill be done moored to a pier with riggers, shipfitters, and their debris littering our decks!"

But he knew we would be at least a fortnight in this condition, and allowed Henry a few days leave to visit his kin in Providence, just a day's carriage ride away. I went with him, seeing the short journey as an opportunity to renew, in person, my relationship with Ann Perry. Writing her regular letters, and receiving hers, was wonderful, to be sure, but here was a chance to see the lady in person, smell her sweet scent, and watch the sunlight create lovely highlights in her flowing mane. And I might just surprise her. Wouldn't that be splendid!

I surely could not sleep in the carriage, as Henry did, and engaging in idle chatter with the first lieutenant during his wakeful moments, no matter how strong our friendship had become, seemed inappropriate. Instead, I closed my eyes, perhaps feigning sleep, and conjured up images of my darling in all the places we had been together, including on the deck of *Chesapeake*. My, it seemed so long ago, and so long since I had actually held her hand and enjoyed her pleasant fragrance!

Perhaps I did sleep, as I became aware of Henry jostling me into wakefulness and saying, "We are here in Providence, Oliver. You must change coaches for the run down to Newport."

I simply looked at him stupidly, not at first comprehending his words.

"Perhaps you would like to stay the night with my family and take the morning stagecoach down to the coast. Or you might find a vessel heading that way which might drop you in Newport." He waited, expectantly, for me to regain my senses.

I shook myself into wakefulness and considered my choices: stay here in Providence with Henry's family or arrive in Newport without a place to stay or any thought of how I might get myself to the Perry's home in South Kingston. And, depending on when I might find a conveyance, the hour would be hardly respectable to go calling on a lady.

"I shall accept your invitation, Henry, to spend the night so I might travel fresh tomorrow to the coast. You are most kind to offer it and I thank you." I smiled gratefully to, not only my superior officer, but also my good friend.

"And welcome you are, Oliver. I am sure my stepmother will be most accommodating. Grab up your dunnage and follow me. It is but a short walk from here to my father's home."

I did as he instructed, slinging my scant bag over my shoulder, and followed him. We walked but a few minutes and arrived at a pleasant looking house with brick steps and a brick front on it. I was a bit surprised when Henry thumped on the door and waited for it to be answered. Why would he not simply open it and walk in? This was his family's home, after all.

Nonetheless, a pleasant looking woman, introduced as Henry's stepmother, invited us in most cordially and, after explaining that Mister Allen was away on some business errand, offered us tea and some sweets. Not wanting to intrude on his time with family, I begged fatigue and retired to a comfortable room in the back of the house where I fell asleep planning my next day's travel and my reunion with my dear Ann.

And wonderful it was, indeed. Her welcome was heartfelt and we picked up right where we had left off those long years ago. I knew the short few days we spent together would sustain me for many months, as it would have to.

CHAPTER TWENTY-TWO

A full month later, our captain still fretted about getting his ship back to sea. Now, he wracked his brain determining how he might "trump Hull's ace" and bring his own ship (and himself) some acclaim.

Decatur poured over charts, our very scant intelligence reports, and wrote letters to Secretary Hamilton seeking sailing orders. Of course, the ship, along with her now famous sister, *Constitution,* had been enjoying the ministrations of the Navy Yard at Charlestown for, at least in the latter's case, some well needed refitting. *Old Ironsides,* as she had become known since her battle with *Guerriere,* needed attention to her rig, masts, and Cabin; *Old Wagon* (even men from other ships now referred to our grand frigate by her uncomplimentary sobriquet, to Decatur's continued dismay) received the attention of the riggers with the hope they might improve her sailing qualities. Time would tell.

And for a fortnight after our return, Henry plied me with questions about my visit with the Perrys, how Ann's brother Oliver was faring, and how did I find Ann. Did she welcome me back with the same feeling she had when we parted two and more years before? He wanted to know all the details and was frustrated when I would tell him nothing except that Oliver Hazard Perry was well and back ashore in Connecticut. His frustration grew as I simply smiled, saying not a word, when asked about Ann and our relationship. Finally, Henry, busy with the day-to-day management of the work on our ship and training the men, lost interest in his quest and stopped badgering me.

In mid-September, Commodore Rodgers, William Bainbridge, who now commanded *Constitution,* and our commander all received letters from the Secretary instructing them to form three squadrons and sail independently of each other: Bainbridge would have *Constitution, Essex,* and *Hornet;* Rodgers in *President* would sail with *Congress* and *Wasp;* and Decatur would command *United States, Chesapeake,* and *Argus.*

The captain was overjoyed; this was exactly what he had been advocating since before the war began. Now, his fever to leave the confines of Boston Harbor reached its zenith; he hounded the yard workers still aboard, not only in our ship, but also still in our consorts, to finish their work quickly. He was a constant flurry of motion, pacing up and down our own decks, then being rowed to *Argus* and *Chesapeake* to personally oversee their own preparations.

Adding to the confusion of our refit, new men were reporting aboard, including a replacement for our surgeon who had left the ship immediately upon her arrival in Boston, claiming "family issues" which required his attention.

The new man was a sight to behold: stunted in growth, he wore a full beard that grew to below the first button on his waistcoat. His eyes, behind the small spectacles he wore, were piercing, but rheumy and red-rimmed, even at midday. He sported a bulbous nose, which appeared over-large for his face even with the beard. Perhaps that it looked a bit like someone had stuck a fat ripe strawberry on the end of it caused it to seem out of proportion to his face. He suffered from a slight tremor, most visible in his hands. I fervently hoped I would escape the opportunity to experience whatever medical prowess he might possess! And I pitied any unfortunate enough to require his ministrations. Eldridge Appleby's whole appearance suggested some of the gnomes I had seen illustrated in books while a child. But he settled in quickly and seemed to all of us a kind soul who had experienced more mayhem and death than any should have to endure. He was not overly verbose, but engaged in conversations that held some interest for him. Doctor Appleby seemed a welcome addition to the gunroom.

Finally, in the second week of October, all but two ships in Rodgers' and Decatur's squadrons were ready to sail. *Constitution* would still need the further ministrations of the shipfitters in the Navy Yard and would sail later, when the work was complete to Bainbridge's satisfaction. Rodgers, as the senior commander, made the decision to head to sea. *Chesapeake* and *Wasp* would catch up as best they might, or leave when Bainbridge took his squadron out. Of course, the word of our imminent departure traveled quickly to all parts of the city. There was high celebration in Boston the night before we sailed, the people hungering for another victory, and the sailors and officers eager to provide it for them.

Edward, for the moment, was not sorry to be remaining in port; the devastation and carnage of his last cruise still lingered in his mind. But he did come aboard *United States* to say goodbye to me and his childhood friend, Stephen Decatur. His wishes were heartfelt, as was his desire to see us return safely and victorious.

Flags whipped in the cool air and guns reverberated across the harbor as the four vessels sailed past Castle Island, fired salutes and received them in return. Those sailors in *United States,* not suffering from the ill effects of an excess of ardent spirits consumed the night before, offered *huzzahs* to the other ships and those ashore. Feelings were high and the grim determination was gone from our commander's face; in its place was a smile, filled with eagerness, and hope. We would come back with glory!

Within three days of our departure, Rodgers and Decatur had determined to separate and cruise independently, the *President* and her consorts heading to the east, while Decatur took *United States* and *Argus* to the southeast. The very next day, we sighted a sail.

"She's showing American colors, sir. Ship rigged she is and heading toward the west." Willy O'Donahue reported to Henry when he returned from the masthead.

"Very well, Mister O'Donahue. Advise the captain of our quarry, if you please." Henry kept his own glass focused on the ship.

"But, sir. She's flying the American flag. Do you think they're under false colors?" Willy looked to his superior for guidance.

"Very possible, indeed. Quite common in these times of runners, the war, and all the smugglers that seem undeterred by our efforts. Now go and inform Cap'n Decatur, as I instructed you."

I stepped onto the quarterdeck from where I had been checking our stern chasers.

"You think we might have something here, Henry? Or just some merchant heading home? I did not have the benefit of his long glass, but could make out the tops'ls of the vessel just above the horizon.

"Who knows, Oliver? But with the cap'n chafing at his lines for a prize, we can ill afford to let anything get by us."

As if in confirmation of his eagerness, Decatur appeared, wearing his homespun shirt of some indeterminate color, loose trousers, and a straw hat. He had adopted the "uniform" as his at-sea wear, eschewing the standard uniform as too formal and confining. Midshipman O'Donahue followed close astern.

"Well, Mister Allen. What have you found for us? A worthy prize?" Decatur picked up his glass from the rack and studied the stranger for more than a minute. Without removing the glass from his eye, he gave his orders.

"I think she might well be American. Tops'ls and her t'gallants seem right. And surely not a warship. Let us close with her then fire a leeward gun to bring her to. We'll see what she might be. And we'll beat to quarters, if you please." Decatur's voice betrayed none of the emotion he surely must be feeling at the prospect of an engagement with a worthy adversary.

The crew and officers echoed his enthusiasm, responding quickly to the Marine's drum as it beat out the insistent call to battle stations. Topmen were in the rig ready for the order to shorten to battle sail even before the gun crews had all mustered. But first, the captain ordered more sail set in order to close the distance more rapidly.

When we were about a cannon shot distant from the stranger, she responded to our leeward gun by heaving to as required. We shortened down, then backed the reefed topsails to heave to near at hand. The American flag on her mizzen gaff still fluttered in the easy breeze while her topmen, still aloft, gawked at us, as we did at them. She was obviously a merchant. Decatur kept our own crew at quarters, our guns run out, and ready for a ruse, should there be one. The merchant crew put over a boat in anticipation of being summoned to the frigate, and presently, it made its way across the half-mile of rolling sea to our side. All the while, *Argus* tacked back and forth, her guns an obvious threat, as if our own weren't enough!

"Mister Devon. Please take the quarter boat and a party of Marines and see what Captain Henderson might have aboard his ship." Decatur ordered after he had spoken with the merchant's nervous first officer who had climbed aboard the frigate, carrying his vessel's papers.

We watched as our boat made the side of *Mandarin* and Judd and his Marines clambered up her side. He made his way aft and disappeared from view; the Marines remained on deck, watching the sailors who lounged about waiting for the order to make sail. While not exactly pointing their muskets at any of the merchant seamen, it was easily seen that the Marines were ready for any surprise.

Presently, Judd reappeared and waved. He held some papers aloft, but obviously we were unable to see them, even with the glass. He stepped onto our own deck after the quick boat ride from the merchant and strode purposefully to the quarterdeck.

"She's carrying for British account, Cap'n. And has a large number of British licenses for grain to be shipped to Spain and Portugal. I brought them with me." Judd handed the sheaf of papers to Decatur, who studied them closely.

"It would appear, gentlemen, we have caught us a 'runner.' These we will hold," he waved the papers in front of him, "and send her into Norfolk. Likely won't sit well with the cap'n; he thought he was going to Philadelphia!" Decatur smiled.

"Send for Mister Cochran, if you please." The captain ordered his first lieutenant.

Henry shot me a look, puzzled at the instruction, but quickly packed off the messenger to find Peter Cochran.

"Sir? You sent for me?" Cochran was a bit breathless as he stepped onto the quarterdeck.

"I did, Mister Cochran. As you know, we have stopped a merchant, American, but carrying contraband under British license. I am sending her to Norfolk, and putting you aboard to ensure that is where she indeed goes. You may gather your necessaries while I pen a letter to her commander."

Cochran was dumbstruck. Not only was he getting off the frigate, but he was heading for Virginia, only a short carriage ride from Washington City! A smile appeared then was replaced by a more serious, businesslike expression.

"Aye aye, sir. I'll see she gets into Norfolk. And perhaps, I should take the licenses, there, to the Secretary. He would want to know about them, I suspect."

"Yes, Mister Cochran. That is exactly what I had in mind. You think you might manage that chore for me?"

"With pleasure, sir." Cochran saluted smartly, tucked the papers carefully under his arm, and departed to get his "necessaries" together as instructed.

And that was the last we saw of our friend Peter Cochran! He rode to *Mandarin* sitting in the sternsheets of the quarterboat as stiffly as when first we had seen him arriving aboard *United States* on that rainy day with the captain back in Hampton Roads.

Mandarin made sail even before our boat was back aboard and *United States* and *Argus* continued to sail to the southeast in the hopes of finding something more worthy. And two days later, Decatur shouted new orders to *Argus* as we lay hove to side by side.

They were to sail independently to the south, while we would head to the southwest. Perhaps separately, one of us would find suitable prey.

Now quite alone, not a sail to be seen in the full sweep of the horizon, Henry and I wondered whether sending the brig off by herself was a wise decision.

"You know how Decatur feels, Oliver. According to his thinking there isn't a ship up to a seventy-four in the Royal Navy we couldn't take in an hour or less. Besides, Hull was quite alone when he took *Guerriere*—and in only half an hour, if one is to believe the accounts we heard—and I know the cap'n is convinced our gunners are superior, even though the ship is not as handy as *Constitution*."

"Yes, but what about *Argus*? Were she to engage with a frigate of *Guerriere*'s strength it would be folly." I was concerned about my first ship. The thought of her being turned into matchwood by a British frigate was unsettling.

"*Argus* is a fine ship, weatherly and fast. I suspect should Cap'n Sinclair discover himself in an untoward position, he will exercise his command's fine sailing capabilities and scurry to safety. Do not fear, Oliver; little *Argus* will not come to grief." Henry smiled and patted my arm in a solicitous manner, ending the discussion.

"Tell me, Henry," I said one evening at supper. Something had put me in a most jovial frame of mind. "Do you miss our colleague? Gone nearly four days now, he is."

Henry shot a glance at me. I noticed Tom Goodwater, sitting across the table suppressing a smirk. Quite certainly *he* didn't miss Cochran! For my part, I tried to maintain an even expression so as not to give away my mindset.

"Oh my, Oliver. I do hope you are joking with us. Miss Peter Cochran? The pride of *three* Navy Secretaries? The very one Secretary Hamilton *bribed* our commander to take off his hands? The self-same . . ."

I interrupted his dissertation, incredulous. "Did you say *bribed* the cap'n to take aboard? How long have you known this, Henry? And why, for heaven's sake, did you wait until now to share it?"

"Oh, the cap'n told me some time ago. He'd been trying to figure a way to get the man out of the ship without offending the Secretary when he shared the whole tale with me. Didn't think passing it on to you fellows would serve any useful purpose." Allen laughed at our expressions.

He went on to explain. "Reckon the Secretary couldn't abide the man any more than we could! Either he offered Cap'n Decatur something wonderful or called in a favor Decatur owed him, but either way, we got to enjoy the man for two and more years. Likely scarred some of the mids permanent-like! I know young John Thayer was terrified of him. But now he will be the Secretary's problem again, if he'll have him back! And you witnessed how eager our late second lieutenant was to get those shipping licenses to Washington City!" Henry laughed at the recollection.

We all joined in, our fine sense of camaraderie restored, the prospect of finding a British ship to fight or take as a prize filling us with anticipation. The meal was filled with happy banter and good claret, which Henry had ordered our steward to break out as a form of celebration.

The next morning, right at daybreak, my lookout hailed the quarterdeck.

"On deck, there! Sail! Sail to weather. Four or five leagues distant."

Maybe this was our chance! I sent Willy to the maintop with a glass and waited impatiently for his return, glassing the sea to our windward side myself in vain hope of discerning what might be out there.

"Sir: she is quite large, under a press of sail, and heading on about the same course we are. Sir." O'Donahue reported even before he had gained the quarterdeck. As his feet landed on the planks of the quarterdeck, he added, "Might be a Spaniard out of the Azores from her size."

"Very well, Midshipman. Kindly inform the captain." I held my nervous excitement in check; it might only be another merchantman.

But what if it is a warship? And more powerful than us? Willy said she was large and under a press of canvas. Could it be a seventy-four? And here we are, by ourselves with no one to look to for assistance should we need it.

Stop it, Oliver! We can handle whatever is out there. We have the best gunners in two navies! And Stephen Decatur as our commander.

Before I could resolve my own confused emotions, the captain stepped out of the companionway fastening the buttons on his homespun shirt. The straw hat was tucked under his arm, mashed flat.

"Well, Mister Baldwin? Mister O'Donahue mentioned something about a large contact under full sail to our wind'ard. Have you determined what she might be?"

"Uh, no, sir. I expect in a few more minutes she will have closed enough to see more of her rig and . . ." I stammered. I thought it best not to guess or offer Willy's conjecture of her being Spanish.

Before I finished my thought, Decatur was on the bulwark and into the mizzen ratlines, his long glass slung across his back.

"Bring her up a point, Mister Baldwin!" Decatur's voice drifted down from the mizzentop.

"Aye, sir. Bring her up a point!" I responded and gave the necessary orders to the quartermaster on the helm and the heavers on deck. And gradually, we began to close with the stranger.

With our ship's lethargic pace—obviously the riggers in Boston had done little to improve her sailing qualities—Decatur ordered more sail set.

"No doubt, Mister Baldwin. She's a warship. As I watched, she bore up a trifle so as to close with us, even as we did. I would wager she will be British and spoiling for a fight!" The captain rubbed his hands together in anticipation of action.

Who's spoiling for a fight? I can't speak for the Brit, if that be what she is, but I can see Cap'n Decatur is!

"We'll have the men fed promptly, Mister Baldwin. Can't fight on an empty stomach. Then to quarters immediately. Won't be two hours before we're engaged."

I ordered the bosun's mate to pipe the hands to their breakfast, at the same time ensuring that their hammocks were neatly rolled in their nets along the bulwark. I was never convinced that those rolled bits of canvas would actually stop a bullet, but, as I would be on deck for this engagement, should that turn out to be what happens, I thought it best not to take too many chances. And suddenly, I realized I was nervous about a contest that might prove our own mortality. I fished my silver watch from my waistcoat pocket and glanced at it.

I didn't particularly care about the time, but noted it was not yet seven. I fondled the watch for a bit, recalling the day I left my parent's home in Philadelphia back in eighteen-three when my father had presented it to me. And having it stolen, then recovered, in Boston. Oh! How young and inexperienced I had been then!

The first lieutenant appeared shortly, offering to take the quarterdeck for me so as I might get a bite of beef and biscuit prior to the action; I readily agreed.

Hardly had I finished the last dry morsel of ship's biscuit, washing it down with strong coffee, than I heard the drum's insistent beating. I raced to the spardeck, quickly checking to ensure that Judd and Tom Goodwater had everything in hand below. I suspected that Midshipman Holt might be less than useful should ball and grape begin to fly, but was confident in the ability of the forward gun captain, a man I knew to be steady and skilled in his employment.

From my station for battle at our stern chasers, I could see that indeed our quarry was a frigate of the Royal Navy, and of size sufficient to satisfy even Captain Decatur. The long red battle streamer stood out against the morning sky like a slash of blood on a white shirt. I tore my eyes away from her as I made my rounds, ensuring that the gun captains had readied our two long twenty-four-pounders and their companions, a pair of ugly, short-snouted carronades per side, each capable of throwing a forty-two pound ball some one thousand yards. Of course they were indeed ready, tompions removed, side tackles cast off, fresh powder cartridges laid out carefully, and all manner of projectiles stacked neatly in the shot racks.

Sand had been spread to soak up any blood that might get spilled as well as provide traction for the men; cutlasses, boarding pikes, and battle-axes were stacked in their racks at the mizzen mast and also, I could see, forward at the main and fore masts. Nets had been rigged to catch any debris that might fall from on high, should the enemy attack our rig. Marines had made their way aloft and a handful was loading their muskets in the fighting tops of each mast. All the way forward, I could see the powder monkeys running the felt cartridge bags of powder to the bow chasers under the control of young John Thayer. Amidships, the heavers and haulers were on station, exposed to enemy fire, but ready to trim sails as the first lieutenant directed. No doubt, they, as I, hoped the hammocks neatly rolled in the netting would protect them from the musket balls fired at them by the Royal Marines in the enemy's tops. Of course, even the landsmen among them knew those hammocks would hardly slow down a load of grape or solid shot.

At each gun station, I encouraged the men, checked our powder and shot, and peeked at our adversary.

She had borne up further, intent on closing with us while maintaining the windward gauge. Noting our relative positions, I realized that if Decatur holds his course, we would pass to leeward and ahead of the British vessel allowing us to offer her a raking fire while only her bow chasers might bear. Even though we might not gain the advantage of being to windward, we would surely be better positioned to open our broadside than they would. And I could see that the Brit was a good bit faster than our *Old Wagon*, even with the extra canvas Decatur had ordered so as to close with our adversary more quickly.

Suddenly, from across the water came the dull *boom* of cannon fire. I watched, in thrall, for the shot; the range seemed long to me. I smiled, pleased with my "eye," as I noted two splashes some five hundred yards distant.

"Hold your fire, lads. We will make our shots count. No point in wasting the powder!" Decatur's voice easily reached to the fo'c'sle and, I am sure, below to the gundeck.

We waited, watching. As the enemy continued to close, I noticed that our captain and first lieutenant were deep in conversation, each gesturing, describing what could only be maneuvers of the enemy and our own ship. Suddenly, Henry's voice rose above the sounds of the sea and squeaks and groans of our rigging.

"Prepare to wear ship! Heavers to the braces and sheets."

The sailing master and bosun directed the spardeck activities as the ship slowly began to bear off, turning her stern to the wind and the enemy. And then we were sailing in the opposite direction, well ahead of our adversary, and clearly out of his range, as he was now out of ours.

What is Henry doing? Decatur must have told him to wear, but why? We are moving away from the enemy!

And then it began to make sense, even to me, inexperienced in this sort of engagement as I was. Decatur was going to let the Brit catch up and we would be alongside, broadside to broadside, with our superior weight of metal. I imagined that when the enemy frigate had used his greater speed to overtake us, Decatur, using our own lack of speed, would slip under his stern, gain the windward gage, and rake him as we went by. A brilliant plan, it seemed to me.

"On the gundeck: Mister Devon, you may fire as they bear!" Decatur's voice rang out clearly.

"Mister Baldwin: as quickly as the carronades will reach, you, too, may commence your firing. Do not waste your powder." His voice, carried aft to me by the wind was as calm as though he might be inquiring about the ship's speed.

I shot another look at the enemy; she was indeed closing with us! We would be firing directly. I felt the ship ease her bow up, closer to the wind.

Henry is bringing her up a bit to close the distance separating us. Good! We'll be firing all the sooner.

"Stand by to tack! Take in hand the braces and sheets! Topmen, clew up the courses. Mister Sailing Master: get those men moving!"

Tacking? Why on earth would we tack now? We should be opening fire!

But tack we did. Still we had not yet fired a shot. I watched the British frigate; she was off our starboard quarter and coming on hard.

The carronades and stern chasers will bear!

"Stand by the carronades! Long guns, check your train tackles! Gun captains, blow on your matches." I gave the orders I had been trained to give and noticed Henry turn to make sure I wasn't wasting powder and ball.

"Good job, Oliver. Let 'em have it!"

They were in range; I peeked down the barrels of the long guns, watching the enemy, as the ship appeared perched on the end of each gun.

"Long guns: FIRE!" I shouted, more out of my own zeal than any necessity, as *United States* lifted her stern on a wave.

BOOM! BOOM!

The two big guns spoke almost as one and I watched for some indication of my success . . . or failure; either a splintered hole in the side of the enemy, or a splash in the water between us.

"Nice shot, Mister Baldwin. Keep it up as long as they will bear!" Decatur's voice seemed almost quiet, yet I could hear him, even with the temporary ringing in my ears from the firing. I turned, and stuck my elbow squarely into his midsection!

"Oof. Seems to recall your actions when first we met, Oliver!" Decatur, taking no offense at my clumsiness, was smiling.

My goodness! He still remembers that horrible day in Boston when I slammed my sea chest into him.

"Oh sir! I am so sorry. I didn't . . . that is, I thought . . . you were forward, sir."

"Don't worry, son. That was nice shooting. You got a piece of him. Keep it up." He smiled once more and turned, heading back to the quarterdeck.

And keep it up I did. The men fired, swabbed out the bores, reloaded, and dragged the massive guns back into battery as quick as ever they had. Our shots scored more hits than misses. Even the carronades were hitting, though, I suspect, with little damage inflicted due to the extreme range. But even over the half mile separating us from our quarry, I could see the men and officers in her working their own guns as they tried to inflict as much or more damage to us and scurrying about, seeing to the damage we . . . *I* . . . had created. And then we were again out of range.

Decatur watched the enemy through his glass, waiting for their next move. Suddenly he turned to Henry and spoke loud enough for me to hear.

"My stars, Allen! That's Carden! That's *Macedonian*! We shall make matchwood of her. I wonder if Carden has realized whom he has met. Now we shall see about the 'pride of the Royal Navy!'"

I instantly recalled the boastful and brash remarks the British captain had made about his ship at the captain's home only some eight months back. I also recalled Decatur's answer and the wager Cap'n Carden had offered. Now we would determine which ship was the stronger and which had a better crew! There was little doubt in my own mind, but in battle, chance frequently plays a role, and we would have to wait for the whole of the encounter to run its course. I remembered that *Macedonian* carried a lighter broadside than did we, and also that the British relied more on their carronades.

As I watched the British frigate, she wore around, still maintaining the weather gauge, a distance off of a bit over a mile, and now sailed the same course as we did. While behind us, I knew she would catch us up soon enough and encouraged my gun crews to stand ready.

"She'll be alongside quick as you please, lads! Stand by your matches. We'll show them who's the better!" Henry shouted to the spar deck gunners.

I am sure the fellows below, eager to get into the fight, heard his words as well, as they let out a lusty *huzzah* and were immediately joined by my crews as well as those on the fo'c'sle. Rammers and sponges were brandished aloft, a further demonstration of the enthusiasm for the coming fray.

Meanwhile, *Macedonian* continued to gain ground on us. I studied the ship as she approached and wondered why Captain Carden did not bear off a bit to close the range for his lighter eighteen-pounders, but I could fathom no reason for his action.

Maybe he doesn't yet realize who we are. Thinks we're gunned the same way he is and wants to stay a safe distance from us 'til he is ready to move in for the kill. Won't he be surprised!

One part of my brain continued to wrestle with the tactics while another checked my guns and carronades, making sure all was in readiness for the imminent fight.

Decatur ordered our sail reduced to the battle canvas, reefed tops'ls, jib, and mizzen. He did leave up the mizzen stays'l as well, likely figuring that with our slower speed, it might be helpful to have just a bit more than might otherwise be necessary. And as the sails were reduced, the British frigate gained on us even more quickly. But, still, Carden maintained the same span of water separating us.

"Stand by, lads. Be ready to fire as you bear!" Decatur's shout was easily heard, our well-disciplined crew maintaining complete silence throughout the ship.

I watched the Brit, knowing full well that my guns would be the first— again—to offer iron to the enemy.

"Mister Baldwin, I believe your twenty-fours might reach. You may fire when you are ready." The captain spoke only as loud as was necessary for me to hear him.

And ready we were; I sighted down the barrel of the nearest long gun to confirm the gun captain had trained the carriage around to aim at the Royal Navy frigate. And the seas were starting to build some more. I waited a heartbeat than cried out.

"Fire!"

A split second later, as *United States* lifted her stern on a wave, the larboard twenty-four-pounder roared out, momentarily extending her nine foot iron barrel with a six foot stream of orange flame. We were loaded with solid shot and I watched a section of bulwark, forward on *Macedonian's* starboard bow, explode in splinters, followed a moment later by a satisfying *thud* that resounded across the water..

For a moment, I pictured the mayhem and destruction those flying splinters would bring to the unfortunate souls near at hand. I would never forget the cruel wounds, the blood, the broken bodies that the iron shot from HMS *Leopard* wreaked in *Chesapeake* when *their* twenty-four-pounders unleashed their fury on us.

Now we're repaying that kindness, Oliver! Think of it that way. I admonished myself for taking momentary pity on my enemy.

Boom! Boom! Two shots fired by *Macedonian* drew my attention away from my thoughts and I watched as a pair of splashes momentarily marked the water with fountains of white foam where the balls fell, well short of our side. And then the lower deck guns on our ship spoke, firing from the aftermost guns first then each joining in as they could find the target. I thought of Tom Goodwater down there in the tight confines of the gundeck.

The heat, smoke, noise, and constant motion of the guns bucking back in recoil, the crews working feverishly to swab, load them, and haul them into battery so the cycle could begin again, must be some daunting for the Massachusetts man. Regardless of how much time at sea he had and how many times he had witnessed our battery firing in practice, there is little that can prepare one for his first actual combat encounter. And I knew he would be waiting for the first enemy shot to come crashing through our own side, throwing splinters everywhere, piercing any who had the misfortune to be in the way. I was glad to be topside where I could stand up, see my enemy, and breathe air without the choking smoke that fouled the air on the gundeck.

Our guns below continued firing at a frenetic pace. Smoke, tinged with lavender, and smelling of sulfur and the acrid, nose-searing odor of burned black powder, wreathed our sides, obscuring our view of the enemy until the wind blew it clear. I am sure we must have appeared to be on fire to the British, so heavy were the smoke and orange flames shooting out from the gun barrels. And through it all, the enemy maintained a slower rate of fire back toward us.

The few shot that actually hit *United States* had so little energy left that they scarcely caused any damage. Certainly a few splintered our bulwarks and several rounds of bar or chain shot parted some of our rigging, not so badly as to cause concern, however.

One of my larboard long guns roared out and I heard the gun captain exclaim, "Lookee there, lads! We have made a brig of her!"

I looked in time to see *Macedonian's* mizzen topmast fall, dragging with it all manner of cordage and timber.

"Huzzah, huzzah! We've made her into a brig!" One of the men repeated, his whole body echoing his glee.

I laughed and shot a look forward to where Decatur and Henry Allen were calmly studying the action. The captain must have heard the comment about making the ship into a brig.

"Take down her foremast, lads, and she'll be a sloop!" He shouted from the quarterdeck and waved a congratulatory hand.

"Mister Baldwin, change your shot to chain shot, if you please! And lively. With any luck, we will take down the others." Henry called out, using a speaking trumpet to ensure his generally quiet voice would carry over the cacophony of the battle.

I waved to him, and gave my men the orders. I heard him issue the same order to our crews below and watched as, after a moment or two, the deadly double round shot, held together by a length of chain, began to decimate the standing rigging of the enemy. And then the main topmast tumbled down, its shrouds cut by our effective fire and the use of chain shot.

The captain stepped aft to where I was directing the fire of my two long guns; the carronades had yet to be called into service as we were still beyond their effective range.

"Mister Baldwin: I propose to take us in closer and give her hull a pounding with the forty-twos."

"Aye, sir. I will see to it." I responded, reaching up to doff my hat in a formal salute.

It was gone. I have no recollection of how or where it might have parted company with me; a casualty of the battle, I assumed. Decatur, seeing my effort to acknowledge his order in proper fashion, smiled and doffed his own, the old straw hat that had seen better days. When he returned to the quarterdeck, he conversed with the first lieutenant briefly, whereupon the latter stepped to the hatchway leading to the gundeck and disappeared.

And close her we did. Within a few minutes, the carronades could reach out and send their forty-two pounds of destruction into the wooden sides of the British frigate. The fire we received in return was sporadic and ineffective. I could imagine what their gun and spar decks must look like, with rigging and spars littering the latter, dismounted cannon and wounded men littering the former. In spite of the chaos they experienced, it was apparent, at least in *my* mind, that Captain Carden did not put the same effort into training his men in gunnery that our esteemed commander did. And further, they had no Henry Allen, our expert in naval gunnery, and responsible for the training our men received.

A few shots—they still fired solid shot—hit us and splintered bulwarks forward. One knocked a bowchaser off its carriage. Many of their shots flew over our heads, sounding like tearing canvas as they flew by, to splash harmlessly in the Atlantic Ocean. And then I heard a different noise: it sounded like the buzzing of bees, a whole swarm of them.

"Get down, sir. Their Marines have the range now." Wright, a sailor assigned to work the breeching tackle on one of the long guns, shouted at me.

I glanced at him as a fountain of gore erupted from his upper arm. Before I could get to him, the gun captain had ripped off his own neckerchief and wrapped it tightly around his wounded comrade's arm, stanching, for the moment, the flow of blood. I turned back to my post by the forward-most carronade. Suddenly I felt a sharp blow to my midsection, like I had been punched by a giant.

I fell back, knocked off my feet and stunned at the realization that I had been hit by the very thing the sailor had warned of: a Marine's musket ball. My vision blurred; I didn't seem to mind, though. The noise of the battle seemed to grow distant, cannon fire merely dull thuds that caused me no distress at all. Images of my parents, Edward, and my dear Ann floated before my eyes. They all seemed to know each other and appeared quite content in their surroundings. Thomas Wheatley, my nemesis from the schooner *Enterprise*, drifted into the picture, laughing at my plight. Then, as an illusion created by a clever magician might do, he simply disappeared. Ann continued to smile lovingly at me, and I knew it was her hand I felt on my cheek, soothing and cool. It was all very peaceful and harmonious. That I should experience this in the very midst of a battle seemed not a bit odd to me. There was no sound save the gentle lapping of water, like a mountain brook burbling its way around the rocks and stones in its bed. And there were no ships, no sails, no chaos; only a brilliant azure sky and my loved ones watching over me.

". . . hit his watch, I reckon. Won't be much good for tellin' time now, I'd say, but likely saved him from havin' me pokin' around in there with forceps while his life blood spills out. Nothing seems to have penetrated his body. No blood on him. Might have busted a rib or two, but he'll be good as new in a few days."

As the words filtered through the mists of my consciousness, I became aware of smelling rum. The images I had been watching, Ann, Edward, my parents, all faded, to be replaced by the thuds of cannon fire that seemed to get closer and sounds of men shouting, distantly. And overhead, sails, some full, some backed, and some clewed up to their yards replaced the beautiful bright sky I had so enjoyed. I shut my eyes, screwing them down tightly in an effort to return to my earlier images, but to no avail. And the slightly sour odor of rum was most insistent.

Surely the captain would not have issued spirits during the heat of battle! Why would I smell rum? We don't even have any aboard. And what was that about my watch? Has that rascal from the Boston waterfront taken it again?

I struggled to sit up and felt strong hands grab my shoulders.

"Take it easy, lad. You can sit up in a moment or two." As I heard the words, I again smelled the distinctive aroma of rum, this time closer.

I opened my eyes, made the effort to focus, and found myself staring into the hirsute face of Eldridge Appleby, our surgeon. His strawberry nose, supporting his spectacles, loomed close as he peered into my eyes and his rum flavored breath fouled the air between us. Behind him, I saw Henry Allen standing with Captain Decatur, each wearing a concerned expression. The sounds of the battle returned now in all their harshness and I could distinguish the sharp roar of our long guns, the heavy, deep-throated *clump* of our carronades, and, now, the crack of musketry, apparently fired by our own Marines in our fighting tops. I tried again to sit.

This time, no hands held me back, but the sudden pain in my side caused me to cry out and clutch at my midsection.

"I warned you about sittin' up, Oliver. Just catch your breath, there, and you'll be fine. A bit of pain, to be sure, but nothin' that might bring you to grief. Your friend Holt wasn't so lucky as you; splinter from the forward bulkhead went through him—through and through—right into his heart. Likely was dead afore he hit the deck." The thick beard and his quite dirty glasses obscured Appleby's expression, but his tone seemed to imply that he was saddened by the loss of our midshipman.

"Holt?" I asked stupidly. "Is the ship badly wounded?"

Holt's station was below on the gundeck; if he had taken a splinter, a fatal splinter, we must have received a shot into the hull there, near his battery.

"No, son. The ship is barely scratched. But Holt was topside, just aft of the fo'c'sle when he got hit. No tellin' why he didn't keep his post. Just bad luck, I reckon." Appleby patted my shoulder and, saying a few words to the captain and Henry, headed forward. From his hand dangled my watch. Or, more accurately, the *remains* of my watch. Before I could call out for it, he returned and put in my hand the ribbon fob from which dangled the ruined timepiece. I mumbled my thanks, I think.

"Can you stand, Oliver? Here, let me give you a hand." Henry bent down, offering his extended hand, which I took gratefully, and managed to get to my feet. The pain in my side seemed no less and I found it worse when I took a full breath. Tentatively, I prodded my ribs and belly. The former produced a sharp pain and I resolved not to do that again.

Now I remembered my watch, dangling from its ribbon, in my left hand. I held it up before my eyes and my heart sank! The beautiful silver watch given me by my father was destroyed! The case was stove in, the cover hanging by a single hinge, and the crystal and face unrecognizable. Of the hands, there was no trace. I was stunned! My watch had been stolen in Boston when I was just a raw midshipman and returned to me by a kindly warrant officer in *Argus*. It survived that and over a year fighting the corsairs of Tripoli only to be smashed in a frigate battle in mid-Atlantic. And, apparently, it had saved my life!

As I turned to Henry, it felt as though there was something else in my waistcoat pocket; likely a few bits from the corpse of my watch, I thought. I fished around in the depths of the damaged pocket, trying not to rile up the throbbing pain just behind it, as Henry grinned at me.

"That must be some lucky watch. Saved your life, it did. That bullet would have likely gone right through you, had your watch not caught it. Wrecked the watch, but you're still right side up! Well done, Oliver."

He turned to return to the quarterdeck as I pulled an object out of my damaged pocket, clearly not any part of my watch. Turning it over in my fingers, I realized it was the musket ball intended to be my undoing, and resolved to save both remnants as talismans of good luck.

My personal ordeal now behind me save for the pain in my side, I looked about, not sure what I expected to see; I had no idea how long I was "out of action," only that the battle continued. *Macedonian* was close aboard now and our forty-two's were pounding her without mercy. The intense fury of our cannonading filled the air with smoke, even in the fine breeze; the noise blotted out everything, even making it difficult to think. I could only imagine what it must be like below in the confined space of the gundeck and, in spite of the musket fire of the Royal Marines, was glad to be topside. I looked closely at our adversary.

Her foretop was hanging by its shrouds, and her jibboom absent; only the stub of her bowsprit remained. Even a cursory glance showed many places in her hull where our shot had penetrated and she seemed unable to sail.

"Boarders, stand by!" Henry's cry caught me by surprise. It had looked as if the enemy was done, incapable of carrying out further fighting. Why board?

"Wagoneers! To the waist and make ready!" The bosun's shout and his use of our fine ship's rude nickname made me smile in spite of myself.

"Mister Comstock!" Decatur could not have missed it. "That will do. You and your men will arm yourselves and stand ready, should we need to board her. And show a little respect for our ship, if you please. She has done us proud and will bring us to glory!"

His tone was not chastising. Decatur was in fine humor; it appeared that he had beat a most worthy opponent and would sail back to Boston a conqueror, just like his friend Isaac Hull. His ship was barely harmed—a stove-in bulwark forward and a shattered mizzen t'gallant mast—and only a handful of his crew wounded or killed. But he was far from finished.

I watched as the men assembled in the waist, armed to the teeth with cutlass and pike, cheering each other, our guns, and our fine ship, and jeering at the British man-of-war we had apparently bested. And then, with a crash, our fore t'gallant mast fell, bouncing off the web of running and standing rigging to land safely in the netting strung above the spar deck for just such an eventuality. To a man, they ducked, then laughed at each other, relieved that no serious harm had befallen us.

We continued to fire, our carronades throwing forty-two-pound shot into the *Macedonian's* hull from a scant two hundred yards, while the long guns kept up a steady fusillade of chain shot into her rig. When the British mizzen—what was left of it—went over the side, victim of our twenty-fours, the enemy vessel became completely unmanageable. The spar and cordage dragging overboard caused the ship to bear off, even as the helmsman fought to hold his course. And *United States* began to pull ahead.

My goodness! He is going to bear off across her bows and rake her with a broadside! That should certainly finish the job! The carnage . . .

My contemplation of the captain's strategy was interrupted by his own shout. "Belay the boarders! Back to your posts. She is done, lads!" Decatur stood on the bulwark at the quarterdeck, clearly a target for any with a musket on *Macedonian*.

With our adversary disabled, unable to steer, and with barely a mast on which to hang a sail, our *Old Wagon* quickly pulled ahead. All the while, the captain watched his enemy, never taking his eye from the long glass he kept focused on their quarterdeck. He did not bear off to offer a raking broadside as I had anticipated he would, but instead turned away from the hulk.

"Stand by to tack. Men to your stations for tacking." Henry Allen called out and received a wave from the sailing master in acknowledgment.

Then we were back alongside, now facing in opposite directions, and hove to, waiting to see what the pride of the Royal Navy might do. It appeared that chaos reigned supreme in her; men rushed about, sorting through wreckage. Bodies were thrown overboard, and the cries and screams of the wounded and dying drifted across the water to our own ears, causing more than one of us to shudder involuntarily.

"Lookee there, boys! She's struck!" One of the sailors in the waist cried out, his glee at the British action undisguised.

Indeed, the colors, the British battle ensign, had been hauled down from the stump of the mainmast, leaving the wallowing, unmanageable hulk vanquished by *United States* and her valiant crew!

"Mister Allen, take a boat with a boarding party across and bring Cap'n Carden here. A few Marines should answer nicely. Mister Baldwin, you will accompany him, if you please." Decatur, still in his homespun shirt and straw hat, neither any the worse for their wear, stood on the quarterdeck, his glass tucked under his arm.

My ears were still ringing from the gunfire as I boarded the boat, following the Marines, each with a loaded musket slung over his shoulder, down the manropes. We were rowed across the heaving seas to the side of the drifting ship.

Not a soul on deck even acknowledged our presence; no boarding ropes were dropped, nor any threw us a line to secure the boat. There was a great deal of shouting, cursing, moaning, and the scraping of fallen spars being dragged across the deck above us. Without warning, a body slid over the side, splashing into the water just astern of the boat.

Henry surveyed the scene and directed the cox'n to ease the boat up to where the main chains were attached to the ship's hull. Stepping on the torn remnant of an open gunport, he clambered onto the channel and, using the shrouds, pulled himself up to the shattered remnant of the bulwark and landed lightly on the deck. I followed his action, and quickly we had the boat secured and our Marines aboard the British ship.

The sight that greeted us put me immediately in mind of Edward's description of what he found on the deck of *Guerriere:* sailors, some quite obviously drunk, staggered about the deck; others dragged broken spars and cordages around, seeking fallen messmates, while still others, some cruelly wounded, cried out for help. Surrounding all this motion and noise, shattered bodies, limbs, and bits of flesh lay in great pools of drying gore. Cannon barrels, dismounted from their carriages, lay askew on deck, one covering part of an obviously quite dead sailor. To my horror, I espied a head, or most of one, lying under the pin rack that surrounded the stump of the foremast. I swallowed hard, trying to suppress the bile that rose in my throat, as I quickly looked away, studying intently a ragged furrow along the deck, dug by one of our shot.

No officer or warrant officer seemed in charge on deck. Finally, Henry pointed to the quarterdeck where they all stood, waiting, it seemed, for us to take charge.

"Cap'n Carden? I am William Allen, First Lieutenant in *United States.* Cap'n Decatur has asked me to bring you across the water to our ship, if you please, sir." I noticed that Henry used his proper name and saluted as he addressed the beaten British commander.

"Very well, young man. You look some familiar to me. Hmm, did we not meet some months ago at your captain's home in Virginia?"

"Aye, sir. We did. February of this year, sir, it was. Please come this way." Henry turned and led the way to where our boat, now secured to the side of the frigate, rose and fell with the still heaving seas.

As Captain Carden climbed down into the boat, Henry said softly to me, "You want to stay here, or come back with me? I am not sure you will be assured of your personal safety here, what with all these drunken louts running about. Must have broken into the spirit locker, the whole lot of them. Some discipline!" Henry smiled the smile of a victor.

I went in the boat, more curious to see what would transpire when the two captains met, than concerned for my safety. After all, there were eight Marines, armed, to protect me should it be warranted.

As the boat pulled across the water, Captain Carden studied his ship. She was a perfect wreck! Her rig mostly down, her hull broken by our heavy carronades in well over two-score places that I could count, and bodies still being thrown into the sea, she made a most forlorn sight.

"Where is Captain Decatur, Mister Allen? I would have expected him here to meet me in some manner of a civilized naval commander." Carden spoke to Henry immediately after setting foot on the clean planks of the American ship, his arrogance still unchecked.

He did not look at Henry, but cast his eyes all about our ship, taking in the order and lack of serious damage we sustained in stark contrast to the chaotic mess he had just left.

"There, sir. He is on the quarterdeck, awaiting you. I will take you there." Henry pointed.

"I see no captain on the quarterdeck . . . or elsewhere, young man. Are you quite sure he is not below, in his Cabin?"

"Yes, sir. He is just there, by the bulwark, starboard side." Henry pointed again, then set off, expecting Carden to follow.

"You mean that . . . figure . . . that caricature . . . in the straw hat and homespun garment? Surely even *your* Navy is not so desperate as to allow a captain to appear in such . . . garb!" Carden sputtered, both furious at being beaten by upstarts like us Americans, and outraged that the victorious captain would not deign to greet his guest in proper uniform.

"Aye, sir. That's him. And I reckon what he's wearing ain't likely to change the outcome!" Henry was simply not going to put up with this man's arrogance; did he not lose the contest, and badly?

Decatur, clad in homespun and straw hat exactly as the Royal Navy commander had observed, returned Captain Carden's salute with a smile, then greeted his former guest most civilly.

"I am sorry we meet again under these circumstances, sir. But it would appear, that the question posed in my home has been answered, at least to my own satisfaction!"

"Hummph! Indeed! I offer you my sword, sir. You fought well. It appears that I am forced to wear the unseemly distinction of being the first of my service to lose in single ship combat to your Navy. Would that it were not so." Carden lowered his tone, his head, and his arrogance.

"Oh mercy, no, Cap'n. That is not the case at all, sir. Your colleague, Cap'n Dacres of *Guerriere* fell to our *Constitution* under *my* colleague, Isaac Hull, late in August. It would appear you are the second, sir. And I will not accept your sword. You fought a fine and honorable contest." Decatur spoke with sincerity, as if he could feel the man's humiliation.

"My goodness, Dacres . . . how dreadful!" Carden uttered, clearly not as bereft at his colleague's loss as he was pleased at not being the first to strike to the Americans.

"Mister Allen, take another boat and the surgeon, if you please, and you and Mister Baldwin send back the other officers, the severely wounded, after Mister Appleby has had a look at them, and see what you make of the wreck. Take Comstock with you; I am sure he will be of help." Decatur dismissed us to continue his conversation with the defeated Royal Navy officer.

And back we went. This time, the officers seemed less hostile and even sent a midshipman forward to direct a few of the more sober seamen to assist our crew in securing the boat and heaving down the manropes for our ascent to the deck. Little else had changed, however, from our first visit; drunken seamen staggered around the deck, searching for fallen comrades as they heaved and hauled on all manner of debris; spars, dismounted guns, rigging, and wounded sailors still lay mostly where they had landed during the battle. And the officers continued to maintain their position on the quarterdeck, not in any order, but in groups of two or three, seemingly by rank, talking among themselves and watching us with sideways glances as we made our way through the chaos toward them.

Henry seemed immensely pleased with the result of our cannonading. He smiled and muttered praises for the men he (and I) had trained in gunnery. When he approached the group of lieutenants standing by what remained of the wheel, one detached himself and strode angrily forward, as if to intercept us from approaching his fellows. He wore a bloodied bandage wrapped around his head but seemed unconcerned about the wound. Several others, officers all, showed signs of having received offerings from our gunners and marksmen.

"What, may I ask, sir, is your intent, now that you have made a perfect wreck of my ship?"

"Sir. Are you, perchance, the first lieutenant in *Macedonian*?" Henry asked in perfect civility and courtesy.

"I am he, sir. And you are. . .?"

"I am William Allen, First Lieutenant of the frigate *United States*. This is Lieutenant Baldwin, Third Lieutenant in that vessel. We are to see you safely across, with your more serious wounded, to *United States*. Our surgeon, Mister Appleby, is already examining those of your wounded still on deck and, I am sure, he will seek out your own surgeon, to offer whatever assistance he might, when he has completed his rounds topside.

"Our boat awaits you, sir, and I would be obliged were you and your officers to make your way to it. I assure you, your treatment on our ship will be as courteous and civilized as any you might expect." Henry pointed to where our longboat bobbed in the still heavy swells at the break in the bulwark.

"You surely do not intend to send me," he paused a moment, glancing at his messmates, then continued. "And my colleagues, away without our baggage?"

Henry looked the man squarely in the eye. "You do not suppose to have been taken by privateersmen, sir?"

"I do not know by whom I have been taken." The lieutenant glowered at Henry as he offered the insult.

It suddenly dawned that I had met this arrogant fellow before; he was Lieutenant Hope and I further recalled that when I had visited this ship in Norfolk, I had noticed that many of the crew and junior officers were quite afraid of him.

"Sir: you will conduct yourself and your officers into the boat, if you please." Henry's voice had hardened. It no longer bore the earlier civility and courtesy I had heard at first.

As the officers made their way forward to the boat, Henry spoke to me, loudly enough for the British officers to hear plainly what he said. "Oliver, assign two of the Marines as guard over the officers' baggage, if you please. Direct them to use whatever force they might need to protect it."

"Aye, sir." I doffed my hat (recovered from the carriage slide of a forty-two-pounder carronade, where it must have landed just before my watch was shot) and went to carry out the order, noticing as I did so, that another boat—this one was filled with American sailors—was approaching the British frigate.

When I returned from my errand, the deck was a hive of activity. American and British sailors (those who were unwounded and of sufficient sobriety to help) seemed bent on sorting out the mess, moving the wounded, and, already, a spirit of camaraderie and order was taking over. I learned, during the course of the afternoon, that many of our men and many of the Royal Navy sailors were acquainted. Surprised at first, it occurred to me that we had several British seamen aboard and, of course, the Royal Navy ship would have pressed Americans in their own ship's company; it seemed quite natural that some might indeed know each other and, of course, they shared the common bond of being sailors.

We all worked with a will. Henry, Mister Comstock, bosun from *United States*, and I directed the efforts of the combined force of sailors with the assistance of a handful of Royal Navy petty officers. By nightfall, and blessed with continued fair weather, we had made surprising progress, not just with the spardeck, but with the structural damage to the formerly British frigate as well.

To be fair, a few fights had broken out between the American and British sailors, spurred on by the sense of outrage felt by the vanquished tars at losing a combat to those "damnable upstart Yankees." I am proud to offer that the Americans kept their good humor and soon mollified their Royal Navy counterparts. Those Americans who would remain in *Macedonian* over the night were welcomed into messes and a fine sense of camaraderie seemed to prevail.

Henry and I returned to *United States* for supper and were invited to join the captain in his meal. Captain Carden was in attendance as well, seemingly over his bout of misplaced arrogance, and, considering his circumstances, quite jovial at the hospitality offered him.

"Well, Mister Allen. How did you find the frigate?" Decatur asked after the initial formalities ran their course.

"Sir. She is cruelly wounded, as you have seen, and the hull has received more than one hundred of our shot, by my count. The rig is mostly down, lowers alone on fore and main are in place, but not unscathed. The carronade batteries forward as well as those on the quarterdeck are mostly dismounted and more than half of the eighteen-pounders below have been rendered useless. "The seamen bore the brunt of it, sir. Their surgeon and Mister Appleby told me there were thirty-six men killed immediately and another thirty-seven or so with wounds severe enough that both medicos doubt their survival 'til morning. Another group, thirty and more by count, are less severely hurt and Mister Appleby, at least, feels they will survive their wounds. He mentioned in addition, sir, that the

British surgeon is a credit to his profession." As Henry spoke this last, he looked directly at Captain Carden and smiled.

Carden acknowledged the compliment with a modest inclination of his head, but said nothing, nor did he smile.

"Is she safe afloat, Mister Allen? And can you and Mister Baldwin restore her ability to navigate?" Decatur clearly had a plan in mind.

Henry paused thoughtfully, though I am quite sure he anticipated the question since we had discussed that very topic only hours before.

"I believe so, Cap'n. It will take some time to jury rig topmasts and a new mizzen as well as plug the holes in her sides. As long as the weather holds fair, we should be able to manage it in perhaps a fortnight."

"Splendid! Splendid!" Decatur smiled broadly as he digested the news. "I am not sure I can afford you as much as a fortnight, Henry. No telling what the weather might have in store for us in these latitudes. November can be troublesome, you may recall."

The captain was absently rubbing his hands together, something I had learned he did when agitated. Now, with the smile spread across his face, it appeared that the action spoke only of his joy with our accomplishment and his eagerness to finish what he had begun.

Then, almost under his breath, he added, "Yes, we will bring our prize home. It would be shameful to sink such a fine vessel."

He had, in his own mind, trumped his colleague's ace.

CHAPTER TWENTY-THREE

It was not, in the event, a fortnight; five days saw us with a rig of sorts, patches covering the lowest and most dangerous holes in our sides, and a prize crew composed of British prisoners of war and American sailors, Lieutenant Henry Allen commanding. I was named first lieutenant.

All during the days and nights of our reconstruction, *United States* lay close by, her sails clewed up and, while not at battle stations, the gunports remained open and the dangerous working ends of our main battery were fully exposed. Boats shuttled back and forth, carrying men and supplies, timbers, spars, and cordage for the repair work.

Captain Decatur made several trips of inspection to his prize, being shown every part of the ship, either by Henry Allen or myself, should Captain Allen be otherwise engaged. At the midshipmen's cockpit, still utilized as a hospital by both surgeons, he stifled a gasp and briefly turned away; the smell of putrefaction and decay was initially overwhelming, and the groans and cries of the men suffering the agony of amputations and a myriad of other distresses, most daunting.

But enter he did and spoke to each of the men who was conscious, offering condolences and encouragement. I was most impressed with this display of even-handedness to the sailors of our enemy. But this was Decatur!

Finally, Captain Decatur, on the invitation of Captain Allen, made a more formal inspection of his prize and, after some deliberation with Henry, deemed her fit for the twenty-two hundred mile trip home.

"It will be truly a miracle if we do not encounter a vessel of the Royal Navy." Henry declared. "The seas are alive with cruisers. One encounter could undo all we have accomplished."

"Mister Allen . . . excuse me, *Captain* Allen. As *United States* will be in company with you, I fear any encounter with a cruiser of the Royal Navy would only result in more grief for the British. We have taken the pride of their frigate fleet and can surely add to our catch, should the opportunity present itself." Decatur openly relished the thought.

"I am more concerned," he went on, a scowl crossing his face, "with foul weather showing up than with cruisers. That, I can do little about and, in the weakened condition of your command, sir, I fear the outcome, should weather of some severity appear. We will have to trust to God for His good Grace and mercy on that score."

I surely was not gladdened by the commodore's grim prognostication, but, with Henry, consoled myself that God would protect us. After all, has He not done so, and quite nicely, so far?

The next morning dawned clear and mild, the breeze fair and the seas easy. We had enjoyed a final supper the night before with Captain Decatur on *United States,* punctuated with any number of toasts to our conquest, a successful voyage home, and Henry's first command. I was surprised that Captain Carden, late of his Britannic Majesty's frigate, *Macedonian,* was not in attendance; he had elected to sup with his officers in the gunroom. As the sun showed itself on the eastern horizon, the bosun turned out the crew on the United States frigate *Macedonian.* He saw to the placement of hammocks in the netting, and parceled out the short-handed crew to the jobs necessary to sail our prize home. The cook, technically a prisoner, but happy to serve under our flag, fixed a hearty breakfast consisting of burgoo and hard bread for the men. Henry stood on the quarterdeck surveying his domain, while I and our American sailing master, Mister Maples, sent the topmen aloft to get some sail on our jury-rigged masts and yards.

Looking at our rig, I was happy not to be spending my time up there! Only the fore and main masts carried topmasts, ingeniously crafted from a pair of mainyards, while the mizzen, salvaged from over the side where it had led to the British demise, was rigged only with a fore and aft sail, called a driver. Shrouds had been tightened and, while it was unlikely that, with mild weather any of it would come down, nobody knew what might go wrong in the event of a turn for the worse. We could only hope.

As the square sails dropped from their yards and the driver was hauled out, *Macedonian* fell off on a larboard tack with *United States* slightly ahead and keeping station to our weather side. Her gunports were closed, as were ours, but we all knew Decatur would be ready for any opportunity to engage another British warship. We were headed home, not just as victors, but with a prize of wonderful stature. Surely this feat would garner ample honor and glory for our commander. Thinking about it, I could barely suppress my grin. But there were over two thousand miles to be sailed before any of that might accrue!

The first week passed quite uneventfully. Sailors, both British and American, became shipmates, a more important relationship than nationality. They faced common threats, problems, and simple pleasures together, bonding them, for the most part, into a crew. Officers—there were only two of us, Henry and me, but we also had, at my request, Willy O'Donahue, midshipman, to help out, stand watches and act as another officer. To that end, Captain Decatur agreed to give him the temporary rank of lieutenant, something that quite overwhelmed the young midshipman.

We all worked together to keep our prize sailing at a pace acceptable to Henry, as well as to keep her afloat. On the second morning, we noticed that *United States* had pulled significantly ahead of us, even with her courses clewed up! To suggest that Decatur reduce sail even further was clearly not within Captain Allen's capability. I offered, only partly in jest, that it might make the commodore smile to see our signal requesting that he retard his progress, in the light of *Old Wagon's* reputation; Henry did not find it amusing.

So, while some men worked the pumps, others continued to patch holes in the hull, and still others worked aloft, rigging sails to makeshift yards, adding shrouds and stays, and attempting, unsuccessfully, to rig a topmast on the mizzen. Between pumping overboard the water in the hold and adding some additional sail area to her, we managed to get *Macedonian* to show us some of her superior sailing abilities and began, slowly, to overhaul Captain Decatur.

Henry was pleased and congratulated Bosun Comstock and our new sailing master, Mister Maples. He ordered an extra ration of "Jamaican" (as the American sailors called the rum issued by ships of the Royal Navy). Decatur, when we came within hailing distance, was equally pleased and, standing on the bulwark of the quarterdeck as was his wont, said as much to us, shouting through his speaking trumpet.

"Try not to get too far ahead of us; wouldn't do to have the prize arrive before her captor, now would it?" The joy in Decatur's voice carried well across the water, even distorted through the tin speaking trumpet.

"Not likely to be a problem, sir. I don't know how long she'll take the strain. Should the breeze pipe up any more, we'll be obliged to hand some canvas, but in the meantime, we're working at shoring up these lowers," Henry pointed at the fore and main lower masts, still scarred from a number of our hits. "Mizzen ain't likely to take any more canvas, but we have managed to close all the holes in her hull. Seems to be staying fairly dry below. Pumping for only about ten minutes a watch."

In fact, Henry had ordered Comstock to remove the fothering canvas we had early on hauled under the hull, to slow the influx of water, as the carpenters worked from the inside patching, caulking, and restoring the ship's integrity.

Our daily sun sights, when reduced to give our position on the globe, showed us making good progress, often one hundred miles and more during a noon-to-noon run. And nary a sail had we espied! A fact that Henry and I spoke of and had toasted with some fine wine (previously belonging to Captain Carden) more than once.

Two weeks into the trip home, and still over one thousand miles from New York, Willy sent his messenger to wake me early in the morning. I stumbled to the quarterdeck, trying to pierce the early morning darkness and hoping not to see trouble aloft. I breathed a sigh of relief when nothing seemed out of place. I squinted forward through the blackness and could make out *United States'* light winking something over a mile off our weather bow. What could be wrong?

"Mister Baldwin, sir. I am sorry to have bothered you . . ." Willy was never really sure of himself but had gained some confidence during his sojourn in *Macedonian*. He seemed to be taking well to his temporary promotion.

I cut him off, perhaps a bit abruptly. "Willy: I am sure you had a perfect reason for calling me. Now, stop your apologizing and tell me what has happened."

"Yes, sir. I think we might be in for some weather, sir. Looks right dark—I mean . . . even darker up ahead. Ain't stars showin' and feels like the wind mighta hauled a bit. Seas have changed, too. And sir, the glass has dropped some in the past hour." He stepped to the rail and peered down into the inky water moving past our side.

I studied the darkness, realizing that he was quite right: the wind had veered slightly and the sea had changed its mood. As to a deeper blackness ahead of us, I would withhold judgment. It all looked dark and, without a moon (we had not enjoyed an unobstructed view of her in the past several nights), any increase in clouds was difficult to determine. But Willy had been up here for some four hours and might be better able to discern building weather.

"Good job, Mister O'Donahue. I believe you might be right. Call out the watch and reef the courses. I will rouse the captain and tell him what we are doing." I left him to carry out my orders and headed for the scuttle to the Cabin.

"Got some weather building up, Oliver?" Henry spoke from the darkness before I could say a word.

"Yes, sir. It would appear so. Willy's got the watch and called me when he got concerned. I think he's right and told him to reef the courses for now." Henry must have felt the different motion of the ship.

"Wise choice. Our rig ain't likely to stand much strain. Did you think to signal the commodore as to what was actin'?"

I had not and, in the darkness of the Cabin, blushed at my oversight. "Not yet, sir. I will do so at once."

"Just haul small a moment, Oliver. I'll come up and see for myself. Then we'll signal the commodore."

By dawn, the seas had built significantly; waves broke against the weather bow and sent icy spray flying down the deck. Comstock had rigged lifelines on both sides of the spardeck; the courses were double reefed, and we had, on Captain Allen's orders, handed two of the stays'ls. Still the ship creaked and groaned like a person possessed.

United States had shortened down, but not to the extent we had. And she was, once again, opening the distance between us. A lookout in the foretop bellowed down "Signals on *Old Wagon*, sir." He was obviously one of our former shipmates in the American frigate.

I swung my glass and focused on the flags whipping stiffly in the strong wind. A quartermaster, as well as our prize captain was doing the same. But I called them out first.

"Commodore says not to press our luck; shorten down and he'll wait for us."

"There's a relief! I was about to order another reef in the tops'ls my own self. Glad he's encouraging us to have a care!" Henry turned at once he had spoken to me and ordered Comstock and the sailing master, Mister Maples, to tie in a second reef in both tops'ls.

Even as our men hastened to carry out their orders, climbing the ice-laden ratlines to the tops, I saw Decatur's men working their own way aloft in *United States*. Apparently, he would continue to act as our protector, as he had signaled.

As the day progressed, *Macedonian's* timbers and rig protested more insistently; the hull creaked and groaned like a soul enduring some hideous torment and the wind's keening in the rig grew louder. Ice had begun to form on the deck as well as making a shiny, dangerous coating on our shrouds and spars.

"Oliver, I think we need to get this ice off the old girl. It's weighting her down and straining everything. Tell Comstock to get some men aloft and let the watch handle the decks. Is the galley fire still lit?"

We had earlier debated whether or not to put out the cook fire due to the weather and decided that, as about the only source of warmth in the ship, to do so would be inhuman.

"Yes sir. As far as I know it is. I have not told the cook to secure it."

"Good. After you get the bosun started on the ice, tell the cook -what's his name? Oh yes, Walters, or something like that—to see what he might provide in the way of hot food for the men. Probably ought to give the prisoners a bit extra as well. Heaven knows, it's likely cold enough in the hold."

Considering the well-being of the British sailors and a few petty officers who had no desire to help us bring their ship to America and were, subsequently, locked in an empty sail locker, had not occurred to me. I remarked on that to my superior.

"Well, Oliver, Cap'n Decatur always insisted on treatin' his prisoners fairly. I think it's a good policy for us, too. Someday, the tide may be turned and I'd like to think we might get treated decently by them, should that come to pass."

I had heard stories of how the British treated prisoners during the War for Independence; it was not anything I ever wanted to experience, but reasoned that, should America gain a reputation for treating fairly its prisoners of war, any of us who might suffer the misfortune of capture stood a better chance of surviving the experience.

"Aye, you're likely right. I'll see to extra rations for all hands, prisoners and ship's company alike."

The remainder of the day and into the night passed cold and stormy; the seas remained boisterous and Aeolus blew his cold, wet breath at us from the north. The crew got their hot food, an extra tot of spirits, and continued their backbreaking job of chipping the ice off the ship before it could send us to the bottom. To add to our woes, we began to take on water at a faster rate as the ship worked in the heavy seas. The squeak and rattle of the chain pumps became a part of the constant noise on board; the timbers protesting, the rattle of the blocks aloft, the groaning and, occasionally, the screaming of the wind, the rush of the seas past our laboring hull, and now, the rattle of the pumps being manned for three out of every four hours—around the clock.

Decatur would signal from time to time, inquiring as to our "health" and each time, we answered properly, showing lights or flags as the time of day dictated. We were managing to weather the storm, which we all hoped would blow itself out soon. Intermittent snow added to the misery as it insinuated its icy wetness between collar and neck, under gloves, and, at times, aided by the wind, stiffening one's face to the point of being unable to form intelligible words. But we continued to make progress toward America and, we reminded ourselves frequently, the untoward weather made it more difficult for the enemy cruisers to find us. We endured, having little choice in the matter, and finally, after three days and nights of torment, we found calmer seas, moderating temperatures, and a warming sun. Every man aboard breathed a bit easier, knowing the ship had withstood the strain—at least this time.

"SAIL! Sail broad on the lee bow. Looks 'bout two leagues distant and headed this way." The lookout's cry interrupted our little celebration of the return of moderate weather and was greeted with a sudden silence from all.

I grabbed a glass, slung it over my shoulder, and ran to the main shrouds, shouting at O'Donahue to send a messenger for Henry.

The ship, when I focused my glass on her, was clearly not British; her high poop and short masts marked her Spanish or perhaps, Portuguese. And she was making headway on a course that would intercept our own and that of *United States*.

"Signal the commodore, quartermaster: vessel two leagues to my starboard. What instructions?" Henry didn't even wait for my report.

"Cap'n, I would wager she's a Spaniard. Small. Maybe a trader?"

"We'll let Cap'n Decatur investigate her, Oliver. Not likely we can do much should she prove unfriendly. What are there, five serviceable long guns and maybe two crews that might be able to fire them? Not the odds I'd like to face. But *Old Wagon* can turn her to matchwood quick as ever you please." He smiled at the thought.

"*United States* bearing off, sir. Headin' 'cross our bow." A decidedly English voice drifted down from the foretop as the lookout there reported that, indeed, Decatur would handle the intruder.

We watched as the big frigate bore up near the strange ship and shivered her tops'ls. A puff of white smoke blossomed out from her bow chaser, followed quickly by a dull thud as the sound reverberated across the water.

"My stars, Cap'n! Is the commodore firing at her already? Must have seen something he didn't like!" Willy stared slack-jawed at Decatur's open hostility.

"No, no, Mister O'Donahue. He's simply signaling her to heave to, just as we did with that ship we stopped to put Mister Cochran on," Henry winked at me. "A lee gun with a half charge and no ball. Nothing sinister about it at all. And it appears to have been successful. The carvel, if that's what she is, looks to be heaving to."

I couldn't help myself. "I would imagine seeing that heavy frigate showing her teeth would be inspirational to them!"

A boat appeared from under *United States'* quarter and made its way to the other ship, now stationary barely a pistol shot distant from our frigate. And, after making the side of the stranger, it returned, made yet another round trip, and then was hoisted aboard.

"What do you suppose *that* was all about? I can't imagine Decatur would send a boat across to them. More likely would be the other way 'round!" Henry continued to watch the two ships through his glass as both hauled their braces and were quickly underway.

We wondered about the strange behavior of both ships for several days until, during the first watch one afternoon, we received a signal from the commodore inviting our captain to sup in the flagship. The weather, while still very cold—the calendar was well into November, after all—was moderate and we continued to make steady progress toward the New England Coast. Henry accepted with alacrity, admonishing me to call him should *anything* unseemly arise. It was after he left that it dawned on me I was now the *senior officer* aboard the prize! I paced up and down the quarterdeck, prowled the spar and gun decks, and, afraid to leave the deck for more than a few minutes at a time, wolfed down some melted cheese and bread for my own supper.

Is this what it feels like to be the captain? How do they do it? How does Henry manage to sleep at night and seem so . . . in control *all the time?*

Mister Maples took the watch that evening, listening seriously to my recitation of Henry's caution to me, and Willy, until he noticed the hour, followed me about the ship like a pet dog, trying, I am sure, to assuage my burden of command. It was almost a relief when he departed to take his own meal in the gunroom.

And when the lookout cried out that a boat was approaching from *United States,* I hurried to the waist to greet my captain with a silent prayer of thanks that nothing had gone amiss.

"Well, I found out what acted with that cruiser a few days back, Oliver." Henry reported immediately on his return from Decatur's table. "And you were right: she was a Spaniard and heading for Cadiz." He pronounced it *Cadeeth.*

He continued, quite unaware of my joy at his return.

"Decatur put the purser off *Macedonian* in her and with him, the Royal Navy pay records for their crew. Figured he could get his own self to England with 'em and make sure the Brits got their pay. Kind of speaks to what we were talking on the other day, 'bout treatin' prisoners proper and fair."

That both surprised me and didn't. Why would anyone, beyond other Brits, care whether the British sailors and officers got paid? That Captain Decatur did could only be explained by the fact that he was Captain Decatur, the very soul of fairness and equanimity.

Henry had more to tell. "Cap'n Carden—he's still taking his meals in the Cabin, you know, and the officers in the gunroom—spoke to me. Said quietly that he'd put a letter to the Admiralty in the purser's hands telling 'em what a gentleman is our captain and how gracious he treats his prisoners. And seems almost likeable now, compared to the way he was acting when we brought him across to meet Decatur! Reckon that first lieutenant of theirs, Hope, has been brought down a bit as well. Was quite civil to me. A most pleasant evening, Oliver.

"And you'll want to know that Decatur asked after both you and O'Donahue. Told him you were standing up to the job quite nicely and Willy . . . well, Willy is Willy and I just said he'd likely welcome a return to the cockpit and the other mids once we get in!"

"Oh Henry! That wasn't fair. Willy is doing fine. Remember he is only a midshipman even though we think of him as a lieutenant. And he's only been aboard a short while. I know he's young, still a boy, in fact, but we all were when we were midshipmen." I sprang to my young colleague's assistance quickly.

"I will be sure to mention that when next I see the commodore, Oliver. I am sure I must have said something about him behaving admirably or something." Henry grinned at me.

It suddenly dawned on me that he might have enjoyed a bit more wine than normal and was simply having sport with me. I smiled back at him and excused myself, claiming the need to relieve Mister Maples on the quarterdeck.

It was only about ten days later that we began to watch for the appearance of land on the western horizon. And the very next day, a fog rolled in, wet, thick, and cold, and obscured everything beyond the jib boom. While the temperature was not yet at the point where everything turned to ice, the fog and cold made the entire ship, from orlop deck to spardeck, dismal. I began sleeping in my greatcoat, trying in vain to shake off the wet from topside whenever I went below. Willy O'Donahue suffered in silence, rarely complained of it, but was humorless in his demeanor. And we all spoke through clenched teeth, necessary to keep their chattering from obscuring our words.

United States, shortened down to allow us to sail alongside, hailed and through the swirling mists, Henry and I watched as Decatur mounted the bulwark and raised his speaking trumpet to his mouth.

"Mister Allen: Should we become separated, do not try for New York. Most likely the Sound is alive with British cruisers. 'Course, should this weather persist, I suspect you would have little difficulty evading them!" We could hear his chuckle quite clearly across the fog shrouded one hundred yards of calm sea that separated us.

"By my reckoning, we are on a line that will take us just east of Montauk. It will be far easier for you to sail straight into Newport from there and I can find you quickly should I need you. But you will not linger there longer than necessary; I expect to make for New London, wait for your arrival, and then we will take our prize to New York together. God speed. And mind the bars and currents around Block Island, should you find yourself in that place." The commodore's voice seemed to come from several directions, muffled as it was by the fog.

"Newport! Henry that would be wonderful! I could see Ann again and you, your parents. Would it not be splendid to sail past Castle Hill and surprise the good folks with our glorious good fortune!" I was enraptured with the thought, one half of me picturing our triumphant entry and one half of me fearing the possibility of becoming separated from our protection and getting through whatever British ships might be patrolling those waters east of Montauk.

The fog persisted, swirling and teasing us by lifting enough for us to catch a glimpse of the big frigate, now well ahead of us, then descending over us again like a blanket to plunge us into a world of solitary whiteness, wet, and cold.

"By my reckoning, Oliver, I make us about fifty miles east of Block Island. Were it not for this cursed fog, I would think our lookouts might spot the high ground there at first light." Allen appeared to have made up his mind to sail *Macedonian* into Newport. Block Island was an easy day's sail from Narragansett Bay.

We had been sharing a nice bottle of Captain Carden's wine in the Cabin, discussing our progress and trying to guess whether we might see *United States* at any time soon. Was she still there, watching over us, or had Decatur, assuming we were still wallowing in the light airs and fog, borne up for New London? We talked about firing a half load of powder to let him know we were still there but decided it would also let anyone else know of our whereabouts as well. So we sailed on, blind and cautious, making our westing, and hoping to see the highlands of Block Island before we discovered the bottom!

Ever since Decatur had offered us the choice of going into Newport, my thoughts, those that weren't focused on my duties in the ship, were consumed with Ann. Had I dreamed of our conversations and promises during my all-too-brief visit to Newport some months ago? No, I thought not; they were too real in my mind. At night I dreamed of her lustrous hair, sweet mouth, and musical laugh; in the daytime, I peered through the fog, often climbing to the foretop, in the hopes of seeing the rise of a small island some forty miles off Narragansett Bay. And I wondered where the commodore might be. As we drew closer to my Ann, I hoped we would not find him, thereby relieving us of the need to sail to New London.

With the light and often contrary breezes, we did not, in the event, sight Block Island until mid-morning of December third, the day after Henry had forecast its appearance. The fog had lifted during the night and the early winter day was as crisp and clear as any might want. A breeze blew in from the north, allowing us to pass the island on its deeper side and bear off for the opening of Narragansett Bay. And there was not a sail to be seen in any direction!

As we sailed past the bluffs of the island's northeast end, a tops'l schooner appeared from behind the headland. Her sails were sharply etched into the deep blue sky and, behind her, a feather of white marked her path across the brilliant sea. She was clearly taking full advantage of the fair breeze!

"Sail! Sail off the larboard quarter and making for us," was the lookout's cry.

In an instant, Henry was into the mizzen rigging, focusing his long glass on this fast closing vessel.

"She's showing American colors, Mister Baldwin. Stand by with our own, if you please. And let us get what after guns we might man in the event this is a ruse and she turns out to be other than what she appears." The commander's disembodied voice drifted down from the mizzentop.

Macedonian turned into a hive of activity, led mostly by Mister Comstock. A pair of guns from the starboard side were dragged across the gundeck to replace those rendered useless by our cannonading in October; powder was found and shot carefully rolled to remove any rust that might impede a true flight, and a few topmen went aloft, ready to shorten sail should it prove necessary. All the while, Henry watched the approaching schooner for any sign of treachery.

As he had instructed, I prepared our colors: the American ensign and immediately below it, the British Cross of St. George. There was not a sail in sight, save the schooner and, even in our weakened, undergunned and undermanned condition, I felt confident we might stand off this small ship. The schooner would most likely be armed with six-pounders and only a few of them on top of it. A few hits from the British eighteen-pounders would, hopefully, convince the schooner's captain to seek easier prey.

"Put 'em up, Mister Baldwin. I think he is just what he appears to be." Henry stepped off the bulwark, speaking as he gained the quarterdeck.

It must admit, I felt a certain pride watching our flag go up above the British colors, telling any who saw that the ship was an American prize. I smiled at the bits of colored cloth as they whipped in the stiff breeze, then sobered as I recalled the cost, both American and British, involved in gaining that distinction.

BOOM! A single gun spoke from the schooner, the remnants of the white smoke from its discharge quickly carried away in torn wisps.

"Look, Henry! She's shooting at us. Can you imagine what that fool must be thinking to take on a frigate? Seems right stupid . . ."

"HOLD YOUR FIRE, LADS. She's not shooting at us. Hold your fire." Henry ignored me for a moment, shouting his command down the ladder to the gundeck.

"He's saluting us, Oliver. There was no shot in that. He's responding to the way our colors are showing. Have the lads fire a half charge to acknowledge." Henry was smiling, clearly enjoying his role as prize master.

BOOM. The deeper throated roar of an eighteen-pounder answered quickly and we heard a faint cheer float down to us from the schooner.

339

The little ship drew close, coming under our stern and easing up to our weather side. Her captain luffed her sails to match our pace and the smart, well-managed vessel loafed along to starboard of us, just a half-pistol shot off our beam.

"What ship are you, sir? Who's prize is that?" A voice, perhaps the captain of the schooner shouted across the water.

Henry leaped onto the bulwark and, cupping his hands around his mouth as we had often seen Captain Decatur do, shouted back. "We are the prize of the frigate *United States,* Stephen Decatur commanding. She was formerly His Britannic Majesty's frigate *Macedonian.* And who, sir, might you be?"

Another cheer rose from our escort and we could plainly see most of her crew lining her leeward rail, waving their arms and hats in celebration of our victory.

"I offer you my heartiest congratulations on your victory! I am Edwin Taylor, master of the private armed schooner *Majestic* out of Providence. Where are you heading, sir? And who might be in command?"

"We are making for Newport, sir. I am Lieutenant William Allen, prize master."

Another lusty huzzah, a few ragged cheers, shouted commands, and the schooner sheeted in her sails and flew by us.

"Do you suppose she's heading into Narragansett, Henry? She'll surely be there long before we get in."

"Aye, that'd be my guess. You might let the crew stand down from quarters. Won't likely be having to defend ourselves now!" Henry smiled, glanced down at the water, then added, "See if Maples might get a bit more canvas on her, Oliver. I'd like to set our best bower before dark today if we can."

There was an order I could carry out with a will! Thoughts of my dear Ann filled my head as I found Maples and passed on Henry's orders. The dour sailing master even smiled at the thought of ending this long slog that had taken us, shorthanded and in a damaged vessel, across over two thousand miles of ocean. What a relief to finally be safe in an American harbor. And what a ride it had been! Watching for enemy cruisers, a storm that hammered at us for three days, standing watch and watch, ice forming aloft and alow, almost constant pumping, and trying to repair the damage our own guns had wrought! And, with our arrival in the safe haven of Newport Harbor, I would find myself in the safe haven of Ann Perry's embrace.

Chapter Twenty-three

Show us some speed, Macedonian. *Get us across this last forty miles quickly!*

The men seemed to feel the same excitement at an imminent arrival. They turned to with a will, carrying out Maples' orders quickly. A t'gallant pole appeared from somewhere and was hoisted aloft followed by a jury-rigged yard. The scrap of sail went up next, hauled to the top of the mainmast by eager hands, British and American alike working side by side. The topmen, working at the dizzying height of the new t'gallant, bent the canvas to the slender pole and the heavers on deck, responding to Comstock's gruff commands, sheeted it home. The sailmaker, a British fellow of an age more suitable to pensioner than seaman, found a spare foretopmast stays'l and Maples added its spread to our rig, further straining, even in the modest breeze, our precarious masts and shrouds. And through it all, Henry paced up and down the weather side of the quarterdeck, watching the water as it now moved faster past our side, each additional knot broadening his smile.

"This is a fine-sailing vessel, Oliver." He said as I returned to the quarterdeck. "I can only imagine what she might be capable of undamaged and with a full rig. I'd warrant Decatur would happily trade her for his *Old Wagon* given half a chance!"

I laughed in agreement, both at Henry's use of the less-than-complimentary nickname, as well as at the thought of passing Castle Rock in short order.

Of course, our additional speed and our heel created more strain on the patches along our leeward side, but the men worked the pumps without complaint and managed to stay ahead of the water coming into the ship. Even the lookout's cry of "Land!" did not interrupt their rhythmic strokes.

When up-spirits was piped, it was a happy throng of men, chattering and laughing, slapping each other on the back, who queued up with their tin cups and, even though we all knew supper would be delayed by our arrival, there was not a complaint to be heard.

Henry had decided to carry all the sail we had up into the entrance of Narragansett; a proper, seaman-like arrival would be remembered and something that Captain Decatur would take pride in. And we would be in the lee of the high cliffs of Castle Hill, once in the entrance.

"Looks like there's people all along the cliffs!" The man in the foretop called down to the deck as we closed with the mouth of the harbor, leaving Point Judith and the shallows safely to larboard.

Henry and I both swung our long glasses around to look; indeed, throngs of people were on the high cliffs facing the sea and more seemed to wrap around the shoreline along the cut that would take us past Breton Point and into the harbor. As we drew closer, the crowd changed from just indistinct masses of humanity to individual shapes. And from somewhere, we could hear the pealing of bells.

"I'd reckon Mister Taylor must have made good time to the harbor, Henry. Looks like word of our arrival beat us in by a wide margin. Seems like the whole town turned out to see us in."

Indeed, it did look as if the whole town had turned out, but I cared not a whit for the whole town; my thoughts were centered on only one person as I slowly swung my glass over the shoreline, hoping to see her.

As the daylight began to fade, and with it, the breeze, *Macedonian* made her way smartly past the line of rocks that extended seaward from the point.

"Take in the t'gallants and stays'ls, Mister Maples. Mister Comstock, make ready our best bower and a cable, if you please." Henry's orders sent all hands, save the cook and the prisoners still confined below, into a frenzy of activity.

I went forward with the bosun to oversee the preparations for anchoring as Willy O'Donahue stayed amidships, assisting the sailing master with the heavers on deck. I had slung my glass over my shoulder and used any spare moment to sweep the throngs standing on the rocks lining the entrance and above them, on the high cliffs that overlooked both the Bay and the sea. We could all hear the cheering, huzzahs, and whistles as the crowds watched us sail past, the American flag still flapping above the British ensign in the failing breeze. Cries of "Decatur" and "*United States*" floated in the evening chill.

This is even a greater spectacle than Constitution *coming in to Boston after her great victory! We're bringing in a prize, the pride of the Royal Navy frigates!*

I am a bit embarrassed to admit that my mind barely comprehended the work being done around me, so intent was I on studying the faces lining the shore as they passed by.

As I swung my glass across one group, each muffled against the cold December evening with coats, scarves, and cloaks, I stopped, tried to sharpen the focus of the telescope, and centered it on one figure. Could it be?

She was wrapped in a burgundy cloak, hooded, but not sufficiently to hide the long auburn hair framing a lovely face, not quite sharp in the circle of my vision. I lowered the glass and found her again with my eye. As I did so, the figure waved enthusiastically with one hand, while with the other, she swept the hood off her head. The hair that I remembered so well, no longer held captive by the hood of her cape, responded to the breeze, and blew across her face.

Is that her? Surely looks like her. Oh, miss, move that hair away from your face. I must know!

I raised my glass again.

The noise of the crowd, the cacophony of church bells, and the cheers of our own sailors in response, seemed merely a dull distraction to my efforts. I found the face in my glass again just as her hand swept back her hair. And there she was!

Oh thank you, thank you. It is you!

It was she! It was my Ann! I waved my own arm frantically, trying in vain to keep the glass focused on her. And then, in a rush of enthusiasm, love, anticipation, and relief, shouted her name.

"ANN! ANN PERRY!" And waved both arms over my head.

I was still holding my long glass in one hand and, in my efforts to attract her attention, inadvertently banged it against the starboard fore-shroud. It dropped into the water with a silent splash. It barely registered in my mind.

Now unencumbered by my long glass, I continued waving and shouting. My voice was only one of the hundreds cheering and shouting, but it was the only one calling her name. She must have heard me; with a wonderful smile, she looked right at me, waved frantically, and called out.

"Oliver! Oh, Oliver!"

The noise of the crew, the cheers of the citizens of Newport, the bells still ringing out their welcome, and the shouted orders of our bosun and sailing master, all faded into the background. I heard her sweet voice as though she were standing almost next to me.

I was home.

AUTHOR'S NOTES

While this book is technically a work of fiction, the reader should note that the historical events depicted are accurate; in some cases I have changed a date to ease the flow of the story, but I have not altered history.

Obviously, Oliver Baldwin, his family, and many of his shipmates are fictitious. Historical characters such as Stephen Decatur, John Rodgers, William Henry Allen, the officers on Barron's court martial board along with the civilian attorneys, John Carden, David Hope, and many others are real. While I, in essence, "put words in their mouths" they represent utterances that I tried to keep within the character of the person. Naturally, there was no scribe following these individuals around jotting down their every word for posterity!

The reader should be aware that the incident subsequently referred to as the "*Chesapeake/Leopard* Incident" did actually occur as described in Barron's court martial and its delayed resolution has been considered by historians to be one of the causes that led up to the War of 1812. *Chesapeake* did, in fact, go to sea with "lumbered" (cluttered) decks, short of crew, and with virtually no training. Henry Allen is credited with firing the only shot offered by the American frigate during the confrontation and, though unconfirmed, is reported to have carried a live coal from the galley stove or camboose in his bare hands to touch off the cannon. The officers of *Chesapeake,* including First Lieutenant Ben Smith, who did die after the incident (from illness, not from any injury sustained during it) are real people who acted as depicted.

For the benefit of any who are curious, an excerpt from Admiral Berkeley's Order to his Captains of the North American Station and, in response, the text of Commodore Barron's letter to Captain Humphries of *Leopard* is set forth below:

"... *that each and every vessel of his squadron should take by force, if they could not be obtained by other means, any British deserters that could be found onboard the* Chesapeak [sic], *and that on the part of the Commanders of the ships of his Squadron, a search should be admitted for american* [sic] *deserters...*"

"*I know of no such men as you describe, the officers that were of the recruiting service for this ship was* [sic] *pa[r]ticularly instructed by the Government, through me, not to enter any Deserters from his B.M. Ships, nor do I know of any being here. I am also instructed never to permit the Crew of any Ship that I command, to be muster'd by any other but their own Officers. It is my disposition to preserve harmony and I hope this answer to your dispatch will prove satisfactory.*

Signed JAMES BARRON

AT SEA June 22nd 1807
To the Commander of his B M Ship Leopard"

The court martial of James Barron, Charles Gordon, Captain Hall USMC, and Gunner Hooks occurred as written (save, of course, for Oliver's testimony) and the outcome was also portrayed accurately. That outcome would ultimately lead Commodores Decatur and Barron to the field of honor in 1820, resulting in Decatur's death. As a matter of interest, portions of Barron's monologue at his trial were taken from the transcript of that trial.

USS *Chesapeake* was indeed considered by many to be a "jinx" ship. Her history as told in the story is accurate to the point at which it ends; on June 1, 1813, under command of James Lawrence, the American frigate was lost in a short but bloody battle to HMS *Shannon* off Cape Ann, Massachusetts. (See **A Fine Tops'l Breeze** by William H. White, Tiller Publishing, 2001) The ship was, indeed, carrying at least four deserters from the Royal Navy at the time HMS *Leopard* fired into her and Lord Townshend's threats, as testified to in the court martial, were accurate.

Upon *Chesapeake's* arrival in Hampton Roads following the incident, the officers wrote and sent ashore a letter to Secretary of the Navy Smith detailing what they termed the "disgraceful behavior" of the Commodore. Henry Allen was one of the signers of that letter. Again, for the benefit of historical accuracy, I offer the complete text below:

"The undersigned Officers of the late U.S. Ship Chesapeake, *feeling deeply sensible of the disgrace which must be attached to the late (in their opinion) premature surrender of the U.S. Ship* Chesapeake *of 40 Guns to the English Ship of War* Leopard *of 50 Guns, without their previous knowledge or consent, and desirous of proving to their country and the World, that it was the wish of all the undersigned, to have rendered themselves, worthy of the Flag under which that had the honor to serve, by a determined resistance, to an unjust demand, do request the Hon. Secretary of the Navy to order a Court of Enquiry into their conduct.*

"At the same time they are compelled by impervious duty, the honour of their flag, the honour of their Countrymen, and by all that is dear to themselves, to request an orde may be issued for the arrest of Commodore James Barron, on the charges herewith exhibited, which the undersigned pledge themselves to prove true, Viz. 1st On the probability of anEengagement, for neglecting to clear his ship for actions. 2ndly For not doing his utmost to take or destroy a Vessel which we conceive it his duty to have done."

> *[Signed] Ben Smith 1st Lieut.*
> *William Crane Lt.*
> *Wm. H. Allen 3rd Leut.*
> *Jno. Orde Creighton Lt.*
> *Sidney Smith 5th Lieutnt.*
> *Sam Brooke Master*

During *Chesapeake*'s cruise to enforce the embargo following the trial (Stephen Decatur commanding) the crew witnessed the first steamship to make an open ocean voyage in America. As represented, *Phoenix*, under Col. John Smith, did make the voyage from New York to Philadelphia. I took liberty with the year; it was not 1808 but in fact 1809 that the momentous event occurred.

Newport, Rhode Island, a town enormously dependent on the sea trade for its economic prosperity, was suffering when Oliver and his shipmates arrived there. Jefferson's embargo had kept many of the town's ships rotting at the piers and, without question, there was enormous resentment, not only in Rhode Island, but also throughout all of New England. The Vernon house, described by Oliver, still stands today and was used by French General Rochambeau as a headquarters during the American Revolution. While the building housing the "grand ballroom" has been torn down, records and other period homes would indicate its description is accurate. Oliver, however, was misled, intentionally by the builders, when he mentioned the house was built of stone; the house is of wood, cut and formed to appear as though of stone. The process is called "rustication," a relatively common practice in eighteenth century America, designed to mimic the stonework of Europe.

That Oliver Hazard Perry had a sister named Ann is fabricated. He did have three sisters, but none named Ann. His mother was, indeed, descended from William Wallace, the famed Scots rebel who, in the late 13th and early 14th centuries, led his people against England's Edward I. The movie, "Braveheart" told Wallace's story in somewhat fanciful form. The Perrys did live in South Kingston; Captain Christopher Perry sailed, during the Quasi War, with his midshipman son who later had the difficulties detailed. Of course, O. H. Perry met his glory on Lake Erie in 1813. And Matthew Perry, who Oliver met at the ball, would go on to his own fame and fortune.

Henry Allen's account of the *Dragon/George Washington* encounter did, in fact, happen as he described it and was one of the major factors, along with the *Chesapeake/Leopard* Incident, which contributed to Allen's hatred of the British. Lieutenant Allen subsequently commanded the United

States brig *Argus* in heroic actions against English shipping in British waters. He died in single ship combat with HMS *Pelican* there and was buried ashore with full honors. His grave is still maintained in a churchyard in Plymouth, England.

When John Rodgers attacked HMS *Little Belt*, he was in fact seeking the larger British frigate, *Guerriere*. That ship, along with others, both English and French, had been harassing American shipping in the area of New York Harbor. Of course, the United States frigate *President* made short work of the smaller ship before Rodgers discovered his error; during the brief night action, *Little Belt* (or *Lille Belt*, as she was properly known) suffered major damage to her hull and rig, nine men killed, and twenty three wounded. A Court of Inquiry was convened and lasted for twelve days, examining more than fifty witnesses. It ultimately exonerated Rodgers based on the determination that *Little Belt* had commenced the exchange. The English rejected the ruling and, to this day, Captain Bingham's (*Little Belt)* version is widely accepted as the true version, at least in Great Britain.

HMS *Macedonian* did call at Norfolk in February of 1812; President Madison had opened our ports to foreign shipping and it was not uncommon to see warships of other nations riding to their anchors in American harbors. Decatur and several of his officers, including Henry Allen, had been invited to visit the ship, which they did. Stephen Decatur and his wife, Susan, held a party at their home in Norfolk for Captain Carden of *Macedonian* and his officers and, while the conversation following the meal between Carden and Decatur is as represented, the wager of a beaver hat is unsubstantiated in fact. Decatur's answer to Captain Carden's offer, however, is clearly within his character.

Edward Baldwin's description of *Constitution* being chased by British cruisers off the New Jersey coast is accurate. The same ship was subsequently chased in Massachusetts Bay, escaping into Marblehead after using her boats in much the same manner as she did off New Jersey.

Oliver's description of Isaac Hull's arrival on Long Wharf is taken from a contemporary account written by Moses Smith, a sailor in *Constitution*. It was published some years after the event in *Naval Scenes in the Last War, Or, Three Years Aboard the Frigates Constitution and Adams, Including the Capture of the Guerrière*. Boston: Gleason's Publishing House, 1846.

Of note also is the Army general to whom the intoxicated citizen of Boston—he couldn't quite remember the name—referred in connection with the surrender of Fort Detroit. It was, in fact, William Hull, a fifty-nine-year-old veteran of the Revolutionary War and governor of Michigan Territory. He was Isaac Hull's uncle and adopted father. Isaac obviously restored some credibility to the family name!

The description of the engagement of *United States* and *Macedonian* was taken from letters written by the commanders of both ships to their superiors following the engagement. A subsequent letter from Captain Carden spoke eloquently of Decatur's fair, and even generous, treatment of his prisoners while they were aboard *United States* en route to New London. This ultimately paid handsome dividends as, when Decatur, commanding the frigate *President,* fell in with English warships off Sandy Hook, New Jersey in January of 1815 (the war was officially over by then, but that fact was, of course, unknown in America). He was forced by overwhelming opposition to strike his colors and, while naturally the ship was taken as a prize, he and his officers were released in consideration of the treatment British prisoners had received at his hand.

While Henry Allen did take his prize into Newport (where Master Commandant O. H. Perry was in command of the Naval Station), he subsequently sailed her to New London, where he rendezvoused with Commodore Decatur and sailed in company with him to New York City, arriving there to great fanfare and celebration, on 16 December. At a reception in Washington City (to which Decatur traveled by coach from New London), he presented *Macedonian*'s colors to First Lady Dolley Madison, who was representing her husband. Congress subsequently voted gold medals to the captains of *Constitution* and *United States* and silver medals to their officers in commemoration of their victories. A representation of the medals given to the officers of *United States* can be found within this volume.

Macedonian, fully repaired and commissioned a unit of the United States Navy, became Decatur's flagship for a Mediterranean cruise in 1815 to deal with Algerian troubles. The ship led a productive life in the Navy, ultimately being abandoned in City Island, New York (well after the Navy had sold her out of service to the firm of Wiggin & Robinson, who paid the princely sum of $14,071). After a quarter-century passed, the hulk was broken up and her timbers (purchased for $25) used by a Jake Smith to build the Hotel Macedonian on City Island. On June 9, 1922, a devastating fire destroyed what remained of this heroic vessel.

William H. White
Rumson, New Jersey